"The essence of being human is that one does not seek perfection, that one is sometimes willing to commit sins for the sake of loyalty, that one does not push asceticism to the point where it makes friendly intercourse impossible, and that one is prepared in the end to be defeated and broken up by life, which is the inevitable price of fastening one's love upon other human individuals."

George Orwell

1

Magnificent displays of brushstrokes, commanding sculpture and creative passion awaited, just a matter of hours away. Dubbed the Oscars of Art, the biannual Manchester Art Conference was set to be the biggest event of the year for Peter Brockland. It was his chance to alter his waning fortunes and rebuild his reputation.

Da Vinci, Rembrandt, Picasso, van Gogh, even Andy Warhol; lengthy, and he was certain costly, negotiations had paved the way for masterpieces from across the world to be sanctioned for a never-before-seen one-week display.

Peter Brockland loved all things art but had struggled to maintain that passion through his decade of inane tabloid journalism. Despite his relentless efforts, art had always been more of a hobby for Peter than a specialist subject. He had never been deemed to possess the intellectual capacity necessary by those within the field to understand the deeper significance of the paintings he enjoyed reviewing so much.

He was not ashamed of it; he may not have a framed PhD in Art History in his hallway or the experience of a four-year internship at the Louvre courtesy of inherited wealth, but he had just as much right as anyone to appreciate the genius of Da Vinci or the audacity of Picasso.

Peter had just as much right as anyone to enjoy how a painting made him feel – though the company he often had to keep in his line of work made it difficult to. He would never forget one of his university Art History lectures, where he had been openly derided at his suggestion that the Mona Lisa looked confused.

"Thank you for such a deep insight into the works of Da Vinci, Mr Brockland," a visiting arts expert had said sarcastically, to the muffled giggles of the surrounding students. Peter had persevered, achieving his degree before turning to journalism, rising slowly within the tabloid industry. In the past few years, he had even convinced his editor to stray from the dead zone of the celebrity fodder middle pages and extend him a de facto position as an arts correspondent, with the freedom to write stories on his terms. It had been this move that gained him some public notoriety, engaging readers with no artistic expertise in the arts.

Peter had effectively become the self-appointed arts editor of the newspaper with no arts section. The intellectuals of the industry had not taken to his light-hearted articles with much verve; his work had always been to them, in even their politest critiques, a cheap art review. Peter had grown to harden himself from such opinions after a time, aided by the relatively warm reception he received from numerous amateur art enthusiasts in the online forums. He had even managed to secure a monthly spot discussing art on a daytime television show, though its teenage target audience had done little to enhance his reputation.

"The nine-nineteen service to Manchester Piccadilly has now arrived at platform four," the station tannoy announced, startling Peter from a particularly ruthless online comment.

Peter locked his electronic tablet, scowling, and lifted himself from the platform bench. He stood beside the train doors, smiling politely as the disembarking passengers forced their escape, before striding into Carriage D.

His mind wandered to the various receptions he might receive as he stepped into the large Manchester conference hall, and he winced at the memory of his last conference. His attempt to network with the industry's best had not been aided by a recent television appearance, where he had been punished with a deluge of green slime for his incorrect answer to a teenager's art question.

"You're the gunge guy, right?" one visiting American professor had asked, his wry smile bordering on pitiful.

Peter desperately hoped that his work in the previous two years, which had even attracted some kudos from noted curators, would be enough for him to at least avoid open derision from colleagues.

Peter shook himself and walked slowly through the carriages, searching for a seat not tainted by any of the usual must-avoid train passengers. It took three carriages worth of polite nods and awkward aisle squeezes before he was able to find a space not occupied by over-perspiration, culinary pungency, or a passenger speaking far too loudly on a phone call deemed too important to wait.

Peter groaned as the words "my best friend's new puppy is just gorgeous…" escaped a young passenger's mouth, at a decibel level that would not have been lost in a sports crowd.

As the train slowly jerked its departure, Peter eventually found a spot opposite an attractive female commuter, immersed in her latest travel novel. He tried to catch her eye as he settled himself down, perhaps slower than was necessary, into the window seat.

Peter had never been particularly successful in the dating scene. At five-foot-ten and in fairly average shape, he was distinctly aware of being a very average-looking man, aside from his striking green eyes. With restless brown hair, a rounded jaw, a slightly stout nose and a hint of stubble, Peter fell soundly within the category of what the police would class as a 'bog standard IC1 male'.

He had not quite yet been cast into celibacy though, with his television appearances helping prop up his online dating prowess.

Peter had begun to formulate his icebreaker when his phone began to vibrate. Fortunately, he had left it on silent; he was not sure that a fully-grown adult answering a Macarena ringtone would have done much to spark an attraction.

Peter looked down at the caller ID – Cyril. If it had been anyone else, he would have allowed it to ring out but, ruing his hypocrisy, he answered.

"Pete? Pete? You there mate?"

Cyril was one of Peter's oldest art contacts, in every sense of the word. He had been the first man Peter interviewed after printing his own unofficial 'Arts Editor' business cards and a friend ever since. At seventy-three years old and with more than fifty years of experience in the industry, Cyril had always acted as a safe voice of reason for Peter's work.

Having had a successful career in his own right as curator of the National Gallery for more than twenty years, Cyril was an expert that Peter could count on, particularly as he was one of the very few respected figures in the field that attributed any value to his work.

"Cyril… I suppose you've got there already have you?" Peter asked quietly, looking around the carriage for any signs of disapproval.

"Oh, yes!" came Cyril's enthusiastic rasp. "I took the earlier train to catch a private viewing."

Cyril had agreed to chaperone Peter at the conference, but with his long-standing reputation in the arts sector, Cyril was always given priority service when it came to events such as this. This, combined with Cyril's compulsive need to be early, likely meant his catching the 'earlier train' meant that he had arrived days before the event had even been set up, and sure enough...

"I've been here a few days already, chap."

"You're unbelievable," said Peter, his voice tinged with jealousy. "How is it?"

Cyril sighed and for the next five minutes took great pleasure talking Peter through the artistic talent on display. As he casually narrated descriptions of extraordinary sculptures, long-lost artistic discoveries and the boldest of abstract paintings, Peter struggled to contain his wonder.

His awe must have been obvious, and he quickly slipped out of his trance when the woman opposite let out a small chuckle. Peter blushed, rearranging his jaw, imagining how ridiculous his vacant expression must have looked.

His blushes were soon cut short as a sharp nudge to his shoulder interrupted his opening line, quickly followed by searing pain, spreading through his crotch. A heavy-set man continued briskly through the carriage, seemingly oblivious to the fact he had knocked Peter's coffee all over him.

Peter cursed and stood up to assess the damage. He was unfortunate enough to have done so at the same moment the woman opposite had noticed the commotion.

She lowered 'Wolves by the Fire', only to find herself at eye level with the now sodden frontal area of Peter's jeans. Dabbing at the stain instinctively, Peter rued his last-minute decision not to have worn his black trousers.

"Coffee," Peter mouthed, as he awkwardly addressed her shocked expression.

"Hi coffee," she said, forcing back a giggle. "I'm Sarah."

"I'll be back in a second," said Peter, smiling as he turned away. "Do you mind?"

He pointed towards the rucksack beside him and she nodded. He smiled his thanks and turned to walk down the carriage as the train began to slow, nearing the next station.

He was inherently aware of the several eyes looking intently towards him as he advanced, and one area in particular.

He continued at pace, only to find his frustration further exacerbated by an occupied toilet.

Peter continued through the connecting carriages impatiently and in a bid to avoid further awkward acknowledgements of passenger gazes, turned to look out of the window. The train had halted at the next station and, to his surprise, he found himself staring directly at the very man who had caused his embarrassment. He stood still, staring intently back at him.

The man was tanned and well-built, with wild, black hair unable to hide the visible scarring on his face or the unnerving glare.

The man stood deathly still, unwavering, with no expression to accompany the intensity of his gaze. Peter shook his head in disgust at him, indicating towards the damage he had caused, all to no avail - the man offered no reaction.

It was not until Peter turned to walk further down the carriage that the man's face betrayed a flicker of anxiety. Peter continued as the train edged slowly back into action, brushing aside the strange encounter, and eventually found a vacant toilet. He entered swiftly, still red-faced, and closed the door behind him.

Peter sighed as he looked down again at the stain on his crotch. Not the icebreaker he had hoped for. He grabbed the paper towels and began to dab again at his jeans.

It happened in an instant. Peter had changed tact to apply the lukewarm air of the rusted hand dryer to the stain when he felt the train lurch. He turned, panicked, his feet trembling as a rushing sound approached, followed by a further violent jerk, a blinding light, and an unmistakable, searing heat.

2

Peter opened his eyes slowly and his mind whirred back into action. What had happened? A dull ringing filled his ears. He had been dabbing the coffee from his jeans and then, what? He blinked groggily, his head spinning.

As his vision gradually regained clarity, he realised he was staring directly upwards. He lay flat on the ground, his body circled by thick grey smoke.

He tried to roll to his side, groaning at the pain of the effort. He could not see anything, hear anything, but for the slowly billowing grey surrounding him.

After a few moments, Peter found the strength to drag himself to his feet, made ever more difficult by the increasing aches coursing through his body. He looked around him weakly, in the hope of gaining some comprehension as to what had happened. He could feel the wet grass beneath his feet - one piece of the puzzle - though that did little to abate his confusion.

"Hello?" he shouted gruffly into the smoke, coughing violently at the effort. Though he felt the vibrations of his throat as he shouted, he could not hear the words escape him.

He wiped away the damp grass clinging to his dishevelled shirt and tried desperately to massage his ears back into action. He was unsuccessful. As he looked around once more, he noticed the smoke clear in parts to reveal in brief, merciless intervals nothing short of utter devastation.

It took Peter several seconds to even contemplate an acceptance of the horrific scenes emerging around him.

He stood, shaking violently and sweating profusely, in a muddy field, thirty feet or so from what appeared to be a twisted mass of melting steel - but it could not be.

A terrible inferno rose from the wreckage of what he feared may once have been his train, as thick smoke continued to cloud the remaining limitations of his vision. Peter waved the smoke aside, walking aimlessly towards the mass ahead. His feet sank into the muddy ground beneath him as he approached, and he was horrified to find that his initial assumption was true. He halted, his face draining of colour, to stare up at the slowly melting, scattered remains of the nine-nineteen to Manchester Piccadilly.

A furious panic threatened to take hold of him. Peter stumbled, his feet sinking into the mud, and fell backwards. With a dull squelch, he imprinted into the ground beneath him, his eyes stinging as the smoke connected with his bulging eyes.

His hearing was still impaired by the tenuous ringing in his ears yet, mercilessly, nothing but the brief darkness of smoke lessened his vision. Aimless shadows emerged from around him, running in every direction, their blurred faces full of expressions of shock, fear, and anguish.

Peter pulled himself up again, hearing only the thumping of his heartbeat and the dull rushes of his heavy breathing. He waved towards one of the figures approaching him, but as the growing figure of a woman appeared from the smoke, she completely ignored him and sprinted past, her face manic.

"Hello?" he shouted again into the smoke. Again, he heard nothing.

Peter turned back towards the remains of the train, ignoring the heat, desperate to offer any degree of assistance. Adrenaline was all that was keeping Peter upright as he pulled his feet from the sinking depths beneath him. The pain spreading through his body should have been more than enough to immobilise him.

He felt his foot collide with something beneath him and stopped instantly, terrified to look down. He kicked slightly again at the obstacle, obscured by the smoke – there was no response. Gulping, he looked down and brushed aside enough of the smoke to reveal a bloodstained, lifeless face. It was Sarah. Her body was sprawled unnaturally across the ground, her left leg hanging below the knee by just a thread of skin.

Peter doubled over and struggled to restrain himself from vomiting. Mortified, he continued to look around the scene as more and more desperate figures continued to run aimlessly in all directions. He felt tears forming and threw his arms out in the hope that someone might need his help, but no one approached. He looked back towards the train again, helplessly, and through the smoke, saw a dim light grow clearer and clearer, larger and larger, louder and louder.

Peter's hearing had returned to its full capacity as the light evolved into the harrowing figure of a young man running through the smoke, his body engulfed by flames. The high-pitched screams were the first thing his returning sense was exposed to, piercing into his bones; they were screams he was sure he would never forget.

The figure died away as it tore through the smoke, the flame diminishing more and more before coming to its inevitable stillness. The young man's dying screams had only been replaced by other growing shouts and abandoned cries for help coming from all directions. Through the opacity around him, survivors called out desperately for loved ones or howled in the agony of their grief.

Peter stood helplessly, turning from side to side. What could he do? How could he help these poor people?

His senses heightened, Peter heard sirens approach from afar, offering some sense of hope. But as he looked around again at the lifeless bodies and scraps of steel littering the scene around him, he knew that there was none.

A faint gleam by his side drew his attention, and he looked down to see that his arm was scarlet. Pulling back the remains of his sleeve, he noticed that a fragment of steel had impaled his forearm.

As though it had only needed him to see it, pain instantly took hold of him. He dropped to his knees as unconsciousness took him once more.

3

Peter woke suddenly.

He lay motionless, breathing rapidly as cold sweat trickled slowly down his forehead.

He threw off his bed covers and jumped towards his bedroom window, clutching his windowsill. His heart thumped uncontrollably, and his rapid breaths misted up the cold glass.

Almost a month had passed since it had happened. But still, he could not escape the nightmares. Peter's dreams seemed likely to be evermore doomed with helpless fiery figures screaming in the darkness, molten fragments of bubbling steel, and Sarah's lifeless eyes.

Peter shook himself and wiped his breaths from the glass to scan the scene outside, searching for a calming distraction. Aside from a pair of eager early-morning joggers, the street outside his second-floor apartment seemed devoid of activity.

Peter's arm throbbed painfully. He looked down upon the crescent-shaped scar, where the debris had impaled him in the attack – as he now knew it had been.

Peter had watched the reports from his hospital bed for days following the incident, bemoaning his lacklustre food selection. All of them told viewers of a bomb, thus far unexplained, having been left on the train at some point throughout its journey, dooming the lives of thirty-five men, fourteen women, and a twelve-year-old schoolgirl.

The young girl had become the face of the tragedy; her death and the tragic interviews with her surviving mother had ignited a collective fury that Peter had never experienced before. The public was baying for blood and desperate for the authorities to find those responsible.

The police had been investigating the explosion under intense scrutiny for the past few weeks but had uncovered few leads. With little evidence remaining, or indeed recovered, from the scene, they had been forced to conclude that it had most likely been a terrorist attack. Yet, with no organisation taking ownership, it looked increasingly as though their theory had been a wild stab in the dark.

Peter picked up his mobile phone from the bedside cabinet and looked at the time – 6 a.m. It was an hour or so earlier than he might usually have woken for work, but it was his first day back; the extra hours' preparation time might help to settle his nerves.

He reached for his painkillers and swallowed a tablet with a prolonged swig of water. He tossed his sweat-drenched pyjama bottoms aside and jumped into the shower, his mind still plagued by anxieties for the day ahead.

Peter imagined the influx of questions and sympathy. He did not know what answers he would have for them; he could not bring himself to tell anyone about the horrific scenes - the melting steel, the fleeing engulfed figures. Peter shuddered. He would have to find a way of forcing himself not to focus on those thoughts.

Twenty minutes into his brilliant relaxation plan, refreshed somewhat by his warm shower and dressed in smart-casual attire, he was no less anxious.

Pottering aimlessly through his apartment, Peter tried to calm himself with some breakfast television. He settled with a groan into his front room sofa, clutching his cereal in one hand, remote control in the other.

Again his plan had failed. As he surfed the channels, he was forced to switch some six times to find one not directly speculating which terrorist group might have been responsible. Channel six had not even settled before the picture of the train wreckage appeared, but he stopped his move to change the channel. This bulletin was not one of the usual media hypes that had surrounded the incident, discussing the ineptitude of the authorities to identify the culprit.

Beside the image of the wreckage was a woman's face. The newsreader reported that the woman, who had survived the initial explosion, had committed suicide. Peter threw the remote control aside and leant forward into his chair, racking his memory painfully; he had seen that before. It was her, the woman who had ignored him as she tore through the devastating smoke, screaming out for someone.

He felt an odd twinge. It was strange; he felt an intense pity for the woman.

Peter had been nothing but relieved following the incident, so much so that his appreciation of life had found new heights. But, as he rubbed his arm, he could not help thinking. How could someone have evaded death so spectacularly as she had, only to take their own life a matter of weeks later?

The report failed to elaborate in any further detail if she had lost anyone in the explosion, but he remembered that she had been shouting out for someone. Or perhaps it was not for someone in particular. His mind was still foggy. Perhaps she had just been instinctively crying out for help. Perhaps the nightmares had become too much for her. For that, he certainly had sympathy.

Peter grumbled; television had been a terrible idea. This latest bulletin would do nothing to deter the scrutiny he was inevitably set to receive at the office.

He was not wrong.

With a twinge of anxiety as he saw it approach, Peter opted to avoid the train. He turned away from the station and instead faced a tedious bus journey, plagued by the stares of schoolchildren closely examining, without any apparent recognition of his annoyance, the hint of burns he still had on his face.

Stares continued from other onlookers as he walked towards the glass-paned Chronicle building, and even the security staff ogled him as he pulled out his pass.

There was no escape, albeit he had been prepared, as he buzzed his key card to enter the office floor of the Chronicle. The room all turned eagerly towards him, falling silent.

"Peter!" came the booming voice of his editor. He walked briskly towards him, breaking the initial awkward silence as he brushed aside his colleagues and pulled him into a tight one-armed hug.

"How are you?"

His editor appeared to have opened the floodgates, and the other journalists flocked towards him. All wore expressions of concern, sympathy, or just downright curiosity. Then the inevitable questions came.

"So Peter, what happened?"

"Do you know who it was?"

"Can I see your injury?"

"Can I get an exclusive quote for my column, Peter?"

"No, of course you can't," his editor had interjected, pushing the young intern aside.

"That's for me, right?" he whispered into Peter's ear playfully.

Peter forced a weak chuckle. He took their questions reasonably well, he thought, given the situation.

As the juniors passed him a stale coffee and helped him into an open chair, he delivered his briefly-rehearsed account of the jerk and the heat, and that he had no idea what had happened, or who was responsible.

After what must have been the twentieth question, Peter saw his opportunity to escape and slowly emerged from the hot seat. He slowly edged towards his office as questions continued to fly in, continuing to palm off, as politely as he could, other staff members offering their sympathies. By the time he reached his office, he had spent a full twenty minutes trying to avoid any particularly difficult, or indeed distressing questions.

"Ok, guys, let's give Peter some space," his editor had called out to the room, all still staring eagerly at him. "I'm sure he's got plenty of emails to catch up on."

"Thanks," Peter whispered, as they walked towards his office.

"No problem, Pete," he said with a wink, as Peter opened his office door. "Let me know when you're ready to give me that quote…"

Peter laughed and turned to look at his office for the first time in weeks. It had not changed at all, but for a light hoovering of the carpet floor, and a large 'Get well soon' balloon tied to his chair. He turned back to see the expectant faces staring back at him through the office glass and forced a smile in thanks.

He docked his laptop to the computer monitor, acutely aware that the eyes outside his office were still fixed upon him, and began to work through the sizeable email inbox.

Perhaps unsurprisingly, Peter's day continued to be plagued by sympathy and questions. Things really got out of hand when Julie offered to make him a cup of tea; she usually limited their brief workplace interactions for the sole purpose of sneering at the latest negative comment on one of his articles.

Even as he kept his head down, his earphones in, and trawled through his inbox, he found himself chancing looks out across the office floor to see that his colleagues continued to whisper nervously and stare up towards him. At points, he felt as though he were the latest tropical exhibition at the circus, but he supposed their behaviour was understandable. If for nothing else, they must be wondering what sort of mental state he was in, taking sweepstakes on how long he would last before he tossed his computer monitor from the second-floor window.

Peter turned back to his computer and replied to an email from Cyril, one of the many asking how he was doing, grateful that he had not elaborated on how fantastic and record-breaking the conference had been. Most of his day, however, Peter had distracted himself by delving further into the news story of the woman from the train who had committed suicide.

Oddly, he found himself growing more and more suspicious as his research continued, trawling through news accounts and her social media presence.

Paula Stratten had been a married mother of three, whose husband had also survived the explosion with her – evidently the person she had called out for as she ran past Peter. She had escaped the greatest jeopardy of her life and not only that, her husband had survived too – surely, with three children, she had everything to live for.

Yet only a few weeks later, she appeared to have taken the drastic decision to end her life, leaving a suicide note citing the 'inescapable nightmares' as the reason behind her need to 'escape'.

Peter certainly understood what she had meant; he had not slept more than a couple of hours at a time since the incident, his sleepless nights plagued by visions of burning skin, sounds of terrible screams and bubbling steel. But his ecstasy and relief at having survived had given him the drive he needed to take the slow path of moving on.

For Paula though, it seemed, her relief had not been enough.

He clicked through the emerging interviews with her husband, standing outside their house, politely requesting privacy whilst expressing his grief and utter shock at what had happened.

"She had been doing so well," he had said to the various journalists. "I had no idea that she was having these thoughts. I thought we were both happy and getting through it. I thought we both felt like we had a future to look forward to."

The day continued to move slowly, his journalistic instincts returning with a purr as he continued to investigate, but Peter could not have been happier when he finally saw 6 pm. He looked up from his monitor to see his editor waving frantically at him for him to go home.

Peter smiled and nodded gratefully, grabbing his laptop.

He walked out, again to the stares of those who had waited for his departure. He perched himself on an empty bus seat and stared out of the window as it began to rain, still unable to shake from his mind the woman's face, screaming in the smoke.

Peter must have left himself on autopilot for a while, and he soon found himself approaching the front door to his flat. His relief was short-lived. His mind had already been on the six-pack awaiting him in his fridge when he pulled his keys from his coat pocket and discovered, to his horror, that his front door was already open.

4

It had been more than twenty-five years since he had last been in close contact with the boy, but it seemed now that it was finally time for him to emerge from the shadows. They had forced his hand. He would have to break the rules this time to keep the boy safe; he had no choice.

He had almost been too late.

Any naïve hope of a coincidence had been dashed when he watched the stolen CCTV footage when he had seen who stood at the platform.

So it was to be then. He had no choice but to tail him and guard his every move, whatever the cost; after all, the boy's death would be entirely his fault. The weeks following the train explosion had been relatively quiet, he thought. He had tailed him diligently, watching from a distance.

Seeing him every day, watching him struggle with the trauma of the explosion… it had taken considerable restraint not to give in to the urge to console him. After so many years away, he could not shake the warmth of being so close to him. He was desperate to help, desperate to tell him that everything would be ok, as he used to do, but knew that keeping his distance was critical, at least for as long as he could.

He stood calmly at the window of a second-floor flat opposite the boy's, wielding his binoculars. He observed the boy's nervous expression closely as he exited the building for his morning commute. He wondered, fleetingly, how much his disappearance had affected the boy, how bitter and resentful he must feel.

As the boy walked further out of sight, he noticed a flicker of movement shortly ahead of him, forcing any regretful musings from his mind. He saw a figure fifty metres away, similarly hidden from view and paying similarly close attention to the boy's movements. Was it time? Had they finally made their move?

He gripped the binoculars tightly, screwing his eyes in his effort to determine the culprit.

The man was tanned, with short black hair, and a hint of stubble hiding a sharp, scarred jawline. It was him, the assailant from the station, skulking in the alleyway dividing the apartments opposite the boy's.

He packed away his binoculars and pulled the rifle to his shoulder, preparing to take the shot, but paused. The assailant showed no intention of attacking or indeed approaching the boy. Indeed, he chose that moment to fade deeper into the shadows, further out of sight.

Odd, he thought, and he continued to maintain his aim through the rifle scope as the two passed each other, his finger gently poised over the trigger.

The boy continued his journey, diverting from the station to approach his bus, but the assailant maintained his position. As the boy got on, and the bus pulled away, the assailant edged out slowly. He glanced around, inspecting the exterior of the boy's apartment building and surrounding areas. He was planning his attack. He followed the assailant's gaze, trying to prejudge his plan. Whatever it was, his movements suggested that it was only a matter of time before the assailant made his move. It was going to be today.

He strapped the rifle to his back, pulled up his backpack and opened the window. Too far to jump, but he needed to be quick.

He turned back to search the apartment for anything that might help him and his eyes darted towards a laundry basket in the kitchen, with several duvet covers poised, and smiled.

Scanning the scene outside for any eagle-eyed neighbours, he tied the ends of the duvets together and secured the end to the window-side radiator, praying that the fabric would not rip under his weight. He climbed tentatively out of the window and looked up towards the boy's apartment. The assailant had reached his floor, approaching slowly.

He sighed and pulled tentatively at the duvet covers. He estimated an 80% chance of success. He had improvised in worse situations than this, he thought, as he lowered himself slowly. Inhaling, he allowed his full weight to pull at the duvets. It held.

Sighing, he abseiled the brick exterior quickly and hit solid ground.

He looked up again towards the boy's apartment; the assailant had edged his way through the front door. He followed hastily, opting to defend from the back entrance.

He glided swiftly to the back of the building and looked up; a piece of cake. The boy appeared to have left one of his back room windows open.

Grabbing for the exposed window ledges and askew brickwork, he climbed acrobatically up the back wall, clutching the first-floor balcony for support, and reached the boy's bathroom window.

He paused for a moment, holding his pose. He allowed himself to hang from the ledge for a second before risking a look. The assailant was walking through the apartment towards the boy's kitchen.

Cursing, he lifted himself to the window, silently berating the boy for being so careless with his home security and pulled himself up, forcing himself through the gap.

He fell to the floor silently and glanced around. He crouched down and pulled his rifle from his back as he approached the kitchen, observing every inch of the boy's apartment for any signs of tampering. His nose burned.

"How original," he scoffed to himself, as gas began to work its way through the apartment. As soon as he had said it, he knew he had been too loud.

The quiet sounds of scuffling in the kitchen had stopped suddenly. Cursing himself for the slip-up, he moved silently towards the ajar door, gripping the rifle, and peered through the gap.

He watched tentatively as the assailant scanned the kitchen until - through the small gap in the door - their eyes met. They stared at each other for a split second, and a slight hint of shock seemed to come over the man's face.

Instinctively, he pulled up his rifle and took a shot towards the assailant, but he had not been quick enough. The man dodged the shot and sprinted towards the door, slamming it open into his face.

He dropped the rifle and growled in pain as blood began to spurt from his nose, but the assailant did not stop, taking another swing at him. He rolled away from the assailant's lunge and composed himself, rubbing at his nose and rising slowly to set himself in position.

They circled each other without a word, breathing heavily, staring intently at each other, planning their next moves before once more they engaged.

5

Why Peter had even contemplated opening the door to investigate, he would never be able to explain. He had read enough news stories and watched enough late-night television to know that situations such as this only ended badly. But the explosion, and particularly having survived it, seemed to have given Peter a newfound sense of courage.

He reached a hand out tentatively and pushed the door open.

"Hello?" he shouted instinctively.

That's right, he thought, cursing his stupidity, let them know you're here. Nobody answered.

Peter edged his way inside the apartment, his heart thumping uncontrollably.

"Hello?" he tried again, though this time with little more than a squeak. Again, nobody answered.

His terrified anticipation withered away as he progressed through the apartment; it seemed at first glance to be in exactly the same condition he had left it. A bit untidy, though for a bachelor pad, he imagined, not too bad.

Perhaps he had just forgotten to close the door behind him when he had left for work that morning - he was battling a bout of anxiety after all. He sighed and placed his keys in his door-side bowl, before gently closing the front door. It had been a long day, that was all; he just needed a drink.

Peter looked around again before moving eagerly towards the cold six-pack waiting patiently for him in the fridge but stopped instantly. The hairs on the back of his neck stood on end. His eyes widened.

He looked more intently at the scene and found his initial conclusion had been entirely wrong.

He glanced at the framed picture of his mother, neatly positioned in the centre of his coffee table, metres away from its usual position.

He continued to look around. Whilst there were no major differences, various items appeared to be just out of position, rearranged as though someone had made a forensic effort to recreate Peter's flat from memory. They had almost achieved the feat.

Peter's heart began to race quicker still. He did not know why he had doubted himself; he knew he had closed the door that morning. Someone had been there, could still be there.

Peter hurtled towards the kitchen, grabbing blindly for the first object to hand, and turned back to make his way through the apartment. He drew his mobile phone from his pocket and began to dial, but something had shifted in the corner of the living room. He looked up, and it did not take long for him to discover who had been responsible for the change of decor.

"Put the spoon down boy," came a deep, calm voice.

He turned with a start, lifting his arm. It was only then that Peter realised his chosen defensive weapon had been nothing more than a metal ladle.

Though the embarrassing revelation removed any element of defensive strength, he maintained his position and focused more intently on the man's face.

His hair was shaggier, his face more lined than the one Peter remembered, as though it were from another life. Sitting in the armchair opposite him, he was for the first time since he was five years old, staring - ladle in hand - at his father.

Peter gaped silently for a moment, lowering his defence.

"What..." he choked, struggling for breath. "What are you doing here?"

"Keeping you alive boy," his father responded curtly, pulling himself up from the living room chair. "We need to go, now."

Peter glanced down at the gun his father had been caressing on his lap, and back up to the rifle strapped to his back.

His mind raced back to primary school. He was lying on the concrete playground floor and the other children were laughing, circling him and shouting - 'loony, loony, Brockland!' He was sitting on the chair outside the headmaster's office, crying gently as his mother spoke inside. "Don't worry," she was saying, with a consoling smile as they drove home. "It's all lies."

"What do you mean?" Peter stammered back, forcing himself from his memories as his initial shock subsided.

"What? No! What are you doing here?" Peter continued, gripping the ladle tighter. "Where have you been?"

Peter had not seen his father since he was a boy. The few photographs his mother had kept after his disappearance was all he had as he grew up, keeping the memory of his father alive.

Since his mother had passed away, still having never fully explained his father's disappearance, he had all but given up any hope of finding out what had happened to him.

Peter had been forced to grow up listening to the various media accounts of his disappearance, each more confusing than the last. Though, however wild, they all seemed to agree on one thing - Peter's father had lost his mind during military service, attacked a commanding officer and escaped into hiding.

His mother had always refused to entertain the story and in the very few times that she had indulged after a glass of wine too many, she would say nothing more than the story was a lie, his father had been given no choice, and that he should never speak of it again.

"Peter, I'm sorry. I know you must have questions but we can talk about this later. Right now I need to get you somewhere safe."

Disbelief and anger flared, as they had not done in years. Peter looked at his father, who stood before him, preparing to leave, seemingly flippant of the near-three-decades desertion of his son's life.

"What are you talking about?" Peter responded in exasperation. "No. I'm sorry, you need to leave. Get out."

It soon became clear that his father had not expected this response, which made Peter even angrier. He stared back at Peter, puzzled.

"Peter," he pleaded, edging closer towards him. "I know you must be angry, confused… but your life is in danger. It is essential that you listen to me. I need to keep you safe."

He moved to pull Peter towards the door, but Peter resisted, tearing his hand from his father's grip.

Peter could not comprehend the ease with which his father seemed to believe he could stroll back into his life, with some ridiculous story of his impending peril.

"What you need to do is leave," said Peter flatly, opening his front door. "Just go."

Years of confusion and bitterness had resurfaced in the space of their five-minute encounter, and perhaps unsurprisingly, Peter was not taking too well to his father's strict demands.

Peter stood his ground, staring at his father. He maintained his trembling grip on the handle of his now wide-open front door.

His father stood for a few moments, assessing the situation, before he gave a weak smile and nodded, defeated.

He sighed heavily as he approached the open door, scanned the hallway outside, and turned to place his hands on Peter's shoulders.

"I never left you, boy," he said, smiling, and with a final curt nod, he turned to walk out of the apartment.

"Keep your eyes open," he muttered, without turning back. "They aren't done with us yet."

6

"Make it clean," came a stern voice, commanding through the phone. "No more mistakes."

"Yes, ma'am", the agent responded.

He cut the call and peered up towards the second floor of the building, attaching the suppressor to his pistol.

A17 had not returned or even attempted contact following the first attempt earlier that evening, and there had been no indication of what had delayed his return.

Something, or someone, had disrupted his mission. It was crucial he remained particularly vigilant this time.

He looked up towards the sixth-floor window of the building to his left and pushed his earpiece intently.

"I'm moving now," he said.

"Copy that," he heard back.

After A17's disappearance, likely death, they could not afford to make any more mistakes. The two standby operatives would provide adequate cover for him as he attempted to complete the mission and determine the cause of A17's disappearance.

Affording a swift nod towards the two shadowy figures at the window, he gripped his pistol tightly and walked briskly towards the front entrance.

7

Peter sat silently within the warm embrace of his favourite armchair, his mind transfixed upon the evening's events. However rampant the lights dancing from his television screen, however many bottles he sank, he could not distract himself from his father's strange, sudden reappearance.

That in itself would have been quite enough for one evening's worth of shock. But for him to have visited not to grovel apologies for his childhood absence, instead deliver some fantasy of Peter being in immediate danger... it was ludicrous, outlandish. Yet, he could not help but try, harder than he might have expected, to justify his father's warning. Peter felt like that confused, eight-year-old child again, longing for his father back.

His mind fixed on his mother again, to her perpetual insistence that they never discuss his father's disappearance. Peter had always believed she always found it too painful to talk about, and, having had no desire to cause his mother unnecessary pain, Peter had always relented.

What little she did say, when pushed, was that he had simply been forced to leave, that he had no choice, and that was that. He remembered even now the chaos that had gripped them when he had disappeared: the visitors, the reporters, the police. It was no surprise that his mother had decided to relocate them, away from the hubbub, leaving any faint source for information or questioning behind.

It was perhaps out of respect for her that he maintained his apathy towards his father following her passing, or perhaps it was just the passing of time. But to see him again in person tonight, his return, forced his repressed childhood curiosity and frustration to the surface.

Peter pulled himself to his feet, leaving his empty bottle on the side table, and prepared himself for yet another sleepless night, this time contemplating the night's events, when he sharpened.

For the second time that evening, the hairs on the back of his neck stood on end. The room suddenly felt ice-cold; his heart began to race. An intense panic began to flow through him and he focused intently on the steadily quickening footsteps in the hallway.

His father had warned him that he was in danger, and in that split second that he decided to trust that warning.

Peter sprinted towards the kitchen and had only just managed to close the door behind him when the front door burst open.

Peter was certain that the orchestral thumping of his heart or his heavy grunting breaths would soon betray his position, but he forced himself to remain crouched and still. He rested his head gently against the kitchen door and listened as the intruder stepped through the now-unhinged front door and out into the apartment.

Peter turned to scan his kitchen for a weapon, anything with which he might have some chance of defending himself. With a slight grin, in spite of himself, his eyes rested upon the metal ladle now hanging in its proper position.

Listening carefully for any sound of movement from opposite the door, he stood slowly to investigate his makeshift armoury and was astonished to find a gun lying on his sideboard.

Peter crept towards it, anxious to hide the sounds of his footsteps and picked it up timidly. Had it been a parting gift from his father?

He turned it from side to side in the palm of his hand. Peter had never held a gun before. It seemed to give him a strange, comforting sense of power in his moment of panic.

Applying his relatively little knowledge of armaments gained from hours spent playing computer games, he released the safety lock and gripped the gun tighter.

Peter moved tentatively towards the kitchen door, listening again for any sounds on the other side. Silence. The intruder seemed to have moved away. Peter imagined he would have a matter of seconds to, well, what? He could try and shoot the man, he supposed, but what if he betrayed his position? He would have to make a break for the open door. He listened again. Still silent. With a deep breath, he braced himself to take an investigative glance.

His face drained of colour. Peter felt his grip upon the gun slip within his steadily sweating palms; a rustling had come from behind him. The intruder must have circled him. This was it.

Peter closed his eyes and took a deep, steadying breath. He would have to be quick. He gripped the gun again, his finger poised on the trigger, and turned, petrified, to find himself aiming the gun at his father.

Recognising Peter's shock, his father raised his hands calmly and gently lowered Peter's gun. They looked at each other for a second, both still, both listening intently. Still, there was only silence in the front room.

Peter's father raised his hand and gestured for Peter to stay in the kitchen and remain quiet.

Peter nodded slowly and moved aside to allow his father a path towards the kitchen door. He followed, and the both of them listened for the intruder's movements on the other side.

Peter heard rustling from the front room. Whoever it was that had unceremoniously granted themselves entry, was now perusing Peter's scribbled desk notes - musings on the stories surrounding the suicide of Paula Stratten.

Peter's father turned back to look at Peter briefly and, with a wink, turned towards the door and stormed into the front room.

An instantaneous succession of gunshots filled the room, fuelling Peter with another rush of adrenaline.

For one whose limits of excitement so far in life had resided within the analysis of paint strokes of accomplished artists, the evening's events should have crippled him; but he remained resilient.

He heard scuffles as the two engaged and heard the loud bangs of what must have been his furniture being tossed aside. Peter stood sharply, contemplating his decision – risk the gunshots and stray furniture to help his father or continue to cower within the relative safety of his kitchen.

He felt an unexpected thrill, bordering on excitement, fill him and quickly came to his decision. Peter's recent brush with peril, rather than cripple him, seemed instead to have birthed reckless courage.

Peter grasped the gun tightly, breathed in heavily, and followed his father into the front room.

He instantly regretted his decision.

Within seconds of his entry, he felt a whoosh of air accompany a stray bullet from the intruder, narrowly missing his right ear.

Peter threw his arms up instinctively and looked in the direction of the gunshot, to see the intruder and his father engaged in an intense grapple. The man was large, dressed head to toe in black, with a thin balaclava covering his face. Peter watched in horror as the intruder extricated himself from his father's grip and lifted his gun for a second shot.

Peter launched himself behind his displaced sofa and, in the brief moment it had taken for the intruder to take the shot, he heard him release a low grunt. Peter's father had tackled him to the ground.

Once again, they engaged in fiercely skilled hand-to-hand combat, as Peter crouched helplessly behind the sofa, yearning for his previous dose of courage to return.

A minute or so passed, with only the grunts and slaps of the two butting rivals to interrupt the silence. Feeling it safe enough to chance another glimpse of the action, Peter stood slowly from his spot. Both had each other by the throat and Peter could see the intruder's eyes reddening through the gap in his balaclava. Taking advantage of their distraction, Peter raised his gun, ready to shoot.

Peter froze. As he looked around the room, he saw two red dots dancing across the apartment walls, scanning the front room from outside, eagerly hunting their prey.

"Dad!" Peter shouted, pointing towards the lights.

His father pushed the intruder backwards, allowing himself a moment to look. His face drained, recognising them instantaneously to be the target lights of the supporting agents' rifles, prompting him to force the grapple away from the threat of the window. He had not moved quickly enough.

Peter's father winced as a shot came through the window, jumping at the opportunity.

The intruder rolled away and pulled himself to his feet, bruised and panting heavily. An evil grin spread across his bloodied face. He poised himself, pointing his gun towards Peter's father.

A shot fired.

Even seconds after it happened, Peter could not remember having done it.

Trembling and breathing heavily, Peter lowered his gun and looked upon the scene he had created.

The intruder lay sprawled on his front, blood oozing onto the carpet around him, a faint expression of surprise etched upon his steadily whitening face.

"Come on, quickly," his father commanded, moving towards Peter and cradling his wounded arm.

He dragged Peter towards the front door as the target lights continued to search and shoot, but Peter seemed not to hear him; his senses had numbed entirely.

The pair's sprint through the corridors of Peter's flat complex breezed through Peter's mind as the shock of what he had just done overwhelmed him.

He looked up weakly, responding to an echo in the distance. They had reached the front doors to the building. His father stood ahead of him and scanned the car park outside, apparently looking for an escape plan.

"Stay here…" came his father's voice, echoing again from a distance.

Peter simply looked back at him blankly.

His father walked towards him briskly and gripped Peter's shoulders, shaking him from his trance. "Snap out of it boy, we're not done yet."

Peter nodded weakly. With a wink and a consoling smile, his father released his grip and moved back to his escape plan.

Peter remained still, confused, his arms hanging stupidly by his side, grasping the gun.

He looked down at it and threw it away instinctively, in disgust. As it clattered across the foyer floor, he looked back as his father walked aimlessly from side to side, still formulating their escape.

With a sudden turn, he sprinted through the front doors and out towards an SUV parked only a few metres away outside.

He was met by another array of gunshots and forced into an impressive display of athletic ducks and rolls.

Peter continued to look blankly upon the scene, his shock slowly starting to subside. Comprehension washed over him. He had just killed someone. He had pulled the trigger and ended the life of another human being. Peter felt a growing heat inside him and crouched over, retching violently.

Breathing sharply, Peter allowed himself a moment to recover. He pulled himself back upwards and wiped away the remnants of his shock. He blinked away the tears and, as he looked around again, stopped to stare at the concierge desk. Emerging, egg-like, from behind the computer monitor came the balding head of Gerald, his ageing landlord.

He stared wide-eyed towards Peter and then out towards the scene outside as the gunshots continued to rain in.

"What the fuck?" he mouthed.

Peter tried to explain, so far as he could, but it seemed that in the excitement, he had lost the ability to speak. He simply looked blankly back at him, only able to offer a faint shrug.

Peter heard a low rumble from outside and looked back out towards the car park to see the glowing halogens of a huge SUV accelerating towards them.

Peter had expected the car to skid to a halt outside, and perhaps that was part of why his feet remained plugged to the ground beneath him, but instead, his father drove straight through the glass doors.

Peter threw himself out of the way just in time as the car skidded to a halt, glass and debris flying everywhere.

"Get in!" his father shouted through the shattered remains of the passenger-side window.

Peter did not need to be told twice. He chanced another look back towards his landlord, whose face was contorted in an almost comical look of shock, before turning to sprint towards the car. He wrenched the passenger door open and threw himself into the seat before fumbling to buckle himself in.

Peter looked at the devastation scattered across his apartment foyer and saw Gerald still peering out from behind the desk. Peter offered an apologetic wave towards his landlord, who offered his hand back, still perplexed. Peter felt the car jerk from beneath him and clutched at the inside door handle for dear life.

His father reversed at speed back out of the gaping hole in the entrance and back out to the ensuing gunfire outside.

Shots hailed in on the car, clanging relentlessly against the exterior as they advanced to the street outside and sped hastily away. Peter chanced a look at the side mirror to see that the shooters had risen from their crouched positions and were running towards a car of their own.

"They're coming!" Peter shouted, still clutching the door handle.

His father glanced towards the rearview mirror and turned violently onto a right slip road, narrowly avoiding an oncoming car. After a few more frantic looks in each of the car mirrors, he began to steady their speed.

"Dad?" Peter muttered, as they settled amongst the traffic, his breathing still erratic.

"Not now," he replied firmly, still eyeing the car mirrors.

"But, what is going on?"

His father remained silent; instead, he continued to glance frantically around for any signs of the shooters.

Just minutes later, as Peter's breathing had finally started to steady, he noticed his father's body tighten. A white Citroën hatchback swerved violently around a junction to join their road, approaching at speed.

His father had noticed them first, and before Peter could shout, he had stamped down on the accelerator, thrusting them forward.

He managed to weave his way through two cars ahead of them before they were held up by another. He hooted furiously, cursing as the Citroën approached nearer and nearer through the traffic behind him. The driver seemed not to care for the safety of the other drivers as he battered them onto the side pavements as they forced their way through.

Peter looked fearfully at his father, who appeared to have come to a snap decision.

"Hold tight," he said, and Peter was stunned to find a wry smile creep its way across his father's face.

He accelerated hard into the car in front and it instantly swerved to the right, giving Peter's father a slight opening.

He pulled the steering wheel left and mounted the pavement, blaring his horn and shouting through the smashed windows at the pedestrians ahead. They threw themselves out of the way one by one, all screaming profanities at the lunatic driving towards them.

Peter's eyes were wrenched shut, but he risked a look through his father's window as they passed the driver they had hit. With wispy white hair, covered by a purple knitted hat, and glasses that Peter could tell instantly rendered her unroadworthy, she could not have been any younger than 80. Her bespectacled eyes, magnified through the lenses, stared angrily back at him as they passed and her middle finger was dutifully poised.

Peter could not help but laugh and, with another jerk, they continued to tear past the traffic before rejoining the road ahead. The situation was just so mad, so unbelievable. Just yesterday he had been anxiously praying for sleep, worried about going to work the next day. Today he was playing a real-life Grand Theft Auto game.

Fortunately for Peter, the SUV appeared to be considerably faster than that containing the mysterious shooters, and they had managed to leave them several vehicles behind.

As they sped ahead, Peter looked back to see their predators abandon the route and turn into a side road.

Peter sat back in his chair, closing his eyes and allowed himself a brief moment to relax and catch his breath. "I think we lost them."

Peter's father scoffed and as he turned to offer his retort, Peter caught a glimpse of white moving swiftly towards his father's side of the car.

Before he could scream out, the car swerved sideways as the Citroën collided with them.

Their SUV tipped onto two wheels briefly, before crashing back to the ground. The Citroën pulled back a moment to avoid an oncoming car before returning for its second assault.

His father had been prepared, braking suddenly. The shooters swerved into the space he had left ahead and mounted the kerb, scraping the edge of a nearby lamp post.

Peter's father pulled back into first gear and accelerated, this time taking the offensive approach. He drove into the back of the shooters, thrusting them forward towards a crossroad ahead.

Shots fired out from the back window of the Citroën in response, forcing them to duck. Peter's father continued to accelerate until they had forced the Citroën into the crossroad.

He stopped the car suddenly and they screeched to a halt. They both looked up, breathing heavily, to see the Citroën skid to a halt, stranded in the centre of the crossroad.

The shooters locked eyes with Peter and his father for a second and raised their guns before they turned hastily. A large, red delivery truck had failed to brake. The truck smashed into them, thrusting the Citroën sideways. It rolled several times, pieces of the car flying off in different directions before it came to a halt on its side.

Flames began to stir from inside and the terrified crowds began to edge backwards, but there was no movement from inside.

Peter's father spared no thought for the dying shooters and pulled into reverse, accelerating backwards.

"Now we've lost them," he said, offering a weak smile.

As brave onlookers edged towards the battered Citroën to offer any help they could, they began to drive away from the scene, past the incoming sirens scrambling to investigate the carnage.

"They're…" said Peter, tailing away.

Peter's father looked in the rearview mirror, a hint of menace in his eyes.

"Dead," he replied calmly. "Yes, they are."

As blue lights continued to rush past them, apparently oblivious to the damage to their car, Peter's father typed a postcode into the GPS and tuned the radio. He sat back into the driving seat, with a long sigh before he began to hum along to the latest track, his face spread with a look of utter contentment.

They continued to drive for an hour or so in near silence, but for his father's humming and groans of appreciation for the heated seats. Peter spent the time trying to come to terms with the Hollywood movie that he seemed to have found himself thrust into, between nervous glances for any further followers as they continued.

They advanced out of the city centre and further into the remoteness of the suburban countryside, ignoring the stares of pedestrians eyeing up the damage to their car.

Peter's heart had only just returned to its usual rhythm when they had begun to pull down a narrow broken-up road towards a hillside river, towards what must have been their destination.

Peter looked at his father inquisitively as they continued to edge towards a small, secluded cabin, a slight hint of ember from inside lighting it up against the darkening evening sky. With one final look in the rearview mirror, his father slowly pulled up beside the cabin, sighed and rested his head back into the seat.

"Where are we?" Peter asked, looking around at the scarce surroundings.

His father threw open the car door and walked towards the cabin, indicating for Peter to follow.

"Home," he shouted back as he reached the cabin, and entered the wooden front door.

Peter got out of the car slowly and looked around, allowing himself another short moment to settle.

The cabin seemed to be the only sign of life for miles. Vast, green hills surrounded them, offering a secluded location, further protected by a crystal-clear stream, slowly meandering through the hills with a harmless glimmer.

It was beautiful, he thought to himself, appreciating the safety that the locale seemed to offer.

"Are you coming in or what?"

Peter turned back to the cabin and followed his father inside.

Though the warmth of a growling log fire was a comfort, further investigation of his father's cabin immediately led him to the conclusion that he had walked into the living quarters of an insane escaped convict.

The space inside was larger than he had envisioned from the outside, though the clutter did little to accentuate it.

Pictures of faces, plans, documents and red cotton connection lines filled the wooden walls. Peter looked around, his jaw agape, and read through some of the news clippings. Most seemed to detail various worldwide tragedies or high-profile murders, and all of the clippings and documents that wallpapered the cabin linked to random faces and unusual symbols.

His attention immediately turned to one dated the 5th June 2029: the day of the train explosion. Peter looked closely at the story and noticed a series of cotton lines leading out from it. He gripped one of them gently between his thumb and forefinger and followed the first link towards the image of a brooding man, slightly tanned with short black hair. It was him – the man from the train platform, the one who had spilt his coffee.

He felt his father scrambling around behind him, but continued to follow the various cotton links and spotted one area to which all of the others seemed linked. It was a picture of a middle-aged man, beside a strange symbol.

The man looked well-built, with a noticeable scar poorly hidden beneath extensive white facial hair.

The bizarre cabin display reminded Peter of some of the crazed private investigators he had met in his line of work, obsessed with finding bizarre, conspiratorial links between devastation and death.

He looked again at the cotton links to find some looked completely random, linking stories of environmental disasters and minor news stories on suicides. Again, all were linked to pictures of faces and documents.

Peter turned towards his father, who had slumped into a bed in the corner of the room and had begun to remove his boots.

Something caught his eye and Peter looked towards a side table to see that his father had propped up a small framed photo. It was a much younger Peter, standing beside his mother and father, all of them gleaming. His heart warmed; he had not forgotten them entirely in his life of madness then.

"Dad, what is all this? What's happening?" Peter asked, pointing towards the walls.

His father cricked his neck and looked up at him with a resigned expression, thinking hard amidst his exhaustion. He suddenly looked old and tired. It was no longer the face that Peter had learned to forget, the face that appeared in the frame beside him; no longer the face that Peter had stared out of his bedroom window waiting for, for weeks as a child, yearning for its return.

"Sit down," he said, motioning towards an old armchair. He let out a long sigh and ran his hands through his hair. "I suppose it's time to tell you everything."

8

R47 looked upon the devastation.

The car lay crumpled, now completely ablaze, the other agent dead, and his corpse burning inside the wreckage as foolish bystanders and firefighters sought to calm the scene.

How had they failed again? She would be furious this time.

He had only just managed to escape the wreckage with his life, but when he told them what had happened and, more importantly, who it was that had helped Peter Brockland escape, he was not sure that his life would be worth much living.

He reached for his phone and dialled, wincing as he lifted his broken wrist to his face.

"Yes," came the sharp voice.

"Ma'am, Peter Brockland has escaped again. M12 deceased."

"Fuck," came the voice on the other end. "How has this happened again?"

"Ma'am, he had help. It was…" he paused. If he was wrong about this, he would be toast. But he was sure of it; he had seen his face many times before on their target list: a high-profile deserter.

"Yes?" the voice asked, impatient.

"Ma'am, it was Red 7. Repeat, Red 7 helped Peter Brockland escape."

The line was silent for a moment, the only sound remaining the crackling of the flaming wreckage in the road beside him and the mutterings of curious onlookers.

"Ma'am?"

"Yes I understood," she responded. "Good. Clean up the scene and report back for a debrief immediately."

The line cut out and he lowered his arm, wincing.

If half of the stories about Red 7 were true, he could count himself extremely lucky that he was still alive.

9

Peter's ears sharpened.

Finally, it was time to hear where the madness of the past few weeks had started and why he, a random small-time art journalist, had been pulled into it.

Peter gripped the arms of the chair and pulled himself down. He sat tentatively opposite and stared up at his father. Clearly exhausted by the evening's events, he had pulled himself into an uncomfortable seated position on the edge of his bed, seemingly considering how best to begin his story.

"I'm not quite sure where to begin," said his father, confirming it.

He sighed deeply and stared aimlessly towards the walls of the cabin.

"I suppose it all began twenty-seven years ago. I was engaged with the military on an operation in Kuwait."

A dark expression came across his father's face as he sat in deep thought, recalling the period with obvious discomfort.

"I was twenty-nine and I had been promoted into a special forces unit with guys with a decade more experience than me, real hard nuts. Looking back now, to have been placed within such an elite unit... was crazy. I think they thought so too, but at the time, I was buzzing. I was the youngest recruit to have ever been recruited to Special Unit."

He paused, thinking.

"I was skilled; even those guys couldn't deny it. I was perhaps even on par technically with them, but there was no way I should have been there. On my first mission, we had been tasked with breaching the defences of a rough local militia. We had intelligence that they were holding several UK nationals hostage. The first attempt was a complete disaster. We were outnumbered, at least three to one. The intelligence had been completely wrong; we were totally unprepared for what we came up against. Even worse, the complex was home to disavowed members of Kuwaiti Special Forces, not some local brute force. We had no chance. It was carnage - I watched my team gunned down in front of me. Only three of us managed to escape."

Again, he paused, running his hands through his hair.

"The three of us barely got out ourselves. Battered and bruised we were, but somehow we dragged ourselves to the extraction point. Even then, we had to wait for hours for any support. Something was wrong; I could see it on their faces."

He stood up from the edge of his bed and began to pace the room.

"They did pick us up eventually of course, but it was barely two weeks after that I was deployed on another operation. Again, the intelligence was poor. Again, members of my team were lost, and again I barely escaped with my life. I couldn't keep doing it. I had your mother, and you to think about," he said, looking up at Peter.

"I hadn't been there long, but I kept telling myself that the next mission would be my last. I was paranoid, terrified. I knew something wasn't right. At each stage of my operational career with Special Unit, I was being placed into unnecessarily high-risk scenarios, with poor intelligence putting me and my team at risk. I was certain that someone was trying to get me killed."

He looked up again, imploring Peter to understand his state of mind at the time, that he had not been crazy.

"I had to do something."

Peter intensified his gaze and sensed that his father's story was approaching its climax.

"But something even stranger happened; my commanding officer joined us on a mission in South America. He had never come before. A commander stayed at home and, well, commanded. It was unheard of for one to come anywhere near an international operation, but given the recent cock-ups, the others didn't think it was that much of a surprise. We had started to engage with our targets in a small town in Chile when he indicated that he and we should advance, just the two of us. I knew this was the time. The others had no reason to be suspicious, but there was only one reason that he could have been there - for me. We advanced together, but before he had any chance of unleashing his plan, I knocked him out and restrained him in our vehicle. I radioed back for the others to retreat, that we would follow, and I drove for miles with him in the back. Eventually, I found a secluded village and an empty hut. I took him into a back room and we, well, we talked..."

Peter raised his eyebrows sarcastically but did not interrupt.

He was not quite sure what to make of his father's story. On the face of it, he sounded like a paranoid maniac and Peter had found little in his father's recollections to negate the media reports he had heard as a child. Had he just made a huge mistake in trusting him?

"Well," his father continued, recognising Peter's bemusement. "He talked. It took a while, but he soon spilled. He told me all I think he knew, all I needed to know."

"What did he say?" Peter asked, breaking his silence.

His father stopped his aimless pacing and approached the wall hosting the strange broadsword symbol, staring directly at it.

"He told me that he had orders from his commanding team to ensure that I did not survive my missions. He had been told to place me in high-risk situations where my chances of survival were bleak, to make it look like an accident."

"What do you mean?" Peter asked.

"I was not supposed to come back from my missions, boy. They meant for me to die," he answered, stroking one of the cotton threads.

Peter's mind raced. The story just sounded so farfetched.

"But Dad, this makes no sense. Why would the military try and kill one of their own?" Peter asked again.

"It took a little longer to get that answer," he replied.

He walked towards an ageing desk on the opposite side of the cabin and pulled open the drawer.

"Want one?" he asked, extracting a dusty whiskey bottle and two glasses.

Peter nodded impatiently, eager for his father to continue his story.

"He said he didn't know much about them other than what he had learned in his limited communications," he said, handing a glass to Peter. "And I'm fairly sure that he was telling the truth, given the pain he was in. He said they were powerful - a secret organisation that had infiltrated major worldwide institutions, including the British Army."

Once again Peter raised his eyebrows in disbelief, and once again his father smiled, taking a large swig from his glass.

"Quite," he said, exhaling heavily from the effects of the whiskey. He briskly poured himself another. "I had the same reaction. Even in my state of paranoia, I thought perhaps I had hit him a few times too many, but he stuck with his story. Something in him convinced me that he was telling the truth.

He told me it had all started when he had been ordered by a superior officer, some 'mysterious woman', to ensure that a recruit was 'disposed of'."

He pointed towards a small news clipping on the wall behind Peter.

"Young recruit found dead in barracks," Peter mouthed, reading the headline.

"I had heard that story a few years before," his father continued. "Young guy, horrible. I asked him why he had killed the boy, and he claimed that his family were in danger, that they would have been killed if he did not follow their orders. He had no idea why the boy had to die, just that his family's lives depended on it."

"But why?" Peter asked, frustrated by the lack of answers.

Peter's father waved his hands impatiently.

"Well after I left him, I ran for it. I came home and explained what I could to your mother. I told her she needed to move you both away, that she needed to go along with whatever story might come out from the army, to ensure that you would both remain safe. I made a few arrangements and I left. I allowed the media to paint me as some deranged criminal. I think your mother thought I had gone insane, that's certainly the story that went out."

He drowned his glass again and stared at the framed photograph, a hint of sadness forming over his face for the first time. Peter leaned forward.

"It was hard to lay low," he continued, pouring a third glass. "My commanding officer was found the next day with a bullet in his head. Naturally, I was in the frame, but I left him alive. Someone else must have killed him and framed me, but it was me hunted as a paranoid, dangerous murderer who had suffered some psychotic break whilst serving."

Peter remembered brief glimpses of the various newspaper reports as a child with his father's face splashed across the front pages before his mother had snatched them away. He remembered how people in the street would turn and stare as he and his mother walked down the street. He remembered the evenings of television when his mother had found herself constantly flicking through news reports to avoid any mention of him.

It had not been long after his disappearance that they had relocated; had this been the cause of their move? Had his mother really kept this story from him, allowing him to grow up resenting the maniac who had left to protect them? Or, had she believed that his father's story was a fabrication and that he had indeed suffered a break from reality?

Oblivious to Peter's contemplations, his father continued.

"They found me from time to time, this secret organisation. But I was always prepared – more so each time."

Peter's father stood up and walked towards the desk. After a few moments of rummaging through various documents in the drawers, he pulled out an old, crumpled piece of paper.

"I had to fight them off a few times before I was able to get this," he said, passing the document to Peter.

Peter held it up to see it featured an almost page-size image of his younger-looking father, with the caption 'INCOMPATIBLE' below it, in bold, capital red text.

"Incompatible…" Peter muttered, staring blankly at the text. "What does that mean?"

Peter's father smiled and walked over to an area of the wall where almost all the cotton lines connected and prodded a sketched image – it was that strange symbol.

"Each of the men and women who came after had this same tattoo," he replied.

"I've never seen it before," said Peter, standing up to look at the symbol in closer detail. "What is it? It looks like some sort of wired sword."

"Thanks for the expert opinion," his father responded, forcing a slight grin from Peter.

"It's a broadsword, entwined by a double helix."

"Like DNA?"

"Exactly DNA."

Peter frowned, still confused. Before he could once more utter his frustration, his father interrupted. "It will make more sense when you see Exhibit B."

His father walked back to his work area, opened up the laptop that had been sitting patiently and inserted a flash drive.

"I acquired this with even greater difficulty," he said.

Peter wandered towards him as his father clicked away, opening a document folder on the screen.

Peter managed to glimpse the titles of further digital subfolders, detailing dates and names before his father stopped at the folder: '2006/07/23_Kenneth_Adams'. He clicked and indicated for Peter to come closer for a look.

Peter moved forward and stared at the screen. His father pushed the laptop towards him and Peter scrolled through the file. It seemed to detail everything that you might ever need to know about Kenneth Adams – his birth records, marriage certificate, phone numbers, and even the pin code to his mobile phone.

His father nudged Peter aside and scrolled down into the file, to show Peter what appeared to be an extensive list of scientific data - numbers, charts and report summaries, with some areas highlighted in red and again the word 'INCOMPATIBLE' footing the data.

"What is this?" Peter asked.

"This is a genetic assessment of a man called Kenneth Adams," he replied. "And not a very good one."

He pointed towards the summary at the foot of the data.

"This was my first glimpse at what the organisation hunting me was really about. Can you see the bottom?"

Peter looked towards the summary text at the end of the data, to see the familiar bold, red 'INCOMPATIBLE' result.

"Mr Adams seems to have failed their process of 'genetic compatibility', and as such..."

Peter's father walked to the opposite side of the room and pointed out another news clipping – 'Onlookers watch on in horror as man throws himself to the Thames'.

Peter followed and read the news story.

'Mr. Kenneth Adams, of Bermondsey, London, threw himself into the dangerous currents of the River Thames yesterday lunchtime. Paramedics were unable to revive Mr Adams...'

"They are a fanatical organisation," Peter's father continued from behind him. "With widespread capabilities to extract and assess the genetic material of, well, at least all of these people."

He waved vaguely towards the many faces strewn across the cabin walls.

"Who knows how many more, thousands maybe. They seem to follow a strict code as to what makes for an 'acceptable human being' and ruthlessly deal with those deemed not to be – the staged suicide seems to be a favourite of theirs."

He looked for a short time at the news clippings with an expression mixed between pity and disgust.

"That's all I know," he continued. "Or all I have cared to know. I've just been running, hiding and keeping an eye on you when I can."

Peter's heart warmed. In accepting his father's story - his wild, completely unbelievable story - he might finally be able to relinquish himself of the self-doubt, the resentment and the pain of his childhood. He could finally solve the mystery of his father's disappearance.

"Did Mum know?" Peter asked bleakly.

Peter's father looked back at him. His eyes seemed to glisten at the mention of her.

"I told her what I could in the time I had. She knew I was in trouble and I think she believed me. At least, I hope she did."

He looked at Peter intently again.

"I was there, you know, at the funeral... you did great. I just wish I could have said goodbye properly before she went."

Peter turned away to look back at the cabin walls and his thoughts turned to his mother. She had been forced to live with this, raising Peter by herself, surrounded by the cacophony of media speculation and prying neighbours.

He imagined how difficult her life must have been, managing their lives in the absence of a husband caught up in some elaborate conspiracy. Whether she had believed the story or not, she had carried on, keeping her husband's secret, keeping it all to herself.

Peter took a deep breath and collected himself; the sudden flash of appreciation for his mother brought on a raw grief that he had not experienced for years.

He looked around the cabin again, towards the faces of mysterious figures and reports of strange incidents. If his father's story was true, these people had dominated the events of Peter's life, without him knowing anything about them.

He thought again about his mother's struggles and felt a sudden rush of enraged passion. It was time to believe his father's story.

"So what do we do now?" he asked, turning to stare directly at his father.

"Now?" his father mimicked, staring at Peter's impassioned expression with confusion. "Now we do what I have been doing for years. We keep you out of trouble, we keep you safe."

"What?" said Peter, incredulously. "We can't just run from this, Dad. If this is true, we have to tell people. We need to expose them!"

Peter felt the juices of his journalistic instinct resurging.

"Expose them?"

His father chuckled.

"I don't think you've quite got it, boy. As far as I know, these people are everywhere. I wouldn't be surprised if they had people in the press. I would put this cabin on it. You wouldn't have a chance."

"We can't just do nothing!" Peter shouted.

His father walked towards him and placed a consoling hand on Peter's trembling shoulder.

Surely, he must understand how Peter was feeling. At some stage, his father must have felt the same as Peter did now, desperate to rid himself of the faceless organisation's pursuit, desperate to avoid forevermore being a marked man.

"I'm sorry, boy; there's nothing we can do. It's taken all my abilities to just keep myself alive all these years, let alone help run this revolution of yours."

"There must be others that know," Peter pleaded, weakly. "Others that can help?"

"Other survivors? Others that have worked out what is going on?"

"Sure," his father answered. "Could be, probably is. But think about it. If they are lucky enough to have not only escaped but worked out and believed what is happening to them, they aren't likely to go out of their way to make themselves a public target are they?"

"We have to do something," Peter uttered again, noting the desperation of his plea.

“I’m sorry,” said his father, and he grasped Peter’s shoulders tightly. “There is nothing I want to do now but keep you safe. Nothing else matters.”

Peter nodded weakly, accepting his father’s conviction. But as his father smiled back, he knew that he was certainly not going to accept his conclusion.

How could Peter possibly allow this group to continue? How could he stand by and allow others’ lives to be as dramatically affected as his had been? How had they managed to remain so secret?

Peter felt his conviction strengthening. He had to, and he certainly would, do something.

“We need to sleep,” he heard his father say, jogging him from his thoughts.

Peter turned towards him and nodded with a weak smile. His father smiled back, almost apologetically.

“Sleep on it. We can talk more tomorrow. You’ll feel differently soon, I promise.”

He rummaged beneath the bed and tossed a blanket towards Peter, before slumping. Peter caught it instinctively and sat down on the small sofa towards the other side of the room.

He remained drawn to the surrounding news clippings, focusing intently on the report of his own train crash story.

Had his coffee not spilled, had he not moved carriages, Peter would have been nothing but another successful statistic for this genetic protection group, or whatever they were.

Peter’s eyes flickered to the names of other survivors, from interviews at, and after, the scene. He followed the cotton threads to news clippings on either side and saw that two of those interviewed in the aftermath had ominous red crosses by their names. Both stories were accompanied by what must have been his father’s scrawl in the margin - ‘suicide’.

One was the woman he had spent most of his first day back at work investigating – Paula Stratten. How many more would there be?

"These survivors..." Peter murmured, bringing a stir from the bed. "They don't know anything, do they? This group, they'll still go after them?"

Peter's father turned to his side but did not look towards Peter.

"They'll never stop," his father mumbled back, which prompted Peter to make his ultimate, wild decision.

10

The man that gripped the steering wheel of the battered SUV as it tore through the wilderness was a very different Peter Brockland than the one that had entered his father's cabin the night before.

His personality seemed to have experienced an evolution in the limited hours of sleep he had allowed himself, as his subconscious obsessed over his fellow train survivors. Many would be oblivious to what had happened to them, sleeping calmly as dawn approached, unaware of what might be coming to finish the job.

Peter had made his decision quickly. He knew something within himself had changed that night. The knowledge that a secret group was after him did not particularly frighten him, but rather refuelled his journalistic instincts. Who were they? What did they want?

Peter had waited patiently for his father's snores and pulled himself to his feet, quietly, grabbing the news clipping from the wall before tiptoeing out of the cabin. He had brushed aside any hints of guilt as the SUV growled into life and drove away in the early hours of the morning with a distinct, heroic intent.

As he pulled onto the main road, Peter pulled the news clipping from the passenger seat and read it again. He scanned down the column, flicking his gaze intermittently every so often to check the road ahead and focused on a particular paragraph detailing the survivors and, more importantly, their addresses.

Why had the reporter deemed such personal information appropriate? It was almost as if he was inviting someone to... and then it made sense.

"They really are everywhere..." he muttered to himself.

It felt like a personal affront to Peter to think that one of his own was complicit, but, with his father's story in his mind, things began to connect. On the off chance that this organisation had not already been aware of their victims' addresses, it appeared that they had people within the media in their employ, aiding wherever they could.

It was clear that the survivors detailed in the clipping were in serious danger, and Peter felt an overriding personal responsibility to ensure that they at least knew, were at least prepared for, what was coming for them.

Peter checked the addresses in the clipping and clicked open the map in the car's GPS.

Lucy Fisher, 29, of Shere in Surrey, proved to be the closest survivor to him and set to be the first fortunate recipient of his newfound heroism, or so he hoped.

He reprogrammed the GPS, his excitement building, and set his mind to a deeper contemplation of the new world in which he found himself so heavily immersed.

Driving towards danger to save a woman he had never met before from a secret society. It was like another scene from the bizarre Hollywood blockbuster he pictured himself in; all he was missing at this point was a cape and a mask.

Before his mind could drift to thoughts of superhero names and catchphrases, Peter imagined the countless deaths and disasters that this group might have been responsible for in their quest for - what? Human perfection?

Wild thoughts of potential activities or random celebrities and high-ranking officials who might be linked to the group made his journey pass by quickly and belayed any gut-wrenching guilt he might develop towards his stranded father.

Before long, the GPS notified him that he was just ten minutes from his destination. His proximity to Lucy Fisher began to sink in, pulling him abruptly from his conspiratorial daydream. He felt his heroic surge dwindle.

As he scanned the houses outside, he realised that he had driven there with absolutely no idea what he was going to do or say to her.

The insanity of his lack of planning was quickly dawning on him. What had he expected to do? Was he just going to knock on the woman's door and hope for the best? What could he possibly say?

'Hi Lucy, sorry to bother you, but a maniacal secret organisation is coming to kill you because your genetic code doesn't quite shape up.'

He took a glance in the rearview mirror and pictured the scene playing out, pictured the woman's bemused expression. For Peter, it had taken the shock return of a long-lost father and two assassination attempts before he had even begun to contemplate the validity of his father's story.

All he was doing was walking up to this woman's house, armed with a scribbled newspaper clipping to exhibit a questionable data privacy violation.

"You have reached your destination," came the calm, robotic voice of the GPS.

Peter pulled to a stop and scouted out for number forty-seven – the article had certainly been specific.

He had to do something, he thought, regardless of the insanity of his approach. There was no time. She could be targeted any day now; he had to do something.

He spotted Lucy before he found the door number, recognising her bright, pink hair from the train as she walked past one of her upstairs windows.

She had been one of the few to look at him with polite amusement, rather than outright derision, as he had advanced crotch-sodden through the carriage.

Peter stared up and watched as she rustled around upstairs, completely unaware of the danger that she was in. He took a deep breath and cut the ignition.

"Now or never," he muttered to himself, checking his car mirrors nervously for any sign of movement from outside.

Peter unbuckled himself and stepped out of the car quietly. With another glance up and down the suburban road, he began to make his cautious approach towards Lucy's front door, his 'evidence' clutched tightly in his hand.

When he explained the events that he had been through and the story his father had told him, she would surely believe him. Besides, she may have even had a narrow escape herself.

Peter took a steadying breath as he reached Lucy's front door and opted to allow his subconscious to decide upon the opening line as he carefully pressed her doorbell.

He heard the chimes echo from the other side of the door and he looked around anxiously, waiting for her response.

The street was deadly quiet, though he supposed that was perfectly normal for three o'clock in the morning. He wondered what Lucy was doing awake at all.

He listened again for any movement inside. There was no reaction; not a murmur; not a sound.

Peter pressed the doorbell again, gritting his teeth anxiously. He heard the chime reverberate through the house again and out towards the silent street behind him. Finally, muffled footsteps approached, creaking as Lucy walked down the stairs inside.

He turned again to look up and down the street outside, his paranoia taking hold of him once more. Still, a deathly silence.

For the second time in his life, Peter felt an intense heat on his skin. He was thrust backwards, forced from his feet, and landed in a crumpled heap several feet away.

He heard a familiar ringing in his ears, deafening all else. His body felt broken, and his mind completely disorientated.

He could barely move but managed to lift his head slightly to see slowly twisting clouds of thick, black smoke disrupting the night sky above.

Peter let out a growl and felt pain shoot through his body at his attempts to move. With an immense effort, he managed to lift himself to rest upon his elbows and saw the remains of Lucy Fisher's small village home, engulfed by flames.

He had been too late.

Peter's neck weakened, and he fell back to the spongy grass beneath him.

He lay still, utterly defeated, his strength leaving him, his eyes starting to water.

The dull sound of alarms interrupted his bout of tinnitus, but just as his hearing began to return, the black smoke continued to blacken his vision.

He was sure that the pain would soon see him pass out, and it would all be over. Some heroic spell, he thought to himself.

Peter turned his head weakly towards the street outside, as he felt the blackness take over him. He managed to make out the faint blurred outlines of shocked onlookers frantically running from their homes to offer whatever help they could.

He tried to shout out, to tell them that it was too late, that Lucy was gone, but he had lost the strength even to speak.

Peter felt his eyes become heavier as unconsciousness closed in, but before darkness took him, he noticed one of the blurred figures edging closer towards him.

The figure approached slowly and stopped ahead of him, sinking the ground beneath Peter. Peter watched helplessly as a hooded figure leant down, and through his blurred vision made out a hint of a grin before he fell into nothingness.

11

Peter's mind buzzed. As he slowly regained consciousness, he began to feel intense stabbing pains in his temples.

He had been standing outside the front door of Lucy Fisher's house. He was about to warn her, tell her about the existence of the strange organisation seeking to murder her, but then everything had gone blank.

Peter tried to reach for his head in an attempt to nurse the pain in his head, only to find himself unable to move his hands.

He struggled, pulling at what appeared to be tight leather straps clasped around his wrists. He pulled again, more panicked, only to be met by the clanging of his restraints. Despite his inability to open his eyes, he tried to work out where he was.

Peter was sitting upright, he was sure, apparently strapped into the arms of an uncomfortable metal chair. He tried to move his feet to feel for the ground beneath him, only to find that his legs had received similar treatment.

He shook his head to shake the still stabbing pain from his temples and sensed cloth on his face, covering his eyes. He had been blindfolded and strapped to a chair, neither offering much cause for hope.

He felt something stroke his cheek and, growing increasingly alert, his nose tensed at a pungent aroma of smoke.

He coughed violently and as the smell subsided, felt his blindfold lifted roughly from his face.

Peter opened his eyes slowly and found himself instantly blinded by an intense white light. Blinking away tears, he caught a blurred glimpse of a large, well-built man sitting opposite him, wielding what appeared to be a large cigar.

"Hello, Peter Brockland," came his deep, controlled voice. "You have managed to cause us quite a bit of bother."

Peter's vision steadily readjusted to the room's glow. As his eyes cleared, he saw his captor and the room in which he had been imprisoned.

The room was square and practically empty but for the two of them, with pristine, padded white walls, interrupted only by a large rectangular mirror, an ominously poised metal toilet and an opaque glass door.

Peter appeared to have found himself tightly bound in what must have been the cleanest prison cell on the planet.

"Do you like your new room?" the man asked, his voice oozing with smooth power. He took another drag from his cigar.

Peter turned to look at his captor. Behind the shroud of cigar smoke sat a well-built, middle-aged man, perhaps ten years older than his father. He was dressed smartly in a fitted black suit, with a slight grin etched upon a stubbled, strong jaw.

His whitening beard failed to hide evidence of a recovered scar, two or three inches long, across his cheek. Peter looked defiantly back at the man, thoughts racing through his head as to who this person might be. He looked strangely familiar.

They had caught him; it had to be them, whoever 'they' were. His father had warned him, he had done his utmost to protect him, but Peter's hot-headed sense of heroism and journalistic curiosity had got the better of him.

"Where am I?" Peter asked, staring directly at the face of the man opposite.

His senses began to clear, making the man's face seem more recognisable still. He had seen this man before, on the walls of his father's cabin. He had seen his face hanging prominently in the cotton spiderweb, with almost all threads leading to him.

The man did not answer Peter but instead looked inquisitively at him, taking another deep drag from his cigar.

They looked at each other silently before, with one final drag, the man flung the butt of his cigar towards the glass door, blowing the remaining smoke towards Peter. His eyes watered again. As the smoke cleared, he saw the man perusing through a small bundle of papers.

"What do you know?" the man asked, his gaze fixed intently upon the documents in his hands.

"What?" Peter asked. "What do you mean? Where am I?"

With a rapidity Peter would never have expected, the man had risen from his chair and struck Peter across the face.

"What do you know?" he asked again, louder, yet still measured. He maintained his gaze upon the documents.

Peter glared at him, holding back his retort, and felt blood trickle from his lip. The man grinned once more.

"Alright," he said, accepting Peter's refusal.

He stood from his chair again and laid the documents in his empty seat, before circling Peter. "Where is your father?"

Peter's suspicions were confirmed.

Though his being taken by someone else was unlikely, the man's question confirmed it. He had been captured by the organisation he had only hours before accepted the existence of.

Sighing with an anxious resignation, he knew that in his current predicament, he had little chance, if any, of it ending positively for him. But the resilience Peter had shown when faced with the events of the past few days and weeks had surprised him, and it was the same again here.

Rather than quiver at the prospect of almost certain death, Peter felt a sense of calm determination. He looked back at the man resolutely and again refused to answer.

The man struck him harder, almost lazily, forcing Peter to gasp.

"Why are you doing this?" Peter asked, struggling against his restraints and shaking his head to rid himself of the slowly circling stars.

The man looked at him curiously before he sat down again, grabbing for the documents. He offered Peter a penetrating stare.

"It is important that I know what you know, and it is equally important that I am aware of your father's whereabouts."

He looked towards the blood trickling from Peter's lip.

"And I'm afraid in my experience, pain is quite often the most effective way of getting answers. So I will ask you again Peter, how much do you know about us? I assume that even in the short time he has spent with you, your father will have told you something."

Peter stared back and felt another pang of guilt as he thought of his father. He imagined how terrified, even angry, he must have been when he woke to find that the son he had risked his life for, again, the night before had deserted him.

Peter looked back at the man and nodded.

"He told me who you are, what you do," he replied, offering his captor a look of revulsion. The man chuckled.

"I see."

He laid back into the chair and folded his arms, apparently very interested to hear Peter's account. "And what did he say?"

Peter felt oddly as though he was being reprimanded by an old headmaster, after having been caught trading prohibited materials with classmates. The feeling did little to help ease his anger.

"He told me everything," said Peter. "He told me how you target people based on their genetics and murder those you deem incompatible."

Peter felt foolish talking with such confidence about something which he, in truth, knew nothing about - and which was more complicated than he had the scientific knowledge to explain.

"He found out about you, escaped you, fought you, and you have been hunting him ever since."

The man sat back and maintained his glance towards Peter, thinking.

"Well, I suppose in its basics that is our purpose, yes," he began, shifting in his chair.

"We source genetic material, through a series of operations and with agents expanding all areas of the key structures within society. We assess that data through our central mainframe to determine its value to the progression of the human race."

Peter stared back blankly, and the man opposite smiled.

"Yes, it is actually quite complicated, and it's not very often that I find myself having to explain the scientific complexities of our agency, so I must apologise. I'm sure the lab guys would explain our methods with more justice. I'm just the president."

Peter continued to look at the 'president' with mixed confusion and disgust, prompting the president to continue.

"We are the 'Progressive Human Race Order'," he continued. "Though that name is rarely used – we refer to ourselves as PHROX."

Peter stared, still confused. For such an organisation as this to have a name like PHROX seemed almost comical. Recognising the hint of a sneer on Peter's face, the president offered a slight grin.

"Yes, well like I said, we rarely use the name – I'm sure you'll agree the X makes it sound ever so slightly cooler than PHRO though."

"What you want to call yourselves isn't what concerns me," Peter retorted, struggling against his ballooning lips. "More the heinous activities."

"Heinous!" the president exclaimed, jumping to his feet in agitation.

"Heinous, you call it? We are protecting the future of humankind, Peter. We are eliminating disease, progressing strength. Our turbulent fight against nature for survival was once all that stood to protect humankind from the plague of weakness and degeneration. Weakness has become too well-protected in this modern world, too burdensome. The ease with which the afflicted can procreate and pass on their burdens can not continue."

The president was breathing rapidly, a mad gleam in his eye, possessed by his fanatical passion. "It is our duty to protect human potential, to strive for perfection."

The president looked intently at Peter, calming from his tirade. He offered Peter a meaningful smile. "It was once your father's."

Peter's heartbeat intensified at the comment. His mouth appeared to have evaporated of all moisture too, and he stared back at the president blankly, the blood draining from his face.

Surely he had misheard him.

"My…" Peter choked, struggling for words.

"Yours," the president replied with a grin.

Peter's mouth grew dryer still, and he shook his head, unable to accept the president's words.

"No," said Peter, weakly. "I don't believe you. My father wouldn't, he never..."

The president had stopped smiling and instead looked again at the documents he had brought with him.

"Dear boy, I have very little interest in what you want to believe and what you do not. Your father was once an agent of mine, a bloody good one too before he deserted us – couldn't handle the pressure anymore, I thought, until, ah..."

He raised one of the papers in his hand, shaking it.

"Until this."

He flipped the document to face Peter.

The document showed a photograph of Peter, set alongside the now-familiar sight of personal information and scientific data. But as he scanned further down the page, he could see that the document had been captioned bluntly at the end with the red, capital 'INCOMPATIBLE' result.

"Your name appearing, given your father's history with the Order..." The president ran a hand through his whitening hair. "Was very strange. It prompted my direct involvement in the case and I did a bit more digging."

The president held up another piece of paper, older and yellowing. It showed a picture of Peter again, a much younger Peter than the first, again alongside the same scientific data and the haunting 'INCOMPATIBLE' result.

Understanding quickly dawned on him, and Peter recognised the conclusion that the president must have come to and, more worryingly, a conclusion that seemed entirely plausible.

"It would seem that your father came across your record when you were first found to be incompatible and covered up the result. Indeed it seems the discovery that his own son was incompatible pushed him to question the entire ethos he had lived by for years."

Peter's blood ran cold. Everything was happening so fast.

It had taken him a great effort and two wild assassination attempts to believe his father's original story, and he was alarmed by the ease with which he was believing this stranger's alternative account. It all seemed to make sense.

His mind raced to find flaws in the story.

"How could my name have been missed?" he managed. "Surely, my father would not have been the only person to know."

"Indeed," the president agreed. "How indeed. A question I am afraid I still have no answer for. He must have had help, sure, but how he managed to keep it so quiet when so many were, are, involved in the process is quite something."

The president rose from his chair with a sigh. He looked down probingly upon Peter's shocked demeanour, as though scanning him one final time for any hint of deception.

"It seems we will just have to wait for your father to come to us then. He will have worked out we have you by now I am sure, and he knows where we brought you of course."

Peter forced his face into a look of anger in an effort to hide his dread. Peter hoped too, in spite of himself, that his father would indeed come and save him from almost certain death, again. He also knew that by doing so, his father would not only confirm the president's story but almost certainly see the death of them both, rather than just himself.

The president picked up the documents and walked towards the cell door. He placed his hand on a section of the wall, and the door reacted in an instant. With a low hiss, it slid open.

"You're going to kill me then?" Peter shouted, ignoring the crack in his voice as he did so.

"I imagine so," the president responded matter-of-factly, without bothering to look back. "Though, we are not the mass-murdering fanatics you seem to think we are. Death is not always the only way; sterilisation and imprisonment are often more useful methods. You, however…"

The president turned back to look at Peter, staring intently at him. His face offered a look of almost reluctant resignation.

"You know too much I'm afraid. And from what I have gathered about you already, you do not strike me as the sort of person to let things go."

Peter looked down at his knees, energy draining from him.

It was an odd feeling to be given a death sentence. He had learned so much over the past few days and developed such an embedded sense of justice and a passion to save the world. Yet here, in this pristine white cell, it appeared as though it would meet an abrupt end.

"I'm sure you will see your father soon," said the president darkly, and he turned back to walk out of the cell door.

Peter took a deep, steadying breath as the door slid shut.

The lights in the room began to flicker and Peter heard a faint hiss from below him. He pulled at his restraints instinctively and looked down to see a white gas creep its way up through the small gaps in the floor.

Panic-stricken, Peter wrestled against his restraints again, but with each struggle, his energy waned further.

Was this it? Were they murdering him now?

His vision began to cloud. His arms numbed.

All that he had learned, all those people he had been unable to save…

He pictured Lucy Fisher. He pictured his father, who perhaps even now was risking his life again to protect him. Peter's head lulled backwards. With one final breath, he was thrust into darkness again.

12

"Peter."

But for the pounding in his head, Peter's senses had deserted him. A distant voice drifted through his mind. He must be dreaming. Or was he dead?

"Peter," came the voice again, clearer.

He felt a grasp on his shoulders, shaking him firmly, and groaned.

"Peter, come on boy, snap out of it," he heard his father's voice say frantically. "Wake up. We need to go."

"Dad," Peter groaned weakly, emerging painfully from his unconsciousness. "No, Dad… trap."

"Come on," said his father, slapping his face gently. He pulled a knife from his pocket and cut at the leather straps before lifting him to his feet. Peter stumbled, but his father caught him on his shoulder.

Peter's legs were weak from the after-effects of the gas. He felt as though he was learning to walk again. He stumbled again. His father pulled Peter's arm over his shoulder, hoisting him up.

"Come on boy, let's get out of here."

"Dad, I'm sorry," said Peter, as they moved towards the cell door. "I should have listened, now they have us both."

"Don't worry about that."

His father pulled at the door, which had been opening and closing against an obstacle that looked oddly like an arm.

Peter's father poked his head outside and searched the corridor for any signs of resistance. Peter hastened a look too and found that two guards lay crumpled outside the cell, the arm belonging to one whose face looked particularly brutalised.

"No one's got us yet boy," said his father, nodding towards the unconscious guards. "We'll be just fine."

Peter nodded back, but his gut told him that his father had not believed his own words. As any father might, Peter could sense that he was trying to reassure him, to protect his son from panic. Peter could not see how they possibly escaped this.

Peter felt a pull at his arm, and they both moved swiftly through the winding corridors, passing opaque glass door after opaque glass door. Peter tried to catch glimpses inside the other cells but could not see anything.

He wondered how many other helpless prisoners sat inside, how many they were leaving behind in their own bid to escape. Though after his last feeble attempt at heroism, Peter restrained himself from any weak plea to help them, trusting his father to take control.

They gained speed as Peter's strength returned, and as they had advanced into a near sprint, they turned another corner to be met by three guards. All turned abruptly to stare at them, startled by their sudden appearance.

They wore thick, tightly-fitted, white body armour, all heavily built and frighteningly well protected. The armour looked strong, yet slick and rubbery at the same time. The design appeared to offer a dangerous combination of effortless movement and solid protection.

Completing their ensemble were pure white helmets, connected to the suits at their naves by the same rubbery material, protecting the back of their necks.

As though that level of protection was not daunting enough, they were also heavily armed. An assault rifle was strapped to each of their backs, and in a white utility belt, Peter could see each of them held two pistols. Peter looked down towards their white boots and saw two knives, strapped in the sides of each boot.

Peter felt his father rustle beside him. He caught a glimpse of a tinted visor covering all but the mouth of one of the guards, which had opened into a wide gape before he was thrust back towards the adjacent corridor.

Gasping, Peter picked himself up from the floor and peered around the corner to find his father engaging with the guards with ruthless brutality and indescribable speed.

Peter noticed amongst the rapid movements that, branded into the white armour of each of the guards, was a black emblem on the right side of their chest. It was that symbol again – the broadsword with the DNA spiral.

In the chaos, a shot had fired, hitting one of the guards beneath their visor. Instantly, they crumpled against the wall as blood oozed down their chest. His father had not hesitated.

Peter continued watching in astonishment as his father kicked another in the chest, with such force that the guard was forced to the floor. Whilst he turned to fight the other, Peter heard the guard groan from the ground and move a hand towards the side of his helmet to reach for something.

"Control, control…" the guard had managed gruffly, breathing heavily, still winded from the attack.

Peter acted on instinct and ran out from his cover. He flew at the guard, forcing them to the ground again, and threw wild punch after wild punch in his attempts to restrict their efforts at communication.

Those few punches that did connect seemed to have little effect, whether by his lack of force or the heavy protection of the armour. In fact, Peter was sure that he was causing more damage to himself than the guard.

The guard reacted quickly and reversed the grapple, pinning Peter to the floor. The guard made another attempt at communication, pushing at the side of their helmet.

"Control, control," came a low, robotic voice. "He's here. Confirmation, Red 7 is here."

The guard had barely finished the sentence before a boot had connected with their jaw, cracking through the visor and crumpling them instantly.

Peter listened as the weak remnants of voices seemed to respond urgently from the guard's visor.

Peter rolled over, breathing heavily, and looked up to see his father sweating, blood trickling from his nose. The second guard lay lifeless on the floor behind him.

"Take the gun," his father ordered, pointing down at the guard as alarms began to sound around the complex.

Peter did not question him; he looked wild and dangerous. The consoling father had been replaced by the rogue ex-agent.

"Come on," he ordered again, making a move forward.

Peter followed without thought, raising the gun with both hands to mimic his father. They continued through the narrow passages, his father silent, entirely focused on the route ahead.

Whilst terrified for their safety, Peter could not help but focus on the president's story, and the right time to confront his father. He was desperate to release the pumped-up frustration that the revelation had built within him, desperate for his father to combat it with an equally believable truth.

The cold ferocity his father was exhibiting to save his son, though useful, seemed only to reinforce Peter's imagination of his younger self – the fierce, detached assassin.

"Dad…" he began blankly, unable to contain it any longer.

"Almost there," his father responded quickly, still intently focused on the route ahead. Peter paused for a moment and took another deep breath.

"Dad," he said again. "They told me. Their president told me that you were one of them."

His father slowed to a halt, and his shoulders slumped. He sighed and raised his gun abruptly. He moved a few paces ahead to scout their route.

Content that they were both momentarily out of imminent danger, he turned back to face Peter, his face pale and his eyes sunken. The alarms continued to blare around them, yet the concentration between them seemed enough to dull the sound.

"He told you, did he?" he asked rhetorically. He sighed again. Peter remained silent, unsure of what to say.

"I was young," his father continued. "I was a young, stupid recruit and I loved it. The comradeship, the action, the fights, all of it – and I was good. By the time I was twenty-eight, I had been involved in three major conflicts and countless other operations and excelled in them all. But conflict often came at a price. My parents were gone; the men and women I fought with were family. Every time we lost someone, it was like a knife to the heart. I lost friends, good friends, right in front of me. After a while, I struggled to cope…"

Peter listened without interruption but struggled in the wake of the pain that seemed to spread across his father's face.

"One of my commanding officers had become a close friend. He was a rock to me there; it was like I had my dad back. He helped me get over the loss and the pain. He kept me sane, kept me focused. But by the time we had returned from my third major tour, I was broken – fewer than half of us had returned. I was done.

"Two campmates had been caught by an IED out of nowhere, metres or so ahead of me. I will never get those images out of my head. But rather than console my grief, as he had always done before, he told me they had been weak, that I had survived because I was meant to. He told me that their weakness could have caused all our deaths, and that weakness needed to be eradicated to ensure that we continue to build.

"At first I was horrified, angry. He had just insulted my brothers – blamed them for their deaths and I did not take it well. We didn't speak for days. But he continued to persuade me. After a while, he began to make sense. It was a dark time for me. Weakness became something that I despised. Weakness caused failure; weakness caused pain. He taught me the ways of the Order, a great society dedicated to protecting the human race. Soon after, I became the youngest agent for a century."

He looked up at Peter, and his face dropped as he saw disgust spread across his son's face.

"You must understand I was young, naïve, grief-stricken," he said apologetically. "I didn't know what I was signing up for, not really. I had been through so much pain and loss, but now I had been offered a higher purpose. I was a protector of the human race, with my new brothers in the Order, ensuring that weakness could no longer cause me, or anyone else more pain.

"It took a while before any sense started to come back to me. I had become good – very good. I was well on my way to becoming the youngest president the Order had seen. I married a beautiful woman and had a son. Life seemed perfect."

He hastened another look towards Peter.

An odd atmosphere had developed between the two. His father appeared to have released perhaps for the first time his inner secrets but was also desperately trying to justify himself.

Peter felt as though he did not know who this man was anymore, disgusted by the confirmation of the president's story. He had been one of them, a 'very good one', he had said. Images of murdered men and women flooded his mind.

When he thought about it, Peter hardly knew his father at all. He had only known him, really known him, for a couple of days and in that time he had built him up as being some sort of brave hero. He had been entirely wrong.

"But then..." his father continued. "Then your name came up as a target."

He raised his hand to his head and ran it through his hair.

"That's the trigger I seemed to need to snap out of it. I began to question everything I had done, everything I stood for. How could a small child, my boy, be any threat? When I discovered that you could be a target, the questions I began asking myself, I could see amongst others. I was blind before, determined in my purpose, but as I began to question the principles of the Order, I found that others were too.

"It seemed there were members everywhere who were not there through blind faith in the movement, but through forces outside their control. Whilst they gave me a degree of comfort, if I had spotted this, had the Order too?"

He paused momentarily, ignoring the continued look of revulsion on his son's face and moved back towards the turn in the passage ahead, listening out for signs of activity. Content, he turned back.

"Some may have been forced into it," he continued, hastily. "Some may have just fallen into it. Some may have been sold by the idea and converted, like me. I grew close to a tech in the labs, one of those in charge of processing genetic material. He was the one that brought me your name. He took a huge risk to do that, and all he asked in return was that I help him to escape and keep him safe. He told me about a hide-out, people who had escaped the Order – old targets, old members who had gone into hiding. He asked me to take him there and pleaded that I join them with you and your mother.

"I knew that I couldn't. We were always told that no rogue agent had ever managed to remain at large for long. I couldn't risk putting those people in danger. My future would have to be alone, even from my family. I helped him to get out, and then I had to plan my own way out. I was given an assignment in Kuwait, to eradicate the population of an entire village, supposedly genetically susceptible to a contagious virus.

"I took the job. I got out there and kidnapped and bound my partner. I had to make it look like I had lost my mind, to keep you safe. I tried to convince him that family meant nothing to me anymore, that you and your mother had just been a cover. I tried to convince him that I believed the Order's idea of weakness was not enough, and that I was breaking away. The Order pursued me of course. What you must understand is that they are fanatical, they do not see what they do as murder but a service to humanity; they follow a strict code - no divergence, no discrimination. They truly believe that what they are doing is serving the best interests of the human race.

"I knew they would spare your mother if I played my part well, and unless your result came through again they would have no reason to harm you. I came back and told your mother everything; I told her never to allow genetic samples of you to be taken, to be careful with whatever you both did and I ran. I was global news for a time, a defecting military maniac, but I managed to avoid them. I've even been able to check on you and your mother from time to time."

He stopped and stared at Peter. The length of his pause this time suggested that he had completed his account, imploring for some sort of understanding, of acceptance.

Peter was dumbfounded. His mind simply continued to race. He vaguely remembered how his mother had always been so cagey when they had visited doctors or dentists. She had always made sure that nothing was left behind, and that nothing invasive was carried out. Peter had always thought she had been overly motherly but had this been why?

His father had done everything in his power to protect him, or so he said. But still, Peter could not escape the terrible truth - his father had been one of them. How many innocent people had he maimed, or murdered, on the orders of this fanatical organisation?

"I know it's terrible," said his father, grabbing Peter's shoulders as he broke the silence. "The things I did. But you have to believe that I am not that person anymore. I haven't been for a very long time."

Peter thought about just nodding, just accepting his father's story, but he could not do it. He could not forgive his father; how could he?

He thought back to the shadowy figures sprinting aimlessly through the smoke at the train wreckage. He thought of Lucy Fisher's house engulfed by murderous, black smoke. He thought of Sarah's lifeless face in the grass. His father had done those things.

Peter flinched and pulled away from his father's grasp.

"Peter…" his father pleaded.

"There!"

A voice boomed out from behind Peter; they had been still for too long. Reacting instinctively, his father pulled Peter behind him and pushed him forward into a run, before a shot fired out.

Peter looked back in panic at his father and saw him wince, clutching his side. His anger towards him seemed to dissipate as quickly as it had formed.

"Dad!" Peter exclaimed.

"I'm fine, go on!" He pushed Peter forward and fired his gun waywardly behind him towards the pursuing Order guards.

They sprinted around the corner, his father behind him, shouting out their next direction. Peter sprinted hard but looked back with every other pace to see blood dripping from his father's side.

His father still seemed to move quickly, even with the wound, and they lost the guards momentarily. They weaved through a series of random routes until finally, they reached a dead end.

"Shit," said Peter, panicking further still, staring around for an exit. "Shit!"

He bent over to catch his breath, before turning frantically back towards his father for the next instruction.

His father moved past him calmly and pressed his hand on a section of wall, leaving behind a faint, scarlet handprint.

Instantly, part of the wall slid open, revealing a narrow passage. Peter stumbled through and turned to pull his father behind him.

"I wasn't sure that was going to work," his father said, smirking with relief.

Another shot fired. The smile drained from his face. He gasped and clutched a point in his lower back, pulling back his hand to see it covered in blood.

"Turn right," he panted, struggling for breath as he leant against the wall. "Keep running. There's a car outside. Go!"

"Dad no, come on!" Peter argued, pulling at his arm.

His father took a deep, rasping breath and used the remainder of his strength to push Peter away, out towards the concrete passageway.

"I'm sorry boy," he said, forcing a smile. "Forgive me."

He pressed at the same point in the wall and the opening slid shut.

Peter lay on the cold concrete, stunned, his hands covered in his father's blood. He stared at the wall as a cold breeze approached, cursing himself with a deep self-disgust.

At his father's most vulnerable moment, Peter had been unable to tell him, and now perhaps never would, his father who had done so much to keep his family safe, to keep Peter safe, that even after everything he had done, he had of course forgiven him.

13

Simon Brockland winced and clutched at his steadily reddening side to stall the pain. Blood oozed from the wound, warming his fingers. He had escaped them so many times before, but not this time.

He turned away from the wall to face his shooter head-on but felt himself fall back as the strength left his legs. His body slid slowly to the floor, leaving a trail of blood against the wall behind him. The pain in his side seemed like nothing to him really, a fair trade when compared with the certain knowledge that he had just seen his son for the last time.

Simon was breathing heavily. He had faced a gunshot many times before, but this time he knew there was no escape. Glancing down at the wound again, he saw the blood pooling faster – he was bleeding, a lot. There was not much time left.

He looked up to see the Order agents, headed by the president, approach slowly. He chanced a look to his right and spotted his gun, agonisingly out of reach. He tried to move his arm towards it, but his strength had left him. His arm tingled. Even if he had been able to reach it, what use would it have been? Energy had drained from him; it was too late.

"Simon, it's been a while, friend," came the smooth, powerful growl he had not heard for a long time.

The president's hands were clasped ahead of him as he slowed to a halt a metre away from the dying ex-agent. He noticed Simon's weakly outstretched arm and kicked the gun away.

Simon smiled, trying desperately to hide any hint of the searing pain spreading through his abdomen.

The president dropped to a crouch, face to face with his former protégé and glanced towards the wound in Simon's side, still oozing.

"You're dying, you fool…" he said quietly, with a menacing stare.

"Ah," Simon sighed, betraying a wince as he pulled himself up slightly. "We all do in the end."

The president continued to look at him as though still trying to convince himself that they had actually caught him: the man who had deserted them, who had thwarted so many of their operations, who had evaded their clutches for so long, the man who had betrayed him.

He stood up abruptly and pulled out a gun from his holster, aiming it directly at Simon's forehead.

"I'm sure you won't mind me brushing over the small talk," said the president, his smile faltering slightly.

"Not at all," Simon replied, forcing another smile as he tried to pull himself into a comfortable position. The president would be sparing him an agonising death. "Make it clean, won't you?"

Simon felt life draining from him. His lips had gone dry; his limbs felt cold. His vision started to blur.

He thought back to a time when he had last felt truly happy. He was sitting with his wife at the park near their home as the sun blazed from above. Both watched as their little boy ran around with his toy aeroplane.

"The boy…" said the president, looking around for any sign of him. "We will get him. It won't be long."

"You will try," Simon replied defiantly, the images of that perfect day still playing in his mind.

He remembered the days that had followed that one, days that would change everything. He imagined how many more of those days at the park they might have had, how many days together they might not have missed if it had all gone differently.

The president forced a weak smile and stiffened his aim.

Simon knew that his death would haunt the president. Though the head of perhaps one of the most dangerous organisations in history, the president was the doctrinal epitome of their purpose.

Killing Simon, a compatible, went against the code, but it was the price that agents paid for their betrayal. Simon was not only a rogue agent to the president; he was his greatest achievement - his protégé before he had deserted them.

"Goodbye, Simon," said the president tersely, his reluctance spread across his face. He slowly squeezed the trigger.

Simon smiled and closed his eyes, his mind fixed upon that blazing hot, perfect day.

14

Peter's fists had numbed from his countless attempts to punch through the opening. His wrists and knuckles had begun to bleed, bruises forming, but the gunshot had been enough to snap him out of his frenzy. It ended him for a moment.

Peter had known his father, really known his father, for just a matter of days. But in no time at all, it was all over, and it was his fault. He heard shuffling from the other side of the wall, pulling him from his sense of almost unbearable emptiness. He was still in danger.

Peter turned from the spot and ran through the passageway, wiping away his tears. He forced himself to ignore the sharp clutches of grief; he needed to focus.

His father had once again risked his life, this time losing it, to ensure that Peter would remain safe - he would not betray his father's sacrifice again. Peter sprinted obediently along the course his father had described, twisting around several corners before he reached the fire escape. Still at a sprint, he thrust open the door, stumbling into the cold air outside.

It was dark, but for the glimmer of moonlight edging its way out from a cloud above. Peter had escaped into a courtyard outside, lit by floodlights surrounding the facility perimeter. Just a few yards ahead, he spotted the SUV that his father had stolen, still crumpled from the effects of their car chase.

His mind still racing, Peter sprinted towards it.

"Oi!" came a shout from behind him. "Who's that?"

Peter stopped suddenly. His hand trembled violently as it gripped the handle of his gun.

"You there! You aren't supposed to be out here! Stop!"

Peter turned slowly to see a man dressed in a knee-length, white lab coat, pointing towards him between nervous glances towards the building behind. Their eyes met for a moment, both awaiting each other's movement as the faint sounds of the alarms rang out. The man moved first, flinging his cigarette to the floor beside him before moving towards his pocket.

Peter reacted in an instant. He raised his gun to shoulder level and fired. The man stumbled back against the wall behind him, his wide-eyed expression of shock fixed upon Peter. Peter did not stop and continued to walk briskly towards the man, firing shot after shot, as though possessed, until the gunshots became empty clicks.

He stopped a metre or so away from the man and stared down. The man lay crumpled on the ground, his lab coat stained in blood. His face had contorted into a look of intense fear, barely recognisable from the damage Peter had caused.

Peter looked down at him with utter repulsion.

He had just murdered the man in cold blood. Regardless of what he had been and what he had stood for, Peter had just brutally killed an unarmed man without a second thought. The man now lying awkwardly at his feet might have a family. He might have been there against his will, blackmailed, as his father had told him many had been.

The sound of the alarms seemed to blare louder, re-energising Peter from his confused train of thought. Breathing heavily, he turned back towards the car. Thankfully, the door had been left unlocked and he pulled at the handle, delighted to find that his father had left the keys on the driver's seat.

"Where the hell do I go now?"

Peter looked around the inside of the car for inspiration and found that his father had provided the answer.

The GPS blinked into life, programmed for him to go directly to 'Home', wherever that was. Peter turned the ignition, and with one final glance towards the bloodied corpse behind him, sped out of an opening in the perimeter fencing and down a narrow track in the surrounding woodland. He followed his directions towards a road indicated nearby, not daring to look behind him for any sign of life.

Hours passed by in a blur.

Peter's singular thought as he followed the calm, robotic instructions, was of his father - his intense guilt, the relationship they had missed out on. He thought too of his father's final revelation - that he had been one of them, one of the Order, before turning against them.

The harrowing image of his father's anguished face disappearing behind the sliding wall was inescapable. He felt that he would never forget that final weak smile that had begged his forgiveness – and he had not given it.

Desperate to shake the image from his mind, he looked out the car window to see if he could recognise where his father was leading him. The surroundings became increasingly familiar as he meandered deeper into the remote countryside. With another pang of emotion, he soon recognised the hills peering out in the distance and the emerging sight of a small secluded river. The GPS was leading him back to his father's cabin - home.

Peter drove down the familiar secluded side road towards the growing figure of the cabin. He approached slowly and parked outside with a heavy sigh.

He wondered how long his father had been hiding there, how long he had sacrificed everything to keep his family protected.

Peter sat quietly for a while, gripping the sides of the steering wheel, and staring aimlessly into its centre. He tried again, and failed, to clear his mind of his father's face, disappearing behind the sliding wall.

Peter took a deep, steadying breath and cut the ignition. He stared up at what he supposed must now be his 'home'. He had nowhere else to go; nowhere was safe now, but here.

Peter got out of the car and walked tentatively towards the cabin, looking nervously around him. The crunches of the stony ground beneath his feet seemed to echo in the silence as he walked. He gripped his gun tightly, cursing himself for having emptied the rounds.

He pulled it to shoulder height, more as a precaution than with any defensive intention, and slowly pushed open the front door.

Peter let out a sigh of relief; nothing had changed. The inside was just as it was when he first entered; just as cluttered, just as manic, but safe.

He closed the cabin door behind him, set the gun on a side table and walked towards the welcoming arms of the sofa. He slumped into it as exhaustion threatened to take hold of him.

Peter looked around and felt an odd, comforting sense of belonging as he looked again upon the document-strewn walls and the cotton web of red connections.

Peter had become a part of this world now and would need to start preparing himself for it. He felt his head lull backwards as another wave of grief and exhaustion began to weigh upon him, urging him to sleep. He had almost yielded to it but straightened at the sight of a blinking USB flash drive plugged into his father's open laptop. He looked closer and saw an envelope lying calmly on the keyboard.

With an intense effort, Peter pulled himself from the clutches of the sofa, life seemingly shocked back into him and walked towards the desk.

Peter picked up the envelope and felt an uncomfortable jolt as he recognised his father's handwriting, addressing it to his son, 'Peter'. He opened the envelope with difficulty, his hands shaking, and pulled out a folded note.

'Son,

If you are reading this, I am probably dead. Please don't blame yourself. Your passion to save others and to tell the world about the Order is one I wish I shared. I have been running too long, my boy. Perhaps it is time to fight back, but I'm not the one to do it.

If my plan has worked, the laptop will have created an encrypted link with the Order's mainframe. The names they see, you will see. The link won't remain hidden long, but perhaps you can help some of them better than I could. It should give you the evidence you need. Use it.

Don't blame yourself for my death and don't spend your days pining. I chose my path a long time ago and if I have kept you safe, I would not have had it any other way. I'm gone Peter, but you still have a fight on your hands.

I hope you never have to read this, but if you are, you need to be strong. They will be hunting you. They will never stop.

You should be safe here for a while, but when you are ready, there's an address programmed into the car: 'Base'. Follow it, take the weapons under the bed and anything else you might need. Burn the cabin and follow that route. Ask for a man called Indici and tell him everything.

I'm sorry that we didn't get more time together. Your mother would be so proud of you.

Goodbye my boy, go get them.'

Peter did not know whether the stains on the page making the end of his father's letter so difficult to decipher had been his father's tears or his own. He gripped the note tightly, his hands still shaking.

His father had believed in him in the end, that it was time to fight back, and he trusted his son to do it.

Peter's body, now wholly on autopilot, had moved back into the clutches of the ageing sofa. He grasped the letter, reading it repeatedly until finally, exhaustion got the better of him.

15

Coming to terms with his father's death proved almost impossible in the days that followed. The mission was aided in no small part by his father's scribbles, haunting him from the documents strewn across the cabin walls. It was like his father was still talking to him, teaching him the secrets of this new world from beyond the grave.

The loneliness did not help. Peter would often find himself staring for hours at the documents, searching desperately for connections, for answers. He was alone, planning for the rest of his life, planning his fight back against the Order.

Paranoia quickly set in, and Peter was almost consumed by the crushing realisation he was now a hunted figure. Every crack, every whisper of the wind, and every sound out of the ordinary caused him to jump and grab the closest gun.

On the occasions when his mind threatened to implode, Peter would find some solace in his time sitting beside the stream outside. He would sit with his father's fishing rod extending uselessly ahead of him, watching as the ripples swam casually past.

Television proved to be no mercy either. He had been horrified to discover, when turning it on for the first time, that his face was being pushed out across all of the broadcast news channels. Peter had watched on in dismay as reporters lined up to read out the accusations - it was he, Peter Brockland that was responsible for Lucy Fisher's murder and, perhaps worse, for orchestrating the train explosion that had set his new life afoot.

As though being hunted by the Order were not enough, he would find little respite now from the police or the public now.

Though his sudden disappearance would be suspicious - even without the sighting of him lurking outside Lucy Fisher's residence - he had hoped the notion of him being a terrorist would be ludicrous to those that knew him. But as the story developed, interviews broadcasted with his ex-work colleagues did not allay his hopes.

In what was a revelation to him, Peter had always been 'a bit weird' and had always given his Chronicle colleagues the impression he was 'up to something'. He might have expected something like that from the juniors - anything for a bit of extra cash - but not his editor. Though never one to turn down free PR, his descriptions of Peter's 'very suspicious' first day back from the explosion, and his always being a 'bit of wrong'un', was hard to swallow.

How could these people have turned on him so quickly? They were journalists. What evidence did they believe that they had?

Peter could only justify it as further evidence that the Order had extensive influence within the broadcast media - his father had been right again. Peter's dramatic plans for a nationwide exposé were hanging by a thread.

In efforts to distract himself from his bouts of bitterness, Peter would engross himself in the contents of his father's laptop, continually awed by his achievement. His father had managed somehow to link his laptop with whatever it was that produced the Order's targets - their 'mainframe'. Peter could see the names of all the targets and, more ominously, those that had been dealt with.

He would often sit staring at the names as they trickled through, trying to make any sense of the scientific data that had deemed them 'compatible' or 'incompatible'.

There seemed to be no pattern, no clear distinction between those determined to be 'compatible' and those who were not.

Whilst some predictable indicators emerged, blacklisting those with hereditary conditions, many appeared to have no obvious traits that might trigger a psychotic organisation to eradicate them.

There appeared to be no prejudice, no racist or particular ableist intent. Their method seemed to be without pre-determined political motive, determined entirely by whatever algorithmic and scientific decisions the 'mainframe' provided. The prospect of this daunting digital presence handing out death sentences swam uncomfortably through Peter's mind, holding sleep at bay.

Peter felt helpless as he sat in the safety of the cabin, watching as the death sentences came through: George Philips, married father of two; Karis Ikoje, single mother and primary school teacher; Louise Weybridge, an apparent drug addict from Glasgow.

Peter had to do something. He could not just sit there and watch the names of these people come and go without doing something to help – he needed a plan.

Peter thought wildly back to his school history lessons, to books he had read, to films and documentaries he had watched. How do you start a revolution alone, against something that no one knows exists?

He would have to expose them first. He would need to bring the Order's existence into the public domain before any notion of a dramatic fightback took shape. But approaching the media directly, perhaps even those within his own publication who had not yet sold him out would be far too risky. Who would believe him now anyway, whatever he did and however convincing his story, particularly now he had become public enemy number one - so how?

The solution evaded Peter for days on end, until he finally gave up trying to find one for himself. He decided once more to trust his father and meet the contact his departing note had suggested. It was time to visit 'Indici'.

Whether truly ready or truly convinced, or whether his growing lack of edible food had helped shape his decision, he did not know. But as the sun rose on his fifth morning, he loaded the car with as many of his father's weapons, ammunition and documents as he could.

Peter stood in the heart of the now bare cabin holding a small jerry can of petrol. Without his father's work lining the walls, it looked small and empty.

He looked down at the jerry can tentatively. His father had told him to burn the cabin, but it was only now as he stood in its centre, that he appreciated why his father had called it 'home'. Peter's days there, though tinged with guilt, anxiety and frustration, had provided him with protection and a welcome solitude from the new chaotic world he found himself in.

With a brief nod, he began to pour a line of petrol on the cabin floor, slowly leading out of the front door. He continued to edge back further from the cabin and paused to look at it in its entirety once more. Among the secluded woodlands around him, it was beautiful. Peter struck a match.

He held it for a short time, taking one final look before he threw it to the petrol trail. The petrol reacted instantly. Peter stood with his hands in his pockets as a small flame glided across the dirt, up through the door and into the cabin.

Smoke soon emerged as the flames embraced the wooden interior and ravaged the furniture.

Peter backed further away, covering his face against the smoke. He watched solemnly as what had become his home in the past few days slowly began to char and lose its structure before the flames consumed it.

An overwhelming catharsis took hold of him and he felt an intense sense of release. Burning the cabin felt like he was burning away his grief - his final farewell to his father.

Peter smiled weakly and stared down at his father's note, clutched in his hand along with the bedside photo he had taken from the frame.

"Bye Dad."

Peter turned away as the smoke soon became overwhelming, and moved towards the car.

This was it, the start of his new life, the start of his mysterious future as a fugitive. Just as his father had been nearly three decades before, Peter was on the run from the Order, with no idea what would happen next.

Peter got into the SUV and drove away slowly, watching in the rearview mirror as the cabin finally yielded to the flames and crashed to the ground with another expulsion of thick, black smoke.

Peter searched the GPS for the pre-programmed 'base' and, with one final look towards the blackening remains of his father's cabin, set off on the next stage of his journey.

16

Peter pulled the car to a halt and sat quietly, staring blankly out of the passenger side. The GPS had to be wrong; this could not be the place.

He had spent most of his journey picturing some grand residence of defence, some dramatic secret hideaway on the city outskirts. Instead, he had parked in a narrow street, staring at a small, dingy terraced house. Peter struggled to imagine the place being large enough even to house a small family, let alone mount a resistance movement.

He stared again at the GPS, almost urging it to tell him he had arrived at the wrong destination, but nothing changed. The green tick confirmed that he had arrived at his destination - 63 Prethwick Lane, 'Base'.

He looked out again at the underwhelming setting. The downstairs window was badly smudged and what little front garden there was had been left entirely to the elements. Ivy crept up the outside wall, trailing past cracks to form a half arch over the upstairs window, which was just as grimy as the one below. Could this really be the place his father felt Peter would be able to begin the great fightback?

Specks appeared on the car windscreen as rain began to fall. It was now or never. Peter grabbed his jacket from the passenger seat and stepped into the rain outside. With a nervous glance up and down the street, he jogged lightly towards the front door, his father's letter clutched inside his jacket pocket.

Peter slowed and approached the front door tentatively before he knocked twice. As the rain began to fall more heavily, he listened for a response but heard nothing, prompting him to knock again. Scuffling and rushed footsteps came from inside.

"Hello?"

There was silence for a moment before Peter heard the clicks of several door locks opening. The door opened a few inches to reveal half of a man's pale face.

"Hello," the man said politely from the gap, as his eyes flickered swiftly left and right towards the street outside. "How can I help you?"

"Uh, hi," Peter responded, shouting against the sound of the rain. He followed the man's gaze, before turning back sharply. "I'm looking for someone called Indici."

The man's face dropped. Peter had barely a moment to react before he found a gun thrust into his forehead. The door was thrown wide open, shedding light upon the inhabitant.

The man was an inch or so taller than Peter, slightly overweight and bearing an untidy hint of stubble. His wild, shoulder-length ginger hair had begun to matt and in the rain, threatened to conceal the pale face below, which looked at Peter, contorted with rage.

"Who are you?" the man asked sharply, pushing the gun further into Peter's forehead. "And how do you know that name?"

"Please," said Peter tiredly, with a degree of calm that seemed to surprise the man. "I have had quite enough of people pointing guns at me. My father gave me your name and told me to find you. Simon Brockland. Here, look."

The man's expression remained stern, but his dark blue eyes widened at the sound of his father's name.

Peter fumbled in his pockets and pulled out his father's letter, offering it to the man. He took it swiftly, maintaining his gaze upon Peter for a few seconds before, with the gun still loosely poised at Peter's forehead, he glanced down to read.

Peter stood quietly, staring into the barrel of the gun. As the man read, Peter felt the force against his forehead falter before the gun slowly dropped to the man's side. He looked up at Peter as he finished reading, an unmistakable look of pity spread across his face.

"You must be Peter then," said the man, eyeing him up and down with a sympathetic smile. "Come in, I am Indici."

"Indici?" asked Peter, with a nod of thanks.

"Code name," he replied, smiling. "Come on, in you come."

Indici moved aside and motioned for Peter to enter.

"Most of us have them," he continued as he scanned the street outside. "For safety."

Peter nodded and walked further inside.

A narrow, gloomy entrance hall lay ahead of him, leading directly towards a narrow staircase to the right and a closed door to the left. Peter turned to see a large mirror breaking up the dark purple wallpaper and noticed black smudges on his face, remnants from the cabin fire. He wiped his face and turned towards Indici, who had closed the door behind him, bolting the door shut with three separate locks.

The lighting inside was dim, offering an almost haunting introduction. The place was passably clean but gave Peter the distinct impression that those who lived there had not invested too much time in interior design. He supposed, judging by the paranoiac way Indici had answered, and locked, the door, that it was expected; they might have to escape at any time.

Indici turned to smile at Peter. He pulled his coat from his shoulders and pointed towards the door to the end of the hallway. Peter obeyed, walking slowly along the hallway, as

Indici shook the rain from Peter's coat and hung it on a small coat stand by the door.

Peter glanced at the doors on either side and noticed them all open slightly, with eyes staring out from the darkness.

Peter smiled nervously as he saw people, lots of them, sitting around the rooms inside, all staring up nervously towards him as he made his way through the house.

"Come on," said Indici, urging Peter forward with a gentle nudge.

Recognising Indici's approval, the inhabitants became more animated. The children jumped up to see who had visited - some emerging from hidden openings in the floor, some through disguised doorways that Peter would never have guessed were there.

Peter stared in amazement as more and more people began to emerge.

"Tea?"

Indici stood at the end of the hallway, the door now open to reveal the kitchen. Faces continued to stare out from the rooms, some still curious, some terrified, some smiling.

Indici offered them a playful smile and closed the door behind Peter, chuckling.

"Erm, yes, please," said Peter, nodding, and Indici rustled through the cupboards for ingredients.

Peter moved towards the large wooden table in the centre of the kitchen and sat down. Though the design echoed the parts of the house he had seen so far, this room appeared to have seen far more activity. Empty glasses and mugs were scattered around the room, and several papers were strewn across the table.

Peter looked at the surrounding walls as Indici clambered around the kitchen searching for sugar, and found himself drawn to a strange framed image of a steel shield entwined by a double helix.

"What is this place?" Peter asked as Indici pushed a steaming mug towards him. "Who are those people?"

Indici sighed and settled down beside him. He took a swig from his drink and gave Peter a short, inquisitive stare, as though assessing his worthiness of an answer.

"They are survivors…" he began, putting his mug down. "Refugees if you like. Some are targets who manage to escape PHROX agents, some are people we have identified and aided, and some are ex-employees like me. We hide as many as we can here, along with a few other safe houses around the country."

"How do you manage them all?" asked Peter, incredulous.

How had these people lived in safe houses without anyone realising, for so long? How had they not said anything?

"Ah," Indici chuckled, brushing his comment aside. He picked up his mug for another sip. "We get by. We all pitch in, I'm sure we will find something for you to do when you join us here."

Peter looked back at Indici and cleared his throat nervously.

"Indici, I'm not here to hide."

Indici lowered his mug slowly and looked at Peter, confused.

"Then why have you come?"

"You read my father's letter. I'm here to fight back," Peter responded, sitting up straighter. "I've come here for help."

Indici looked back at Peter blankly.

"Fight… fight back?" he mumbled. "What do you mean?"

Peter pulled the flash drive from his pocket and placed it on the table. Indici stared at it a moment and back at Peter, still perplexed.

"This flash drive contains information about PHROX's genomics programme, evidence of their members and their crimes. It has everything we need to expose them," said Peter.

Indici's eyes widened momentarily as he stared back at the flash drive but quickly returned to their normal state.

"Your father?" asked Indici, nodding towards it. Peter nodded back. "Impressive. But what do you expect to do with it?"

"Use it," said Peter. "He also managed to link a laptop to their mainframe, somehow – it releases names of some of their targets. We can protect them, release PHROX's plans, expose them and destroy them."

Indici laughed as though Peter had suggested one of the most ludicrous ideas imaginable. Peter glared back; he was not quite sure what he had expected from his journey here, but he had certainly not come all this way to find his plans ridiculed.

His father had told him in his final letter that this was the place for him to come and start the fight. He had not even considered that he would need to convince those that the Order had forced into a life of hiding and fear that they needed to fight back.

"Peter, people won't believe the contents of one flash drive, particularly on a story as far-fetched as ours. Do you know how many conspiracy theories are doing the rounds on the internet these days? How can we trust that the names produced are valid targets? You are speaking as though what you are suggesting is easy."

"We have to make people believe!" Peter shouted back, quickly losing his temper.

A few anxious seconds passed before Peter raised his hands in apology. He rubbed them together with a sigh, calming himself down.

"Think of all those people who have died and will continue to die because of the Order. If my father was able to convince me it was all real, then we can convince everyone out there."

Peter picked up the flash drive and shook it at Indici.

"My father died to get me this information because he believed it was time for the world to know."

"Peter, I can assure you that you do not need to lecture me on the actions of the Order…" Indici replied calmly. "You've known them for a few days, we have all lived in fear of them for years." Indici motioned towards the hallway. "The people in this house fear for the lives of their families, their friends; they aren't interested in protests and rebellions, they just want to be safe. They want to stay alive."

"They will never be safe as long as this group exists!" Peter hit back.

Indici looked back at him with a hint of pity.

"Peter," he began in the same calm tone. "Your passion is admirable, but if it were as easy as you suggest, do you not think we would have done something before? Those people in there..."

Indici pointed vaguely again towards the rooms Peter had passed minutes before.

"They have all seen enough. They have all been through enough. Peter, I don't have a house of soldiers; I have a house of frightened families. We risk our lives every day simply by stepping out of this house for food and supplies. You would have us all, hungry and scared, fight a rebellion against an enemy that has people everywhere?"

"Yes," Peter responded bluntly, staring back at him. "Because we have to."

"Here, here," came a deep, booming voice from behind them.

A tall, heavily-built man had crept through the kitchen door with a silence unbefitting his stature. The man had seemingly eavesdropped on the latter stages of their conversation.

"Oh for goodness sake," Indici sighed. "Peter, this is Dux. He forms part of the small security team we have been able to put together."

Peter nodded his introduction.

"Peter's right," said Dux, nodding back as he moved further into the room.

Dux's physical structure offered an imposing figure. He must have been close to six and a half feet tall, with arms the size of Peter's legs. The dim light glistened off his clean-shaven head, and his dark, brown eyes were possessed by passion as he turned to look at Indici.

"Indici, we've been talking about this for months now. We have increased our numbers, and the Order is growing far more active. It's time we did something."

Peter nodded at Dux again, this time in thanks and turned back to look at Indici.

"Can you at least consider it?" Peter implored. "Whether you help me or not, I promised my father, and he died to help me, to fight back."

"I will help you," said Dux, offering his hand.

Peter nodded his appreciation and shook it, shaking his hand slightly afterwards at the force of Dux's grip.

Indici looked intently at them both for a moment, thinking, before he moved towards a small television in the corner of the room.

"Peter, have you seen the news recently?" he asked.

Anticipating what he was about to see, Peter sat back as Indici switched on the television. Unsurprisingly, they did not have to wait long before a news bulletin appeared with Peter's face - the police's 'number one terrorist target' was still on the run. Indici cut the channel and looked back at Peter.

"What do you expect to do against these people? Every time you step out of that door, millions will know your face. And they won't be friendly Peter!" he said, throwing up his arms.

"Most of them see you as some crazed anarcho-terrorist, the same person responsible for the death of that schoolgirl. They will not hesitate to report you, damn, attack you even."

"It doesn't change anything," said Peter, scowling. He knew that Indici had a point, but it did not alter his desire to act.

"Indici, these people cannot live out their lives in the rooms of this house, hiding every time that a knock comes at the door. Walking out that door for supplies and not knowing if they will return... that is no way for anyone to live. I refuse to live in a world where I am forced to run and hide from some secret organisation who have taken it upon themselves to decide who is and isn't worthy of life. Neither should you!"

Dux nodded slowly from behind him and sat down to face Indici, who sat with his head in his hands, slowly massaging his temples.

"You know he's right, Indici," said Dux. "We have more people than ever; we have more fighters and we can get more. The Order's increased activity has only increased the number of people we have been able to save. We have a decent number of ex-military now; we can finally start thinking about how to get rid of these people."

Indici looked back at them, a glint of excitement in his eyes ebbing through a face etched with concern and worry. He sighed.

"It's not up to me. I made it my job to protect these people. It's the people in there you need to convince," he said, pointing towards the rooms. "It's their lives, their family's lives that you are asking them to put on the line. If you can convince them and those in the other safe houses, then maybe we can start to think about how we do it."

Indici stood up and looked at Dux.

"Dux, if we are even going to consider this we will need to get the others on board. Can you do the rounds?"

"Sure," said Dux, smiling.

He stood up and nodded towards Peter and Indici, before turning to exit the room. Peter noticed in the brief moment that the door had been open that the people outside were still staring intently, whispering amongst themselves. Had they heard them talking?

Peter tried to get a feel for their facial expressions, keen to determine whether they looked agreeable, excited, or scared.

Dux closed the door behind him, hiding them from sight. Peter turned back to see Indici looking at him, rubbing his hands, but with that same hint of excitement in his eyes, shining through his anxiety.

"Peter, if we are going to get everyone on our side, we need to start doing some serious thinking."

17

Peter's next few days were not filled with the rebellious activities he had expected. He spent most of his time introducing himself to as many refugees as he could, bonding as they carried out their delegated household tasks.

With every new face, he would introduce his story, his father's story, all in his efforts to softly promote his plan to fight back against the Order.

When not cooking or cleaning, Peter would spend time in the kitchen 'control room', agonising over lengthy debates with other resistance figures, as they hammered out potential ideas for the fight ahead.

The ideas ranged from the radical to the ridiculous, with very little in between. Evening lagers followed morning coffees, and the effects of too much of both contributed heavily towards a variety of outlandish plans that people had for their future.

The house was torn; many grew excited and hopeful at the prospect of a better future, but many still possessed a terrible fear. Peter listened intently to their stories of death and dismay, many who had sought to tell him their troubles to convince him not to mess with the Order. But all it did was fuel Peter's desire to dispel them.

He met mothers who had lost daughters, fathers who had lost sons, and brothers who had lost sisters. It seemed as though every horror imaginable could be found within the experiences of those he now shared his living quarters with.

Though disheartening, he was not surprised to find his passion for rebellion was not universal. For some, this new Peter Brockland fellow was just another mischievous troublemaker, for others, worse, an imminent threat to their safety.

The terror that many of the people living at 63 Prestwick Lane held for the Order was palpable, and the atmosphere grew increasingly tense. For some, the absolute safety they felt in the safe house was far too much for them to put at risk.

Scepticism appeared equally prominent in the other safe houses, as Dux's rounds for volunteers led to no explosive early success. His reports more often told of increased PHROX activity than any increased enthusiasm for their resistance movement, though there was some optimism.

"We've got 12 strong military guys signed up to join the Shield Force," said Dux, in one such report, with an air of optimism. "And we've got willing learners. Not many, but the early signs are good."

The 'Shield Force' had been an idea of Dux's in one of their early kitchen get-togethers, in reference to the symbol of unity they had been using - the shield and double helix, a direct opposite to the Order's emblem. He planned to develop a strong, core quasi-military presence within 'The Resistance', as they had begun to call themselves, to carry out any of their more dangerous missions.

Whilst the emergence of an experienced military unit was encouraging, Peter was aware that, whatever plans lay ahead, they would need far more than twelve to take on the Order.

The support they had managed to gain had been of great use for morale. Even those who were not supportive of the idea of revolution could not argue against the fact that the increase in defensive support for their families could only be positive.

It took them a couple of hard-fought weeks' work, but growing reports of unified support for action from other safe houses were starting to create the domino effect Peter had been hoping for; more and more people were warming to the idea of a fight back.

"Come on," said Peter to one such recruit as they approached the kitchen to tell the others of his plan. "You'll be fine."

There was perhaps no more important recruit to emerge than the recent university graduate, George Younger. Peter met him on his first night, as he settled into a small space in the corner of his new room next to him. They bonded over their sarcastic love of tight sleeping spaces and, since then, had talked for hours about Peter's 'crazy' plans and relived both of their experiences with the Order.

George had been brought into the safe house just months after his graduation, after his family had been brutally murdered. George told him how he had remembered waking up one night to the sound of screaming, before a woman had come into his room holding a kitchen knife.

The mysterious woman had seen George in his bed, catatonic with fear, and walked towards him slowly. George told him how his face had been covered by a foul-smelling cloth, before everything went blank. Before falling unconscious, he described his glimpse of the woman's emotionless face and a strange, twisted tattoo on her wrist.

George came around the next morning covered in his parent's blood to find armed police officers at the foot of his bed. The police had not believed his story of the strange female night visitor, of her lifeless eyes and strange twisted sword tattoo. George's youth, perhaps more, looked likely to be spent within the confines of a prison cell.

But it appeared that someone had believed him.

George had been on his way to the courthouse when the police van stopped abruptly. The back doors had swung open, and an electric pulse shot at the guard, who had crumpled to the floor.

Into the van entered a well-built man, Dux, tailed by Indici. He had been hiding at the safe house ever since, avoiding the television reports, avoiding the nightmares.

Peter opened the kitchen door and pushed George gently inside.

"Put your beers down," said Peter, smiling as the group welcomed them both inside. "George has an idea."

"Ok kid," said one of the burlier Shield Force soldiers, pulling up an empty chair. "Can't be any worse than some of the others we've heard tonight. What have you got?"

The group had endlessly discussed how they might use the media to help them with an exposure campaign. Social media divided generations. Younger members talked of Twitter trends and Instagram virals whilst older members nodded aimlessly or stared back in utter confusion. Television, Peter had suggested, might offer the best agent for them to expose the group on a wider scale. But with the mainstream still baying for Peter's blood, George had come up with a way to do it.

"A hacked broadcast…" George stuttered, drawing bemused glances from the room. "We could run a hacked broadcast."

One of the resistance figures at the table laughed, taking a sip from their beer. "That's the best you've got, kid?"

"Come on guys," said Peter, nudging George forward. "I think this could work."

Indici looked up from the table and stared at Peter.

"We've been talking about plans for weeks now Indici," said Peter, shrugging. "We need to do something to get this thing moving."

"I thought hacked broadcasts were for pranks, hoaxes and stupid alien stories and things?" said one resistance figure.

"Yeah, like that Ropey Joe thing a few years ago," said another, referring to the strange incident five years before. Peter remembered the story vividly; a student had managed to interrupt an MTV music video with a five-second clip of him rapping obscenities into his laptop webcam.

"If we can get something out, even if it's laughed at, it will get people talking, right?" said Peter.

Indici turned to look at George.

"Surely we would need equipment, access to broadcast towers or something. Is it possible?"

The group all turned towards George now, following Indici's lead.

"It's possible," George answered, pushing his broad-frame glasses up the ridge of his nose. "But it will be difficult, and dangerous."

18

After a long week, Nigel Hadley found no greater pleasure in the world than relaxing in the clutches of his favourite armchair, eagerly awaiting the Saturday night home game.

A few months short of sixty years old, Nigel's clubbing nights were, in truth, all but over, however much he tried to convince himself otherwise. He clutched at his lower back, thinking back to the previous weekend's dancefloor antics with a grimace.

His wife had recently taken up an evening dance class to keep in shape, though he imagined that Sandro, the chiselled Spanish dance instructor, probably had more to do with it. Unfortunately for him, Nigel appeared to be the test subject for her new moves, and the previous weekend had been a particularly painful example of how the two of them had come to differ in rhythmic capabilities.

This weekend would not be a repeat. With both of their children now grown up and living in places of their own, Nigel had full ownership of the house and, more importantly, the television. Albeit, of course, until his wife returned.

Nigel looked lovingly towards the six-pack of lager gleaming in the ice box nearby and grabbed a bottle. He laid back into the smooth leather upholstery with a groan, completely relaxed.

He smiled and took a swig of lager before reaching for the remote control. He flicked to the sports channel, only to find that his perfect evening had taken a dark turn. His least favourite presenter had been given coverage duties for the pre-match build-up.

Nigel scowled and, opting to avoid the pain of watching the sub-par interview technique and shoddy football analysis decided to substitute the pre-match coverage with something else.

His gamble had not paid off. A local news story on rabbits found in a local sewage system fared little better than Paul Otterman's cringeworthy presenting ability. He took another swig and prepared to change the channel again when the screen flickered suddenly. It rested upon a few seconds of static before returning to the news story.

The news reporter looked momentarily perplexed.

"We apologise for that slight technical diffic-"

She had hardly managed to issue her apology before the crackling background appeared again, this time accompanied by a long, high-pitched tone.

Nigel groaned and pulled himself up from the chair, preparing to give the TV a swift whack, but the screen had changed again, this time displaying a test signal. A few seconds passed, before a series of random pictures appeared. Infamous natural disasters, high-profile suicides and high-profile accidents silently presented themselves, one after the other.

The screen flickered every so often within the minute's silent period of imagery, as though trying to sustain the connection.

Nigel pulled his hand back and stared at the screen. The eeriness of the display sparked the hairs on the back of his neck and a strange, unexplainable sense of an unnatural fear set over him. The episode reminded him of various tv shows and films, where televisions had been used by extra-terrestrial invaders. But, this surely wasn't…

"You are deceived," came a low, distorted voice.

The images stopped suddenly and the screen switched to a bright white background.

Nigel rubbed his eyes, and the screen flickered again. This time, screen grabs of people, some hugely prominent world figures, some living and many deceased. Though not particularly knowledgeable in current affairs, Nigel had been comfortably able to pick out more than a few influential government figures from the photo reel.

"You are deceived," the voice repeated in the same low, distorted voice. "They are amongst you."

A strange image rose slowly from the bottom of the screen, translucently covering the flurry of faces. It looked strangely like a sword surrounded by squiggles.

"They are PHROX," the voice continued.

Nigel knelt on the floor, just inches away from the screen, almost hypnotised by the strange interruption.

The screen flickered again to white noise. The faint outline of a featureless face appeared suddenly, matching the crackling background in such a way as to appear as though it were protruding outside the screen. Nigel jumped back, clutching his chest.

"Prepare for the resistance…" the voice said, though this time the distortion had waned slightly, replaced by a clearer, male voice.

The face was interrupted by a high-pitched beep and the test signal once again, with a brief apology note from the broadcaster:

'We apologise once again for the technical difficulties we have faced this evening. We hope to resolve the problem shortly.'

Nigel sat on the lounge floor, cross-legged and stunned. He waited to see if the strange event was indeed over.

He pulled himself to his feet after a minute, as the television maintained the test screen and walked towards his front window. He pulled back the curtains to look outside for signs of similar abnormality.

The neighbours had started to gather, all staring around at each other, some conversing excitedly, some nervously, but all had evidently seen the same thing.

Nigel pulled the curtains shut and sat back into his armchair. Something strange had happened that evening; this was not just some stupid prank. He pulled up another beer and allowed his mind to wander. Something big had begun – but what?

Meanwhile, in a satellite station just a few miles away, Peter Brockland sprinted ahead of the Shield Force, all laughing at their success.

19

By the close of the following day, it was clear that the hacked broadcast had achieved its desired effect.

Stories of what had happened travelled pandemically. The frantic retelling of the protruding face, the distorted voice and images of famous faces and terrible events appeared unable to escape one eager ear of the public.

Children ran through primary school corridors at the angst of their teachers, pretending to be the alien invader that had taken over their televisions.

Social media had not escaped the hype. Various channels had witnessed an avalanche of posts; some even reacted quickly enough to report on the event live, adding their unique atmospheric feel to their followers. Most continued with their post-match roundups, sharing clips and opinions about the bizarre event. It had not taken long for the hashtag #AlienInvasion to become the latest social media trend.

Things had reached such a climax by the week's close that a Home Office minister was forced to divert his explanation of the Government's latest policing measures to respond.

"I'm afraid I am quite too old to understand the nature of these online trends," she said with a chuckle. "But, needless to say, I can confirm for your enthralled breakfast viewers that there is no imminent threat of an extra-terrestrial invasion."

Whilst most believed the hack to be the result of some student activist prank or a spontaneous brand promotion campaign - certainly, nothing to worry themselves about any further than a day's light-hearted discussion - some processed the event with an intense foreboding.

'Mysterious revelation leaves government minister dumbfounded', came the tagline of one prominent fringe reporter's latest podcast in response to her breakfast television interview. 'The conspiracy is real!' came various others.

Their paranoia seemed almost justified for some by the noticeably limited media coverage in the days that followed; most had not even registered the event as remotely newsworthy. As the Resistance had expected, whether due to the pressure of well-positioned Order figures or through senior executive's embarrassment at being hacked, the primetime media had completely ignored the episode; it was as though nothing out of the ordinary had happened at all.

"Music to our ears," said Peter at one of their follow-up kitchen meetings, as they sat glued to the television. "If they aren't reporting it, people are bound to ask why. And if people keep questioning why, they will soon understand."

The atmosphere in the safe house, previously tense with news of Peter's plans, had changed drastically. People beamed as Peter walked by, congratulating him. For the first time, they had witnessed the capability of the Resistance to mount a credible defence.

"The trouble is," Indici would often say at their roundtables, in his predictable efforts to nullify any excessive positivity. "The more active we become, the more active they'll become too. Look at Q17."

It was true that their positivity was not universal. The loss of the 'Q17' safe house had been a huge blow to morale, particularly as stories spread of the brutality involved.

There had been no indication of how they were found, but just two weeks after the broadcast, the Order discovered the existence of their hideout. In a ruthless display, the Order had sanctioned six of their agents to storm the residence in the dead of night and leave none alive.

Peter felt that he would never forget that evening. Many of them had been crowded in the kitchen, laughing, preparing to call it a night as the call came in on speakerphone. Their faces had dropped as they heard Q17's representative panting through the speaker as she sought their help. They listened in horror, helplessly, as agents stormed in and gunshots fired out.

Indici was right to be anxious. The brazen display of a previously unexpected resistance movement had clearly startled the Order.

They spent the following days in an intense state of anxiety, eager to avoid further safe houses from being discovered, and restricted activity solely to monitoring the online response. Though online chatter largely deemed key political figures as part of some strange conspiratorial group hogwash, and with primetime media still notably quiet on the issue, there was little cause for hope. Yet, there was some glimmer as smaller, independent outlets and video blogs started to broach it. Some had been actively discussing the event and the surrounding topics to avid followers – who were this strange 'PHROX' force, and who were the hackers?

Then the story broke.

'Renowned anarchist Peter Brockland linked with hacked broadcast'.

The headline filled the broadsheets and the tabloids, the morning and the evening television bulletins. CCTV footage confirmed Peter's beaming smile, leading the Shield Force as they escaped the broadcast studio. His name trended across social media, and he became the central topic for pub conversations and tearoom workplace chats. This time, the media did not hold back.

Peter Brockland, the 'deranged anarchist with a familial history of mental illness', had been targeting the authorities in efforts to shape the country into his warped vision of a world without government interference. His father's story had resurfaced too – the soldier who had lost his mind in combat, attacked his commanding officer and gone AWOL, presumed dead. The traumatised young Peter Brockland had reportedly grown up blaming government institutions for his father's descent into madness and was seeking his revenge.

It was never a more dangerous time for Peter, but the Resistance seemed to revel in the publicity. PHROX, albeit portrayed as a figment of a crazed anarchist's imagination, were now wholly thrust into the public arena.

Though dangerous, Peter's continued appearance amongst all of the Resistance would be critical in maintaining the near-universal passion for the fightback. Often under the darkness of night, Peter travelled with the Shield Force from safe house to safe house, spanning the country, pleading with them all to find their courage and to help with the fight back against the people who had destroyed their lives.

Was this how they felt, he would often think to himself in periods of reflection cramped in the boot of a car, those famous revolutionary figures of history?

With Dux's imposing figure beside him, backed by the eleven-strong armed guard, Peter hoped that his rousing speeches - sharpening with each delivery - were doing what was needed. With each safe house he visited, he was welcomed with more and more reverence, enhanced when they heard of the latest near-miss with Order agents as they travelled.

Peter found that he was developing a resoluteness; he was no longer frightened. He felt it his duty to visit those he was asking to fight for the cause. Though it was uncomfortable for the previously desk-bound, ridiculed, art journalist to admit, he was quickly becoming a cult figure.

"Resistance, we need a greater public presence," Peter's rehearsed speech would open, drawing worried expressions from most of the watching groups. "We need to be in people's faces every single day."

As he stood back, scanning each room to look out at the men and women in front of him, he could not help but notice them hanging on to his every word. Peter Brockland had become a leader, their leader.

"I will not lie to you," Peter would continue, thriving in the tense atmosphere. "The road ahead will be dangerous. I cannot and will not guarantee the safety of anyone in this room; I cannot even guarantee the safety of myself. But it is only together, us here, our friends in the other safe houses, and the public when they are enlightened; only together can we finally be rid of the Order. Who are they to say we cannot live in this world, that we are not worthy of it? We here will decide if we are worthy, we here will decide our futures, together!"

Peter grew more and more confident each time he delivered the rallying call, and the safe houses were growing more and more receptive to it. Without exception, his speeches would draw cheers as he looked around.

"I," he would pause again, looking intently at the men and women beside him, and out to the people hanging on to his every word. "We… cannot ask any more of you than you can, or are willing, to give. But I promise you that we can win this fight. We are going to take back our lives!"

The rooms would cheer, all of them, raising clenched fists into the air. A spine-tingling sense of solidarity took over each and every room. For the first time since he had arrived at Indici's safe house, Peter felt the full force of the people, his people, behind him.

20

October 2029 saw the beginnings of a revolution.

An emboldened Resistance would regularly situate themselves amongst the public - in high streets, shopping centres, sporting events - all wielding placards or wearing printed t-shirts. It soon became not unheard of for one to have stormed a public speech to advertise the spread of 'the Order' to packed, often confused, crowds.

All donned in black hoodies, faces concealed by the same eerie, blank white mask, the Resistance quickly made themselves recognisable as the followers of this strange new movement.

They would stand deathly still, their placards raised and their printed hoodies revealing slogans such as 'they are amongst you', 'eugenics has returned' or 'protect yourself from the Order', all footed by the hashtag #resist, or #phrox. Some simply wielded sketches of the double helix entwined with the broadsword, or photos that revealed the involvement of famous society figures in the Order's activities.

Most passers-by thought them public nuisances, part of that 'deranged, cult-like following' of Peter Brockland. Many laughed and applauded at what they believed were just harmless, albeit creepy, marketing stunts for a new clothing brand that had made full use of the growing attention for the strange 'anti-PHROX' movement.

The façade of a peaceful protest, or some marketing stunt, quickly subsided. After a few weeks without incident, the Order grew weary of the brazen public displays. The authorities, undoubtedly leant on by infiltrating Order members, seemed to have grown weary too. Without warning, sirens would blare and cars screech to a halt as officers shut down any sign of the Resistance's public displays, not often without violence.

There were reports too of 'exasperated members of the public' taking matters into their own hands and violently attacking the protestors – Order agents in disguise. Increasing violence unavoidably led to Shield Force presence, which in turn ensured escalation, often resulting in open street brawls.

Primetime media could no longer avoid coverage of the debacle, as video clips of the protests and violence spread virally from mobile phone to mobile phone. What had begun as a bizarre television hack from a fringe 'activist group' had in just a matter of weeks become front-page news.

The Order had lost its battle to keep the Resistance movement contained and was forced to change tack. Instead, they sought to tackle the Resistance head-on, promoting them as mindless anarchists taking to the streets as part of a fad. It was a message that many bemused government officials were, in their ignorance, happy to advocate.

The media continued to refer to 'domestic terrorist' Peter Brockland, the cult leader of a group of disenfranchised rabble-rousers, inciting civil unrest, protesting against an increasingly 'authoritarian' political regime.

"Just another immature student union level protest," officials would say when interviewed. "And while we of course wholeheartedly support the freedom to protest, there comes a line. Peter Brockland is a dangerous threat to our way of life. Any support for him or his actions is completely unacceptable. Further violence from these protestors will not be tolerated."

Whilst media reports seemed constrained by whatever influence Order figures or government officials were able to impose, if indeed they were not the same thing now, the public was not so easily convinced. Videos spread across the mobile phones and tablet screens of teenagers and adults alike - Resistance figures addressing crowds in secret locations, exposing the eugenics group responsible for the deaths of hundreds of thousands worldwide in their quest to perfect humankind.

The Resistance fought back with videos of their own, promoting the stories of various of their victims. With the graphic design prowess of George and his team, they quickly brought to life the conspiratorial links to high-profile deaths and disasters. Their work was certainly gaining success; the noise that the Resistance had been able to create was deafening.

Several iterations of Peter Brockland social media accounts had been created and shut down. George, and others that helped form the Resistance's 'social media division', had been frantic in their efforts to 'like', 'share' or 'retweet' any public mention of the Resistance - so much so that #PHROX or #whoarePHROX would often be trending topics of the day. Though to their dismay, they found just as often mentions of Peter and his 'disciples' accompanied by hashtags of #crazy or #shutthemdown.

To avoid capture, George and the team would spend only a matter of days in the same location, hopping from IP address to IP address, making communication with the wider group increasingly difficult. It soon became normal for Peter to spend days anxiously awaiting news from George and the team in the hope that they had continued to evade the clutches of the Order or the police.

Internet clampdowns were not limited to the Resistance either. As stories of the Order spread from account to account, whether mocked or seriously considered, accounts would be locked and their posts wiped. It quickly became standard procedure for any mention of Peter Brockland or PHROX to warrant 'emergency monitoring procedures' by the police and warnings dutifully given.

Free speech it seemed had become a muse of the past when it came to mentions of Peter Brockland and his 'dangerous, incendiary lies'.

Peter took a deep gulp of his coffee and looked up from another of his black and white newspaper mugshots. He gasped and cursed as the coffee spilt down the front of his shirt. The president of PHROX, in the guise of 'an intelligence chief', was on television, explaining to a reporter the danger that Peter Brockland posed upon society. Peter shouted out for the others to come and see, as the president continued to explain the importance of bringing in exceptional measures to prevent his message from spreading to vulnerable minds.

"We are not calling for a restriction on free speech," he said in that deep booming voice as Indici and the others tumbled into the kitchen, themselves looking up at the television in shock. "This man is incredibly dangerous. It is our job to stop him from influencing vulnerable minds with this wild conspiracy theory. For the murders of Lucy Fisher and those people in the train attack earlier this year, we must bring him to justice. These proposed restrictions are essential for us to do this, for national security."

"They are crumbling!" Indici proclaimed as they watched. "They've even had to pull the president out!"

Peter smiled back weakly, still rubbing the stain from his shirt. He did not quite share the same level of excitement. The last time he had seen the president, he had been minutes away from murdering his father. Whilst many in the room drew strength from their belief that the president's appearance indicated weakness, Peter had been unnerved.

In Peter's brief interaction with him, the president had placed an imperative focus on the Order's secrecy; his emergence as a public figure was a drastic move. This was a dangerous sign of intent.

Peter sat in the safe house kitchen again the following day, looking up in dismay as the news broadcaster replayed the president's interview. Putting down his newspaper, which had again displayed his familiar mugshot on the front page, Peter looked around in anticipation, waiting for the other members.

Indici had called a special meeting, with the promise of something that would help change their fortunes, a 'game-changer'.

The door opened and other members of the Resistance began to fill the room, nodding towards Peter as they found their seats, rustling for drinks as they waited for Indici's announcement.

"You all need to watch this," came Indici's voice excitedly, pushing open the kitchen door.

The room watched, bemused, as Indici walked towards the television and inserted a disc into the DVD player. He sat in the remaining chair and grabbed the remote control, clicking for the disc to start.

The monitor buzzed into life to reveal what appeared to be grainy, black-and-white CCTV footage.

"What is it?" asked one of the Resistance members, drawing an abrupt shush from Indici.

It appeared to show the inside of a luxury hotel room, with the date printed on the bottom right-hand side of the screen - 17/09/2010.

The room watched intently as the clock turned 23:17. The door opened, and a man and woman entered. The woman staggered through the door, kicking off her heels; the two of them had clearly enjoyed their evening.

"Indici, have you really called us in here to watch some couple hooking up in a hotel room?" came a groaning voice from the corner.

"I'm not complaining!" came another.

Peter looked at the man and laughed, taking a gulp of his coffee, but the atmosphere in the room quickly changed.

The man stiffened. As the woman began to undress, he looked nervously around before moving out of sight. They saw the light dim as the man closed the curtains off-screen before he emerged again. He stood still a moment before the woman staggered towards him, completely undressed.

Peter could not see the man's face clearly, but as the young woman drew closer, she seemed to slow nervously; she was frightened.

In an instant, the man swung his fist into the side of her face and she staggered backwards. There was no sound to accompany the footage, but Peter could see that she was screaming. She tried desperately to drag herself to the door, but the man had been quick. He grabbed her face, covered her mouth, and dragged her into an adjoining room.

"What the fuck is this?" Peter asked, looking at Indici after a minute's silence had passed.

Indici did not look back. He continued to stare at the screen. He fast-forwarded the footage until the clock moved to 23:48. Reverting to normal speed, they watched as the man emerged from the side room. He was rubbing his hands down his front, covered in dark stains – blood.

They continued to watch in horror as the man moved aimlessly around the room, running his fingers through his hair frantically. He was visibly appalled by whatever he had just done.

Indici pointed the remote towards the screen and paused the footage as the man stared blankly towards the room door.

"On the 18th of September, 2010, the morning after this, a 23-year-old prostitute was found dead, lying in a bath of her own blood, at the Dorchester Hotel in London," Indici began. "The perpetrator had used an empty hotel room and somehow avoided any of the hotel's CCTV cameras. He was never suspected, never even questioned. The young girl was found with a razor in her hand, and the police concluded that she had committed suicide."

"But you've got the CCTV," said Peter, perplexed. "It clearly shows this man assaulting her."

"This…" said Indici, pointing up to the television, "is not hotel CCTV."

"What is it then?" asked Dux.

"Who is it?" asked another.

"This footage was sent to me this morning at great risk by one of my old contacts in the Order. This footage was recorded by a hidden camera placed in the hotel by the Order, spying on this agent as he carried out his first mission. That man…" said Indici, pausing to point up to the screen, "is now our Foreign Secretary."

The room seemed to collectively gasp at the revelation.

"But how do you know it's him?" Peter mumbled as the room sharpened.

"I had been in the Order for years before he was recruited," said Indici. "I was part of the team responsible for providing names to the agents. I'm afraid I gave him his first mission…"

Indici's voice tailed off. He averted his gaze from the intrigued eyes around the room, clearly disgusted with himself.

"I gave him his first mission," he repeated.

The room remained silent. Indici rarely spoke of his time in the Order, unless providing information.

"I had been trying to break away for a while, but I had to keep my cover. I gave him his mission, but I could tell he was not convinced. He was just a boy; he was terrified. He was not as driven as the other recruits. It was a huge risk, but I told him he did not have to do it. I tried to convince him that there was a way out.

He just looked at me, pale-faced. He probably assumed it was another test. He took the information and left. You can see what he did then," he said, pointing weakly towards the screen.

"But how could you help someone like that?" a young woman in the room asked.

"I didn't know what he was going to do," he said defensively. "I only knew that he had been given a name. They don't kill everyone, you know that. They try to avoid this sort of mess where they can. But I supposed he panicked, tried to get it done as quickly as he could. That murder…"

Intense darkness appeared to come over him.

"That was it for me – my time was up. That was when a certain Peter Brockland came out of the mainframe."

The room fell silent and turned to stare at Peter. He remained transfixed upon Indici's story. Peter had not made his father's story one of Resistance folklore yet; he was still trying to come to terms with it himself. Many in the room were hearing this part of his past for the first time.

"I had begun to know your father – the real him. When you were born, and I was perhaps one of the few that noticed it, he seemed to soften. I was sure that all he needed was a nudge, and I, perhaps selfishly, took advantage. I kept your result secret and gave it only to him. I said I would keep it hidden, but only if he helped me to escape."

Peter remained still. His father had already recounted the events that had followed, but hearing them again, from another source, somehow seemed to make it that bit more real.

"Well," said Indici, noticing from Peter's expression that he did not want the entire story repeated. "I got out. I never thought I would have to see this."

"And how exactly do you intend for us to use this tape? You can't even see his face."

Behind a cloud of cigarette smoke towards the back of the kitchen, came the ever-suspicious Colombian growl of Q1's most recent Shield Force recruit.

Peter had met Lucia Garrido only a few weeks earlier. Her father had been part of the Columbian FARC and was killed when she was a girl in a failed attempt to rescue her mother from the captivity of a drug cartel. Brought up by her uncle amid armed conflict, she moved to the UK shortly after her uncle had seen the same fate.

Since then, she had been lost, struggling to adapt to life away from armed conflict. That had all changed three weeks ago when she was once again thrust into the fire of combat, only narrowly escaping an attempt on her life. She had overcome two assailants on the walk home from her night shift, with only a glimpse of a strange tattoo offering any clue as to who they were – the sword entwined with the double helix.

Indici looked, if possible, even more uncomfortable as the room turned to look at Lucia, and back towards him, perhaps all thinking the same thing.

"She has a point," said Peter. "What are we supposed to do with it?"

Indici drew a deep breath. "We need the Foreign Secretary," he said bluntly. "Without him, I agree with you, it's just some man we claim is him, murdering this young girl, and us trying to feed it into another wild conspiracy story."

Indici looked around the room and into the faces of them all, stunned by the absurdity of his suggestion.

"Yes," came a familiar Latin purr as Lucia's face grew consumed by her eager smile.

The room's brief excitement dropped as they quickly recognised the gargantuan task.

"His confession gives this clip more meaning," Indici implored, searching the room for agreement. "It will have far more of an effect."

Many in the room laughed, as though they were waiting for Indici to move towards his punchline. But it did not come.

"Wait," said one after a moment's silence. "This isn't serious, right?"

"You're seriously suggesting we kidnap the Foreign Secretary?" came another.

Peter turned to look at Indici and smiled weakly at the desperation in his eyes. The idea was ridiculous, probably impossible, but Peter understood. Indici needed this; it was his chance to make up in some way for that girl's death all those years ago. If they were able to capture the Foreign Secretary, he could finally help get her some degree of justice.

"I think we should do it," said Peter, with a steely, determined look around the room.

The room remained silent, and Peter felt like he could hear the cognitive whirs of their minds as they sought to process the plan - that this was not a joke.

His agreement seemed to be the trigger that many of them needed. After a few minutes of quiet, they began to nod in excitement. "We appear to have some planning to do."

21

"It looks like there's only two of them," Dux whispered, his breath rising slowly through the crisp winter air. Pulling back from the sighting scope of his rifle, he moved back slowly towards the protection of the thick hedges.

Twelve of the Shield Force waited, huddled together and crouched in the darkness of the surrounding woodland, eagerly awaiting Dux's return from the perimeter check.

December's assault of cold weather had removed most of the leaves that might have protected their position, but a thick covering of snow on the ground and the build-up of dead branches around them offered some retreat. Even so, Peter felt a rush of gratitude at Dux's insistence that they wore white.

"Only two?" Peter exclaimed, covering his mouth as his breath clouded in the cold air.

"Two at the gate," Dux replied. "I can't be sure of inside."

The group looked towards Dux, shivering.

For weeks, they had been involved in passionate discussions in the safe house kitchen, planning what they were going to do. Now they were actually there, actually doing it.

Peter pulled a set of binoculars from his side and looked up towards the country estate, squinting at the power of the lights against the darkness of the calm evening sky.

Three floors separated what must have been at least a 30-roomed building, glistening with the elegance befitting a person of such a high position. The brick perimeter walls were fading in colour, stained by centuries of existence, which only made the addition of Christmas decorative lights more impressive.

Huge windows surrounded the building, one which Peter imagined had played host to some of the most important governmental decisions that the country had ever taken. He wondered how many Order agents had infiltrated it in the years that had passed, influencing key policy decisions.

Peter turned to scan the outer perimeter, searching for their entry point.

The building was well protected; a long, gated stone driveway was the only interruption to a several-foot-high brick wall perimeter.

Peter turned a dial on his binoculars to zoom in, first upon the two formidable-looking armed police officers at the gates, and then back up towards the second-floor windows in a search for any sign of life.

"There he is," said Peter, pointing towards one of the larger windows on the second floor. "And he's... ah."

Peter sighed and dropped the binoculars slowly to his side. The Foreign Secretary has walked purposefully past one of the second-floor windows, flanked by the familiar white garbs of two Order agents. He passed the binoculars back towards Dux, who too looked up.

"Order agents," Peter told the group.

"Shit," came one blunt response.

"This is too dangerous," came another.

Peter turned towards Dux, whose gaze remained fixed upon the second floor. "What do you think?"

Dux continued to look around the perimeter, towards the second-floor window, and back towards the armed police officers patrolling the gate.

"I think we've trained too hard and come too far to go back now."

Dux lowered the binoculars and turned back to the group, crunching nervously against the snow beneath them. Some looked back with determination, some with scepticism.

"There's no reason for the Order to suspect he's in immediate danger," Dux continued, staring at them all. "Those two agents can only be there as a precaution. This will be dangerous, but I don't see that this affects the plan too much. We always planned for resistance; we will just need to be more clinical, no messing around."

The group nodded slowly, though again some with greater enthusiasm than others.

"This is the first time they will know that we can bring the fight directly to them," said Dux. "That we can hit them hard. We need this."

Peter looked around at the group and nodded. He looked into all of their reddening faces. They were family now, brothers and sisters in their fight against the Order.

"Let's show them shall we?" said Peter with a grin, offering a hand.

The group looked back at him and, without exception, offered their own hands. As action approached, scepticism had quickly turned to a deep, joint purpose. They all nodded.

"Ok. With me," said Dux, pointing to Acutus and Arma, two of the Shield Force, who quickly rustled from their crouched position.

"On my signal," he said, pointing at Peter.

Acutus and Arma followed briskly, and the three of them made their way out from the protective surroundings. The remaining group watched on, awaiting their signal.

Dux had told Peter fascinating tales of his past life in the SAS, but watching him in action was altogether different. He watched through his binoculars as the three of them approached stealthily, gliding with ease down the snow-dusted hill leading to the estate - invisible, had Peter not known that they were there.

Acutus and Arma had formed part of the same squadron as Dux in their previous life, and the three were by far the best prepared to open the assault. Peter watched as they slowed, nearing the estate's perimeter wall, and hid from the patrolling officers.

Peter felt a brush against his arm and turned to see Lucia standing beside him, clutching her pistol.

"Are you ready?" she whispered, looking intently at him.

Peter lowered his binoculars and stared at her for a second, before turning back. Lucia might be purring at the chance to get back into combat, but Peter had never experienced anything like this.

He was acutely aware, though he had never admitted it, that he was not ready for a full-scale assault on a government official's residence, how could he be? However many speeches he had made to the safe houses, he was an arts journalist; he had no place being amongst seasoned fighters. But fate has dealt him a hand, and with his leading position in the Resistance, he had little choice but to join. In the presence of such accomplished combatants as Dux and Lucia, he did at least feel some reassurance. He could not have been with a better standard of people to begin his combat career.

"I'm ready," he replied, forcing a smile.

Lucia squeezed his arm and followed his gaze towards the estate below.

They watched as Dux, Acutus, and Arma made their move. The three descended on the police officers, striking with ruthless efficiency. In a handful of swift movements, the officers were neutralised and left bound and unconscious. Dux looked around and held up a fist, signalling for the others to follow.

Peter turned to the others and nodded, smiling nervously as he caught Lucia's eye.

Peter took a deep, steadying breath and moved out from the branched covering. As instructed, he kept low within the shadows of the overhanging trees and the remainder of the group followed suit.

His heart thumped uncomfortably as they edged closer. His eyes darted up to the windows with every step, anxious to remain out of sight. But for the laboured breathing of the approaching party, the night remained silent.

Mercifully, the windows remained empty as they approached the perimeter wall. Phase one was complete; they had avoided detection. They halted, as planned, behind a Land Rover parked twenty metres from where Dux and Acutus stood waiting.

Peter heard a short gasp come from his side and turned to see George, pale-faced and trembling. He pulled up his glasses and wiped away at the steam-covered lenses.

"George," Peter whispered, clutching his shoulders. "If you can't do this, I can."

"No," George replied hastily, collecting himself with a deep breath. He pulled his glasses back on. "It needs to work."

Swallowing down George's lack of faith in his technological abilities, Peter nodded.

"No offence," said George, smiling.

Peter grinned and looked up from behind the Land Rover. Dux was looking towards them at the entrance gate, waving for George to hurry.

"Go on," said Peter, pushing George out from the car's protection.

George nodded and ran towards Dux, keeping low, his small laptop bag clutched to his chest. He reached them in seconds, fumbled for his bag, and frantically got to work, setting up several devices with his laptop.

After a few moments, interrupted only by the intermittent need to rub his hands in the cold, George nodded towards Dux. Dux looked down at the laptop screen and nodded towards the rest of the group.

Peter took another deep breath, clutching his assault rifle for support, and moved towards Dux, signalling for the others to follow.

Whilst their white outfits did offer some camouflage against the snow, their emergence from the protection of the Land Rover was unnerving. They stood beside the gated entrance together, pumped and prepared for the assault.

"Good to go?" Dux asked, looking towards George. He nodded.

"Novus..." said Dux, looking back at the group and addressing George by his codename, "...has blocked all radio and wireless signals entering or leaving the house. They won't be able to see our approach on CCTV or call out for help. We have control of their security system for now, but we can't be sure what backup systems they have when they find out we're here, so we will need to be quick. No stupid risks. Our target was last seen with two agents on the second floor. Myself, Acutus and Arma will take the second floor."

"Salvator..." he continued, pointing towards Peter, "will secure the ground floor with Pugnator and Ignis." He pointed to Lucia, who smiled back.

"Venator and Umbra will hold the outer perimeter and prepare our escape, and Culter and Coclear will tail the back and side exits to the building. All understood?"

The group nodded, focused entirely on the upcoming move.

"Remember, tear gas before every room and masks on at all times." He pulled his mask from his side, before pointing towards his earpiece. "Keep your comms on and stay together. Do not panic, do not take stupid risks, and no fuck ups. We take the Foreign Secretary and we go. Novus?"

Dux nodded down at George, who nodded back and began to work away on the laptop. Peter heard a quiet beep, and the gates opened slowly.

Without hesitation, the group moved briskly through the gate and up towards the manor, the gravel driveway crunching beneath the snow as they approached.

The driveway was surrounded on either side by shrubs and small trees, all adorned with lights and baubles to offer a direct, festive route towards their target.

Peter frequently looked up towards the manor to see that the lights only seemed to be on in a couple of the upstairs rooms. A good sign, he hoped.

They reached the broad, wooden front door and collected themselves. Dux motioned towards Culter and Coclear for them to circle the perimeter and they moved swiftly away. Culter set himself at the corner whilst Coclear continued to circle, ready to relay the signal to enter.

"Ready?" Dux asked the remaining group, clutching two gas canisters.

Peter's heart was beating rapidly, but he was ready; he was excited. He nodded back. Dux looked to the corner of the building where Coclear stood. He gave them the thumbs up.

"Masks down," said Dux, pulling down his own to cover his face. The others quickly followed suit.

Dux turned back and smashed the glass door panels with his rifle. In one swift movement, he clutched the gas canisters from his holsters and tossed them inside. Ignis and Pugnator did the same through the other ground-floor windows, and Peter heard the similar distant sounds of smashing glass from Culter and Coclear.

Dux stood in front of the door as clouded gas escaped through the smashed glass and clutched his rifle. With one final nod, he turned to the front door and, with one powerful thrust, kicked it open.

They stormed inside and dispersed, just as they had practised. Peter looked around through the clear plastic of his mask, breathing heavily, his assault rifle held at the ready, and scoped his immediate surroundings.

Aside from the flickering laser sights of his comrades' weaponry dancing through the clouded gas, there seemed to be little reaction to their abrupt entry. The rooms inside remained quiet, but for the sound of the tear gas hissing as it made its way through the ground floor.

Dux, Acutus, and Arma made straight for the stairway ahead, whilst Ignis and Pugnator investigated the room immediately to their right.

Peter grew more and more anxious as he made his way through the ground floor, not at the situation he found himself in but rather the lack of opposing forces. The silence did not just unnerve him, it terrified him. Could the Order have known that they were coming?

Peter jumped as Ignis and Pugnator returned from the room, shaking their heads to indicate no one was inside.

Suddenly, the unmistakable sounds of shouting and gunfire came from upstairs. Peter panicked a moment, looking up before he caught Lucia's eye. Her short, consoling nod seemed enough to spark him back into action. Keep to your job. No fuck ups.

Peter looked around once more and his heart stopped. A white figure emerged above them, their rifle aimed directly at Lucia's chest.

"Duck!" he shouted, moving towards her.

At the same moment Peter had shouted, the agent's gunshot had rung out and Peter turned to aim a shot of his own towards the agent. He fired several rounds as he edged backwards towards Lucia's crouched figure. She had managed to avoid a direct hit, instead receiving a graze to her left thigh.

The agent was thrown backwards by the force of the gunshots but, as Peter pulled Lucia to her feet, he looked back in horror. The agent rose slowly from the floor. The bullets had not penetrated the protective armour.

"Keep moving!" Pugnator shouted from behind them as he continued to fire towards the top of the staircase.

Peter moved towards the next door, dragging Lucia alongside him. He kicked it open and threw in the tear gas canister. They waited outside as the room slowly filled with smoke before Peter pulled her through. He directed his rifle ahead, scouring the room for any sign of life with his laser sight.

There was no one there. As the smoke began to fade, Peter could see that the room was full of chairs, covered in what had been pristine white cloth and pink ribbons, as though they had been prepared for a wedding. He imagined future commercial bookings might soon see a significant dip when news of the famous terrorist Peter Brockland's infiltration spread.

"Are you ok?" he asked, lowering his gun to turn towards Lucia.

"Fine," she said, scowling at him. She pulled a ribbon from one of the chairs nearby and tied up her leg wound. "Keep moving."

Peter heard a loud thud from outside the room. He peered out, terrified. The agent had fallen from the top of the stairway into the heart of the entrance hall, their white body armour slowly reddening.

Pugnator followed them into the room, panting heavily.

"Aim for the neck!" he said, gasping between breaths.

Peter and Lucia nodded back, and they turned to continue their advance through the room, listening intently. Shouting and gunfire continued to seep through the ceiling above them.

Pugnator closed the door behind him and pushed a large cabinet on its side, blocking the entry and ensuring they were not easily followed.

They continued through another door and down a narrow walkway, passing eerily-lit portraits of previous Foreign Secretaries. Peter wondered, as he stared up at their oil-painted faces, how many of them had been influenced by the Order too.

They reached the end of the walkway and were met by two more wooden doors. Peter immediately grabbed the handle of the left side; the others opted for the right. They looked at each other for a moment and nodded.

Breathing heavily, Peter opened his door slowly and threw his final canister inside. The others had entered their room too, leaving him alone to face whatever lay ahead. He felt how he had done when he first held a gun in his flat, vulnerable.

What was he doing here? Doubts crept into his mind as he heard a commotion in the room Lucia and Pugnator had entered. They almost threatened to derail him, when he heard Dux's voice swimming through his head: stick to your jobs, no fuck ups.

What was he thinking trying to take on fully trained Order agents? It was madness, suicide. He heard Lucia shout out and turned back to leap to her defence when he heard a shrill cry behind him.

Peter turned back quickly and noticed a small cot in the corner of the room, illuminated through the smoke by the moonlight outside, shining through a large glass window. It was a baby.

Fearing for the infant's safety, Peter bounded towards the cot, his inhibitions gone, forgetting entirely that he was in an active warzone.

He reached the cot and looked down upon the tear-stricken face of a young girl shouting out incoherently. Her glistening, blue eyes searched frantically in the space above her for a familiar face.

Peter had no idea why, but he felt the overwhelming need to comfort her, to make sure that she was safe. He dropped his rifle to the floor and reached into the cot.

A door to his right flew open. A middle-aged woman, with an otherwise beautiful face stricken with terror and rage, was fixed upon him, the intruder reaching to grab her precious daughter.

"Get away from her!" she shrieked, sprinting towards him wielding a large frying pan.

"No!" he shouted, raising his hands to cover his head. His arms raised, he was horrified to see the woman's fast-approaching figure dotted by small, red target lights.

"No!" he screamed again, this time turning to the window towards whom he hoped were Shield Force members patrolling the perimeter. "Don't shoot!"

He was too late. A shot had fired out, and at the same time, Peter felt a crunching pain in the back of his skull. He fell to his knees as dizziness and nausea set in. The blow had been a hard one, yet, with his eyes watering in pain, his sole focus was on the mother – she had to be ok.

He turned back towards the cot. The child's mother was gasping as blood spread across her blouse. She reached up desperately towards her child through the barriers of the cot.

Culter walked through the shattered glass window, his rifle still aimed directly at the mother.

"No..." Peter winced, gritting his teeth with the pain.

Culter turned to look at Peter.

"Are you ok?" he asked frantically, looking at the growing bump at the back of Peter's head.

"Yeah, fine," he lied, rubbing his head. He felt the warmth of his blood. "Is she alive?"

Culter moved towards her with his rifle still raised. She lashed out, throwing a fist towards his leg and screaming for help.

Her left shoulder was bleeding heavily. Culter laughed at her, somewhat cruelly, forcing a scowl from Peter.

"Oh come on," said Culter, affronted. "She's one of them."

Culter turned back towards her, still gripping his rifle, though he had now lowered it to his side.

"One of who?" she shouted angrily, sobbing from the pain in her shoulder.

"You're going to try and tell us you don't know what's going on around here?" said Culter, incensed. He lowered himself to a crouched position to face her. "With all the Order agents in your own home? Do you take us for idiots?"

"Culter, leave her alone," said Peter, pulling himself to his feet.

Though he still felt the dizzying effects of the frying pan attack, he maintained his glare and they stared at each other. The woman was sobbing silently, staring up in terror at Culter as she shielded her child from view.

They were interrupted suddenly by the sound of quickening footsteps, moving away from them from the floor above.

"We need to go," said Lucia, running into the room from behind them, giving Culter a meaningful look.

"Fine," he said, getting to his feet.

He gave Peter another searching look and turned away from the woman. He moved briskly across the room and back out into the entrance hall.

"Keep sharp," said Pugnator, following him. "It might not be who we hope for coming down those stairs."

Peter moved towards the woman, crouching down.

"Peter, come on, let's go," Lucia insisted from the door behind him.

"I'm coming," said Peter. "Go on. I'm right behind you."

She let out an exasperated sigh and exited the room, following the others, leaving Peter alone with the woman.

"My wife!" came a distant, muffled yell. The sound prompted another anguished look on the woman's face. "What have you done with my wife and my little girl?"

It appeared that Dux and the others had been successful; they had done it. Peter turned back to the woman, who appeared to have poised herself to scream back at him. Peter silenced her, placing his hand over her mouth.

"Don't scream," he said, picking up his gun and pointing it towards her. "Do you know who I am?"

He pulled his hand away and she nodded silently, terrified.

"You're the terrorist, the one my husband they've been trying to find."

Peter shook his head angrily.

"Your husband is not who you think he is. He is part of a secret order…"

She shook her head violently, tears streaming down her face from a mixture of pain and anger.

"He is part of a secret order," Peter persisted. "One that has been secretly assassinating members of the public for years."

"You need to listen!" he shouted, as she continued to shake her head in disbelief. "They will come for you, and your daughter. You need to get away, we can protect you."

He heard a loud bang from outside, shaking the floor. The dull sound of sirens quickly followed, approaching in the distance. The police had been alerted; their signal jam must have given way. Lucia appeared back at the doorway, flustered.

"Mierde," she muttered when she saw he was still crouched beside her. "Peter, get a fucking move on! They're coming! Now!"

Peter looked at the woman with pity and sighed. She showed no sign of moving. He got to his feet abruptly and jogged after Lucia. Peter stopped at the door and turned back to the woman, who sat shaking, cradling her child in her uninjured arm.

"I'm sorry," he said, looking stony-faced.

Peter turned before he could grasp her reaction, and ran after Lucia, past the dimly lit portraits, through the trashed wedding set-up, past crumpled Order agents and destroyed furniture, and out of the large wooden front door into the commotion outside.

Dux stood waiting, firing shots towards the approaching police cars. Peter covered his face and backed up against the wall as he saw the others making their way through an opening in the brick wall, blasted open by Venator and Umbra. They scurried out towards the woodland surroundings towards their getaway vehicles. Peter could see a man hidden amongst them, bound and hooded. They had done it. They had actually done it.

"Dux!" Peter shouted, stepping out from behind the protection of the door.

Dux continued to fire towards the oncoming police cars, now just metres away from the gate. One of the shots hit the petrol cap of the lead car and it shot up in a burst of flames.

Peter watched on, wide-eyed, as the car smashed through the perimeter wall and rolled towards them, crashing just a few metres away from where they stood to block the driveway behind.

"What were you doing?" Dux shouted back, pulling Peter down to a crouched position as they ducked the return fire.

"There was a baby… his wife," Peter replied.

Judging by the contorted expression on Dux's face, it appeared that he had already been told this. Peter had only reaffirmed what Dux had hoped was not true.

"For fuck's sake Peter, we're on a mission. I said no stupid risks. We can't stop for shit like that!" he shouted angrily.

Dux had never acted like this before, particularly towards him. Peter looked angrily back towards him.

"If you think I'm going to let an innocent mother and child die…"

Shots continued to fire towards them. Armed police officers shouted at each other as they crouched behind their vehicles.

The crumpled police car and brick debris that littered the driveway prevented the other vehicles from closing in, but Peter looked down to see that one officer had managed to escape from the inferno. She dragged herself towards them and aimed a handgun directly at Peter.

Dux pushed Peter aside, but before he had hit the ground, Peter had managed to take a shot at the officer's hand. The gun dropped from their grasp, and the officer rolled away in agony across the paved entrance.

Peter pulled himself up and ran towards the officer. Kicking her gun away, as the officer howled in pain, he pulled off the helmet to reveal a young, fierce-looking face, paired with flowing red hair. Her pale face was etched with pain and fear.

She closed her eyes slowly, as though resigned to her fate, expecting a final shot to come, but nothing came. She opened her eyes again and saw that Peter had dropped to her level. She stared at him with a hint of surprise.

"You… aren't going to kill me?" she asked, panting heavily and cradling her injured hand. Peter heard the faint shouts of the mother inside and the officer stared past him, her face etched with concern.

"What's your name?" Peter asked gently, distracting her from the shouts.

"Jenny," she said, still panting. She stared down at her mangled hand and back up towards the woman's fading screams.

"Jenny, I am not the person they say I am. I am not a terrorist," he said defiantly. She looked up from her hand, confused. "You must believe what we are fighting for, it is imperative."

Peter stood to his feet as the smoke slowly began to subside, and what little festive lighting remained glittered through. He looked down towards her.

"Sorry about your hand."

He turned back from the smoke to see that Dux had already reached the others. Peter looked back towards the backup police cars approaching, and back down to the young police officer, who still looked astounded.

Peter offered a weak smile before he too turned to sprint through the gap in the perimeter wall and out towards the darkness of the surrounding woodland.

22

Chief Superintendent Justine Smith walked up towards the Foreign Secretary's countryside residence, her mind still boggling as she tried to comprehend the events of that night.

In the entirety of her thirty-eight-year career, she had never heard of anything like it. A member of Her Majesties' Cabinet kidnapped by an art journalist, who had by some strange manner of hypnotic persuasion outside the realm of her understanding, convinced ordinary people to think it acceptable to cause pandemonium in the streets.

She looked down and covered her mouth with one of her customary pocket handkerchiefs as she walked past the charred remains of one of her officers. She stood still and bowed her head as the officer's corpse was wheeled away, all because of Peter Brockland's 'Resistance' group.

She looked up at the Foreign Secretary's residence. Almost all the windows had been smashed, and the walls shelled by gunfire. With a frown, she watched as Detective Forster and Rogers exited the building, sharing sombre looks. They looked up, noticing her approach, and immediately straightened. Chief Superintendent Justine Smith was not a woman to mess with.

"What the fuck happened here?" she asked them with her trademark brashness as she climbed the concrete steps.

"We're not sure yet ma'am," Detective Forster stuttered, rubbing his hands together in the cold.

"Not sure?" she responded, looking towards him sternly.

"It appears that Peter Brockland was here ma'am," Detective Rogers cut in, saving her partner from their boss's retort. "No witnesses inside as far as we have been able to find, but the coppers are still searching."

"According to Officer Powell…" said Forster, cutting in, eager to make up for his previously beleaguered response. "Peter Brockland was here with a small group of armed men and women."

Justine followed his gaze as he continued his account and saw Officer Powell sitting with one of the paramedics, cradling her arm. She looked at her anxiously. Since her husband had passed away, his niece was the only family she had left.

"She says they bound and kidnapped the Foreign Secretary and took him up there, towards the woodlands. Officer Powell sustained a gunshot wound in her attempted pursuit of-"

Justine's eyes sharpened at the mention of Jenny's injury and, silencing Forster with a raised hand, she moved swiftly towards her.

"Idiot," she heard Rogers whisper from behind her, hitting Forster's arm. "That's Fred's niece."

Justine moved past the wreckage in the driveway towards Jenny, who smiled weakly as she approached.

"Is she ok?" Justine asked the paramedic sharply. The paramedic smiled and nodded back.

"She'll be fine."

"What happened? Are you ok?"

"I'm fine ma'am," Jenny replied, responding as she always did whilst working to maintain her professionalism. She had always wanted to avoid other officers knowing who her uncle's wife was, always eager to avoid murmurs of favouritism.

"It was Peter Brockland. They broke in and kidnapped the Foreign Secretary. They were armed; they were professional. They were..."

"Thanks," Justine said, nodding towards the paramedic, indicating for him to leave. "They were what?"

Jenny rubbed the bandage on her hand as the paramedic moved away, eagerly awaiting the effects of her pain medication.

"He could have killed me," she said weakly. "I was defenceless at his feet, and he could have killed me."

Justine rubbed her shoulders and offered a consoling smile.

"You'll be ok, we'll catch the bastard."

"No," Jenny replied, looking up at her with a strange expression. "He, I don't know, wasn't what I expected. He didn't seem like a killer. He said that people were lying about him."

Justine looked down at her with a weak smile; she was clearly still in shock.

"Ma'am," came a voice from the front door. "We've got two bodies in here. I think it's the wife and child, ma'am."

"Fuck," she muttered. "Forster! Rogers! Get in there and take a look."

Jenny looked up towards the house, confused. "But the woman was still shouting out when they left."

"Jenny, you need to rest. Take a couple of weeks off. That's an order," she said sternly, noticing Jenny's face rile into disagreement.

"Officer," she said, as the man who had announced the discovery walked past.

"Jennings, ma'am."

"Officer Jennings, not a word of this to anyone until we have the facts, understood?"

"Yes, ma'am," he replied with a nod.

Justine stood up and pulled Jenny to her feet. She lifted her uninjured arm over her shoulder and slowly led her away.

This story was going to be huge. Doubtless, she would be blamed, unfairly perhaps, but the buck stopped with her. The Foreign Secretary had always been different to others in Cabinet when it came to security. He has always insisted on having his own security detail, against her regular advice, but it would be the Chief Superintendent that got the dressing down for the failure to protect a Cabinet minister.

They had to catch Peter Brockland and stop this strange cult movement before more people got hurt, before it got too out of hand.

*****

Agent J35 pulled off his bulletproof vest and threw it into the back seat of the commandeered police vehicle, eager to escape before his deceit was noticed.

He heard the SCO19 officer struggling in the boot; he would deal with him soon enough. He started the car and reversed slowly away from the scene, pressing at his earpiece.

"J35," came a crackling voice. "Is it done?"

"It's done," he replied, pulling off the rest of his stolen uniform. "Both dead."

J35 was never gladder than at that moment that he had decided not to have a family. He could not imagine what it would have felt like, had that just happened to him.

"Good," came the voice, without a hint of emotion. "And the incompatible officer?"

"Being dealt with as we speak," J35 responded, looking up into the rearview mirror to see the boot bulging as the man continued his feeble attempts to punch his way out.

"Good. Get back in, soon as you can."

The voice cut out, and J35 pulled away from the scene. As he turned into a small track towards a clearing in the surrounding woodland, he chanced a final glance in the rearview mirror. The shovel remained still, gleaming ominously from the back seat.

23

"Mr Foreign Secretary."

Peter's voice reverberated against the concrete walls of the small cellar room as he moved slowly towards the beleaguered figure of the blindfolded man.

With a start, the Foreign Secretary began to pull violently at the restraints binding his limbs to a small chair in the centre of the room.

Their new prisoner had been left in solitude for three days, with only brief food and toilet breaks to reprieve him from the silent darkness.

His face looked fraught, lined from his hours of shouting out for news of his family's safety.

"It's a pleasure to have you here with us," Dux added, standing in the corner behind him.

The Foreign Secretary continued to shake his head, as though struggling to adapt to the sounds of other human voices. It was understandable; but for the sound of his own desperate shouts for news and help, he had heard little but for the placing of blended food in front of him and the ominous stretching of the plastic straw.

He struggled again against the bonds to his arms.

"Please," said Peter, nodding calmly towards Dux. "There's no point in struggling. There's no escape."

Dux approached the Foreign Secretary from behind and placed both of his hands upon his shoulders, pushing him firmly down into his seat. The Foreign Secretary flinched at the touch and with one final fruitless attempt to struggle, settled.

"I demand to know where I am," he commanded, with the tone of someone long accustomed to authority. "And the whereabouts of my family."

Peter pulled back the chair opposite slowly, allowing the screech of the legs against the floor to force another cringe from the Foreign Secretary. Peter sat down, placed his hands together on the table between them and simply stared back towards him.

"WHERE ARE THEY?" he bellowed, shaking with anger as he tried once more to break free from his bindings. The room fell deadly silent. Peter turned towards Dux, who had been looking intently at him, and nodded.

The previous three days had been awkward for Peter. His behaviour during the mission, particularly the delay in their escape as a result of his desire to help the Foreign Secretary's wife and child, led many to question whether Peter Brockland really had 'the stuff' needed to lead a revolution.

For the first time since Peter had joined Q1, it was not only himself questioning his suitability as their thought-of leader, but others had now begun to whisper amongst themselves. Did Peter Brockland have the stomach to do 'what needed to be done'?

Tensions had not been helped by the loss of Arma who, unbeknownst to Peter as they had escaped, had been shot down by one of the Order agents, moments after Dux had called out for them to leave.

Consumed by grief, Dux had emptied an entire cartridge into the agent before shouting out angrily again for the others. Though Arma's death had not been Peter's fault, there had certainly been a degree of ill-feeling amongst the growing Shield Force 'clique'. And Peter's perceived show of weakness at the scene provided an easy source for them to direct their grief.

Dux had shut himself away for the entirety of the following day, appearing only briefly to intervene in a heated argument between Peter and Culter in the Q1 kitchen.

Though Dux had apologised for his initial bout of anger, reiterating both to the group and to Peter personally that Peter was at no fault from Arma's death, he made it clear that when running missions such as that again, it was imperative that his orders were followed.

Biting his tongue in respect of Dux's grief, particularly when Arma's face was displayed on news channels as a successful kill of one of the 'crazed terrorists', Peter had agreed. Though he had not gone so far as to hold back on several periods of intense discussion with Indici.

The Shield Force's growing attitude had begun to remind him of his father's - cold; callous; ferocious. Peter found himself fighting a constant battle between his desire to retain some sense of humanity, and his desire to possess the ruthlessness required to be a successful part of the fight ahead. Was this cold, ferocious persona what he would need to become? Could he be that?

As his battle raged on, Peter was happy, relieved even, to allow Dux control in situations such as these.

"Your child is fine," said Dux calmly. "Peter saw them as he left, but your wife was shot."

The Foreign Secretary remained silent and rigidly still. After a moment, his head dropped.

"She sustained a minor wound to the shoulder, but Peter says she was conscious as we left. I am sure she is perfectly fine."

Forgetting his predicament, the Foreign Secretary exploded. With a strength that neither of them had expected, he snapped the plastic cable tie binding his hands together. Resurgent, he thrust the table forwards and sprung towards them.

The table hit Peter hard in the midriff, forcing him backwards. He gasped for breath, clutching his stomach. Collecting himself as the oxygen returned to his lungs, he looked up to see the Foreign Secretary lying face down, with the chair strapped to his back. In his moment of outrage he had clearly forgotten that his legs were still bound to the chair.

Dux had managed to avoid any of the table's impact and had quickly moved towards the now-turtled Foreign Secretary.

"Come on," said Dux, pulling the man up effortlessly. He pulled two cable ties from his back pocket and rebound the Foreign Secretary's hands, before removing his blindfold.

The man had evidently spent a good proportion of his time at Q1 crying in frustration. Tears had blotched his skin, the remnants of which had collected in his thick, black moustache. He blinked profusely as his eyes reacted to the light for the first time in days. He stared around before setting a determined, rage-fuelled look towards Peter.

"If anything has happened to my wife…" he began, threateningly.

"I hardly think you are in a position to be threatening me," said Peter, hating the man more and more with every throb in his stomach.

The Foreign Secretary maintained his intense glare.

"Do you know who I am?" Peter asked.

The Foreign Secretary nodded.

"Do you know why you are here?"

He remained still and silent. Peter sighed.

"Do you know why you are here?" he asked again.

"Answer him," said Dux, gripping the man's shoulders tightly.

"You've kidnapped me, terrorist. How should I know what a deranged maniac like you would want with me?" His eyes squinted around the room frantically, as though searching for clues. "Russian involvement I suspect."

He spat at Peter as he finished and once more tried to break free from the chair.

"What have you done with my family?!" he shouted, his eyes bulging.

Peter felt the warmth hit him above the eye and his face tightened.

Dux made another move to settle their prisoner, but before he had even had a chance to stand up, Peter had reacted. He threw a fist directly into the man's jaw, forcing the chair backwards. The Foreign Secretary fell back to the floor, gasping.

"Shit," said Peter, wiping his face before rubbing his stinging knuckles.

"Quite," said Dux, who had turned to look incredulously towards Peter. He crouched down to check their hostage's condition. "Still conscious… I was not expecting that!"

Peter tried, but failed, to hide a slight grin.

"But perhaps we should try and keep him awake for the next bit?"

"Right," Peter agreed.

Dux pulled the Foreign Secretary back up to the table. He looked groggy and his face had begun to swell, but he still managed to fix a derisive glare at Peter.

"What's the next bit?" he asked, eyeing Dux as he spat blood to the floor.

Dux turned towards a small television monitor in the corner of the room. Peter maintained his glance upon the Foreign Secretary and watched as his look of derision turned quickly to confusion, then concern.

Dux pulled a remote control from his pocket and moved back to the table, sitting down in the extra chair beside Peter. "Perhaps you'll remember this," he said, directing it towards the screen.

They all sat silently as the hotel footage began. As the gruesome scene unfolded, the silent intermittent glare from the television accentuated their hostage's look of shock and anguish.

The Foreign Secretary remained silent, ashen-faced as the coverage progressed, opening and closing his mouth, lost for anything to say.

"H...how," he stuttered weakly. He stared down into the table. "How did you get this?"

Neither of them answered, rather allowing him to sink further towards the table. Looking at the man's face droop as the footage played out behind them, Peter felt that the man opposite him was not shocked by seeing the evidence of his actions in the hands of the enemy, but ashamed.

"Philip," said Peter softly, breaking the silence and addressing their hostage for the first time by his name. "We are going to need something from you."

The Foreign Secretary looked up. His face was now so drained of life that, though his expression suggested he was on the verge of tears, Peter was unsure that he could cry, even if he had wanted to.

"What do you want?" he asked, sharply.

"We are going to need a confession," said Peter.

The Foreign Secretary looked up, confused.

"What do you mean?" he asked. "You have me there, on that video. You've ruined me, ruined my career. My life, in that clip, is over. My family's lives, over. What more could you possibly need?"

"The video is evidence you butchered that innocent young woman," Dux replied, holding back his disgust. This was the moment of truth; they needed him. "What it doesn't explain is why."

"We are not here to ruin you, Philip," said Peter, silently thankful that in his discombobulation, the Foreign Secretary had not sought to address how unclear the footage was. "Your career means nothing to us. We are here to destroy the organisation you work for."

A strange look came over their prisoner's face, recognising the game was up. He had not just been a random government target – they knew who, and what, he was. "Of course," he replied, and Peter was surprised to see that he had managed the strength to form a weak grin.

"Your attempts to expose the Order have certainly been entertaining. I should have expected something like this."

Dux and Peter remained quiet, both struggling to adapt to the Foreign Secretary's sudden rally of strength.

"What do you honestly think your small bunch of rebels are going to achieve?" he asked again, sneering. "Even if you manage to convince the world that we are real, we have a hold on every major structure of society. We have people everywhere. Your best case scenario is that the Order simply takes power."

"Our best case scenario," Dux sneered back, "will be the death of you and the rest of your delusional fanatics, and a return to some sort of normal life for the thousands of people driven into hiding. That small bunch of rebels you speak of is, I'm afraid, not as small as your Order believes it to be."

The Foreign Secretary looked back at Dux, breathing heavily from his outburst, with the remnants of a sneer still spread across his face. "There's nothing that you can do to me in here that the Order could and would not do worse."

"You're wrong," said Peter, looking intently into the Foreign Secretary's eyes.

"We have you. The Order has your family. What do you think the Order might do to them? You know them far better than I do, but from my experience, they don't act with a great deal of mercy towards traitors, do they?"

The Foreign Secretary flickered, his eyes betraying a hint of fear.

"What are you talking about?" he snapped. "I haven't told you anything."

"Do you trust them to believe that you will remain silent?" Peter asked.

The Foreign Secretary quickly seemed to realise the truth of Peter's words and his face drained of its remaining colour. The Order were fanatical in their desire for secrecy, even now; it was of critical importance for the president. If there was any potential risk to them, it had to be dealt with, swiftly.

Whatever this man had done and whatever he had stood for, it was clear from the longing in his eyes that his family meant far more to the Foreign Secretary than the purpose he had dedicated his adult life to. Peter understood now why the Order were so against their agents having children; a parent's bond with their child was too great of a burden to their work.

A few moments passed, as the Foreign Secretary considered his remaining options. They both knew that the Order would stop at nothing to keep their existence hidden, even if it meant disposing of their own. The Foreign Secretary squirmed uncomfortably in his chair and bit down on his lip. He sighed dejectedly.

"Can you help me?"

He could not look at them. His eyes had diverted towards the table, his face defeated.

"Excuse me?" Dux asked, incredulous.

The Foreign Secretary gulped and continued to stare meekly at the table. "My family. Can you help me?"

Dux laughed, but as the Foreign Secretary looked up desperately, Peter glanced towards Dux and back at the Foreign Secretary. He nodded.

"We will need that confession," said Peter plainly.

"I'll give you whatever you want," said the Foreign Secretary, quietly. "Just help me get my family back."

His shoulders had sagged and his head dropped.

An abrupt knock at the door interrupted them and Culter entered. He stared at the defeated figure of the Foreign Secretary a moment, before nodding towards Dux and Peter, urging them to follow.

Dux stood up as Culter closed the door. He pulled the blindfold back down over the Foreign Secretary's eyes and followed Culter into the hallway.

"Will you help me?" the Foreign Secretary asked weakly, his voice breaking as he looked aimlessly around the room. Peter left the room without offering an answer, closing the door behind him.

Peter turned in the hallway and spotted Dux's boots disappearing up the stairs. He followed quickly and stopped to see him standing at the kitchen door, his arms folded. Peter edged slowly towards him. It was not long before he sensed the atmosphere inside; something bad had happened.

Beyond Dux sat at least thirty resistance figures, all huddled around the kitchen table, glancing up apprehensively towards the television. Peter walked slowly towards them and as he reached the doorway, all eyes inside silently suggested that he needed to see this.

Sceptical, and fully expecting to see another news story detailing his latest exploits in domestic terrorism, he turned.

Peter scoffed as he saw his now-familiar photograph, but soon fell silent as the pictures switched to show bodies, covered in white sheets. They were being wheeled out from the Foreign Secretary's residence.

'Foreign Secretary still missing, now presumed dead. Wife and child murdered' the sub-caption read.

Peter gaped. How had the Order got to them? It did not make sense. The police had been there by the time Peter and the others had escaped. Perhaps it really was true what the Foreign Secretary and the president had told him, that their infiltration of the structures of their society really did run deep.

Peter had told the Foreign Secretary that he believed the Order would do anything to protect their secret, but even he did not believe they would actually murder his wife and child. He had met the president, heard of his devotion to the cause; even after everything they had done, the move seemed to go so defiantly against his own code.

The barbaric nature of the attack did not surprise him, but it signalled a complete change from what Peter had understood the Order to be – a callous, murderous organisation, but one driven by a devout, albeit warped, ethos; not mindless.

Peter sank into one of the few remaining chairs, staring weakly around at the stony faces in the room. He remembered the woman's distraught face as she sought desperately to protect her child… the child. How could they murder a young baby?

Peter winced. He felt pain in the palms of his hands and noticed he had been clenching his fists so tightly, his nails had drawn blood. He could have protected them, both of them. He could have saved them.

"As you can see, the Order appears to have dealt with our friend's family," said Indici, breaking the silence with his customary precision of stating the obvious. "There's our leverage gone."

"We can't tell him," said Dux, scoffing with frustration. "We've got him right where we want him in there. He's begging for us to help him get his family back. If we tell him his family is dead, he's not going to cooperate. He'll either think it was us that did it, or that he has nothing to live for. Either way, we get nothing."

"He's going to find out eventually," said Peter, with a deep sigh, blood rushing back to his fingers as he released his fists.

Peter had been scorned by many that sat in the room for trying to protect the woman and her child, scorned for his supposed moment of weakness. And now he had been proved right to try - there they were, their lifeless bodies being wheeled out, dead. He was never more certain of his approach.

"Even if we get the confession from him, he'll soon find out and who knows how he will react if he finds out we hid it from him. The confession is useless if he denies it later."

Indici looked at Peter, then Dux.

"So what do we do?"

"If we tell him, we might as well cancel the whole plan," said Dux firmly. "We get the confession and we can think about anything else afterwards. We can keep him here if we need to, he can't deny anything if he's locked up."

The majority of the room nodded in agreement.

"It's certainly tough to sympathise with the man," said Indici, sighing.

The room all turned to look at Peter, who had not indicated his agreement. "I'm sorry, I disagree," said Peter firmly.

Many around the table averted their gaze. They had all heard about Peter's moment of weakness at the Foreign Secretary's manor. He noticed Culter in the corner of the room shaking his head, staring patronisingly up towards the kitchen ceiling.

"We can't keep something like that from him, whatever he's done. We have to tell him," said Peter, defensively. "Besides, if he believes the Order killed his family he'll want revenge; he'll want to help."

The room remained silent. Peter could not help but think back to his own feelings of anger and the impulse for vengeance when his father had been killed. He would have helped anyone at that point to get back at the Order. He knew that the Foreign Secretary would too.

Dux sighed.

"We can't take that risk Peter. We need his confession for our plan to work."

Peter shook his head. If the Foreign Secretary believed that the Resistance had been behind his wife and child's deaths, Dux was right to consider that it was game over. But the deception, and the callous nature of it, did not sit well with him; it felt like an Order move.

"Peter," said Dux with a sigh, "I can't let you back in there if you're not down with this."

A stir echoed around the room. The atmosphere dropped.

Peter had never felt threatened amongst this group of people, until now. His behaviour during the kidnapping and his attitude now – was he appearing weak?

Peter stood up abruptly and scanned the room, searching for allies, but the eyes remained staring at the walls or floor. He turned to look at Dux, who stared directly back at him without a flicker. This was not a fight that Peter was going to win.

"We can't become like them," he said poignantly, staring at the television and back towards the kitchen's embarrassed faces. "I certainly won't."

He pushed his chair aside and walked past Dux towards the kitchen door.

"You're too nice for this fight Peter."

Peter walked out briskly, closing the kitchen door behind him.

24

The 'kitchen incident', as it soon came to be known, changed things.

Peter no longer took part in the kitchen round table discussions, and received little more than a polite nod in the hallway from those aligned with Dux's more vicious vision for the Resistance movement. Peter's role within the Resistance had taken a sudden and dramatic shift.

Without the burden of leadership, he had more time to learn of the struggles faced by those he lived with. Peter would wander the rooms of Q1 almost aimlessly most days, meeting more and more of the inhabitants. He was keen to hear their stories and learn more about the plights that brought them here.

Peter often found himself staring out through his bedroom window too, longingly towards the street below. He quickly became desperate to escape the confines of the terraced house - to walk outside, somewhere, anywhere, just to clear his head. But he knew that was impossible, even without Indici telling him so.

If Peter Brockland had not been public enemy number one before, the daily media reminders of the Foreign Secretary's abduction, and the murder of his wife and child, had certainly made him so. He could not risk being seen; he could not risk betraying their location. Q1 was fast becoming far less of a sanctuary, than a prison.

Peter was not without his supporters though. Many of those he spoke to sympathised with his position. Many had escaped tragedy, fear and violence and had little desire to associate themselves with those experiences again. Though they felt powerless over their futures, they made it clear that they had not escaped the perilous clutches of the Order to find themselves protected by the same sort of people.

Peter found solace in his periods of fragility talking with George and others in their quasi-digital team, during the short periods they found it safe to return to Q1.

He would often sit with them as they scrolled through the various social media channels and online blogs, trying to get a sense of the real public mood, whilst also pushing the Resistance message. Peter had developed an unhealthy obsession with 'Googling' himself and to say that the general public commentary was negative would have been a catastrophic understatement.

"Of course you're going to see negative comments," they would tell him, when Peter read out his latest insult. "You're supposed to be a crazed terrorist child killer, what did you expect?"

When not scrutinising cartoons of his lynching online, Peter would sneak short patrols of the basement corridor to listen out for any signs of success.

By the sounds of the thumps, yelps, and crashes from the other side of the door, it did not appear so. Peter wondered what could possibly have happened; the Foreign Secretary had been so keen to help before – had Dux refused to help him find his family?

Peter felt powerless, knowing that their approach was wrong. He had been part of something exciting before he was shunted aside, a real collective fight against a combined enemy. He desperately wanted to be part of it again.

Peter walked downstairs, brushing past the remaining strands of Christmas tinsel tied around the bannisters. He looked up and noticed one of the younger boys sitting in the front room, playing with one of his new toys.

"Hey buddy," he said, walking into the room and ruffling the boy's hair.

"Hi!" the boy responded enthusiastically, though not enough to divert his focus from his battling action figures.

Peter sat down on the sofa beside him and stared down at the plastic battle scene below, placing his whiskey on a side table with a smile. "What are you up to?"

"Trying to beat the bad people," the boy said, smashing the two figures together. "The bad people took my daddy and I'm going to beat them."

"Ah," Peter sighed, and with a sad smile he took a swig from his glass. "Of course you are buddy."

The boy continued to smash the action figures together, more and more violently.

"I'm going to kill them," he said darkly, his high-pitched voice starting to break. "I'm going to smash them, just like Dux does."

The comment seemed to spark something deep within Peter. It was as though the ember that had been flickering weakly in his mind for the past few days had erupted. He felt, quite unexpectedly, a rush of anger he had not felt since his father's murder.

Peter had perhaps not seen it clearly before, the direct impact of an increasingly aggressive Shield Force. His vision for what the Resistance should be and what it should represent, compared to what it was slowly becoming, was at a crossroads. If he did not step up and fight for his vision, if he did not act now, it might become irreversible.

The Resistance could not become a force dedicated solely to destroying the Order and protecting 'their people'; they needed to be more. They had a duty to re-establish, perhaps even improve, the lives of everyone. With their knowledge of what the Order was doing to people around the world, the Resistance had a duty to restore humanity. It was a duty that Dux and others seemed to have forgotten in their dogged pursuit of revenge.

Peter crouched down to face the young boy and clutched his shoulders. He shook them softly, and looked directly into his tearful eyes.

"We are better than them," he said quietly, a ruthless purpose flowing through him. The boy looked up at him, his eyes still watering. "Your daddy was better than them and you, you are going to be better than them, ok?"

The boy stared back at Peter with glistening eyes. He dropped his toys and threw his arms around Peter, sobbing.

Peter lifted him into a tight hug. He turned slowly and saw the boy's mother standing in the doorway. Peter stared at her, steely-eyed, before passing the boy back to her.

It was now or never; it was time for him to make his stand. It was time now for him to fight not only for his own position in the coming fight ahead, but to shape the Resistance's future.

Peter placed a consoling hand on the mother's shoulder and smiled, before leaving the room. Purpose blinded his senses from any anxieties as he walked directly towards the staircase, down towards the basement below. He saw Culter standing guard outside the interrogation room, and he turned quickly to face him as Peter approached.

"What are you doing down here?" he asked, with a smug grin. "You can't go in, Dux is in there".

Peter was no longer preoccupied by a desire to fit in with Dux's gang. He continued towards Culter, who maintained his smug grin, and drew back his right arm. Peter swung his fist into the side of Culter's face who, not expecting such a move, had left himself defenceless.

Culter fell to the floor with a loud crash, unconscious.

Peter was breathing heavily, momentarily shocked by what he had done. The noise seemed to have startled the people in the room and he heard movement from inside.

Peter did not wait for a reaction. Still breathing heavily, he wrenched open the door to find Dux standing beside the Foreign Secretary. He was still bound to his chair, his face cut and swollen. Blood oozed from his mouth and nostrils, dripping slowly to the floor.

Dux looked up towards Peter, clearly startled. "What are you doing here?"

"Get out," said Peter plainly, looking directly at the distressed figure of their prisoner.

Dux let out a weak laugh. "What..."

"Get the fuck out of this room," Peter interrupted, more forcefully, staring directly into Dux's eyes.

Dux stared back at him for a second, sizing him up. He edged slowly towards him.

Peter looked straight back at him resolutely. It was only at that point that he seemed to appreciate the sheer size of the man making his way towards him. Peter clenched his fists, ready to strike again if necessary.

"Dux," came a muffled voice behind Peter.

Culter had managed to collect himself from his daze outside and had stumbled dizzily into the doorway, clutching the door frame for support.

"He hit me!" he mumbled, through a swelling jaw.

Peter moved directly towards Dux, who continued to stare back at him, diverting his gaze only to look at Culter over Peter's shoulder. Was that a faint impressed look in Dux's eyes?

With one final glance, Peter moved past him and sat in the chair opposite the Foreign Secretary.

"He fucking hit me!" Culter screamed again from behind him, but Dux did not respond.

"I'm going to speak with the Foreign Secretary alone," said Peter, mustering all the authority he could in his voice.

He slowly lifted the man's blindfold and the Foreign Secretary lifted his head weakly.

Peter prepared himself. His next few seconds would be filled either by the sound of his face being smashed against the table by two far larger men, or by the quiet sounds of Dux and Culter leaving the room.

Fortunately for Peter, and his face, no such scuffles came. He heard the door close quietly behind him, muffling the sounds of Culter's complaints. It was just him and the Foreign Secretary now.

He looked awful. His nose was broken and his face so swollen he was almost unrecognisable. His facial injuries were nothing though when compared with the look of resignation in his eyes. He had clearly come to terms with himself that he was going to die in this room, to protect, as he had hoped, the Order and his family.

"I suppose you want me to thank you for removing that animal," he said weakly, through a fat lip.

"Your wife and child are dead," said Peter, ignoring him.

The Foreign Secretary froze. Peter continued to look directly at him, his face emotionless. He allowed the Foreign Secretary a minute to process what had been said, before pulling a small pen-knife from his pocket. He cut the cable ties binding the Foreign Secretary's wrists and legs.

His hands remained clasped together, as though he had not processed the move. Instead he looked up at Peter, his face blank.

"Did you hear me?" Peter asked again. "Your wife and child, they are dead."

The Foreign Secretary remained still, staring at him. He began to clench his fists as the blood circulated back into his hands, strength returning after weeks of restraint.

"Did you hear me?" Peter asked again, louder.

"I heard you!" he erupted, flailing his arms. He shot up from his chair in a grief-stricken rage, flinging the table away.

Peter avoided the thrust of the table and stood abruptly, preparing himself for any backfire to his plan. But the effort appeared to have been too much for Foreign Secretary and he sank to his knees, breathing heavily.

Peter heard the door move behind him.

"Do not come in here!" he shouted.

The door stopped moving. He turned back to the pitiful figure crumpled on the floor ahead of him, shaking violently. He crouched down, a metre or so away from him.

"You killed them!" he screamed at Peter, his face contorted.

"No," said Peter plainly, staring directly back at him. "You killed them."

Peter continued to watch as the Foreign Secretary shook violently, his head cupped in his hands.

"Do you think the Order would have risked your wife telling the truth about them to help secure your escape?"

"They didn't know…" he said weakly, gasping through sobs.

"You know they would not have taken any chances. And they expected us to kill you; they did not think they would need leverage. They, like you, are making the mistake of misunderstanding what this resistance stands for. We are not murderers, nor will we ever be."

Peter looked towards the video camera in the corner of the room, its red light still blinking to indicate the live stream. He knew that members of the Resistance would be watching intently. He wanted to make his point stick. Peter moved back towards the Foreign Secretary, who looked back up towards him, now pale.

"You put your faith in the wrong side," said Peter, "and it has cost you your family. But it doesn't need to cost you your life."

"What life?" the Foreign Secretary said weakly. "My family is gone."

Peter put a hand on the Foreign Secretary's shoulder and was relieved to find that he accepted it.

"Don't waste their memory," said Peter. "The Resistance can never forget the part you have played in ruining so many people's lives, but perhaps you can go some way in making up for it now by helping us. Think of your family, and what the Order did to them. Help us defeat them."

A few tense seconds of silence passed. The Foreign Secretary wiped away his tears and bloodied face with his sleeve and breathed in heavily.

"Ok," he said, rubbing himself down and offering a curt nod. "What do you need me to do?"

25

The muddy fields housing thousands of tents amidst the blissful surroundings of the South-Western UK countryside were once again blessed by the sort of glorious sunshine that the Taunton Festival had become spookily famous for attracting, defying yet again the typically wet and gloomy January weather.

Local hotels and bed & breakfasts had seen record numbers of room bookings. The surrounding pubs had served kegs worth of extra alcohol. And, less exciting for them, the influx of additional litter-picking needs proved an apt task for the local youths carrying out mandatory community service orders.

The Taunton Festival had entered its sixth year and once again outperformed its previous attendance record. More than 200,000 people, young and old, trudged their way through the Norton Fitzwarren fields, set aside to excite travelling crowds with the biggest and best musical acts the world had to offer.

The setting also made for an extraordinary opportunity for the Resistance to spread its message, and one not unnoticed by the authorities. The record crowds faced similarly high numbers of constabulary presence.

It seemed not to phase many of the attendees, instead offering greater opportunities for social media likes as they posed for selfies with the officers, smiling and laughing with tins of supermarket cider at the ready. After all, they lived in dangerous times - the notorious terrorist Peter Brockland and 'The Resistance' were still at large.

The police presence paled into insignificance when the television sets and tablet computer streams of millions watching the event worldwide displayed state-of-the-art drone footage of the thousands in the crowd.

Some had taken full advantage of the sunshine, even with the cool breeze donning little more than was necessary to avoid public indecency charges. It made for interesting outfit decisions when accessorised with the essential wellington boots to counter the previous few days' torrential rainfall.

The Taunton Festival had quickly evolved into a fairground for fancy dress, with outfits ranging from outlandish displays of 80s punk to Disney characters, Halloween leftovers to comic book superheroes. It was no longer a rare sight to see Catholic nuns make their way around the complex in full habit, whether actual or impersonated. The event had certainly become one comfortable catering to the diversified personalities of the British and international public.

The various novelty stalls and tents in the surrounding fields selling anything from hot dogs to glow sticks all led up to the main stage – a huge bubble-shaped structure, enclosed by a semicircle of trees that helped protect the famous site of Norton Camp.

The stage hosted a huge 25-foot high screen, which, when not magnifying images of the artists to cater for those unfortunate audience members at the back of the crowd, relayed pictures of the audience to the watching public.

Now though, the screen magnified the closing moments of US country star Hughie Jackson's set as he cooed into his stool-side microphone. The evening set was nearing its close, and the crowds had become impatient. Some drug and, or perhaps also, alcohol-inhibited, they trembled in anticipation. They would soon witness the closing act that they had all paid their extortionate Saturday night ticket prices to see - Tornado Fire.

Detecting the growing impatience amongst the nuns and punk rockers below, Hughie Jackson opted to close his set with a shorter version of his Top 10 hit 'Three Lines to Freedom' - keen to avoid any projectiles from an increasingly inebriated audience. He certainly did not want the highlights of this year's event showing him facing the same treatment as Danny Jones last year, forced to flee the stage covered in bottled urine.

Only metres away from Tornado Fire's final preparations, Peter Brockland stood with his gun poised at the head of one of the festival's lead producers.

The producer trembled as Peter gazed down, ensuring that he was competently preparing the grand finale of the day that the Resistance had planned for weeks.

"You'll understand why we're doing this when you see it," said Peter, hoping to calm the man's trembling.

The young man could only have been in his early twenties, but even in his agitated state showed considerable technical expertise, pushing and turning buttons and controls in rapid succession, fuelled by the added adrenaline a gun at his head would provide.

"The world needs to see the truth. They need to understand."

The producer nodded weakly, though likely to avoid any harm at the hands of the lunatic behind him - the one he had seen on television for months causing chaos around the country, the one who had murdered all those people on the train, the one who had murdered the Foreign Secretary's wife and child.

"Jason, are we ready for Tornado Fire?" came an excited voice through the producer's walkie-talkie, as she continued to sing along to the closing lines of Hughie Jackson's hit.

Jason turned to look at Peter as the woman continued her sub-par rendition. He nodded sternly back at him. Jason gulped. "All ready to go."

"Good work, let's do it!" came the cheery voice of the production manager again.

"Not until I say," said Peter, pushing the gun into the back of Jason's head.

"Ladies and Gentlemen!" came the amplified Texan accent of Hughie Jackson, breathing heavily as he closed. "It gives me great pleasure to welcome to the stage your final act of the evening... Tornado Fire!"

The crowd screamed in jubilation as the Tornado Fire foursome made their way out onto the stage, to dry ice and pulsing red strobe lights. Peter looked at George excitedly, eager for reassurance that everything was ready, that everything was going to work.

They had planned the festival takeover for weeks, ever since they had discovered that the Tornado Fire guitarist, Julia Starr, had been targeted by the Order. She had taken some convincing, as did many the Resistance tried to protect, but they had persuaded her of their existence and her imminent danger. Her belief had been critical to their plan, allowing them access to all areas of the backstage process in the guise of the band's 'groupies'.

The lead singer had completed the opening verse of number one hit 'Three of Us', and had begun to goad the crowd, jumping around the stage with her microphone extended.

"Is everybody having a good time?!" she screamed to the audience as the music behind her built up to the climactic first chorus. The crowd roared back ecstatically.

George nodded back at Peter.

"Now," said Peter, looking down at the producer. Jason turned weakly to look back at him as though searching within himself for the courage to resist.

"Now!" Peter shouted, brandishing the gun once more at him.

Jason gulped and turned back to the laptops controlling the screen. With the pressing of a small combination of buttons, the amplification equipment on stage immediately shut down. The strobe lighting ceased. The screen behind them went blank.

The screams of excitement and laughter began to falter, and the acoustics died down as they realised that the break was unplanned; something had gone wrong.

Boos rang out amongst the crowd, and plastic bottles were hurled towards the stage. The band looked helplessly towards either side of the stage at the runners, who looked back, equally baffled.

"Jason, what the fuck is going on?" came the production manager's voice through the walkie-talkie. She no longer possessed her nauseatingly jovial tone.

Jason looked up at Peter again. Peter eyed the laptop screen and pushed the gun into Jason's head. Jason turned, shaking, and clicked.

The main screen outside suddenly flickered back to life to show the Foreign Secretary sitting in the small basement room at Q1, staring directly into the camera.

The audience's gasps grew louder as those who knew of the Foreign Secretary's disappearance told those around them who the man on the screen was. The police surrounding the crowd looked momentarily stunned, looking around towards the others and pushing frantically at their earpieces for directions on how to proceed.

"What would you like to say to the men and women in the audience today Foreign Secretary?" came a warped voice off-camera, amplified 100-fold by the surrounding speakers.

The crowd quietened, but for stray vocals of the drunks who had not yet understood what was going on.

"I… I want to tell them the truth," the Foreign Secretary responded on screen. "About me, about everything." He sighed heavily. "About the Order."

The Foreign Secretary gulped and took another deep, steadying breath.

"I am not everything that people think I am."

He paused, collecting himself again. "I am… I was… part of an organisation that has lived amongst you for hundreds of years. The Progressive Human Race Order - PHROX."

Hardly a sound could be heard from the crowd now; even the drunks had noticed that something was very wrong.

"And what is PHROX?" came the warped voice off-screen.

"PHROX is a secret organisation working to maintain and protect the development of the human race. Using genetic technology, they seek to protect those genetic lines deemed compatible to continue the progressive evolution of the human race. They seek to halt and destroy those which are not."

"How?"

"Some are killed, some imprisoned, some sterilised. We did whatever was necessary to prevent incompatibles from passing on genetic defects."

The audience was engrossed now, even the intoxicated ones, and the atmosphere was increasingly frightened. Some had heard of the various 'Order' conspiracy theories from social media and the protests carried out by the so-called 'Resistance', but nobody had taken them seriously, not really. They were fake, dangerous.

"We have people in institutions across the country and worldwide – hospitals, police stations, clinics, anything. Anywhere genetic information can be obtained we will likely have access. We take the genetic information, we analyse it and compatibility is calculated. Will their genes help to develop the human race, make us faster, stronger, more intelligent? Are there any potential weaknesses or defects in their genetic code? They are identified, assessed, and the Order ensures that any unworthy genes do not become a problem for future generations."

"How many people have you killed Foreign Secretary?" the warped voice asked again. The question appeared to have taken him by surprise.

"I... it's impossible to say how many the Order has killed. Thousands, hundreds of thousands maybe."

"How many have you killed Foreign Secretary?" the warped voice pushed again.

"I... I don't know – not many."

"You can't remember how many people you have killed? How disappointing." There was a brief pause before the voice continued again. "How deep is the infiltration of the Order?"

The Foreign Secretary looked distraught. "They're everywhere. They have people everywhere."

"And why are you telling the world now? Why should people believe you?"

"They killed my family," he said weakly. "My wife, my child."

After a brief pause, he stared down at the floor and tears began to form in his eyes.

The picture on screen shook as the video camera was lifted from its position and turned to face Peter Brockland. Peter's face stared directly out to the Taunton Festival audience. The crowd moved awkwardly, drawing gasps of panic again. They pointed up to the screen, whispering at each other loudly, as the police pushed more urgently through them, closing in on the main stage.

They had all seen this man. Peter Brockland had been all over the news, the terrorist, the child killer, determined to destroy the society they all lived so peacefully in. Yet, here he was, with the Foreign Secretary, who seemed to back his story -

the same story they had been told was a ludicrous, dangerous lie.

"We told you they were here," came Peter's voice. "We told you that they were amongst you. You have been told that I am dangerous, that I have murdered people, that I am your enemy. That is a lie. I am a victim, as are many of you. I was just like you, I knew nothing until they came for me. But I was fortunate enough to have help. I am fortunate enough to have the Resistance behind me to fight back. It is time for you to accept the truth and it is time for you to defeat it."

The screen flickered to show pictures of various high-profile individuals, as they had done with the broadcast. Government officials, military leaders, celebrities - all appeared, in various compromising situations.

"We have all been blind to the infiltration of this Order into our society," said Peter's voice, narrating images of high-profile murders and worldwide 'natural disasters'.

As the recording continued, Dux's voice came through Peter's walkie-talkie - "Pete, they're closing in". It was time to go.

Peter nodded at George, indicating for him to leave. "I'll be right behind you." George nodded and ran out of the production tent.

Peter listened to his voice booming at the crowd outside; they had shown them enough, they had been successful. He wondered, as their images filled the screen broadcasting worldwide, how those individuals were feeling now. What awkward situations had they now found themselves in, slipping away from various late-night meetings, family get-togethers and high-end dinner parties?

Peter's mind wandered too to the president, who he hoped was watching on in horror as his beloved Order was so publicly exposed, planning his next move.

Peter moved quickly to tie Jason to his chair, hoping that this would be enough to exonerate him from any accusation of collusion. He heard his voice near the recording's conclusion.

"Those of you still unconvinced by the truth must search within yourselves. Many of you will have been affected; many of you will have been suspicious – you must believe. Those we can help, we have and we will continue to, but we are not enough. We have sent information to all we have been able to, to warn you of any danger you might be in. We, The Resistance, are amongst you now as PHROX has been. We will help you to fight, but we must all fight together to defeat them. Rise up now! We will not let them control our future! Rise up!"

Jason stared at Peter, his face draining of colour as though he had seen him for the first time. "Is that true?"

Peter aimed the gun towards him and squeezed the trigger. Water squirted from the barrel, dousing Jason's face. Peter smiled as Jason flinched, dropped the water pistol, and ran out of the tent.

The video on stage cut out just as suddenly as it had started, leaving a blank screen and a dark, empty stage.

Some might have already believed the crazy conspiracy theories, and many more might have been convinced by the spectacle they had just seen. What was certain was that panic and fear had exploded amongst the 200,000-strong audience, and pandemonium ensued. People were dropped from shoulders and others thrown out of the way as the crowds stampeded to escape the enclosure.

Gunshots rang out as panicked undercover Order agents sought to complete missions, killing those targets they could now that the cloak of secrecy had been removed. Armed police officers sought to shoot those agents down, some thwarted by partners who were also part of the Order.

Wellington boots turned from brown to red as blood oozed into the muddy ground beneath the crowds, as hundreds fell to the ground.

Backstage, Peter and the Resistance drew further away from the scene, having escaped in what vehicles they could find. Peter looked back in horror as he heard the gunshots and screams. They had not expected the response to be so immediately violent, but there was nothing they could do for them now. He could only hope that as many of them as possible could escape into the protection of the surrounding woodland.

The Taunton Festival was certain to have started something. They had done all they could to expose the Order, and they would have to wait and see what would happen. They all sat quietly staring at each other as they sped further away from the devastation behind them, all preparing for what was to come.

*****

Miles away, the president sat amongst other leading Order figures, many of whom had just been exposed, their public disguises now destroyed.

"What the fuck am I going to do now?" came one high-ranking military official, grabbing at his hair.

The president sighed and took a deep drag of his cigar. He stood up and turned to look at a portrait on the wall of his office. He clasped his hands together, rubbing them in deep, silent thought.

The others watched on as he continued to stare at the image, all silently waiting for instruction.

"For many years my friends, many successful years, our Order has worked tirelessly in the shadows to ensure that the human race continues to evolve, to fight the threat of devolution, to strengthen our people, to become better, stronger, healthier."

He looked around into the faces of his associates and sighed. He glanced up towards an agent standing patiently at the doorway of his office and nodded. The agent nodded back and left the room.

"It appears the shadows are no longer big enough to conceal us. It seems now, my friends, that we must reveal ourselves."

26

Chief Superintendent Justine Smith jumped out from the back seat of the Land Rover Discovery, her wellington boots sinking into the ground below.

She looked out towards the field of scattered tents and ahead towards the treeline enclosure with a distinct sense of foreboding. She looked around impatiently and saw two officers trudge towards her. She supposed they were coming to brief her on the situation, but they needn't have bothered; the videos online had been quite graphic enough.

She had watched the early coverage, of course. Even an ageing Chief Superintendent was prone to watching fools dress up on television, especially if Hughie Jackson was involved. She had watched, with millions of others, in incredulity - there was no other word for it - as the jubilant, and she was sure law-breaking, scenes unfolded. She watched as Tornado Fire switched to show no other than the missing Foreign Secretary, coerced into admitting Peter Brockland's story was true.

But the reaction afterwards, the exhibition of mindless brutality by some of the officers at the scene, was unbefitting. It was certainly not protocol for officers of any kind to react with such violence in response to what was obviously a stupid stunt.

Her jaw had dropped further still as she watched the Deputy Commissioner appear alongside Peter Brockland's supposed list of conspirators. It was strange; Justine never possessed a particularly good feeling about the Deputy

Commissioner. A misogynist creep, sure. Ruthless, unquestionably, but to suggest that he was part of some secret Order was farcical.

"Ma'am," came the southwestern twangs of the approaching officers in unison, forcing her from her daydream. "Welcome to Taunton. Shame about the circumstances."

"Yes, quite," she responded, wrenching her boots from the sinking mud beneath her. "Catch me up."

"Officers reported initial gunfire at 11.15 pm. Conflicting accounts though I'm afraid. Some say the audience fired first, some saying it was the officers."

"How can it be conflicting?" said Justine sharply as the officers led her through an opening in the treeline enclosure. "Why on earth would a group of festival-goers be armed with, oh my god-".

Justine had cut her sentence short as she walked into the enclosure. Instantly, she grabbed her handkerchief, overpowered by the smell. She watched in horror as paramedics struggled against the conditions to wheel out the countless bodies, many still dressed in their ludicrous, now bloodstained, outfits.

"Yes, ma'am, we understand," the other officer interrupted. "The reports have been strange."

Justine held up a hand to silence them as she struggled to adjust to the scene.

Her embroidered sky blue handkerchief still held tightly to her nostrils, she led the officers silently towards the main stage. She looked down as they passed several bullet-ridden bodies, repulsed to find that her boots were drenched not only by thick mud, but scarlet.

Pulling herself from visions of excited youngsters making their way there, oblivious to what would soon transpire, she turned back towards the enclosure entrance. Loud clicking and growing voices offered her some merciful distraction until she realised it was the reporters arriving. They had spared no time in capturing their shots for the front pages.

"Officer…"

"Young, ma'am," the young officer responded, straightening.

"Officer Young," said Justine. "Would you be a dear and find a polite way of telling those reporters to fuck off?"

"Yes, ma'am." Officer Young smirked slightly and nodded before turning towards the reporters.

Justine followed the other officer towards the main stage, her handkerchief firmly placed across her nose. The main screen was damaged, cracked by stray gunshots, and speakers and instruments were strewn across the stage.

Her boot hit something on the floor, distracting her from her analysis. She looked down to see an armed officer lying on her back, peaceful and lifeless.

With a pang, she thought of Jenny; it could have been her lying there and for what? She shook herself and had begun to walk away, before noticing that something was amiss.

She pulled a pair of disposable gloves from her pocket and knelt beside the offer. She fumbled with her jacket and picked up the officer's side weapon – a CZ 75 handgun. She eyed it with confusion; it was not a standard issue and, stranger still, the weapon had been fitted with a suppressor. She turned to tell the officer to bag the weapon for evidence when she noticed an odd marking on the woman's left wrist.

"Officer…" she said, waving for Officer Young's partner to come closer.

"Davies, ma'am," she replied.

"Yes, yes," said Justine impatiently. "Come and have a look at this."

Officer Davies leant down beside her and looked at the woman's wrist. "It's just a tattoo, ma'am. Odd one though I must admit."

"But don't you think it looks like the symbol from Peter Brockland's videos?"

Officer Davies looked closer before turning back towards Justine, shaking her head. "Just looks like a cheap holiday job to me, ma'am."

"Ok," said Justine, pulling herself to her feet.

It certainly looked to her like the strange sword symbol that had fronted several of 'The Resistance's' videos. Perhaps after the long weeks of trying to catch him, she had begun to overthink things.

She noticed a couple of paramedics pushing an empty stretcher nearby and waved them over, pointing down at the officer.

"I was told we have the technician Peter Brockland held hostage?" she asked Officer Davies as the paramedics slowly approached.

"Yes, ma'am. Over here."

She looked down again at the lifeless face of the young armed officer as the paramedics slowly lifted her onto the stretcher. Such a waste.

They continued through the field, which was slowly clearing of bodies, towards the large marquee beside the main stage. Justine pulled back the canvas opening and noticed a man shivering in the corner beside another officer.

"You must be the technician?"

She looked towards the officer, who nodded and moved away. The man turned to face her blankly, clearly still overcome by his experience.

"Jason, the technician, yes..."

She pulled a seat towards her and sat opposite the man. He was young, mid-twenties or so and still in a state of complete shock.

"Thank you for waiting, Jason," said Justine, looking at the man. "It can't have been easy."

Jason nodded weakly.

"I'm going to need you to tell me what happened, ok?"

The man nodded again and gulped.

He began to tell his story, fighting stutters. He explained how Julia Starr had asked the production staff to let them bring in a new group of supporters, how Peter Brockland and his group had taken the security staff and members of the technical team hostage, and how he had forced him to play the footage of the Foreign Secretary.

"And then he shot me," he said, and Justine was surprised to find that he had let out a laugh. "He shot me with a water pistol and ran away."

She looked up at Officer Davies to see if she too had heard him correctly, and was relieved to find the same look of confusion spread across her face.

"Ok," she said with a sigh, putting the young man's strange revelation down to shock. "Thank you, very helpful. Get yourself home now and get some rest."

"Thank you, Sir," he said, forcing a smile. "Miss!" he stuttered quickly, realising his mistake.

Justine smiled and led him towards the canvas opening. "Give this man a lift home, won't you?" she shouted towards one of the officers outside.

She felt her phone buzz in her pocket and was surprised to find that it was the Commissioner. She stepped back inside the marquee and stared at the screen; he never called directly. They must have been desperate for news on this one.

"Sir," she answered. "I suppose you want an update on Taunton?"

"Justine, I need you to come back in immediately," came the Commissioner's voice, one that only a well-funded private education could achieve. Yet it seemed strained, terrified even.

"What's happened?"

"There's been a series of coordinated explosions. A few in London, some further out, one near Buckingham Palace, hundreds of fatalities – we suspect Brockland's lot."

The Commissioner sounded as distressed as Justine had ever heard a person sound before. Her mouth dried; she could not find the words to say.

"The Government has recommended the Queen call a state of emergency. We are likely to see martial law in place within hours. I've been shown draft proposals for an emergency government of unity or something to take control under some MI5 guy. The army is camped out at the Palaces of Westminster as we speak. It's fucking mayhem over here. The Met is being officially briefed in an hour – you can dial in on your way back. I need you here now."

She had no words.

"Yes, Sir, straight away," she said blankly, but the phone had already cut out.

What was going on? She was surely in the midst of some terrible dream, a nightmare.

Justine walked aimlessly as she sought to settle her growing anxiety. She shook herself roughly; this was no time for a crisis. She needed to be on top form now.

She looked towards Officer Davies, who had remained in the marquee, eying her with a grave look of concern.

"I need to go back to London immediately."

The officer nodded and made their way outside to ready her vehicle. With a final look around the marquee, her mind racing, Justine turned back towards the opening and out towards the chaos outside.

27

www.xxbeccastewart2014.blogz.com
19/06/2029

My first post

So, here goes. Feels a bit strange writing to a tablet screen, but Mrs Forrester said it would help so here I am, giving it a go. Rumours have been going around school for months now, and the rumours are true. My mum was diagnosed with Huntington's disease in April, and it's broken me. She's always been clumsy, it was always part of who she was, but we never thought it would be as bad as this. Dad won't talk about it, but I can see it in his eyes. I think he thinks that I have it too, but he doesn't want to test me. He wants to focus on mum, but what if I do have it?

- -

www.xxbeccastewart2014.blogz.com
07/07/2029

Mum's check-up yesterday

Five years… I can't believe it even now, a week later. The doctors told my Dad she had about a year until she would begin to lose brain function and five until she would need special care. I'll never forget the look in her eyes when she got home. She tried to smile, tried to tell me everything would be alright but I wake up at night thinking about the look in her eyes. I'll never forget it, that look of fear. At least the new school counsellor has been helpful. He asks a lot of questions about her though…

- -

www.xxbeccastewart2014.blogz.com
15/08/2029

What the hell happened today?!

I can't believe how many of you are reading my posts, the support has been fantastic! Now, I need your help. The strangest thing happened today. We were out walking, trying to help mum get some fresh air when two men wearing masks tried to take her. Did anyone else see? My Dad got hit pretty hard trying to help, but loads of people jumped in and the men eventually ran away. Mum's still scared and confused and we don't know what to do. Who were they? Why did they want her?

- -

www.xxbeccastewart2014.blogz.com
26/12/2029
Attachment: Christmas_2029(3).jpg

Happy Christmas!

I still can't believe you are all actually reading my posts - I hope they are helping all of you with your own problems. Anyway, Happy Christmas! It took a few takes, but we finally got a picture of Mum smiling. It's hard watching her struggle. She's trying to stay happy, or perhaps she's just trying to look happy for me. Dad still won't let me get tested. Maybe he's too scared, maybe Mum won't let him, I don't know. I know I don't want to be as sad as Mum though. Hopefully the Taunton Festival tickets Dad bought her can cheer her up! Who's going?

- -

www.xxbeccastewart2014.blogz.com
09/02/2030

Mum

Sorry I haven't posted in a while. Mum died two weeks ago and we still don't understand how it happened. We've been preparing for her to die from the disease for a while now, but never like this. Taunton was supposed to be a bit of fun, something to take her mind off it all. I've never felt so empty before. How could the police have let all those people die? My Dad is so sad and angry, I think he blames himself. He keeps saying it's some sort of government cover-up, but I don't know. He sounds really scared. He even said that some of the police were actually the ones firing out, did anyone see? And who is Peter Brockland? Dad says he isn't a terrorist and that he's trying to help. He keeps saying that the state of emergency and the new Commander in Chief are dangerous and that Mum's death is all their fault. I'm worried about him. Is he going mad?

- -

www.xxbeccastewart2014.blogz.com
28/02/2030

Worst birthday ever

I turned 16 today, happy birthday to me right? But it's not the same without Mum, it's not the same anyway. What's happening with the world? School has changed completely, no one wants to talk to me anymore. They all look at me like I'm dangerous, but I suppose I might be. The school counsellor keeps asking me if I am having any of the problems Mum had. Dad still won't let me get tested, he says it's too dangerous. They arrested a man with a biological weapon last week, and the Commander spoke about something to do with genetic problems. I don't really understand it, but Dad says it's bad, and that no one is talking about it in the new election, that the Commander is using it to take more powers. The Commander just looks so popular, especially since he took the Queen's role when she died. It looks like he's saved everyone.

- -

www.xxbeccastewart2002.blogz.com
07/05/2030

DON'T VOTE FOR THEM

I still can't believe so many people are reading my posts, but it is so important that you read this. Two men, the same ones that tried to take mum last year, tried to kidnap me on my way home from school. I still can't believe I got away. Somebody crashed into their car and I managed to run away, but I heard them. They talked about the Order taking over, and that the Commander in Chief was their leader. Peter Brockland was right! Don't vote for him, he's dangerous. Please!

- -

www.princessstewart016.blogz.com
30/05/2030

Do not trust them - fight back!

New domain name, but it's still me. They shut down my page after my last post and Dad said we had to run away, that we were in danger. So we're in hiding now. The new Social Control Force almost caught us yesterday, in those scary white outfits. Everything has changed so quickly since the Commander, well the President now, won. The army and the SCF are patrolling every street. The police are different too, and journalists and army generals have all been arrested. We can't let them win, we have to fight back.

- -

www.princessstewart111.words.co.uk
24/08/2030

Believe in Peter Brockland

They blocked my account again. I think they might be tracking us so watch out for my new domain names, I'm getting good at changing them now. Anyway, me and Dad met Peter Brockland last night and he was amazing. We were here when the SCF came to Didsbury, and so were the Resistance. That's why they came - they must have found him, and they destroyed everything. They didn't care who they killed as long as they got Peter. He managed to escape with a few of them, but a lot of people were killed or arrested. They caught one of the main guys too, I saw them take him away.

But Peter managed to save me and Dad from an SCF agent. He said he knew who I was, that he thought my posts were brilliant and that I needed to keep telling people what was really happening. He said it was really important that I tell you all not to go to the new Pregnancy Treatment Centres. They are testing unborn babies and killing them if they are 'incompatible' or something. It sounds horrible. Please don't go, whatever you do. Don't trust anyone anymore, even doctors. Don't take risks.

- -

www.orderevader1.bloghere.org
15/09/2030

Don't watch television tomorrow

I told you they caught one of the main guys from the Resistance in Didsbury a couple of weeks ago. Now they are going to hang him for treason tomorrow, on national television. Don't watch it. Don't let them scare you.
This message has been censored for the protection of national security. Anyone caught reading future accounts from the suspected traitor Rebecca Stewart will be prosecuted.

- -

www.remembertaunton.becca.bloggerthon.com
26/01/2031

Remembering Mum

It's been a year since the Taunton Massacre, a year since they killed Mum and I still feel as empty as I did then. I still can't believe how much things have changed, how we have all let it happen. A part of me feels happy that Mum isn't alive to see how bad it's become. The president is a monster. He tells us that they are 'facilitating the progress of humanity' and eradicating disease, but their brutality is beyond cruel. How have we become a country that no longer allows people to have children without permission? People are sterilised if they are found 'incompatible' with their programme, and still, nobody knows what that programme is!

Dad thinks my blogging is becoming too dangerous too. He's tired of running, but I couldn't not post today. I can't stop thinking about Mum, and how many others have been locked up, killed or sterilised by doctors or the SCF because they don't fit with the vision of this new regime. What's worse is that some people believe what they are doing is right, that picking who can and can't have children is protecting us all - how can they! Or are they just scared for themselves? Are they just trying to protect their families, like Dad and me? Why is no one helping us? We hear nothing about the rest of the world anymore, has the same happened to them? The Resistance has gone quiet too, the Order is too strong. People must continue to fight back, or what will we allow ourselves to become?

\- -

www.princessorderevader293.blogholder.com
28/01/2031

They've found us

I think I made a mistake with my last post - they've found us. I don't have long. I think this might be the last time I write to you all. They just shot Dad, I don't know what to do, I'm trapped. It's all my fault. If you're reading this stay strong and keep fighting, never give up. They're banging on the door now, it's not going to be

\- -

THIS ACCOUNT HAS BEEN PERMANENTLY DISABLED.

28

"They're here!"

His shout reverberated through the silence, growing more panicked with every echo. He turned quickly as red dots tore frantically through his front room, searching for any sign of life inside.

Raj had known it would only be a matter of time before they found out about her. He had been one of many in the months that followed the introduction of the 'Level One Restraint Order', stripped overnight of his right to have children.

Raj and his wife had been struggling for years to start a family and the new, free local birthing support centre appeared to have been the miracle they had needed. Only after they had visited the facility did they begin to hear the rumours – parents restricted from childbearing rights, forced arrests, unborn foetuses terminated.

Raj and his wife had tried, naively, to brush aside the rumours as just part of the crackpot conspiracy theories of Peter Brockland and the Resistance. Their doctor had been friendly and promised to run tests on Raj's sample. He had gone out of his way to help them to conceive.

That was until they received their letter from the Department for Social Control, which had in no uncertain terms, banned Raj from future procreation upon threat of a lengthy prison sentence. More sinister still, the letter had also politely suggested that Raj volunteer for sterilisation 'for the benefit of humankind'.

Raj jumped back from the front room, ducking one of the probing red laser sights, and sprinted back into the hallway. He ducked more spots of red infiltrating through his front door as he frantically sought to collect his family.

"Jasmine!" he shouted. "Danielle!"

He halted abruptly, narrowly avoiding a laser sight coming through a side window, drawing a line directly ahead.

"Jasmine! Danielle! They're here, come on!"

Silent tears formed in the corners of his eyes as his impending doom quickly began to register. But his life did not matter now; he had known the risks and had taken them all the same. He had to keep them safe now. Jasmine and Danielle had to survive.

Raj noticed a flicker of movement at the top of the stairs and turned to see Jasmine holding their daughter at her chest, both faces possessed by terror.

"No!" he shouted as they approached, holding up a hand and pointing towards the target light.

Jasmine nodded silently and lowered Danielle to the floor. She dropped to a seated position and indicated to Danielle to do the same. Danielle obeyed without hesitation, and they both lowered themselves down, step by step, beneath the window and towards Raj's outstretched arms. With an outburst of emotion, he clutched them into a tight embrace.

"We always knew this day would come," said Raj, staring into Jasmine's steadily glistening eyes. He ran a gentle hand through her soft, shoulder-length hair. Now that the time had come to say goodbye, he felt he had never truly appreciated just how beautiful she was.

"You need to hide," he said softly, pressing his forehead to hers. "You and Danielle, now."

She nodded resolutely, wiping away the tears. They had spent months preparing for it, reworking their cellar into a hidden basement concealed beneath a small hatch in the kitchen floor. They should be safe there, for now.

Danielle resisted her mother's effort to move and began to cry; at just two years old, she was oblivious to the peril of their situation.

"Dani," said Raj softly, clutching the young girl's shoulders as he stared into his daughter's blotched face for what was almost certainly the last time. "You need to hide for Daddy, just like we practised, ok? I'll-"

Raj's voice faltered. "I'll see you soon, ok?"

Raj noticed shadows moving outside the front door through the frosted glass, quickly followed by loud bangs as the agents pounded Raj's front door.

"Rajesh Gadhavi," came one of the agent's voices. "You are accused of incompatibility with Law 1 of the Social Control Regulations and with the direct violation of an official Level One Restraint Order. Cooperate now and you will not be harmed. Fail to cooperate, and you will bring destruction upon yourself and all those in your company."

The infamous words of the new Social Control Force agents rang out through the front door, as he had heard many times before, amplified by some electronic device. Raj knew that their cooperation would not be rewarded and that their lives, whatever they did now, were forfeit.

"Please Dani," he begged, clutching his daughter's hands. "Like we practised?"

He forced a smile, hoping it might ease her agitation, though he was sure that even at her age, she could sense the fear in her father's eyes. She threw herself at him, hugging him tightly. Raj could feel her trembling, tears falling gently on his shoulders, almost as though she too recognised it would be the last time she would see her father.

With an almighty wrench, Raj pulled her from him and lifted her towards her mother.

"Be safe," he whispered to Jasmine, and with one final embrace, they shifted away.

"Rajesh Gadhavi," came the agent's voice again from outside. "You are accused of incompatibility with Law 1 of the Social Control Regulations and with a direct violation of an official Level One Restraint Order. Cooperate now and you will not be harmed. Fail to cooperate…"

"I'm here!" Raj shouted back, interrupting the second reading. "I'm coming out!"

"You will cooperate," came the amplified voice from opposite the door but he noticed the shadowed figures move away.

Raj began to unlock the multitude of locks and looked back towards the kitchen. He caught a brief final glimpse of Jasmine's hand vanishing through the opening in the floor and turned back towards the door, with a deep, controlling breath.

He had no real idea what was going to happen to him now. He had heard that Law 1 breach speech many times before at the misfortune of others, in television propaganda and the numerous accounts of others. The problem was that none of those stories had come directly from those who had experienced it – perhaps this really was only set to end in his death.

Raj stood behind the door, releasing the final lock. At least Jasmine and Danielle would be safe, he thought.

He heard a creak in the floor behind him as he began to turn the doorknob. Before he had been offered any opportunity to react, a gloved hand grabbed his face from behind.

Raj struggled against the stranger's tight grasp as the hand pulled him backwards, gripping him tightly as they struggled, but soon realised his resistance was pointless. The agents must have broken in through the back door - had they seen the two of them escape?

"Do it," said Raj, resigning himself. "Make it quick."

Raj screwed up his eyes and held his breath, expecting life to be drawn from him. Nothing happened. He felt no merciless blade against his throat, felt no snap of his neck, but rather a cold object sliding its way into his side pocket.

"You're going to need this," came a rough voice behind him.

He felt the stranger's grip loosen, and the man moved forward to glance out of the side window, his pistol poised.

The stranger was dressed in black, with what appeared to be an entire arsenal tied to his back, over a thick, bulletproof vest. The stranger was wearing that blank, white mask Raj had seen many times before – it was the Resistance.

Raj gasped, struggling for breath. He reached into his pocket to feel for whatever the stranger had given him. He felt cold metal and pulled out a gun.

"What's this?" he asked, still in disbelief.

He heard more scuffles around him and turned to find three, four, five other masked figures filtering into his front room.

"I presume you know what a gun is," the rough voice said sarcastically as he turned back from the door to nod towards the others. They reacted immediately, scuffling around again into kneeled positions in the front room - battle stations.

"It looks like there's four," the man said, peering again through the glass.

The stranger turned to Raj, his piercing green eyes shining through the gaps in the mask. "It's time for you to fight back."

Raj nodded, clutching the gun.

The stranger turned back to the door to look through the peephole and let out a short chuckle. Without hesitation, he raised his gun and fired.

The gunshot tore through the front door, and Raj saw the figure of an agent opposite crumple to the ground.

Immediately, gunshots sounded from outside, shattering the front windows of Raj's front room. Resistance figures took aim from their crouched positions, shooting back as the gunfire from outside destroyed item after item in Raj's front room.

The masked stranger had thrown himself aside as soon as he had taken the point-blank shot, and only just in time, as bullets tore through the front door.

"Are you ready?" the man shouted at Raj, his arms covering his head.

Raj had dropped the gun beside him, throwing up his own hands too, screwing his face as the gunshots continued to fire out. With his eyes closed, his senses heightened, he thought he had heard the man's voice before.

"Raj, are you ready?" the man shouted again.

Raj opened his eyes and scrambled around him. He clutched the gun again and gripped it in both hands. With a look towards the masked man, he nodded.

"For the Resistance and for your family!" the stranger shouted. He threw himself out from the protection of the stairway barrier and out into the gunfight outside.

Through his now wide-open front door, Raj could see two agents crumpled at his doorstep, their usually impenetrable white suits stained with blood. Raj looked across his front lawn and saw another agent firing aimlessly towards the ducking stranger as they stumbled backwards against the gunshots of the Resistance figures.

Bullets bounced uselessly from the agent's suit, which seemed to possess an almost impossible impenetrability, allowing the agent to crawl, clearly injured, behind a car parked on the street outside. Another agent pulled them frantically to safety, through intermittent shots back towards the house.

With an act of courage he would never have expected of himself, Raj ran out towards the car outside, firing shot after shot. He felt possessed, as though the Resistance had finally given him his opportunity to fight back against those who had sought to restrict his dreams of a family with Jasmine.

Raj's rush of impassioned adrenaline had clouded his judgement, and he quickly realised he had run out of bullets. As the clicks of his now barren gun rang out, he saw one of the agents peer up from behind the car, grinning.

Raj stood uselessly in the middle of his front lawn and noticed a small object fly out from behind the car opposite. As though playing out in slow motion as bullets passed him, he watched the object loop from above and drop just a few metres from his feet.

He looked down and gulped, quickly realising the object sitting ominously ahead of him was a grenade. Rooted to the spot, he closed his eyes and pictured Jasmine and Danielle. His blissful reminiscence was short-lived as he felt an immense force collide with his side. The masked Resistance figure had flown into him, and the two of them rolled violently away from the oncoming blast.

The grenade exploded, throwing the contents of Raj's front garden everywhere. A huge blast of air and dirt had left a small crater where his immaculate front lawn had once been. They had managed to escape the effects of the blast but the force of their acrobatics had unmasked the stranger's face.

Raj looked up, panting, his ears ringing from the blast, to see him. It was really him – Peter Brockland.

"We need to go," said Peter, clasping either side of Raj's head in a frantic attempt to shake the shock out of him. "You and your family, you need to come with us. We need to get you out of here."

Peter looked around frantically for the remaining agents. Still shaken from the Resistance's gunshots, one lay slouched by the front wheel of a parked SUV. The other appeared to be firing random shots from behind, repelling the Resistance forces as he held a finger to his ear, calling for backup.

Peter knew that they had only minutes before further agents arrived. They had certainly not planned for a lengthy encounter.

"Raj, you need to get your family. We need to go. Quickly!"

The other Resistance fighters spilt out of the house, shouting out with their guns aimed at the SUV. They approached quickly, dodging stray defensive gunshots, and surrounded the car.

Peter watched as the agent who had called for reinforcements tried to resist, but was shot dead by Culter. The other seemed to have lost all leg function and tried desperately to pull his body away.

"Indici!" Peter yelled towards the car, and a masked Indici looked back. "Start the car! You and Culter take the agent back to Q16; we'll take the family."

Indici nodded back. He and Culter pulled the remaining agent to his feet and dragged him towards their stolen Audi.

"Come on, Raj," Peter muttered, standing anxiously in the open, awaiting Raj's return.

Peter turned to the others and saw Indici bundling the injured agent into the back of the car. He turned back to look at the house - Raj had not reappeared.

"Just go!" Peter shouted back towards Indici, who had stood anxiously at the car, waiting for direction. "We'll follow in one of these."

Peter pointed vaguely towards the selection of the parked cars not yet destroyed by gunfire. Indici looked back with a strained expression, hesitant to leave Peter and the others behind.

A rushing noise came from overhead, slowly growing louder. Peter turned ominously and looked up, to see a helicopter approaching in the distance. Peter looked back at Indici, panicked. "Just go!"

Indici nodded, his eyes widened at the helicopter's appearance. He rushed into the car before accelerating away.

Peter turned back towards the house again. Raj and his terrified family had finally appeared, running out from the front door alongside Acri and Sagitta.

Waving them frantically towards one of the cars outside, Peter noticed some of Raj's neighbours peeking through the curtains of their windows. As the sounds of gunfire ceased, many had clearly thought it safe enough to glance at the commotion outside.

Peter ignored their glances. Instead, he fumbled at the door handle of a parked Volkswagen, but could not help but wonder which of them, if any, had been the one to report Raj's family. If the past year had taught Peter anything, it was that his loathing of the Order's eugenics programme was not as widely shared as he might have hoped.

The seductive appeal of a world without disease; rid of needless child suffering; free procreative support; and various other 'freebie' offers, seemed enough for swathes of the population to turn a blind eye to the darkness that came with the regime change.

The mere fact that in more than a year of fighting, the Resistance had achieved little in preventing the Order's increasing control, seemed evidence enough that there was not a shared societal appetite to prevent the notion of a 'better' humankind, even if it came at the cost of humanity itself. The fight, even if the Resistance did win, would not be over with the overthrow of the president.

The speck in the sky that had once been the distant helicopter was so close now that he could see the white outlines of Order agents hanging out of the openings on either side, clutching rifles.

Peter squinted; he thought he had seen something break away from the helicopter. With an impending sense of dread, he looked on helplessly as the object approached them.

"Missile!" Peter screamed as he threw himself behind the car.

The others followed suit, throwing themselves to the ground as the missile passed them.

A deafening explosion sounded out from behind them. Peter turned, petrified. Just a few hundred metres away, Peter saw a swirling inferno slowly disintegrating the stolen Audi. Indici and Culter were gone.

Ignoring the sinking pang of loss, Peter turned to see that the helicopter had reached shooting distance. The agents had wasted no time in firing, as bullets clanged against the shell of the small Volkswagen. How had this gone so wrong?

Peter sprinted out towards the others and crouched behind the protection of a bullet-ridden family car nearby.

"Raj!" he shouted, flinching as further bullets collided with the car. "Keys! Which one's yours?"

Raj looked up at him through bloodshot eyes. He shook violently and fumbled for the car keys in his pocket; he appeared to have lost all function.

Peter pulled him closer as the shots continued to fire in. Acri and Sagitta were forced to grab Jasmine and Danielle and take cover behind another nearby car.

"Raj, come on!" Peter shouted, shaking him.

Peter heard whistling from above and turned wide-eyed to see another missile flying towards them.

For the third time in his life, Peter felt a thrust of hot air, as he was thrown backwards.

Time, as he now seemed to have become accustomed to, slowed down as he travelled through the air. He landed hard on Raj's neighbour's lawn, unable to move.

He had not been killed, he knew that much, but his vision was blurred, whether by the smoke surrounding him or by the direct impact, he did not know. He was unable to move. Peter winced as he tried to draw breath and realised that the fall must have broken one, or more, of his ribs.

As he tried to recalibrate against the ringing in his ears, Peter found strength enough to turn his head towards the blurred outline of the helicopter, landing through swirls of smoke. Several more blurs of white appeared as the agents began to exit, shooting towards the car where the others had been huddled, defenceless.

Peter tried to pull his body into action, but even as he had thought of it, he felt his strength vanish. Peter could only look on from the ground helplessly as Acri fell sharply, clutching his chest, his body slowly drowning in a pool of his own blood.

Peter heard the faint sound of the young girl's screams force its way through the ringing in his ears. As the pool of Acri's blood oozed towards her, he watched as the girl ran out from behind the car, desperately back towards what she must have thought was the safety of their house.

Peter's desperation to protect the young girl seemed to lend him the strength needed to force himself to his feet. He stumbled a moment as the smoke swirled around him. Without thought of the situation or the pain that plagued every sinew of his body, he tried to sprint towards the girl.

Almost instantly, he felt a sharp pain in his right calf, forcing him back to the floor. Peter's vision began to blur again as the gunshot burned through his leg, but he continued to drag himself forward. He had managed to crawl just a few yards before he fell to his front, exhausted.

Another shot fired out, and he felt something heavy drop beside him. With another terrible sense of foreboding, he turned to his side. The face of Raj's wife stared back at him out of her now lifeless, blue eyes.

Rage seemed to ignite a further rush of energy, and Peter threw himself up, roaring madly. Ignoring the pain in his leg, he fired towards the agents, but his bullets made no impact.

He turned towards the helicopter and saw Sagitta knelt beside two Order agents, both their guns held to the side of his head. Peter turned, breathing heavily. He had no idea what he could do. The agents had moved towards Raj, who was clutching his daughter, trying desperately to retreat towards the house.

Peter raised his gun weakly towards them. From behind him, an agent threw the butt of his rifle into his back, forcing him to the ground. Peter winced and felt the agent kick the gun from his grasp.

Another agent, her long, brown hair tied to one side, exited the helicopter and made her way slowly towards the agents surrounding Raj. She nudged two of them aside and raised her pistol. Without hesitation, she fired.

The young girl's grief-stricken screams tore through every cell in Peter's body. He watched helplessly as the girl stood defenceless, teetering from side to side, with no understanding of what was going on, or why. She pulled at her father's arm, but his bloodstained, lifeless body lay unresponsive.

She ran from side to side again, calling out for her mother, her tear-stricken face searching the scene for any sign of comfort. The Order agents continued to close in, their rifles aimed towards her.

Time appeared to slow down again as Peter battled with his failing senses, and he saw the girl edging away from the agents. He had to get to her; he had to save her. He had to.

With an immense effort, Peter threw back his elbow, connecting with the agent's crotch behind him. The agent winced, and Peter grabbed the knife from the agent's leg-side pocket. He turned sharply and thrust the knife up into the agent's jaw. Blood gushed down his arm.

The agent fell to the ground instantly, but Peter did not wait; he had already turned back towards the girl. He had to save her.

He limped towards her, dragging his injured leg behind him, but managed only a few short metres before he was forced to the ground again. This time the agent held him down, pushing his face into the grass – he would not be getting up this time.

Peter looked up, straining against the agent's submission helplessly, and saw the long-haired agent look back at him curiously. The woman smiled, and her eerily sharp blue eyes analysed him closely.

She raised her gun slowly, her eyes fixed upon his, and, without the effort even to look at her target, fired.

The screaming stopped instantly; everything seemed to stop instantly. All that was left behind was a still, brutal silence. Peter screamed in anger, his eyes bulging with the strain of resisting the agent's grip. His head was surely going to explode.

"Burn the family with the house and hang the other one," he heard the woman shout towards the agents, and she turned to walk towards Peter.

He heard a struggle as three agents pulled Sagitta to his feet and dragged him towards the nearest lamppost.

Peter had lost all fight. He could only watch on blankly as his friend attempted to resist the Order agent's restraints. The agents threw a thick cord around Sagitta's neck as he struggled, and tightened a knot.

Peter locked eyes with him as the agents tossed the other side of the cord over the nearest lamppost. He tried desperately to communicate some form of silent apology with his eyes as his mouth fought against the dirt beneath him.

Sagitta had stopped struggling and looked back at him calmly. His encounter with death seemed inevitable now, and rather than face his end with a fruitless struggle, he had decided to accept it with honour. He nodded briefly towards Peter and took a deep breath.

Peter struggled uselessly, screaming into the dirt. He watched agonisingly as Sagitta was lifted slowly, tug by tug, by the agents surrounding him, the noose tightening with every pull.

Sagitta's reddening face and bulging eyes were soon hidden from sight as the unusually long, sneering face of the long-haired agent blocked Peter's view, gazing down at him intently.

"Hello, Peter Brockland," she said calmly. With a cruel smile, she nodded behind him.

Peter struggled again, with an anger he had never felt before, as his friend's swaying corpse emerged from behind her before he felt a sharp blow to the back of his head and everything went blank.

29

The depths of Peter's subconscious riled with a sudden and terrible burst of activity. Raj's dying eyes fixed intently upon his daughter, cornered and helpless; the young girl's look of terrified confusion replaced by a blank, sudden silence as she fell to the ground; Sagitta swinging lifelessly from the streetlamp; the young mother's ocean-blue eyes drained of light, staring directly back into his own.

Peter shuddered violently. Had it been real? Please, he begged himself, let it have been a nightmare.

His mind whirred back into action, and slowly, his senses seemed to accelerate back into life. Consciousness offered no mercy; the images were clearer in his mind now – the horrors of what had just happened, or had it?

Peter screwed his eyes shut as a pounding, intense pain threatened to take control of him. He suddenly remembered being struck in the back of the head, hard. Instinctively, Peter moved an arm to caress the spot but found that he was unable to.

Where am I, he thought to himself. What happened?

The strain of forcing his eyes shut seemed to go some way in soothing his headache, but not without cost. Playing out across his eyelids, as though it were happening again, were the vivid pictures he had been so helpless in preventing. As the young girl turned once more to look desperately towards him, as he lay uselessly in the depths of the front lawn, he could face it no longer. Peter wrenched his eyes open.

Immediately, he was faced with a blinding light, intensifying his headache again. Peter tried to caress his pounding temples and looked down groggily to find that his arms had been shackled.

Peter looked around, blinking tears from his eyes.

He had been in a room like this before. It was perfectly square, with a soft white floor and pristine white walls disturbed only by a large, rectangular mirror and translucent, glass door. The only difference between this room and his previous stay was an ominous-looking toilet in the corner, and a large television mounted to the wall.

He had not needed evidence of the room's familiarity, or the shackles binding him, to know that he had once again been taken by the Order.

How could he have been so stupid? They had worked so hard and achieved so much in the past year. Surely, his role in the fight did not end like this. Peter's eyes began to readjust, and his spurt of activity seemed to have triggered the television into life. An acidic heat rose up in his chest, and he vomited violently.

Swinging lifelessly from Tower Bridge were seven masked Resistance figures. Their bodies were covered from head to toe in a loose black gown, and their faces concealed by the familiar Resistance mask. The corpses hung by a thick cord, and in the light, riverside breeze bumped lifelessly against the cold stone. Each had been branded with a large white stencilled print across their chests - 'Traitor'.

More sinister still, they had been positioned neatly on the left side of the bridge. The Order was clearly sending a message – the bridge had plenty more room.

Peter could not quite process what he was seeing. The sight was just so horrific that it could surely not be real. It had to be some illusion, some manifestation of his exhausted mind. The people, the authorities, would surely not have let this happen.

Peter yelled out in anger, and silent tears formed. His head seemed not to hurt anymore; nothing seemed to hurt anymore. He was absent of physical feeling but instead consumed wholly by an overwhelming rage.

He roared again, his face straining at the effort of wrenching himself from his restraints. Even for the Order, whose evolution of brutality over the past year had been endless, this blatant display surpassed even greater lengths of cruelty.

Seemingly noticing their prisoner's agitation, blurred figures appeared at the door. One seemed to move a hand towards the wall, and with a low hiss, the door slid open slowly to reveal a long, sharp face.

Peter could not stop himself; he turned to face her, his face aglow with rage. With an incoherent roar, he hurled towards her the wildest of profanities that came to his grief-stricken mind.

The agent simply smiled back. She waved an arm aimlessly behind her and maintained her emotionless gaze upon Peter.

A younger man entered, dressed in a white lab coat, with the unmistakable symbol of the Order on his breast pocket. He approached Peter cautiously, clutching a wet mop.

Peter had not yet lost heart and continued to shake himself violently in his chair, screaming out maniacally. He felt like he could kill any of them, all of them, if only he could free himself of his restraints.

The young man stopped a few metres from Peter, meeting his maddened expression with trepidation. He turned back to look at the other agent.

"What are you waiting for?" she snapped coldly.

The young man turned back towards Peter and began to tentatively mop up the vomit on the floor. Peter kicked out violently and caught the man with a sharp kick to the shin. He yelped in pain.

The other agent moved swiftly towards them and pulled the man back towards the door, throwing the sodden mop after him.

"Idiot boy. Get out," she said.

The man left the room sheepishly, and the door slid shut slowly behind him. Peter, who had shouted himself hoarse, was left alone with her.

The agent circled him slowly, keeping herself just out of the range of his wild kicks.

"Come now, come now," she said jovially, whispering into his ear and gently stroking Peter's face from behind him.

Peter thought he was going to explode; how dare she touch him.

"You must calm down," she hissed as she continued to circle Peter. She stopped in front of him and looked down with that same emotionless smile. "What has got you so worked up then?"

Peter glanced up at the television through bloodshot eyes as his friends continued to swing in the breeze. She turned to follow his gaze before offering him an even wider grin.

"Oh," she said, feigning an embarrassed chuckle. "I do apologise. I must have forgotten I'd left this on! It makes for a riveting watch, don't you think?"

She thrust her arms up into the air sarcastically, before moving towards the monitor. "No, I suppose you wouldn't agree, would you, being one of those traitors yourself. That must have been a distressing watch for you."

She placed a finger on the side of the screen and, with one final pause to relish in Peter's misery, pressed a button to turn it on standby.

"I'm ever so sorry about that," she lied.

Peter stared back at her, his face contorted. The agent had drawn her hair back into a tight ponytail, the strength with which it had been pulled back making it difficult for Peter to guess her age. She was at least in her late forties, and though the suit helped to exaggerate her physique, she was evidently strong.

"Now," she said, moving in front of Peter again. "You've been quite busy since you were last in a room like this, haven't you?"

Peter did not respond, though he was sure her opening line of questioning had been rhetorical. She paused for a moment, her eyes boring into Peter's.

"You've had a bit of fun," she continued. "Caused a bit of a stir. But ultimately, a mistake on your part."

She paused again as though waiting for a response, but again, Peter remained silent.

"I suppose," she continued. "In a strange way, we should be thanking you, Peter. There are some in the Order, myself included, who have pushed for years for us to take a more public approach to our work. Many resisted. There is a great deal of moral sentiment amongst our members you know – they devote themselves to a certain 'code'. The president is one of them – I believe you have met?"

Peter offered no response, instead repressing the memory of their last meeting. The agent simply smiled back and accepted his silence as a yes.

"So," she continued gleefully. "On behalf of those of us with a more hard-line approach to our work, I must thank you. We had not planned for it, but your movement seems to have worked out wonderfully for us!"

Peter pulled again at his restraints, though with considerably less effort. He could not believe that he had allowed himself to be captured again, that he had allowed Indici, Sagitta and the others to be killed.

The ecstasy in the agent's voice went no way in helping to deter the clutch of acidity in his chest. The agent gently patted Peter's arm and began to circle him again.

"But Peter, Peter..." she said, pointing suggestively towards the now blank television. "This resistance to our new society is going to have to stop. You are beginning to take up far too much of our time. We are trying to save the human race, trying to better it. We don't have the time to keep dealing with those unwilling to accept the new regime."

She stopped in front of Peter, maintaining that same smug smile, still goading for a reaction. "What did you really believe that you and your band of dysfunctionals were going to achieve?"

She looked more intently at him. Peter noticed the subtle tactical switch in her voice; she wanted answers now.

In his previous life, Peter had read numerous fascinating accounts of interrogation techniques from his colleagues. His mind wandered to one of them, who had been national news when kidnapped whilst reporting on the dire conditions of a Ugandan refugee camp.

Fortunately for him, the supporting British forces had been ruthlessly efficient in retrieving him before the assailants had been able to murder him. Nonetheless, he endured three long, intense days of interrogation and torture.

The key to his survival, he had always enjoyed telling people as they clung on to his every word, was control. Any restriction upon it, whilst a sure instigation of further aggression, was something he felt had kept him alive, kept him fighting. It was at this moment that Peter decided to heed that advice.

Peter stared back defiantly, silent, attempting to relinquish some of the agent's control. It did not appear to work. Instead, she smiled more widely and continued to stare back; she seemed perfectly content to wait.

"Why am I here?" Peter asked after a considerable period of silence had passed.

"What?" she replied incredulously. "Why are you here? You thought we would simply allow you to escape? You thought we would allow you to continue wandering the streets rabble-rousing?"

She laughed again. "Goodness, how hard did they hit you?"

"No," said Peter through gritted teeth. "Why am I still here? Why am I still alive?"

"Oh, I didn't have you down as a quitter, Peter!" she said, jubilated by his display of weakness.

"I'm… interested," Peter replied.

"Peter, much like the rest of your little club, you continue, even now, to misunderstand our purpose. We don't senselessly murder people; even the hard-line of us follow the 'divine purpose' if you will, we aren't monsters you know."

Peter looked at her wide-eyed. Not too long ago, he had seen this woman murder an innocent two-year-old girl in cold blood. The agent bore into his eyes, avidly trying to read his mind.

"You know this," she continued, with the air of an exasperated schoolteacher. "We only dispose of, or 'neutralise' as the president likes to say, those deemed by our system to be incompatible with the future progression of the human race. You know this."

"But I..." said Peter, stuttering slightly, confused by her reaction. "I'm incompatible."

"Ah," the agent mumbled, another grin forming across her face. "Well, actually no, you're not. Contrary to your father's belief, you were never 'blacklisted', so to speak. You were never actually an official Order target."

Peter's stomach sank. His father had been a central part of the Order when he discovered Peter's incompatibility; how could he possibly have made such a monumental, life-altering error?

"My father spent his life, gave his life, to protect me from your system. He told me that he was given my name by one of the mainframe technicians. He told me..."

Peter felt the weakness in his voice as he stuttered, desperately convincing himself that this version of the story, his father's version, was the only one. "You're lying."

"Your father certainly did believe that you were in danger," she replied. "It was a necessary measure at the time, I'm afraid. Your father, as I'm sure he will have told you, was quite the high flyer within the Order at the time."

Peter looked at her distant expression, confused. It was odd as though she was recollecting Peter's father with reverence.

"He was a fantastic agent. Ruthlessly dedicated and devastatingly efficient. It was only a matter of time before he took the next stage to lead the Order."

Peter gazed fixedly back at the agent as she recounted her story. She leant back on the wall and pulled out a cigarette.

"But I always had an odd feeling about him. He had to be tested," she said, clicking a flame from the lighter.

She closed her eyes, relishing the drag, and sighed heavily, releasing a heavy cloud of smoke.

"Most of those in the Order, particularly field agents, shy away from family life. It is something of an unwritten rule that we should not have children. You can imagine some of the difficulties we might face. Whilst most are fanatical in their belief that we are the guardians of a stronger, safer humankind, you can never be quite certain of the genetic quality of your offspring. Best to avoid any..."

Her voice trailed off, and her face seemed to darken. For the first time, she seemed to exhibit some hint of, was it regret?

Peter watched the agent's first slip of human emotion with astonishment. His experience of her had been one of mindless brutality, murdering a young family as though it were nothing. Yet here she appeared to pine for a family she could never have.

"We both know how this process works – those who do risk it have their children checked and those who fail, well..."

She trailed off again, and Peter noticed her left hand move across her stomach. Peter's mind, though still caged by intense throbs of pain, raced.

The agent took another drag of her cigarette, allowing Peter's mind to wander. He pictured the various protocols the Order might have put into place to deal with newborn incompatibles. He felt sick. The idea that even newborn children could not escape the regime's brutality, even those whose parents were part of it, was horrifying.

"I'm sure there are some who keep families secret. They must live with the fear of them being discovered, or with the psychological torment of questioning the purpose of their work, with the existence of their own child. As I say, we tend not to risk it. Your father, however… we were aware of his relationship with a young woman, your mother, but you – he kept your existence very much hidden. Not the behaviour befitting of a future leader."

She took another deep drag and flicked the remainder of her cigarette towards the corner of the room. Peter followed the line of the cigarette butt and noticed another blurred figure standing stationary at the door.

"I found out of course," the agent continued. "Eventually. Clearly, your father could not be trusted. You required investigation at once, as did he. It was very difficult, very difficult. Your father was a spectacular agent and a huge favourite of the president. I needed to be sure. Your mother was not so adept at keeping you hidden; perhaps she didn't even know you were in danger. I was able to find out where your father had hidden you both. I tailed her for weeks, keeping myself out of your father's sight. I found my moment. I broke into your neighbour's house and started a little fire."

She grinned again, not to Peter but to herself, as though relishing the memory.

"Your mother, hearing the screams, made the quite foolish decision to try and help them. I slipped in unnoticed and took a strand of your hair whilst you slept. I was finally able to run you through the system… and whilst I had hoped so much that you would not be, you were compatible."

Peter contemplated her story, staring at her. He had championed himself, even built his new life upon being a 'leader of the incompatibles' fighting back against the Order. But now, was he ever truly one of them? Was he really one of them now?

He found his discomfort enhanced by an ashamedly deeper, albeit brief, sense of relief. He was not, as he had believed himself to be within the scientific paradigm of the Order, damage upon humanity.

"I was somewhat disappointed, as you can imagine," the agent continued. "It was not the result I had hoped for. The thought that your father could continue to rise within the Order with a child, after hiding its very existence, was something that I could not allow. I was torn between the principles I had lived by for so long and the protection of the future of the Order itself. That is to say, the future Order your father may soon be leading."

Peter looked back at the agent blankly. He could not bring himself to even consider the notion that his father might have continued within the Order, let alone lead it. But could he have done?

Peter knew that it had only been the knowledge of his son's incompatibility that helped his father to snap out of his fanaticism. Had his father discovered the opposite, that Peter was indeed 'compatible', that he had got away with his deception, would he have felt justified in his beliefs? Might he have gone on to lead one of the most dangerous organisations to have ever existed?

"And so I fashioned myself a means of testing him," the agent said with another smirk, noticing Peter's discomfort.

"Your name flagged as incompatible seemed the perfect way to test your father's loyalty. With the unwitting assistance of one of our lab agents, I was able to find a way for your name to be processed as incompatible. That lab agent then took your name directly to your father, pleading for help in exchange for covering up that name."

Peter froze, thinking once more through his father's story.

"But," he stammered. "That would mean..."

"Yes," the agent replied gleefully. "Yes, that would mean that you know the lab agent I speak of. Though I believe you know him by the codename 'Indici'. What a delightful surprise for you. Though… you needn't be too concerned by his betrayal, not least because he was smouldered by our little attack yesterday. I've been waiting to deal with that traitor for a very long time."

Indici, unwittingly, in fear of his own life, in his desperation to escape the Order, had been manipulated. He had been, in part, the reason that his father had turned away from the Order, the reason this whole sorry saga had begun. He had been the reason that Peter's childhood had been so bleak. It had all started with a lie.

"Yes, well your father was incapable of handling the knowledge that his only son was incompatible. He pounced on the lab agent's offer to help and buried the information – his true colours finally revealed. I now found myself in something of a tricky situation. How could I expose your father's betrayal, whilst keeping my own honourable fraudulence a secret? I knew that your father would be planning his escape too – I had to act quickly.

I was not quick enough though - your father acted as I had not expected, causing quite the scene in his final hurrah. I had expected some dramatic attempt to feign his own death in duty, but no. He dealt with his commanding mission agent and escaped. I believe he came home to tend to you and your mother, to hide you, and then he disappeared."

Peter listened intently as the agent took out another cigarette.

"Given you had never been an official target - indeed nobody knew of your existence but the lab agent and I – the Order questioned your mother of his whereabouts disguised as police officers. But it seems he had played his part well and convinced her of his madness. I, of course, could not mention you. The punishment for tampering with our system is death, but it had been necessary to show them all that your father was not worthy. The focus was entirely on the worldwide search and capture of your father, whose fame as an effective agent was soon dwarfed by his ability to evade capture."

The agent scowled.

"I was in charge of his capture, and I'm afraid my reputation took quite the hit thanks to him. I was soon removed, and replaced by agent after agent. All failed to capture him. It's not until my recent discovery of his hand in trying to disrupt our Liberia mission that..."

"Liberia?" Peter interrupted, another sickening feeling rising in his stomach. "You can't mean the Ebola outbreak?"

"Yes," the agent replied matter-of-factly, taking a drag.

"He had somehow uncovered my plan to release the virus into a small village, most of whom shared a damaging genetic mutation. The operation was naturally high-risk given the contagious nature of the virus involved, but I am perhaps more cavalier than my colleagues – I considered the unintended casualty rate to be of minimal concern. However, someone in my team apparently did not share that view. There was a mole feeding information to your father. He sought to thwart us but was unsuccessful. He allowed himself to be seen. He tried very hard to save the mole's life, but they were dealt with."

Peter shivered, imagining the mole's fate. Death was the fate of traitors.

"The knowledge that your father had managed to infiltrate the Order from the other side of the world gave me enough ammunition, I felt, to convince the president that it was time to use you as bait."

"I sought you out and after some searching, found you working for a newspaper. I paid two homeless men to pretend to fight on your way home one night in the hope you might try to break them up. You might remember?"

Peter considered her. Now he came to think of it, Peter did vaguely remember breaking up two men fighting a couple of years ago.

He remembered instantly regretting his moment of compassion, having waded in to help only to find that the two of them reconciled to fight their now joint enemy.

"They were able to acquire some of your hair for me, which was enough. I paid them in kind, though the drugs I gave them packed something more of a deathly punch than they were expecting. I convinced another of my lab agents to forge your results again, and I was finally able to expose your father's cover-up.

The DNA matched that of the infamous Simon Brockland. The president finally knew the truth. Naturally, he was furious. I convinced him that we could use you to lure your father back. I processed your result, in the hope that your father would be made aware you had been found, in whatever way he had been kept informed of our previous operations. His weakness for you ended years of hunting. He came back for you. But I shouldn't take all the credit of course. You did wonderfully."

Peter sat blankly, still trying to mull over the depths to which this agent had gone – releasing a deadly virus amongst hundreds of innocent villagers, recklessly murdering two homeless men. All just to lure Peter's father into a trap. Why?

"Do you truly understand our power now?" the agent asked, sneering at him. "We have infiltrated the highest echelons of world society and had hands in controlling them for years, with just a force of hundreds at our disposal. You think now, as more and more inevitably join our cause, that there is anything your petulant 'rebel force' can do to stop us?"

"We exposed you..." Peter interjected quietly, with a calm passion in his voice. "We exposed you, we fought you, and we forced you out of hiding – that's what our force has done. You are blind to what rises against you – we are many and ever-growing. Your days are numbered; the world will not accept the society you want to create. The people will fight back."

"The people will do nothing," the agent spat back, taken aback by his sudden outburst of passion. "You will do nothing. Don't you understand? The greatest weakness of humankind is the intrinsic selfishness to save themselves and protect their own – they will accept anything if it means their families are safe. Look at your father. You are a fool to think otherwise."

The agent continued to penetrate the determined glare of her prisoner, contemplating.

"Perhaps I give your rabble-rousers an unfair lack of credit," she said, though it was more to herself than to Peter. "You have become something of an inspirational figure for them. But, you aren't truly one of them, are you?"

She sneered again at Peter, who looked up, confused.

"Of course I am."

"Oh no, you aren't incompatible like them. A nuisance certainly, but you are compatible with our societal construct. I wonder… how might they react if they were to find that you are not the incompatible figurehead they think you are, that you are part of the Order's vision for the future of humankind? Why, along with the revelation that you have been working with us all along, I imagine their morale would be crushed!"

Peter laughed, though feigning greater strength than he felt.

"They will never believe you. Besides, it's not my presence that gives them the inspiration they need to fight. It's their families that you want to destroy. You think they are their weakness, I think they are their strength. They will fight to keep their families safe from you."

"Perhaps," said the agent, walking towards the door. "But those few who do believe in you might just resign themselves to their despair. Those that don't need only fight on a little longer until we destroy them. Once again, Peter, you will be responsible for the deaths of countless others – you've become quite good at that now haven't you?"

Peter glared back at her.

He could not detract from the fact that she was right. Peter had been responsible for so many deaths - Indici, Raj, the young girl, and his father, to name a few. It seemed only set to continue.

The agent moved slowly away and rapped lightly on the door. The shadowy figure outside moved. The door slid open with a low hiss to reveal two hefty agents standing patiently outside.

She turned back and gently pressed a button on the side of the television, bringing it back to life to reveal again the lifeless bodies hanging from Tower Bridge.

"We will allow you to watch our progress of course," she said coldly.

She turned back towards the Order agents and waved them inside.

"Leave his face," she said as they entered. "I want him to see everything."

30

The following weeks were some of the most discouraging Peter might ever have imagined.

He had not even one day's reprieve from the ferocity of the two agent's introductions when they had barged inside, without warning, forcing him to undress. They dragged him to the floor and hosed him with a powerful tide of ice-cold water, removing the dried blood from their previous encounter to reveal the growing bruises below.

On his fourth day, Peter had been beaten so badly that the long-haired agent, or 'G' as they called her, had been forced to step in to prevent fatal injury.

"He must be kept alive!" she had shouted, apoplectic with rage before she dragged both agents from the room. "His life is paramount!"

Paramount, he thought, as he lay on the floor drifting in and out of consciousness. At least that was something, though the knowledge that they wanted him alive did little to add any comfort to his stay. Agents continued to visit him, their attitudes towards hostage management varying only in their methods of violence.

It was not even as though his time away from the agent's attacks allowed him any respite. Each night he was forced to undress, hosed down with the same ice-cold wave of water and given a change of clothes before the lights were cut. But for the dim television glow, stuck in a permanent state of life to show the horrors of the world outside, he was left in darkness.

It was not until his second week that sleep deprivation was added to Peter's menu of torture. They no longer allowed him the pleasure of sleep, allowing him only minutes before amplified sounds of screaming children and barking dogs blasted into the room.

Peter's third week improved only in the increasing sporadicism with which he was under the Order's watchful eyes, fists, feet and elbows. The agents slowly limited their visits, and their attacks seemed only to occur every other day. It seemed they were teasing him with a tantalising branch of hope.

Though he was sure he was losing his mind, he remembered, and clung to, advice an old colleague had given. Limit their control. Focus on a hopeful thought, anything, and cling to it. It might just keep you sane.

Though fatigued by pain and sleep deprivation, he remained adamant that the footage played of the outside world could not possibly have been the entire truth.

All the same, as he curled up on the floor nursing whichever body part had withstood the latest beating, watching safe houses stormed by Order agents, and the men, women and children inside being forced into the back of blacked-out vans, was difficult to deny.

Hope was vital, he would tell himself, almost obsessively as he watched. Hope was vital. Hope is vital.

"Food," came a young female voice from the side of the cell, startling Peter from his thoughts.

The cell had been pitch black, but for the ever-present glow of the television, but a gleam of light flooded the cell as the door slid open. An agent entered, more purposefully than the others had, and carefully lowered his meagre food rations to the ground.

This voice had been one Peter learned not to fear. This voice never seemed a prelude to violence but timid and unsure of itself. When he heard this voice, Peter knew he would actually be able to eat. This agent was the only one whose method of food delivery did not involve the deliberate scattering of his rations across the cell floor.

"You don't have to do this, you know..." he said weakly, his eyes still adjusting to the influx of light.

Strangely, Peter had come to appreciate this agent. Whether it had been his decreasing sense of self or just that he had sensed something in her, he convinced himself that this agent might be less certain of her involvement in the cause. She just might be his limited chance of escape.

She had been about to turn to leave, as she always did, but paused momentarily. Capitalising, Peter pulled himself up from his curled position, clutching his ribs with a wince – they had yet to recover from an intense beating a few days earlier.

Noticing his movement, the agent looked up and the eyes behind the visor locked with his own. After a moment, she glanced towards the camera in the corner of the room and snarled before kicking the box of food towards Peter. The force of the kick sent the egg flying out of the box, colliding with the wall behind him.

Peter watched in anguish as the egg smashed, leaving only crumbs for him to scavenge. He turned back towards her, desperate to engage more, but the door slid shut. She had gone.

He heard the camera whir back towards its usual position, mocking him from above. She must have noticed it move towards her as she paused to look at him. Peter was sure, though even now some part of him was convinced that it was food and sleep deprivation, that this woman was the key to his escape, but how?

Peter fumbled in the dark, reaching out for his limited rations, and sharp pangs of hunger shook him from wild thoughts of escape. He found the food box and reached inside weakly to grab the solitary slice of stale bread that remained. But as he felt inside, his fingers clasped around another unspoiled egg.

For the first time in what felt like years, Peter smiled.

*****

Peter's days remained arduous as sleep continued to evade him. His food interruptions remained brief and, whilst it was preferable to the alternative, intermittent beatings no longer took up his remaining hours. The violence had finally ceased, and in its place came a banal solitude.

For hours on end, Peter was left in darkness, alone with his thoughts as he desperately battled to ignore the continual television footage.

Whilst alienating, spending days on end staring at the same spot of pristine white wall, Peter did welcome the amputation of his anxious anticipation of the beatings. Though he was sure that this was not what the Order had intended, this, combined with the gradual revival of his broken body, made his caged existence far more comfortable.

Without the fear of violent interruption, Peter embraced physical meditation. Push-ups, shadow punches and crunches calmed his mind as he sought to retain some form of strength, as the lack of food saw his body wilt away. He had been trained by Dux's men to fight, and whatever fate lay ahead of him in this cell, or beyond, he would not waste it in a bout of self-pity.

It was during one such session of shadowed ju-jitsu that the cell door slid open for what felt like the first time in weeks. Peter recoiled as the slow hiss of the cell door brought with it another sharp influx of light. He fell to one knee, covering his eyes. Any brash hope of escape was quashed as his eyes adjusted to the familiar long, sharp face of G entering the cell.

Peter blinked away tears and looked at himself in the light. His body looked depleted, bruises covering almost every square inch of his body, even after his weeks of solitude. Though his muscles had waned from the lack of food, his training had maintained at least some manner of a physique. G looked him up and down and failed to hide her surprise.

"It appears we have been over-feeding you," she said, turning to an agent behind her with a wry smile. "Let's cut it to once a day, shall we?"

The agent behind her nodded, and Peter forced himself up from his crouched position, ignoring his instant light-headedness.

Though the mystery female agent he had come to depend upon had provided additional food – food he was sure was the only reason he could stand – he was still weak, still aching.

"I have something to show you," said G, smirking again. "And I want to see your face as it happens."

Peter felt an instant sense of dread. He had witnessed many disturbing images in his solitary confinement, however hard he had tried to ignore them, none of which had warranted a visit. For her to come in this time, particularly bearing that grin, had to be something big.

"I do hope that you weren't too busy working out yesterday to see our little exposé on you and your affiliation with the Order?" she jeered. "I almost came in to watch it with you."

Peter had of course seen the story. According to breaking reports, it was he who had been the architect of the Order's policy programme.

Peter's eyes flickered towards the open cell door. He could strike her, grab her gun and make a break for it, and then… well, then what? His eyes appeared to have given away his thinking, and G waved aimlessly behind her, beckoning two agents into the room.

"Hold him down," she ordered.

Peter did not resist, there was little point.

The agents clutched his shoulders and forced him into the chair, holding him tightly. G circled him slowly, without a word, before crouching down.

"As I was saying," she whispered, her lips only millimetres from his right ear. "I hope you saw our little show yesterday."

Peter remained still, staring defiantly ahead at the television. It was one of the few times the screen had remained empty, but for G's reflection. He saw her nod towards his right side. A rustle came from beside him, and an agent swung a fist into his stomach, winding him.

"Still not learning manners, I see," she said smoothly.

"Yes," Peter spluttered, struggling for breath. "I saw it."

G had mentioned their plan to destroy his reputation, but even as Peter watched himself awarded a 'Galton Medal' for services to the State, he had given the story little attention. It was so patently untrue; the Resistance had fought beside him. They knew who he was, and who he stood for. They knew that he was one of them.

"Well, we thought we might follow that up with a more personal token."

Peter straightened, recognising with a deep sense of foreboding the relish that had occupied G's voice.

"We have become aware that the Resistance has manufactured some form of a digital link, at least in part, to the mainframe. Or, I should say, they had."

Peter betrayed a look of fear.

He had told them that they needed to be careful. Against every desire to help, Peter knew that by saving everyone identified as incompatible, the danger of his father's link being exposed grew. The impossible knowledge of all Order's targets would arouse too much suspicion.

"We tracked the link, naturally. But rather than risk an attack, we have been feeding the Resistance false information, drawing your forces out one by one - quite successfully, I might add," she said, smiling broadly. "In fact, we brought one of them in today..."

She looked up towards the still-open cell door.

Peter followed her gaze. He watched as the mother of the young boy smashing action figures together emerged into view, held by two Order agents. She was limp, and her feet dragged lifelessly along the ground as the two agents pulled her past the door.

"We fed them your name," she said. "But of course, the result will not be what they were expecting."

She moved from behind him and crouched at his eye level.

"They will know now that you are not really one of them. We may perhaps have exposed our knowledge of the link, but I think it was worth it. Agents were sent to the establishment in any case, and we were still able to find a few lingerers who had not yet escaped. The building will be ashes I suspect by now."

Peter's head dropped. Q1 was discovered then. The headquarters of the Resistance movement had been destroyed.

"However," G continued, with a glimpse of annoyance. "It appears that the release of your supposed compatibility has sparked something of a public reaction."

She turned towards the screen and, grimacing, clicked it back into action just as a breaking news report appeared.

"This just in," came the powerful voice of the presenter. "We have received reports of a disturbance outside Temple Underground station. What can you tell us, Bob?"

The screen switched to a flustered on-screen reporter, standing to the side of what appeared to be hundreds of protestors marching along the Victoria Embankment directly towards Westminster. Some wore badges depicting the entwined shield symbols, some with white masks, some holding banners reading 'Real Equality', 'Down with the president', 'Life for all!'

Police officers surrounded them, flanked by the customary white uniforms of the SCF.

All seemed relatively peaceful, for now, but Peter had seen the crackdowns of previous weeks. He had seen the violent methods with which SCF agents and supporting police forces had prevented scenes like this from happening – why were they allowing this?

"We are beginning to hear some ominous reports suggesting some in the crowd may be armed. These same reports suggest we may be witnessing an attempted coup upon the Palace of Westminster," the reporter continued, fighting against the noise of the crowds behind him. "The president is currently holding an emergency cabinet meeting to discuss the situation and its applicability to the enhanced Treason Act. He has issued a public statement urging protestors to reconsider their actions and return home. I implore anyone watching the protest today with a desire to join to please stay at home."

Peter felt the authenticity of the reporter's plea and suspected that he too sensed imminent violence as the crowds drew closer to Parliament Square.

Peter watched as the drone footage switched to the path ahead of the protestors and could see the quickly gathering military presence. Soldiers supported the wall of SCF agents as they set up a barricade, complete with military vehicles and two tanks. It was almost certainly a trap.

"Don't do it..." Peter whispered to himself, squirming against the clutches of the two agents, dreading what was soon to happen.

G moved behind him again as he continued to struggle and kissed him gently on his left cheek.

"Your friends are all about to die..." she whispered gently.

Straining helplessly, Peter watched as the crowd came to a halt just metres from the military barricade, brandishing banners and yelling.

The drones continued to span the scene, feeding back the images to the news coverage. The crowd stood, their banners fluttering in the breeze, shouting obscenities towards the SCF agents and military forces. G stood up from behind Peter and ran a gentle hand through Peter's hair.

She pulled out a small communications device from her holster and, with one hand resting upon Peter's head, pulled it towards her mouth.

"Now," she said.

"No!"

Peter tried to wrench himself up and grab the device from her, but he was too late. Seconds later, he heard a gunshot fire out from the scene. There was a brief pause before another gunshot fired, followed shortly by another and another and Peter watched as bodies began dropping to the ground.

"A shot has been fired," came the on-scene reporter's frantic voice, ducking as the drone above continued to display the crowds. "Shots have been fired by the protestors. A soldier is reportedly down. The military and security forces are being forced to respond."

Peter suspected the shots had not originated from the protestors at all. Marches on Parliament had never been part of the Resistance plan, at least this early on – it was too dangerous without the numbers. This had to be a spontaneous public protest.

Peter forced his eyes shut as the drone continued to span the bloody scenes below.

"Open his eyes!" G ordered, and the agents on either side of him dutifully obliged. "This is just for you."

Bodies were falling everywhere. People were screaming. Blood oozed into the ground, dispersed by a steady flow of rain, painting the road beneath them a harrowing scarlet. Protestors dispersed aimlessly, some sprinting into side roads, some throwing themselves into the river, with little success.

Where was Dux? Where was the Resistance? How had they, how had anyone, allowed this to happen? He saw police officers and soldiers, who had only months ago been guardians of the public, standing and doing nothing.

Peter had to get out of this prison. He had to escape; he had to stop this.

With another almighty effort, Peter forced himself upwards, breaking from the two agents' grips. He grabbed the chair and swung it towards one of the agents, who was thrust backwards from the force of the blow. The agent staggered into G, knocking her to the floor. Breathing heavily, Peter swung the chair back towards the other agent, who also fell to the ground. Now was his chance.

Peter turned and ran towards the still-open cell door, but just as he had crossed the threshold, he felt an immense force connect with his chest. The shoulder of an agent outside thrust him back inside.

Gasping, Peter tried to move from his crumpled position, desperate to escape, but the agent outside continued towards him and kicked him in the stomach.

Peter fell on his back and stared up blankly at the white ceiling. So much for his escape plan.

G moved into view above him and wiped away a trickle of blood from her lip.

"Is he conscious?" she asked.

Another agent had entered the room in the commotion and crouched down to look at him. He noticed a soft pair of lips trembling from beneath the visor. This close, he could see her eyes sparkling through the dark tint – it was her, it had to be. She was beautiful, he thought, or was it just the dazzling effect of the stars circling his head?

"I want to help you," she whispered, loud enough only so that Peter could hear her.

"What was that, R24?" G asked sharply.

"Still breathing," she replied quickly. "Stunned, but conscious."

G nudged her aside and crouched down to look at Peter's blank expression.

"You just witnessed the end of your Resistance, Peter Brockland," she said menacingly.

She stood up and beckoned at the agents to follow her. The two agents looked down at him with wry grins and spat at him before they followed her out of the cell.

The woman came into view as Peter wiped his face weakly, looking down at his pitiful figure.

She slowly lifted her visor. She was indeed beautiful. She was young, in her mid to late twenties, and her light skin complemented her fiery red hair, pulled back into a ponytail. She continued to look down at him, her sparkling blue eyes dimming as the cell door began to close, drawing the remaining light from the room.

"I'm going to get you out," she whispered.

Peter looked back at her, still spread-eagled on the floor, astonished by her brash exhibition of defiance. She was tough – he could see it in her eyes.

He nodded back.

31

The unwelcome visits from heavy-handed Order agents soon ceased; in fact, Peter was deprived of all human contact but for the delivery of his meagre food rations.

Peter was surprised by how much he missed the television. Even with the horrific scenes he had been witness to, the coverage helped him feel connected, help keep him abreast of the happenings of the outside world, of the knowledge that the Resistance was still out there fighting back. Now, he had nothing.

Peter rolled to his side, staring longingly towards where the television now sat dormant. He felt his stomach growl.

The increasing sporadicity with which his morsels of bread were delivered had left him weak. The effort alone to clamber towards his food soon rendered him breathless, with only the promise of some degree of sustenance at the end giving him the strength to keep crawling.

Peter longed for news from the mysterious red-haired agent, anything to distract him from the queueing dark thoughts threatening to consume him.

The lack of news, or of any contact at all, was unbearable. So much had it begun to grind on him that Peter almost welcomed another chance to fight off a beating, just for some form of contact. But nothing came. It was probably a good thing; his body was becoming so depleted of energy now that there was little chance of him finding the strength to last more than a few seconds.

Peter knew that they were watching him. The occasional whirring of the CCTV camera in the corner of the room told him so, as it diligently checked that he was still alive, still suffering. He often found some slight enjoyment in those short periods of bread-deprived stupor, by wandering the room, simply to hear the rhythmic whirs of the camera following his every step.

How sad has this got, he thought to himself, as he turned for another lap.

But as he began to stumble, he noticed that the whirring had ceased. It no longer followed his movements. What was going on? It had not stopped tracking him for over a week.

Peter turned to face the cell door and noticed that it had become lighter, or perhaps it was the sudden interruption to his banality causing him to be more alert than he had been in days. He stood facing it and clenched his fists, grinding his teeth to abate his exhaustion, and prepared himself for whatever horror they had planned for him next.

A shadow appeared at the door. Peter watched as the slight figure looked left and right, then left and right again. Peter's heart rate intensified; for better or worse, this person was clearly not meant to disturb their prisoner's isolation.

Peter took a deep breath. He prepared for his lunge as the cell door slowly slid open but stopped as the agent entered. She had removed her helmet as she walked inside to reveal her slightly stubby nose, her porcelain white skin, and the slick flow of her auburn hair.

The door slid shut behind her, and the lights flickered into life, blinding Peter. Though heartened by her appearance, he was still not certain that she could be trusted. Blinking profusely, Peter's fists remained clenched.

She paused nervously, and they exchanged intense, suspicious stares.

"We don't have much time," she said impatiently, breaking the silence.

Peter offered no response. Instead, he continued to look suspiciously at her, his fists still raised.

She sighed impatiently and slowly began to remove her belt. With a click of the buckle, her belt dropped to the floor with a loud clunk. She looked back up at Peter, who stared at the weapons on the floor and back up to the agent in astonishment.

She sighed again and began to unzip parts of her bodysuit. Peter was not quite sure at that moment that he was not dreaming and allowed her to continue only a moment before interrupting.

"What are you doing?"

"I'm trying to show you I'm not here to hurt you, see?"

She had removed the top half of her uniform, allowing it to hang down to reveal a khaki vest underneath and, importantly, no more weapons. She was clearly strong, her muscles well defined, and Peter could see hints of several healed over scars - evidence of her combat experience.

Peter continued to look at her with a dazed expression and, though very much distracted, maintained his defensive position.

"Oh for goodness sake," she said with a sigh. "Well, I'm not taking anything else off."

Peter almost smiled. After one final suspicious inspection, he nodded and lowered his fists.

For the first time in days, Peter could see the state of the room and himself. Without his daily hose down, Peter knew his stay had become unhygienic - the smell by the fourth day had been enough to tell him that - but as he looked down at his pimpled, oily skin, he could see the sustained effects of the agent's attacks too.

Dark, purple bruises scattered around his body, interrupted only by the recently healed cuts and scrapes. Though Peter had felt his increasing weakness, after weeks of malnourishment, seeing his depleted appearance brought it to life. His eyes widened as he stared at the hints of bone beneath his skin.

Catching his breath, he chose to ignore the state of the food-stained walls and worse-stained toilet and looked up at the agent, whose evermore-evident allure in the light made Peter feel distinctively self-consciousness.

She nodded and smiled, thanking him for his defensive retreat.

"Peter, we don't have long," she said, glancing towards the CCTV camera. It had remained stationary and pointed towards the opposite corner of the room. "Maybe five minutes or so before they realise I'm not in the control room."

She looked at him with greater urgency. "Peter, I need you to tell me how to reach the Resistance."

"What?" Peter scoffed. "You're out of your mind!"

"Peter, I can't help you if you don't let me. I need you to help me."

She moved towards him. Peter looked again at her toned figure; this agent was clearly well-trained and more than capable of beating the answer out of him.

"What made you think you could come in here, strip off and expect me to give up the Resistance?" said Peter. "You're one of them, one of the Order. How can I trust you?"

She was only centimetres away from him now, so close that Peter could see the lines in her skin, the small hazel dot in her emerald green eyes, and the reddening glow of her cheeks.

"Firstly, I have not stripped off," she said, affronted. "Secondly, I thought I, I thought we..."

"You thought a few extra slices of bread would soften me to give away the entire Resistance movement? I don't believe that somehow."

"I don't care what you think Peter," she said with a growl. Before he could react, she grabbed him by his throat. "If I'm going to get out of here, and if we're going to destroy this group, you are going to need to tell me how I can do that."

Peter could not help but linger on how close they were, even as she clutched his throat; their eyes were almost touching now. Having spent the week increasingly disdained by the smell of his cell, he was overcome by the rosy scent of her perfume. And, with her athletic figure pressed closely against him, he soon found himself needing a distraction.

Peter pushed her backwards, and she released her grip. They stood opposite each other again, glowering.

Peter noticed a red light flickering in his peripheral vision and looked up towards the corner of the room. His face fell; the CCTV camera had come back to life.

The agent had noticed his glance, and her face too dropped. After a brief moment's calculation, she drew back her fist and flew at Peter.

Peter stumbled backwards as her fist collided with his jaw. He turned back, cursing, and wiped a trickle of blood from his lip. Behind her, he saw another shadow appear in the tinted glass, and the door slid open.

"Rachael, what are you doing?" came the agent's high-pitched voice, her face hidden by their visor as she entered. She sounded panicked and turned anxiously to check outside for signs of any other agents.

"I…" Rachael stuttered back, looking at Peter. "I had to get a piece of him, one on one."

"Come on," said the other agent, staring down at Peter before dragging Rachael back towards the cell door. She picked up Rachael's belt and threw it towards her before looking left and right outside the cell.

"We need to get back," she continued, her voice still panicked. "If G finds out you left your post, she will kill you and probably give me the same treatment as this traitor."

"Charming," Peter muttered, wiping blood from his lip again.

The other agent ignored him and turned back towards the door, still clutching Rachael's arm. Rachael pulled her arm back and looked back towards Peter intently with a playful wink.

"I'm coming," she said, pulling her bodysuit back on.

She gave Peter one last weak smile and pulled down her visor before leaving the cell.

As the door slid slowly shut behind her, the lights cut out. Peter was once again left, nursing his jaw, in total darkness.

32

Fortunately for Peter, and indeed, her, it appeared that Rachael's reckless foray into his cell had gone unnoticed. His next few days were not filled with inquisitions about her presence there, but instead the growing familiarity of darkness and solitude.

Peter was left wrestling with the decision he knew he must make - could he trust her. He spent hours pondering, as the camera continued to growl menacingly in the corner, its red eye gazing down upon his every move.

Was Rachael just part of the act? Was she just the next stage of the Order's psychological chess match? Was she just performing the disarmingly attractive distraction, the 'good cop', comforting him in his time of vulnerability? Was it all just part of the Order's plan to extract every last piece of information he had of the Resistance and their movements before finally disposing of him?

Thinking of the Resistance gave him little pleasure; the lack of information was unbearable. Were they even active anymore? Were they alive? Had their quest to bring down the new PHROX-controlled government been thwarted?

Peter growled, wrestling against the negative thoughts, and paced the room again.

Rachael had asked for information on how to get in contact with the Resistance safely. Her desire to find them, whatever her actual motives, must indicate that the Resistance was still out there, still fighting. Even now, there was still some hope.

Peter was left with two options. He could remain silent and fester, perhaps die, in his cell in the certain knowledge that he had not contributed to the discovery of the Resistance's whereabouts. Or he could put his faith in Rachael, perhaps his only bleak chance at escape. He could put his faith in a woman he had known only for days in the hope that by doing so, he could return to the Resistance and help advance the fight.

Peter did not have long to make his decision.

He sat quietly on the floor, staring blankly towards the cell door as it lit up to signal his latest food delivery. He edged slowly towards the door and saw the shadow of an agent crouch down. With a dull clink, the agent placed his food gently in the opening. Placed. Not thrown, not kicked inside. Could it be her?

Peter grabbed for the food and glimpsed the familiar white helmet and visor staring through the opening. He listened intently; the camera had stopped whirring. Rachael lifted her visor.

"So," she whispered quietly, leaning in towards the opening. "Have you decided if you are going to help me?"

Peter knew they would not have long before the surveillance camera buzzed back into action, perhaps only seconds. He looked at her intently, directly into the glow of her enticing green eyes.

"Can I trust you?"

She remained still for a second, looking at him impatiently. Then, suddenly, she leant further forward and kissed him.

Completely taken aback, Peter stared at her, her lips still on his. His eyes darted towards the camera, which with the dim glow of the light outside, he could see still positioned towards the opposite corner of the cell.

Still processing his shock, he heard a loud buzz as the camera returned to life. He pulled away, his lips still tingling, and stared at her in astonishment.

"You have to," she said.

Peter looked back at her blankly, increasingly aware that the camera would lock on to their interaction within moments. She looked determined, as though her life really did depend on his help. He played through the various scenarios in his mind and, with one final penetrating look, made his decision.

"Lamb and Flag," he whispered, rushing his instructions. "Covent Garden, London. Ask the bartender for a half of the strongest they have on tap."

Rachael beamed at him.

"If you get in trouble, give them this."

Peter reached inside his mouth and began to twist. He had lost his original in a charity rugby event at the Chronicle, and almost lost another in the subsequent pitch-side brawl, but his new screw-in tooth gave Peter an unusual party trick.

Peter passed his tooth to Rachael, who looked down towards his open hand with disgust. Peter smiled as she held out a reluctant hand and took it.

"Not many people are aware of this," he said, as Rachael continued to stare at it.

"Pass the bartender the tooth and tell them it's from Salvator. They will know what to do. If they don't kill you, tell them I'm alive, tell them where this place is, and tell them it's time to end this."

Rachael turned the tooth over in her hand. There was a small black marking on one side – it looked oddly like some sort of small shield. She looked back at Peter, then back at the tooth, perplexed.

"Trust me, they will know what it is."

Rachael nodded and put the tooth carefully into her side pocket. She said nothing; she just looked at him again before rising to her feet.

"You should know," said Peter quietly as she turned away. She paused. "I was going to help you before you kissed me."

She remained still for a second, and Peter could not see her reaction. The opening in the door slid shut, and he saw her blurred outline walk away.

Peter grabbed for his food, searching it ravenously, and was delighted to find that she had once again provided him with extra. He shoved a slice of bread into his mouth and chewed ferociously. Even as he sat back smiling, relishing the sustenance, he could not help but fixate on his hope that a kiss from a pretty girl would not signal the downfall of the Resistance.

33

"Ladies and gentlemen, this is your driver speaking..."

Rachael jumped as the loud, jovial voice reverberated through the carriage, as the train driver woke her from her daydream.

"We are approximately fifteen minutes from London Euston, and I am delighted to say we are on schedule. Please ensure that you take your belongings with you."

She pulled her face from the window and shook herself. She felt something sharp in her palm and looked down to see Peter's tooth. She had been playing with it aimlessly throughout the journey, turning it repeatedly as she contemplated her next steps.

So much depended upon the next couple of hours. Not just for her, but for the future of the Order and the Resistance movement. She may have been able to win Peter over, but would the others believe she was on their side?

Rachael noticed a pair of eyes staring at her and looked up abruptly. A young boy sat patiently beside his mother, staring towards her hands with an evident look of confused curiosity. She smiled back and swiftly put the tooth back into her jeans pocket.

The train soon began to slow and pulled into London Euston station. The clang of the train intercom rang out as the train came to a halt, and as the driver bade his final jaunty farewells to the disembarking passengers, Rachael grabbed for her rucksack and moved out towards the hoard outside.

She advanced nervously, weaving through the crowds. She had practically shoved her ticket through the barrier in her anxious state. Ignoring the exasperation of the ticket attendant - "gently, please madam" - she looked up as the barrier opened towards something that made her blood run cold.

Three heavily-armed Order agents were pushing their way through the crowds, accompanied by two police officers, pointing directly towards her.

Panicked, Rachael pushed her way through the barrier and past the ticket attendant – "Oi!" – and marched towards the nearest exit, her head down. How could they possibly have known? Had they been following her? She had been so careful to ensure that no one had known about her plans, but had they somehow found out?

"You there!" one of the agents shouted, jumping from behind the crowd to take a closer look. "Stop!"

She began to hyperventilate, staring frantically around the station for any source of inspiration. Beads of sweat formed, and she reached into her jeans pocket nervously, fingering the grip of her pistol.

Fuelled by the onset of panicked adrenaline, Rachael considered her escape plan.

She couldn't kill the police officers - well, she shouldn't - they were only doing their job. Besides, even if she could take them down, she was considerably less confident that she could overcome three fully-equipped agents, even with more than one cartridge of ammunition. She had worn that uniform for years; it was practically impenetrable.

"Stop," one of the agents shouted from behind her again. "Now!"

The crowds had noticed the commotion and were eager, if not terrified, to see who had been targeted. She heard the rapid claps of the agents' boots against the station floor grow louder and louder.

She had come so close.

Rachael dropped her bag to the floor with a sigh and moved for the gun in her pocket.

"You there! With the child, stop now!"

The words had momentarily stunned her. She stood rooted to the spot as the agents brushed past her and jogged towards a young man frantically walking his child towards the station exit. He stopped as they approached, shaking, catatonic with fear.

The man turned slowly to face the agents, his face drained of all colour. Rachael did not wait to see the outcome; she knew what was about to happen. Public arrests had become commonplace, and many of the surrounding crowd had begun to turn back to their activities, offering pitying glances towards the young father.

There was nothing they could do. The Order was too strong, too violent. The images of the 'traitors' hanging from London Bridge had certainly done the job. It would take an incredibly brave, or stupid, person to stand up to them in such a public place.

A wave of guilt rushed over Rachael as she watched. She, of all of them, could perhaps do something, but she had no choice but to allow it to happen; too much was riding on her finding the Resistance. Any attempt to help would confirm her betrayal, and for her plan to work, they needed to believe she was still one of them.

She locked eyes with the young man only for a second, enough to see his devastated look of resignation. She offered a brief, almost apologetic, glance towards him before they were led away through the crowds. Rachael watched only a moment as the two of them had their wrists bound amidst angry glances from the crowd before she turned away.

Rachael's brief tube journey was gripped by tension. Not that London tube journeys were famed for outbreaks of spontaneous conversation, but the carriages remained notably silent. Inquisitive, almost accusatory, glances spread from person to person as though searching for the most appropriate culprit to blame for not protecting the man, for not taking the stand that they so desperately wanted to themselves.

Given the chance, and with the right tools, they might all have stood up to those agents. They might all have tried to prevent the young father and child from being taken away. But they had their own lives, their family's lives, to consider, as did she.

Rachael left the carriage at Leicester Square station and walked briskly towards the escalators. She eyed her mobile phone as she ascended, eagerly awaiting the return of her GPS signal to direct her towards her mysterious destination. She jumped the final stairs, feeling the cold breeze of the air outside and stepped out to the street to find two Order agents waiting. They both stood still against the bright backdrop of the theatres behind, scanning passers-by.

She noticed one turn towards her and stared for a moment before turning away to whisper something to their companion.

"I was careful," she mumbled to herself, nodding curtly at them before walking briskly away with her head down. "There's no way they could know."

Rachael continued, obeying the phone directions into Garrick Street, surprised by how many people were still out at 9pm on a Sunday. She looked down at her phone again - the next left. She turned into Rose Street, and there it was.

At the end of a short, narrow, cobbled road, two men sat holding the remnants of their pints in front of a four-storey building with the unmistakable 'Lamb & Flag' text painted in gold.

Rachael turned back to look up and down Garrick Street to see if she had been followed. There were no signs of the Order nearby. With another calming breath, she made her way towards the pub, turning Peter's tooth aimlessly in her pocket.

The two men turned, pausing their conversation to eye her up as she approached.

Could they be Resistance fighters? She slipped her hand towards her jeans pocket and stroked the grip of her gun.

"Alright, love," one of the men slurred before downing the last of his ale. "Can I get the lovely lady a drink?"

"No, thank you," said Rachael with a relieved smile, removing her hands from her pocket. "I'm meeting a friend."

She had not needed to use that one in a while, she thought, as she moved towards the entrance.

"Lucky bastard!" said the other, spilling some of his drink down his front.

Rachael smiled again, hoping that she had arranged her face into an acceptable enough look of flattery, and pushed open the wooden front door.

A distinct smell of stale beer immediately threatened to overcome her as the door swung back to a close. Screwing up her nose, she looked around at the cramped opening to the apparent Resistance hideaway.

The entrance was small, and a television screen played out to the empty chairs to her left, offering a greater source of light than the dimly lit lamps surrounding the bar. A narrow stairway to her right led to an upstairs bar, and a small gap between the bar and the right wall led towards another sectioned-off room, closed off by two wooden doors.

It appeared that the pub had attracted a few stragglers even at this late Sunday hour, as two men and a particularly tired-looking woman turned to face her from the barstools.

The barman looked up, noticing his customer's gaze, and walked towards her, tossing a tea towel over his shoulder. He was tall and brawny, with a hint of a belly protruding from the bottom of his short-sleeve t-shirt. His hair was black, shaggy and unkempt, and a distinctive pair of tortoiseshell glasses covered a set of large bushy eyebrows.

She walked a few steps towards him, still playing with Peter's tooth in her jeans pocket.

"What can I get you love?" he asked in a thick cockney accent.

"Erm," Rachael began, eyeing the beer drafts whilst trying to remember what Peter had told her to say. "I'd like a half of the strongest you have on tap."

The barman stared at her blankly.

"Please," Rachael finished, awkwardly.

"You want what?" he asked, edging closer towards the bar.

The atmosphere in the room had turned, and Rachael became distinctly aware of the silence. She turned nervously towards the stray drinkers surrounding the bar, who all stared intently at her. Instinctively, she moved towards her jeans pocket again.

"A half," she repeated, though, in her nervous state, it had come out more as a question than an order. "Of the strongest you have on tap."

The barman stared again, assessing what she had just said. In a flash, he nodded towards something behind her.

The two men from outside had crept through the pub door and now stood, perfectly sober, blocking her exit. Each had a gun pointed at her – they had played their act well. The other pub-goers had stood abruptly from their stools, and they too aimed guns towards her.

Rachael reacted in a flash and pulled out her gun, moving swiftly towards the corner of the room. She stood still, breathing heavily, her gun moving towards each of them in turn. She knew her situation was bleak. With a defeated sigh, she lifted her gun above her head, conceding, and let it hang limply on the third finger of her left hand.

The barman walked slowly through the opening in the bar towards her and removed the gun from her hand, before throwing it across the floor. He pushed the muzzle of his pistol into her forehead.

"Who the fuck are you?"

34

"Well, everything certainly seems to be in order," came the commanding voice of Chief Superintendent Justine Smith. The young custody officer stared back at her, staring nervously towards her assessment form as she ticked off a final clipboard line item.

Justine returned the young officer's stare for a moment, applying the resolute glare she had long become reputable for, before allowing herself to soften. The officer might even go as far as telling colleagues in the canteen later that day that the CS had offered her the rarest hint of a smile.

The officer's shoulders relaxed, and with a deep sigh, she smiled back.

"This way, ma'am," she said, her voice awash with relief. Raising her arm, she indicated towards the route back down the corridor towards the front desk.

Justine nodded back, reverting to her standard steely expression, and followed the officer through the corridor and past the cell doors.

She halted a moment; something had grabbed her attention in the corner of her eye. Justine turned towards one of the holding cells and saw the small gap in the cell door wide open.

She turned to peer through the small opening and saw a young man sitting cross-legged, almost unnaturally still, staring up at the small window in the corner of his cell.

Justine edged closer and looked intently down at the man. He could not be any more than a late teen, and she was transfixed by the stillness with which he sat staring up towards the outside world.

"He was brought in yesterday," the young officer whispered from behind her, noticing the chief superintendent's pause. "Hasn't moved all day."

Justine continued to stare at the man, whose stillness remained, not fazed even by the strength of the sunlight as it shone brightly down through the window, directly into his face. Still, he sat staring, without a sound, as though possessed.

"Asperger's, they suspect," the young officer continued, leaning in to look through the remaining gap in the door hatch herself. "The SCF brought him in for processing yesterday after his school teacher reported him."

Justine stiffened at the explanation. She turned to look at the officer, who promptly pulled back with an embarrassed laugh, and back towards the young man, still transfixed by the sunlight outside.

She wondered how terrified he must have been, extracted by the SCF in front of his schoolmates for something he could not control, something that not too long ago would have been a celebrated victory over adversity. Now he was punished, even by those supposedly bound by a duty of care.

To think that this was what her police stations had become, not institutions bound by duty to protect the public, but holding cells for those unfortunate enough to be born different, those deemed infectious and unwanted. The public had been sold absurdity in the promise to eradicate hereditary disease, to rid the world of the plagues of cancer, of Alzheimer's. If they understood the evil involved… well, she only hoped they would feel as revolted as she felt now watching one of the countless innocent victims.

"Ma'am?" said the young officer, interrupting her train of thought and indicating again towards the front desk.

"Right," said Justine, turning her gaze from the young man. "Yes, let's go."

They both walked silently towards the front desk, the officer glancing back occasionally towards the chief superintendent, hoping she had not done anything wrong. But Justine was not paying attention.

Her mind wandered back to some forty years before: she stood brimming with pride in a hall amongst her friends and colleagues. She could still remember the ache in her face at the extent of her smile as she had taken her oath. After all the training, all the sacrifices, bar her wedding day it had been the best moment of her life.

Then she thought back to a year ago, as she stood in a similar hall to pledge her oath of service to the new president. She remembered how uncomfortable she had felt, amidst the growing public protest, and all the growing rumour. The oath she had sworn stuck in her throat - to protect the president and to honour her duty to uphold democracy and protect the State.

Could she allow misplaced duty to be an excuse anymore? In all good conscience, could she allow the flagrant abuses of public freedoms to continue, regardless of the validity, or indeed not, of the elected officials?

"Ma'am?" came another voice, startling her from her daydream.

The desk sergeant stared at her from across the desk, holding out a clipboard and pen.

"What? Yes, sorry."

She took the pen from him and signed the custody form. She pictured Jenny with a baby on the way and wondered what she would do if they were marked by the SCF.

Justine leant down to pick up her bag and nodded towards two armed officers as they made their way past the front desk. She turned back to the young custody officer, who had maintained her nervous demeanour.

"Make sure you look after that young man, won't you?" she said, nodding towards the cell door.

"Yes, ma'am," the officer replied, smiling back awkwardly.

Justine nodded back curtly without returning the smile and turned towards the station entrance just as an almighty bang rang out through the front hall.

The entrance doors had flown open, and sunlight flooded the front desk, causing the custody officers to recoil. The armed officers turned abruptly and aimed their weapons towards the commotion, just as Justine grabbed for her own concealed pistol.

Four figures entered - a middle-aged man and a smaller boy, flanked by two SCF agents. As the doors swung closed behind them, taking the sunlight with them, Justine noticed that the man's hands were bound, hanging uselessly in front of him as the agent pushed him towards the front desk.

Justine lowered her pistol and focused her attention on the boy. His face was etched with fright, the distress in his young, tear-stained face matched only by the anguish upon his father's - taut and bleeding as a result of what must have been a typically overzealous SCF arrest.

Justine could see that the young boy had also, remarkably, had his hands bound. His tiny wrists were so tightly bound that his hands began to turn purple.

Justine's face tightened. At that moment, something inside her switched. The brutality with which these agents thrust the man forward, laughing, and the callousness with which they treated this young defenceless boy, no older than five or six, set something off, igniting a wave of anger she had not felt in a very long time.

"What is the meaning of this?" she demanded, lowering her pistol and walking forward to stand in front of the two agents.

"Two incompatibles for processing," said one of the agents as he lifted his visor. He pushed the man forward again. "We need you to hold them here for a while."

Justine glanced down at the terrified boy and noticed his face twitching. She knelt down and smiled at the boy, who stared back with wide eyes, just as terrified of her as he was of them.

"What's your name?" she asked softly as the boy continued to stutter through sobs.

The boy did not answer but instead stared up towards his father. Justine smiled at him softly again and pulled a small penknife from her pocket.

"Well, I don't think these are necessary, are they?" She slid open the penknife and cut through the cable ties binding the boy's hands.

"What the fuck do you think you are doing?" said one of the agents angrily, pulling the boy sharply back towards him by the neck of his t-shirt, before lifting his own visor.

"I am Chief Superintendent Justine Smith," she replied curtly, and she stood up to stare directly back into the infuriated face of the SCF agent. "So it will be what the fuck do you think you are doing, ma'am - even from you."

She heard an excitable gasp from the young custody officer behind her, and the agent stared at her blankly for a moment, then towards the other agent, as though unsure of how to proceed.

The additional powers and public fear of their policies had given the SCF a distorted sense of superiority over the rank-and-file police force, but even they knew better than to question the authority of the chief superintendent. The president knew that the cooperation of the police force was critical, at least in the early stages of their rule. Without them at his side, it would be chaos.

"Why have these two been detained?" she continued, taking advantage of their stunned silence.

"We suspect the boy has Tourette Syndrome," said one of the agents, addressing the chief superintendent with forced politeness through gritted teeth. "He needs to be processed, confirmed and sterilised."

"No!" the boy's father shouted, struggling against the other agent's grasp. The second agent pulled the man backwards and threw his fist into the man's stomach, forcing him to his knees.

Instinctively, Justine drew her pistol again and aimed it directly towards the agent, her face reddening.

She had spent a year tackling her complicity with all of this, as loyalty and honour battled guilt and regret; she could take it no longer. She reacted in an instant, knowing that now was the time to resist, to say no more.

The agent looked up at the barrel of the gun in complete shock. The other agent had moved towards his sidearm, but in an instant, Justine heard a shuffle from behind her; the two armed officers had approached, both aiming their weapons towards the agent.

Justine sighed and felt another wave of guilt; the loyalty of these two officers would almost certainly cost them their own lives too.

The agents looked towards each other and back towards the three weapons aimed at them, and slowly lifted their arms.

"You are so fucked," said the taller of the two, his feigned smile unable to hide the menace in his voice. "Ma'am," he finished, sarcastically.

"Thank you, officers," said Justine, nodding to the officers on either side of her. "Please relieve these agents of their weapons and comms. In fact, I think they can just remove everything."

"Officer Kurdan," she shouted towards the young custody officer, maintaining her glance and aim at the agents. "I am ordering you to take this man and his son and ensure that they are kept safe."

She heard an immediate shuffling behind her, and the officer rushed towards them. With a terrified glance at the stripping SCF agents, Office Kurdan led the agent's prisoners back to the front desk.

Justine nodded in response to the look of thanks from the father as he walked past and looked back at the SCF agents who, without the protection of the white suits, looked considerably less imposing. Stripped of their protective shell - their symbol of fear - these people were nothing.

"I cannot stand by and allow the systematic sterilisation and murder of innocent civilians to continue," she said. "Whatever the consequences for me, my conscience can no longer bear my complicity with this new regime. You may leave and tell your boss that this is my official resignation."

She waved the gun towards the entrance doors. "You may leave. Now."

The two men, stripped to their t-shirts and underwear now, stared back at her, their faces taut at their humiliation. With a nervous glance towards the two flanking officers, whose weapons remained aimed at them, they edged backwards.

"You're going to pay for this," said the shorter of the two, staring back with an ominous grin before they both slipped out towards the street outside.

"Almost certainly," Justine muttered to herself as the doors closed behind them.

Her career was over now, but she felt no regret. On the contrary, for the first time since her husband had passed, she felt an immense weight lifted from her shoulders. No longer would she have to feel shame every time she put on the badge, allowing her self-imposed sense of duty to prevent her from doing what she knew to be right.

"Lock the doors," she said to the two armed officers. "It won't take long for them to bring others."

The officers nodded and proceeded towards the front doors. The now ex-chief superintendent turned back to the front desk.

"How can I ever thank you?" said the young father, his face still pale.

"By staying alive," Justine replied, smiling weakly. "You'll need to find the Resistance, no, sorry..." she paused for a moment, with a chuckle. "We'll need to find the Resistance."

She stuttered as she said it, uncannily aware now that she too was a marked woman. This blatant display of insubordination would not be tolerated by the regime; she was almost certainly set to become the latest addition to London Bridge.

The man nodded, clutching his son, and beamed back.

"You two," she said, turning back to the custody officers. "I'll need to cuff you before they return."

They looked at each other and back towards her, confused. "Ma'am?"

"They mustn't think that you helped me escape," she explained, staring up towards the CCTV camera. "Or they will shoot you on the spot."

"But we want to help," said Officer Kurdan.

"We want to help bring these people down too," said the other.

"Now is not the time," said Justine sternly, shaking her gun towards them. "For now, I'll take whoever they have held here and get them to safety."

Both officers nodded, accepting their order, though they were unable to hide their looks of resentment. Justine moved towards them and placed a consoling hand on their shoulders.

"I need you to help mobilise the force from the inside," she said, reassuringly. "The day will soon come when we will need to stand up and fight for the freedoms we have cherished for so long. And when that day comes, we will need our best and bravest standing with us, on the right side."

The officers nodded, their resentment replaced now by a fire in their eyes. Justine smiled.

"Ok, now I'm going to need to release anyone being held here under an SCF detainment order."

"There's only one ma'am," said the young officer, handing Justine the keys to his cell door. "You saw him earlier."

"Ok," she replied. "Then I'm going to need the two of you to sit down."

The officers nodded and dropped to the floor, facing away from each other with their hands outstretched, and allowed Justine to handcuff them.

The armed agents approached Justine, returning from their task.

"I'm afraid the two of you have rather shown your hands in this one. But I would be delighted if you'd join me?"

The officers smiled back. "Would be an honour ma'am."

She nodded back, restraining an overwhelming desire to embrace the two of them. Unbecoming of a senior officer, even a resigned one.

"Very good," she replied. "Then please escort…" she turned to look towards the father.

"Stephen," he replied. "And this is Charlie."

She smiled at the boy again and noticed that his stutters appeared to have stopped; for the first time, he smiled back.

"Very well, please escort Stephen and Charlie to a suitable vehicle out back and wait for me. I shall grab our next passenger."

The officers nodded, and the four of them walked out through a side door.

Justine heard the screeching of car tyres from outside; they did not have long. She clutched the keys in her hand and moved briskly towards the holding cells, halting outside that of the young man's.

She stared in again through the opening in the cell door. He was still sitting cross-legged, staring up at the sunlight outside, unfazed by the commotion.

She placed the key in the cell door, and for the first time, the man seemed to stir.

No longer could she allow the brutalisation of those deemed incompatible with the supposed bettering of humankind in the name of some supposed betterment of science and society. She could not allow it, even if it meant her own death.

As though the young man had sensed her determination, he turned slowly to face her. She stood at the cell entrance staring at the young man, whose face remained blank, though his eyes seemed to have regained a sparkle.

"It's time for us to go young man."

35

"My name is Rachael Fuller," said Rachael, forcing every muscle at her disposal to remain calm. "Peter Brockland… I mean, Salvator… gave me this location. I've come here to help. Look, I can prove it."

Rachael moved a hand towards her jeans pocket to pull out the tooth but quickly stopped. The room reacted in an instant, thrusting their weapons forward angrily.

"Don't you fucking dare," the barman growled, pushing the muzzle of his gun into her forehead.

Rachael sighed and slowly lifted her hands back above her head.

The barman continued to stare at her, scanning her thoughts, analysing every possible scenario in the search for the truth. After a few moments, he stepped back slowly and nodded towards the hard-faced woman beside him.

The woman nodded back and lowered her gun before moving towards Rachael. Still glaring at her suspiciously, the woman stood behind her and patted down her jacket and jeans.

"Check her ankle Jess," said the barman, his gun still poised.

Rachael groaned; she knew what was about to happen. She felt the hem of her jeans roll up, and beneath the denim emerged a small tattoo on her left ankle – a black broadsword entwined by a double helix.

"Yep," said Jess, staring up towards Rachael's face with an unmistakable look of loathing. Their suspicions had been vindicated. "She's one of them."

"Lock the doors," the barman barked at the men at the door. "Check outside too – we don't know how many others she's brought with her."

"Wait," Rachael pleaded. "Please, I know what this looks like, but I'm here to help."

"Shut it," Jess sneered from behind her, and she continued to rummage through Rachael's jacket pockets.

"Paul," the barman continued, addressing the other man at the bar. "Warn the others, we might need to move quickly. Inform Q29-".

"I haven't brought anyone else!" Rachael shouted, losing her temper.

The room fell silent, all turning to look at her, and none possessing expressions other than complete disgust. Rachael gulped.

"Check my pockets and you will find Peter Brockland's tooth – he gave it to me. He told me what I should say to you. How else would I know?"

The barman looked at her again, considering her with his harsh black eyes. He nodded almost reluctantly towards Jess, who slipped her hand into Rachael's jeans pocket. She rummaged deeper and pulled out keys, a mobile phone, a train ticket, and…

"A tooth," said Rachael, as Jess pulled out Peter's etched tooth and handed it to the barman.

He stared at her a moment, before looking at the rough fragment of polymer in the palm of his outstretched hand. He turned it slowly in his fingers to reveal the small etching – the shield entwined by the double helix.

He looked up at Rachael. Though the barman's stance appeared to have softened, his expression was not replaced by one of understanding but confusion.

"What is this supposed to prove?"

Rachael's face dropped.

Peter had told her that this strange offering would be the key to her survival, all the proof she had needed. Was the barman testing her? Had it all been a trick? Had Peter truly believed she had changed sides or had this been his opportunity to enact some form of revenge?

Rachael felt Jess's grip tighten, forcing her arms into an arm lock. She struggled, immediately regretting her decision to surrender her weapon so easily.

She eyed the door desperately before looking towards the others, all still aiming guns directly at her. She frantically contemplated her options before…

"Let me take a look."

A tall, heavily-built man emerged from a dark opening opposite the bar, his deep booming voice immediately taking control of the room.

The barman obeyed immediately, dropping his gun. He handed him the tooth with a nod and turned back to face Rachael, his gun raised again.

Rachael looked past him towards the new man, who stood calmly, playing with the tooth between his thumb and forefinger. He lifted it up to one of the dimly lit lamps decorating the room to reveal the shield symbol.

Rachael breathed in heavily, still jostling against Jess's clutches, as the man scanned the tooth, carefully. She was acutely aware that he, whoever he was, would likely decide in the next few seconds whether or not she could be trusted, perhaps even whether she lived, or died.

The man lowered the tooth and gave Rachael a brief penetrating stare. With the weakest of grins, he nodded towards Jess, whose grip softened.

"Thank you," said Rachael, smiling.

He did not smile back. "Were you followed?"

"No," said Rachael, grabbing back her belongings from the table. "I was careful." The man continued to stare at her.

"Cauponi," he said, turning towards the barman and addressing him by what Rachael assumed had to be a codename. "We can't be too careful. We need to man the doors and keep a steady eye on any approach from outside. Prep everyone downstairs, they need to be ready for evac at a moment's notice. You…"

The man had turned to point at Rachael. "With me," he said, gesturing for her to follow.

Rachael nodded and followed briskly as he turned back into the dark opening he had emerged from. He stood opposite the door to the men's toilets, holding open the cellar door.

She nodded again and entered. The dizzying smell of stale ale and lemon-scented urinal blocks turned slowly to a fresh, chalky cold as she descended the narrow, wooden stairway into the cellar below.

The haunting lighting of the bar above was replaced by complete darkness. Rachael advanced slowly, her hands held out aimlessly as the stairs creaked beneath her, eager to find some source of light or stability.

Thankfully, she soon felt creaking wood turn to stone beneath her feet and heard a rustling from the man behind her. Lights clicked into action, quickly shedding light upon the scene below.

The room was larger than the bar above might have suggested. Doorways led through to five dark, narrow passageways, as though she had entered the heart of an underground labyrinth.

The brickwork was old, with cracks in the white paint where the elements had worn them away, and cobwebs plagued almost every corner and crevice. Bar supplies and cider bottles were stacked around the room, surrounded by large wooden beer kegs, each through plastic tubes supplying thirsty customers above.

Rachael heard a short gasp and turned to see a young boy emerge from one of the passageways. He stopped still, staring wide-eyed at the man behind Rachael, clutching a mop.

"Nothing to worry about Jim," came the man's deep voice from behind her. He moved past Rachael to ruffle the young boy's hair. "But you need to tell your mum we need to be ready to go as soon as possible, ok?"

The boy nodded, and with a final suspicious look at Rachael, he turned back to run down one of the passageways, leaving his mop behind.

"This way," said the man, resting the mop against the wall.

Rachael followed him into a dark, narrow corridor, which again seemed to lead to other smaller rooms.

Rachael peered through openings in the doors as she followed and saw countless eyes stare back at her, some scared, some curious. Each of the tiny rooms held camp beds or small bunk beds - all, Rachael assumed, offering sanctuary to those targeted by the Order.

"In here," said the man, and he halted outside a small room, barely big enough to house a small sink, kettle and fridge.

Rachael had evidently not lost her fixed look of incredulity at the scale of the pub's underground level as, for the first time, the man offered a hint of a smile.

"This is one of the oldest pubs in London," he said, inviting her to sit at one of the small plastic chairs. "Not many people know, but hundreds of years ago it used to be something of a criminal hideout. Naturally, it made a good spot for us and we've added a few touches of our own since we moved in."

He nodded towards the rooms they had passed, which she had noticed looked fresher than the cellar surrounds, and hastily built.

"There are a lot of people who need our help these days," he said, looking at her again with a penetrative, almost accusatory, stare.

Rachael looked back, trying not to display the sense of guilt that had quickly washed over her.

"So," he said, grabbing two beers from the fridge. "Peter is alive?"

He popped the cap from one of the bottles and slid it across the table towards her.

"Yes," said Rachael, taking it with a nod of thanks. "But I'm not sure how much longer he can last. I offered to help and he gave me this place."

"Ok," the man said, resting back in his chair. He took a large gulp. "My name is Dux, I head up our limited security operation. We had assumed when Peter was taken that he would be killed in an effort to crush the Resistance's morale. We've all been preparing for the sight of him hanging with the others at London Bridge, but it appears they had other ideas. That little Galton medal stunt… pretty clever."

Dux took another gulp.

"People began to panic. They began to question the movement and whether the man they had put their faith in was truly who they believed him to be. Splinter groups started to form, you might have seen the protests near Temple – completely disorganised, spontaneous, stupid. We found out about it too late to do anything; it was a massacre."

Rachael remembered – she had been watching the live footage from Peter's holding cell as G forced him to watch the scene unfold.

"Peter Brockland has become a talisman for our movement," Dux continued. "People just seem to be drawn to him and his story."

Rachael understood what he meant – Peter Brockland was nothing remarkable, not really. She had checked out his background whilst working for the Order when they had all been warned of Simon Brockland's return.

His family history was abnormal, sure, with a reportedly insane father having gone AWOL from a military operation whilst he was a young boy. But, as an averagely-successful arts writer with no obvious public presence, he had certainly not been a charismatic 'Messiah-type', and certainly not the sort of person one would expect to lead a revolutionary movement.

But Rachael had spent time with him; she had watched over him. Above all else, Peter Brockland possessed a spirit she had never witnessed before. Even as the Order agents sought to destroy him, physically and psychologically, he always fought back. Without fail, he always got back up, to fight for those he had come to represent.

Courage, selflessness and, even within the destitution of his caged existence, Peter possessed an infallible desire to help others. Even her, his captor. She could certainly see how he could become a talisman for people, whether he recognised it himself or not - someone they would gladly follow into battle.

Dux appeared to have read something from Rachael's glazed expression and smiled. She fought back blushes and nodded back. She noticed a change in Dux's demeanour. It felt as though he had finally believed she could be trusted.

"So why now?" Dux asked.

"What do you mean?" said Rachael quickly.

"You are..." he paused a second, looking at her again. "You were... one of them, working for the Order. An agent I would imagine, looking at you. Why turn now?"

Rachael shifted uncomfortably in her chair, considering how much she should tell him. Dux may have begun to trust her, but with this, with everything at stake for her, she could not risk putting her own trust in the wrong person.

"They've... changed," said Rachael, purposefully. "Their methods are more direct; they've become more callous than they have been before and they are getting away with it. People believe that they have changed things for the better. But -"

She paused, her voice cracking. "If they only knew what was coming, it's going to change everything."

"What is it?" Dux asked, for the first time possessing a look of real concern.

"They call it Progeny," said Rachael. "The next step in their genetic engineering plan - artificial insemination technology. It analyses the genetic components of two potential parent's DNA, and selects those best suited for each other, designed for a specific societal purpose."

Dux looked back at her, perplexed.

"I'm not the genetics expert, I'm afraid," said Rachael, with a weak smile. "But the Order's plan has always been to proactively manage human procreation, to control the production of children. They want to use Progeny to create the best soldiers, the strongest farmers, the smartest scientific minds. Everyone will be born to carry out a certain role; people will no longer have the freedom to choose who they want to have children with, or which children they might raise together. Mothers will have the genetic material of their future offspring selected for them, if they are lucky enough to be selected at all, based on their algorithms, using the analysis and predictions of the Progeny system. Those who don't comply... will be killed."

Dux's face dropped further and further as she explained, and by the time she had finished, he had shot up from his chair.

"How..." he stuttered, pacing the limited space. "How long have they had this?"

"They have been testing genetic engineering for years, ever since the early technology has been available, on animals mostly. But with their human tests, it never seemed to work – genetics is just far too complicated to predict. The procedures involved are by their very essence unpredictable. There are ways you can eliminate certain genetic traits, but you can never be certain of success; whole-scale genetic engineering to this scale was supposedly impossible."

Rachael looked up at Dux. "But they believe that they have perfected it, and with the power and resources they have at their disposal now -".

"We have to stop them," said Dux, weakly. He gripped the edge of his chair tightly, his expression fraught with shock and concern.

"We've got to move on them before it's too late," he continued, his vigour growing with every word. "One final defence, one final fightback for our futures, for our children's futures. What will Progeny do to the world if we allow it to succeed without a fight?"

Rachael felt the growing passion of his plea and nodded back.

"Ok…" he said, breathing heavily as a renewed purpose took control of him. "Ok."

The prospect of a fight to the death appeared to have been exactly what he needed. Dux paced the room uncontrollably, thinking.

"Did you come here with a plan?" he asked, still fidgeting. "This is going to take scale, organisation. We will need to mobilise every single one of us, anyone still sympathetic within the police, the army. We need to let them know exactly what we are facing."

"There are plenty within the Order not loyal to the cause," said Rachael. "There are many who may have been supportive of the light-touch eugenics; some are genuinely in it with the hope of eradicating needless disease and suffering. But the drastic moves they are taking towards restricting personal freedoms have put many off. They will break away if they think the Order will lose. And people out there, the army, the police, they won't accept this when they find out..."

"I agree," said Dux, nodding aimlessly. "At least, I hope so."

Rachael nodded, but before she had any chance to open discussions on battle plans, quickening footsteps approached from outside. The two of them turned abruptly to see the barman sprinting into the kitchen doorway, panting heavily.

"They're...here..." he managed through deep gasps. "Three of them... walking towards us... right now."

Dux reacted in a flash. He reached into his pocket and tossed Rachael's confiscated gun back towards her with a telling glance, before running out.

Rachael looked down at the gun in her hands, the final indication that Dux trusted her. This was her chance now to prove herself to the Resistance. But, she thought with a hint of anxiety, in doing so, the Order would finally realise her betrayal. Had she done enough to keep her safe?

Rachael threw the anxiety from her mind and pushed back her chair. She ran after Dux, through the cold passages and past the refugees frantically grabbing for their belongings, all being ushered towards the same dark passageway.

Rachael quickly caught up as they reached the cellar, and they both halted, listening for any commotion from above. Dux turned and indicated for Rachael to be silent as the families scurried through the various passageways below. With a brief nod towards her, they tiptoed up the cellar stairs, their guns ready.

Dux halted at the cellar door and turned his head to rest his ear against the wood, listening intently.

"Where are they going?" Rachael whispered from behind him, pointing back down towards the refugees bustling through the opening of the passageway.

"There are tunnels leading to other safehouses," he whispered back sharply, indicating for her to be quiet.

They both listened intently as a voice rang out from the bar in a deep, commanding tone.

"A woman came in here not long ago," the man said, addressing a younger member of the bar staff. "Red hair. Someone of considerable interest to us."

Rachael gulped; they knew then.

She listened as the young barmaid pleaded her ignorance from behind the bar, but Rachael was not really paying attention.

She had come to terms with what turning against the Order would mean, but now that they knew it, now that she was an official target – it suddenly felt so real.

She heard a scuffle from the other side of the door, and the sound of a stall knocked to the ground.

"Don't fucking play with me, girl. Where is she?"

Dux reacted to the threat in an instant. With one powerful thrust of his right boot, he kicked the cellar door open. He moved out quickly, and in one swift move had shot one round point-blank into the back of the agent's neck.

Rachael ran out from behind him and saw the agent slump to the floor, a pool of blood spilling steadily around him.

She looked up and saw the young barmaid shaking, her face completely pale but for a spatter of the agent's blood.

The pub door blasted open from beside them, and two agents rushed in. They stared at the agent lying lifeless on the floor and back up at Dux and Rachael, their lips pursed.

Rachael reacted quickly, and before Dux had any chance to move for his weapon, Rachael pulled her gun. With a ferocious speed, she shot the agents with pinpoint accuracy in the small gap beneath their visors.

They both crumpled, but as one fell, Rachael could see their finger cramping.

"Duck!" she screamed. As the agent's body hit the floor, shot after shot fired in succession.

The lights shattered, the television screen cracked, and the monitor fell to the ground with a crash. Bottles and pint glasses smashed from behind the bar, and shards of wood splintered from the wall and ceiling above. Everyone alive had thrown themselves aside, desperate for any cover.

After a few seconds of madness, Rachael heard the agent's rifle fall to the ground. The agent's finger must have finally surrendered its final act of defiance. The shooting had stopped, leaving behind an eerie silence interrupted only by the shallow breathing of Dux, Rachael and the young barmaid.

Rachael remained still, crouched in the alcove with her gun, listening for any sign of movement. With the sounds of slowly crunching glass, she chanced a look from the alcove and saw Dux crouched behind the bar.

"Just a scratch," she heard the barmaid say, breathing heavily from behind the bar.

"There will be more of them," said Rachael, lifting herself to her feet and peering out towards the bodies sprawled across the bar floor. "They will know they have been killed, they will send more agents."

"You know what to do," said Dux gently to the barmaid, patting her shoulder gently as he helped her to her feet. She nodded silently with a determined smile and ran past Rachael, down into the cellar below.

Dux stood opposite Rachael, staring around at the damage. He seemed to be pondering something for a moment before he turned abruptly, rounding on her.

"How did they know you were here?" he shouted, pinning her to the wall with one strong thrust. His eyes bulged, and his face, only inches from her own, was contorted with rage. "We could have been killed!"

"I don't know!" Rachael fired back, struggling against his grip.

With all the strength she could muster, Rachael thrust herself into the wall behind her, using the force to kick Dux away.

He stumbled backwards, and they both collected themselves, squaring up and glaring at each other.

"I didn't bring them here," said Rachael. "Obviously."

She nodded down towards the agents she had killed. Dux seemed to soften slightly, accepting her point, but he did not deter from his position.

"Why were they after you? What had you done for them to suspect you?"

Rachael stared back at him, his face still full of befuddled anger. Now was the time to tell him the truth.

"It's my daughter," she said with a deep sigh. "All agents who choose to have children are required to have them tested regularly for any signs of genetic abnormality. Since last year, those who have risked it have had it done at the pregnancy screening stage."

Rachael looked up and noticed that Dux's stance had softened further. He looked back at her in complete shock, without interruption.

"Before then, I was supposed to send her for an evaluation on her first birthday, but..." she paused, betraying a look of desperate weakness. "I couldn't do it. What if she had come back as incompatible? I couldn't send my daughter for sterilisation, or termination. I knew then that I had to get out. I had to escape, to keep her safe. I thought that I was helping to change the world in the Order, but when I had Mia, I seemed to snap out of it. I knew they could not be allowed to continue. I had to stop them, and Peter gave me my opportunity."

Dux stared back at her. He tried, and failed, to speak, to offer some consoling words, but instead fixed a sympathetic look. His quest for words was cut short as the sound of quickening footsteps came from below, creaking up the cellar stairs.

The barmaid appeared back from the cellar, breathing heavily. Her arm was still bleeding, grazed by the stray rifle shots, but it had not affected her spirit.

"Everyone's gone," she said. "Scopum and Celeritas are going to stay behind and help fend off the next ones."

"Ok," said Dux, weakly, turning from Rachael. "Make sure that you're clear of the blast range before you detonate."

Detonate? Rachael stared at Dux, but he did not answer. Instead, he maintained his penetrative glare upon the barmaid.

She nodded back, but her face tightened as the unmistakable sound of a car accelerated towards the pub from inside, growing louder and louder.

"Go on," said Dux, frantically waving for the barmaid to leave. "Quickly, go!"

She obeyed, disappearing down the cellar stairs as two women came the other way. Both had long straggly hair, and their faces were almost identical - scarred and resolute, right down to the same determined look.

"They're here," said Dux. As he said it, they heard a car screech to a halt outside. "Fire some warning shots. We'll lead them through the side alley while the others escape. Hopefully, we can buy them enough time."

The twins nodded back and rushed towards the front of the pub, crouching beneath the front window, shattered in places by the dying agent's aimless rifle shots. They peered through the small bullet hole gaps, preparing for their attack.

"Ok," said Dux, turning back to Rachael, with fire in his eyes. "Are you ready?"

36

Days had passed since Peter had revealed the Resistance's whereabouts, with no news, no indication that his trust in Rachael had been well placed. He turned to his side uncomfortably and pulled himself to his feet with a groan, cursing his latest episode of disturbed sleep.

He felt around in the darkness for the small scratch in the floor that pointed towards the cell door, and crawled towards it, reaching aimlessly in the hope that food had been delivered whilst he slept.

Nothing materialised. His stomach rumbled painfully.

Peter leant back against the wall and tried to catch his breath. The demonstrable drop in food rations that had accompanied Rachael's departure had left him weak – even the effort of crawling a couple of metres left him gasping.

His mind raced as his lungs hunted desperately for oxygen. He hoped that Rachael's prolonged absence meant that she had been successful and that the necessary groundwork was being put into place to pull together the offensive.

Peter often daydreamed in his periods of starved lethargy, imagining how the final revolution might play out, of destroying the Order's hold on society and returning to a normal life. But was that even possible now? So much had changed. It was farcical to imagine himself sitting back into the clutches of his middle-of-the-range ergonomic desk chair in six months' time, clutching a stale office coffee as he planned his next article.

It was almost as if his time as an arts journalist had become a shadowed memory of some previous incarnation. The man he was now was so totally different from the one that had spent his days in self-conscious anticipation for the latest reaction to an art review.

The country too would change, whatever the outcome, whoever ultimately won the battle. The Order, however brutal their methods, however loud the public outcry at the lengths they had gone to, had exposed a thread of societal sympathy for eugenics that might perhaps never be woven back into the fabric of taboo opinion.

The promise to eradicate hereditary disease and build a world free of unnecessary suffering had resonated, it must have done; they could not have risen to such prominence so quickly otherwise.

Eugenics, in some form or another, seemed a concept that, with the advances in technology, many in society could sympathise, regardless of its sinister history.

Fortunately for the Resistance, the brutality and despotism with which the Order had continued to consolidate power had worked in their favour. Though their beliefs were fanatically scientific, offering no apparent ideological distinction between class, race or creed, the inhumane lengths that they had been prepared to go to – sterilisation, forced abortion, imprisonment, murder – seemed enough to convince many who had been sympathetic that they were misguided. Or, at least, he hoped so.

If the Order had truly developed technology to eradicate disease and ensure a perfectly functioning, healthy society, were the impositions on personal freedoms something people could stomach? How much would one human life be worth when compared with the good of the human race?

Peter jumped at the sound of rustling outside his cell door. His heart raced as he heard the low hiss of the small hatch sliding open. He pounced, throwing himself towards the opening as a small tray of food was pushed through.

In the limited light offered by the portal to the outside, he was shocked to find a greater quantity than his previous days. Was it her? The hatch slid shut as quickly as it had opened, leaving the room in darkness again.

Blindly, Peter grabbed at the tray, feeling for the bread - two slices this time. He had also been given a small beaker, and with no regard for its contents, he devoured the meal. Ignoring the immediate onset of brain freeze, he felt a euphoric rush of strength; he had almost forgotten what milk tasted like.

He put the beaker down and moved ferally towards the additional chicken leg, unashamedly drooling. As he tore into the salted flesh his hand brushed against something small and cold.

Peter picked up the object and twisted it in his hands. With a click, a light appeared from one end, blinding him.

He blinked away tears and pointed the small torch towards the tray. A small piece of paper lay next to the beaker, with a flurry of rushed handwriting… 'Tomorrow'. He turned the note over in his hands and reached again for the chicken, devouring it too, as he contemplated the note's meaning.

Was it Rachael? Had she returned? Had their plan been successful?

Peter sat back as the chicken leg, bread, and milk curdled in his stomach. He had not eaten that much in one sitting for what felt like a very long time. He leant against the wall and reached towards the note again, allowing his imagination to once again take hold.

*****

Lights flickered, illuminating Peter's cell for the first time in days, waking him from another daydream.

His eyes watered as the lights continued to flicker on and off, on and off.

Peter listened intently. The note had told him something was going to happen tomorrow, but without any concept of time or how long he had slept for, was it time?

He heard the faint sound of alarms ringing out from the corridors, and with the brief seconds of flickering light, saw shadows pass by the cell door, all moving swiftly in the same direction.

Excitement took hold of him, and whether a result of the additional sustenance or the onset of adrenaline, his weakness seemed to abate. He was alert. He was ready for action.

Peter lifted himself slowly and moved towards the cell door, peering through the frosted glass as the lights inside the cell continued to flicker. More and more shadowed figures rushed by as the alarms continued to blare out. Something had happened, something big – it must have done.

The lights suddenly stopped flickering, and he was again plunged into darkness. He continued to listen intently, placing his ear against the glass and heard a faint whirring, growing steadily louder.

Seconds later, his cell lit up, but this time with a dim red glow. It reminded Peter of his early days as a journalist, visiting the various dark rooms the photographers would use to process their art. The facility had been plunged into panic mode. This had to be it.

Peter strolled aimlessly, fidgeting, his mind racing. The Order had to be under attack. What would they do with him now? Would he be left to rot in his cell alone? Would they finally come to finish him for good?

Peter continued to move, unable to remain still. He could not bear to remain with his thoughts in this room any longer, not knowing. The Resistance could be out there, fighting while he lingered in this cell, awaiting his fate.

He moved towards the cell door again, looking around for something he could use as a tool, intent on somehow prising, or smashing, it open. It was as though they had read his mind.

Peter looked up at the glass again and saw three shadowy figures. They did not pass by frantically this time but stood stationary, looking directly at him. This was it.

He stepped back as the door slid open to reveal the long, sneering face of the agent they called 'G'. She was flanked by two burly Order agents, kitted in their slick white bodysuits, their weapons poised.

"Well," she said darkly, edging towards him. "It appears your friends have come for you."

Peter looked directly into the barrel of the gun facing him.

G continued to approach as the door slid slowly shut behind her. She looked angry, her taut expression even more menacing in the dim red light of the cell. Peter raised his hands slowly behind his head.

"I think it's you they've come for," said Peter.

She smiled weakly, staring at him.

Peter had grown accustomed to her arrogance during their exchanges, but as he looked back at her face, he saw it etched with concern. Whatever had happened, she had lost her aura of smug confidence. Yet still, she stood in front of him now, her gun raised, his life at her mercy.

This was it then, Peter thought. He had lasted this long, but his time had come to its dark end, here in the cell he had reluctantly been resident in for so long.

In reality, he had come to accept that his time there would likely end with his death. But knowing that the Resistance was still out there causing the Order problems had given him strength, the same strength his father had possessed, to face his own demise head-on.

"No need to string it out," he said, smiling weakly, and he lowered his arms back to his side.

She stared at him blankly, clearly taken aback. Her finger trembled over the trigger, and her cold eyes bore into his.

Peter took a deep, final breath, accepting his fate, and closed his eyes.

37

Claire Phelan began to slow her march. A light showering of rain began to fall upon a scene wrought with tension, silent but for the rhythmic march of thousands of footsteps behind her. The Resistance protestors were making their way through the narrow streets of Birmingham.

Claire looked ahead, wiping away raindrops as the Bullring emerged from the buildings on either side, and down towards the wall of SCF agents, police officers and military forces. She slowed to a halt and raised a clenched fist, indicating for those behind to follow suit.

They obeyed, lurching to a stop. Claire always did have a way of marshalling a crowd, experience she was sure developed from her days as a headmistress - in another life.

The streets around them remained silent, deserted. Central Birmingham, usually so alive with the hustling and bustling of everyday life, was empty now but for the horde of supporters behind her. The meandering streets of Birmingham had become the battleground setting for the Resistance fightback.

Claire remained alert, clutching her mobile phone in anticipation of news of the others, still marvelling at what the Resistance had achieved.

Just hours ago, the call had gone out through various encrypted methods lost on her, urging those who wished to fight back for their freedoms to take to the streets, tonight, together, in a nationwide stand. And now, here in Birmingham, they had come in their thousands.

The rain clouds above darkened, and, as though offering the starting light for the night ahead, the streetlights slowly flickered into action. With a low rumble of thunder from above, rain fell more heavily.

Claire swept aside her fringe as lights danced across the iconic bubble-like walls of the Bullring, where they knew Peter Brockland was being held, where Dux was planning his escape.

She glanced again towards the ominous defence ahead of them. Hundreds of white uniforms stood tall ahead of an even larger group of police and military forces. If the sheer numbers against them were not enough to deter their resolve, on either side of the front line of agents sat six tanks, all painted white, their guns pointed towards the incoming attack.

Claire's mind wandered back to life just two years ago before tragedy had struck. Even now, there, she found it difficult to process just how much had changed. It had only been weeks after her wedding day that she had first encountered that strange tattoo when the Order had stolen her future from her.

Claire felt her fist vibrate, wrenching her from her thoughts. "What is it?" she asked nervously.

"Choppers incoming," came a rushed voice between deep breaths. "They don't appear to be armed, though."

She cut the line and looked to the sky. On cue, she heard the rushing sounds of incoming rotors from the darkened clouds above.

"You will disperse," came an echoed voice from overhead, only just discernible against the torrent of wind and rain as the helicopter descended. "Return to your homes immediately!"

Claire heard a rustling from behind her; the crowd had become anxious, struggling against the force of the rotor-fuelled breeze. She lifted a clenched fist high into the air again, and silence fell.

A beam of light fell upon the crowd from the searchlight above, blinding them as they scoured the crowd. But still, they remained obedient, unmoving.

"You will disperse!" the voice came again, with greater urgency. "Or you will be treated as enemies of the peace and detained or killed on sight!"

The crowd rumbled slightly at the threat, and Claire heard many nearby reaching anxiously for their weapons. She held her fist in position resolutely, and the helicopter passed overhead.

Many behind her had been seasoned police officers or soldiers, and attended the march in full regalia, having been unable to accept the regime they had been duty-bound to protect. But most were just ordinary citizens, extraordinarily brave ordinary citizens, with little, if any, combat experience. They had all come, young and old, knowing the dangers they faced - to fight for their futures, for their family, for their freedoms.

Claire did not blame them for being nervous, it had only been Indici's last-minute intervention that had prevented her from giving up all that time ago. Picturing herself teetering on the ledge of that twelve-storey car park clutching the images of those she had lost, desperately trying to escape the pain, gave her the strength she needed to fight on.

But she had never escaped that final look of fear in her husband's eyes, as he sprinted towards her in that dark alleyway - before the tattooed stranger had murdered him, stabbed her and left them for dead as she clutched his lifeless body. She would never forget that face.

Inadvertently, her hand drifted towards the scar. Whether the assailant had intended to kill her, or her unborn child, or just intended to cause such damage as to prevent her from having children in future, she never discovered. Either way, with that accurate pierce of the knife, the assailant had achieved their goal.

She felt another buzz and pulled up the phone again. A text had come in from Justine, which had, in typical, curt fashion, let her know it was time – 'Good to go. Good luck.'

Claire slid the phone back into her pocket with a deep, steadying breath. She desperately hoped that Justine was right, not for herself, but for those behind her. Looking out again towards the defensive display ahead of them, if they had not turned, if she had not convinced them… this was suicide.

The beam of light returned, shining brightly in their direction as the helicopter turned from above the Bullring and flew back towards them.

Claire dabbed at her eyes, embracing the rain against her face, and begged for the sound to come. Another rumble came from above. This time it was not the ominous rush of the helicopter rotors; it was time.

"Ready!" Claire shouted, turning to face the crowd behind her. She had never been one for passionate speeches, but this felt enough.

"Ready!" they shouted back in unison. The ground reverberated beneath her as they stomped their feet and thrust their weapons into the air.

She looked out amongst them, men and women dressed in whatever protective gear they had been able to find, and fixed her gaze upon a young, teenage boy. He stood defiantly, thrusting his team baseball bat into the air, his face etched with passion.

Claire hid a sudden onset of melancholy. Many of the people there would die tonight, but she had to remain strong. They had a job to do, all of them. If they were to die, they would do so fighting for what they believed in, fighting for a better world.

Claire turned back to face the Bullring. She gulped, clutching her rifle in one hand, and the photo in the other. At the sound of their roars, the agents ahead had crouched to the ground, battle-ready, their rifles poised. She waited patiently for the final signal.

38

Seconds passed, yet the final shot never came. He was still alive.

Instead, his eyes still screwed shut, Peter heard scuffles around him. He opened his eyes to find the flanking Order agents had turned on G. The larger one restrained her in a tight chokehold, as the other retreated from a flailing kick. G's gun slipped from her grasp and fell just feet away from him.

Peter threw himself towards it. Warmth seemed to rush through his fingers as he grasped the grip; it felt good, as though some form of power had been restored.

The lights continued to flash red, and the sirens continued to blare out from outside the cell. Confused and disorientated, Peter moved backwards and raised the gun towards the agents, his grip shaking as he tried to make sense of what had happened. What was going on? How was he still alive?

G continued to struggle against the larger agent, but with one swift strike to the back of her head from the other, she succumbed and fell unconscious to the floor.

Peter remained confused and still, pointing the gun from one agent to the other until he noticed a hint of striking red hair. The smaller agent turned towards him and removed her helmet. Rachael looked back at him, shaking her head to release her hair from its hold.

Peter's jaw dropped, and the gun fell limply to his side. He had been right to trust her. The wave of relief might well have flattened him were it not for his curiosity as to who the other agent was.

Content that G was subdued, the other agent turned towards him. They lifted a pair of large arms to remove their helmet and revealed a large, bald head.

"Dux..." Peter gasped, and he dropped his gun to the floor.

Dux smiled back and looked him up and down. "You look terrible."

Peter let out a sharp laugh, in what felt like the first time he had laughed in years. With a swift move forward, he embraced Dux in a strong one-armed hug.

"When you are both finished..." said Rachael impatiently from beside them.

"Don't worry," said Peter, still smiling. "There's one for you too."

"We're in the middle of something here," she retorted, pulling G's helmet from her before throwing it towards him."Gear up."

Peter looked down at the helmet as Rachael checked the corridor outside, then towards G's crumpled figure, and back at the helmet. He was not quite sure he liked what Rachael was implying. "Wait," said Peter, comprehension dawning. "I'm wearing..."

His fears were quickly confirmed as Dux knelt beside G.

"Yep," Dux replied as he began to remove G's protective suit.

"Hers?"

"Hers."

"But it won't..."

"Fit?" said Dux, standing up with G's suit in his hands.

He looked Peter up and down again, taking in his famished physique. "I think you'll get away with it."

Peter snatched at the suit as Dux chuckled, glad of the colour of the room to hide his blushes.

He slowly stepped into the white, rubbery armour and found that it stretched with surprising ease to clip in at his waist. Bitterly, he continued. The suit was indeed fitting him, albeit tightly. It appeared that his period of near-starvation had more of an effect on his body than he had imagined, exacerbated further by the reacquaintance with Dux's daunting figure beside him.

"The food hasn't been great you know..." said Peter meekly as he fastened his chest guard.

The suit felt sleek, wetsuit-like, but as soon as the various parts clipped together, the material appeared to solidify, shaping itself to his body. Once fastened, he felt an intense warmth as a current appeared to run through the suit, shocking it into a near-impenetrable state, giving him the look of a far more enhanced physique.

Dux laughed, but Rachael turned towards him with a stern expression. Peter smiled apologetically; had it not been for her additional food rations, his stay in the cell would have been considerably worse.

"Sorry," he said weakly.

She continued to look stern until her eyes flickered to his chest. Peter followed her gaze to find his suit considerably more padded than he had expected.

"Nice tits," she said, unable to restrain a playful smile.

She moved towards him and handed him a gun and knife for his leg pocket.

"You couldn't have found a man to disarm I suppose," said Peter, taking himself in once more.

Though the material had shaped itself remarkably to his figure, the suit was clearly intended for a female inhabitant. Dux chuckled again.

"Come on," said Rachael, stern again as she moved back towards the cell door.

She peered outside, left and right, left and right. After a third check, she nodded back towards Dux, who immediately put on his helmet and pulled down the visor. He turned to look at Peter and with a swift nod, gripped his rifle and moved outside.

Peter slid his hands into G's gloves, surprised by the same rubbery warmth that quickly spread through his fingers, and followed. He stopped behind Rachael, who remained at the door opening.

"You look great," she said with a playful wink, and she pulled down her visor. "Now let's end this shall we?"

Peter smiled and offered an agreeing nod. He pulled G's helmet up from beside him and placed it on his head, no longer surprised to find that it too made for a comfortable fit. He pulled down the visor and gasped.

As soon as it had clicked into place, the inside had burst into life, projecting the scene around him as though he were in some sort of computer game. He had expected only a shaded vision of what stood before him, but instead, the white surroundings of his cell had been replaced by green computer graphics, accompanied by statistics: his heart rate; distances between obstacles; even a percentage indicating the defensive integrity of his suit – thankfully, 100%.

He glanced at his hands and gun to find the helmet analysing the weapon. "Glock 17 Gen 4" appeared in small green text above the green outline of his gun, with "9 x 19mm" to the side – his remaining ammunition.

"Rach," he gasped, forgetting his situation. "The visor… it's, it's amazing!"

He looked ahead at Rachael's now-digitised form, which looked back at him from the cell door. The visor analysed her too, scanning her face and body. It highlighted the limited areas of weakness in her protective suit and identified her weapon, the same Glock 17. The analysis also seemed to hone in on her facial expression, drawing out further green text: IMPATIENT.

Peter laughed. Her name had appeared too, along with her official Order agent classification. As his eyes lingered on her information, it seemed to trigger further analysis, and more details appeared - number of kills, mission counts, years of service.

Opting to overlook the worryingly high kill number, he continued to focus on the statistics. The analysis completed by highlighting her outline in flashing red - DEFECTOR, KILL ON SIGHT.

"You will need to get used to that pretty quickly," she said urgently. "Or else risk your life without it."

Her red outline turned to look back towards Dux, waiting for his signal.

"They know about you," said Peter, weakly. "They know that you're helping the Resistance."

"Of course they know," she replied. "They almost killed me at your meeting place."

"Come on, we need to go," she said, moving towards him. "Here."

She felt into her side pocket and handed Peter a flash drive, his father's. He glanced down at it, lost for words, and watched his visor make its primary scan. Red text quickly protruded from the small green outline – DANGER. STOLEN PHROX PROPERTY. DESTROY IMMEDIATELY.

"It's time we brought down the system, don't you think?" said Rachael.

He looked back up at her, and the visor recalibrated. He turned his eyes back to the flashing red text - DEFECTOR - and focused on it for a second, his curiosity getting the better of him. More text appeared.

FAILURE TO COMPLY WITH MISSION ORDER – DISPOSAL OF INCOMPATIBLE: DAUGHTER.

"Rachael," said Peter, his face dropping with a sudden comprehension. "Your daughter."

He watched Rachael's digitised hand move towards him, and she lifted his visor. She did not look angry, but her face exuded proud defiance.

Like his father, had her loyalty to the Order only faltered when it had been her own family at stake? He had found the strength to forgive his father, albeit not in time for him to know. Could he accept her too; did it matter?

"We don't have time to talk through this."

A few metres away, shots fired towards Dux, pulling them away from the distraction.

Dux had rushed behind a wall opposite to avoid the gunfire and looked up at Rachael and Peter, nodding.

"Let's do this!" he shouted.

Rachael nodded back and grabbed at both her guns. She breathed in deeply. With a nod, she moved out, taking wild shots in the direction of the incoming Order agents. She reached Dux without injury and knelt beside him.

Peter peered out from the cell door, gripping both his pistols with similar vigour. He pulled down his visor, and it quickly drew his attention towards two legs emerging from behind a wall at the end of the corridor. Rachael had managed to hit one of the agents on her way through.

The shots had stopped firing, and Peter took his chance. He took a deep breath and noticed his heart rate on the left side of his visor, though he had not needed the escalating numbers to tell him his heart was beating through his chest. He closed his eyes to calm himself; he needed to be prepared. He opened his eyes and saw his heart rate had steadied - he took a step outside.

The other agent had not yet appeared, and he continued sideways towards the others, his guns still poised to fire on sight. Only seconds away from the others, he saw the Order agent appear. His visor reacted long before he did and, within milliseconds, had analysed the agent ahead of him - SURPRISED.

Peter looked at the agent and saw them peer down, first at Peter's chest before lifting their glance to his jaw. His protruding Adam's apple and overgrowing stubble seemed enough to stun the agent opposite.

In that split second, Peter had been given his chance to shoot, and his visor dutifully identified his target. Without hesitation, Peter shot three rounds towards the agent's neck, connecting with his final effort.

The agent fell backwards and dropped their rifle to grab their throat. The agent writhed on the floor a moment before green text emerged from the, now still, outline – DECEASED.

"This way!" Rachael shouted, moving out from behind Dux and grabbing Peter's shoulder.

Dux ran out and scouted ahead, his rifle poised. Peter followed, still gripping his guns, resisting the almost overpowering urge to explore the visor's incredible technology.

The three of them continued to move until they reached a corridor on the building's outer surface. The famous Bullring exterior was entirely covered by its iconic aluminium disc architecture, but from this side, the wall was transparent, revealing with unwavering accuracy the dramatic scenes unfolding outside.

Peter slowed to a halt. Looking out at the digitised scene outside, the perils of his current situation had deserted him. His mind was awash with stunned confusion, and he soon became overloaded by statistical analysis.

He lifted his visor slowly to look upon the scene with his own eyes, just to see if the staggering numbers on the screen were true.

Marching towards the Bullring were thousands – 11,327 if his visor was to be believed - of people. Not just civilians either; green text erupted with background checks, identifying who the people were. Ordinary citizens - painters, beauticians, shop workers - joined huge numbers of defecting soldiers and police officers, all donned in their uniforms, in direct defiance against the regime.

United in their purpose, they all clutched various weapons of sorts and wore the same eerie white mask that had so eloquently come to represent the antipathy towards the PHROX regime. The Resistance was here, in their united thousands, to take back their lives.

Peter urgently scanned for signs of the Order's defence and was horrified to find that, however many people might be marching towards them, the Order had been prepared. Tanks flanked either side of a wall of white as Order agents stood ominously ahead of police officers and soldiers who had remained loyal to their government.

Peter's mouth drained of moisture. He watched as the Resistance approached, some documenting their approach on smartphones, some flying anti-PHROX banners, some wielding placards of faces, perhaps of those lost to the regime, or symbols of hope and… he blushed as he saw a large banner depicting his face.

Though bursting with pride, he pictured the bloodbath inevitably set to follow. He saw the faces of the crowd and foresaw the scene as they fell to the ground in pools of their own blood. This was it; they could not fail. He could not fail.

He slowly pulled his visor down again and noticed a warning alert - WARNING: INCOMPATIBLE FORCES APPROACHING. ETA 15 MINUTES.

"Peter!" came a frantic voice from behind him. It was a woman's voice, Rachael.

The shock of the scene outside subsided as he felt a pull on his shoulder. He looked back at Rachael blankly and noticed a change in her expression as she too glanced out towards the crowd. For the first time in the limited period he had known her, the calm demeanour had vanished; her face had drained of colour, and her eyes widened.

He felt a rush of hot air graze past his right ear as a bullet rushed past, missing him by millimetres to collide with the glass exterior with a high-pitched crack. Rachael pushed him to the ground and jumped on top of him as Dux fired shot after shot towards the two Order agents.

"Are you okay?" she shouted frantically, checking him for signs of injury.

"Yes," he said blankly, breathing intensely and staring back at her. "Outside… the people outside..."

Rachael ignored him and pulled him up to his feet. She turned quickly and fired towards the now cowering agents.

"Come on!" she said, pushing him towards the end of the passageway, away from the scene outside.

Peter chanced one final look at the marching crowds before the passageway slalomed left. Dux stood over the writhing body of the remaining Order agent, his gun poised.

"Outside," said Peter again, gasping for breath as they continued to run towards their destination. Rachael did not respond. Instead, she continued to advance, searching for something in the outer walls.

"Rachael!" Peter shouted frantically. "Outside! The people. It's going to be a bloodbath!"

"Don't worry," she said, half ignoring him as she continued her search. "It's all part of the plan."

"The plan?" Peter asked, incredulous. "What plan?"

"Peter..." she said, giving up on her search to look back at him. "We are fighting back. Did you not expect a battle? Today, we destroy the Order."

"But, how?" said Peter, blankly. "How are there so many?"

"The Resistance has been mobilising whilst you've been held hostage," came a low voice behind him. Dux had caught up. "Not just here, but everywhere they are marching on the Order."

"No gunshot?" Peter asked.

"He'll live," said Dux with a wry smile.

"They've been pulling troops together for months: social media, personal visits, rallies. You name it, they've done it..." Rachael continued.

"Brilliant," said Peter. "Really, brilliant."

He could not help but be staggered by the amount that they had been able to achieve in the time he had been incarcerated. More so, his faith in the public had been restored. His bleak periods in the cell left him contemplating just how much, if at all, the public disagreed with the regime, how much they might actually support the Order's policies.

"And they are all prepared to..."

"Fight," Rachael interrupted with her customary steely glare. "Fight for our lives back."

Peter grimaced. It all felt so rushed, so real, all of a sudden. He had spent his past few months alone, useless, confined to his cell. But outside, the Resistance had mobilised and marched towards their target, prepared to fight, and die, to defeat the regime.

"But they'll die..." said Peter, his mind racing back to the cold, lifeless eyes of Raj's wife lying ahead of him on the grass. That could be all of them in only a matter of moments.

"Peter," said Rachael calmly, clasping his shoulders. She pulled up her visor and offered a rare consoling look.

He looked back, gaunt at the thought of those thousands about to die outside fighting for the cause he had started, all the while contending with the knowledge that it had to happen; they had to fight. There was no other way.

"Peter, there is nothing particularly special about you..."

Peter snapped out of his brief depression. "I was hoping for something a little more comforting."

Rachael smiled back. "Peter, there is nothing particularly special about you, but look at what you have achieved. All those people out there..."

She pointed towards the outer wall.

"You have helped them to find the courage to stand against this oppression, to fight for their freedoms and their children's futures. It all started with one man who would not accept that he was unequal. One man who would not accept that his father died for nothing. You, Peter, nothing particularly-special you, inspired them all by taking a stand. They know now that anyone can stand up to the Order and take their lives back. Their fate is not your responsibility, but your inspiration to claim their lives back is. You must let them choose their future."

Peter stared back. He knew she was only trying to be kind. Perhaps she had even meant the passionate response, but he would certainly not thank her for reminding him that those marching for their futures might soon die because they had been inspired by his own rebellion.

"They are buying us the time that we need to end this, for good."

She stared at him, a fire burning in her bright green eyes.

"Don't waste it," she said, holding out her hand. "Now come on, let's end this."

Peter looked up at her again and nodded, clasping her hand.

39

How had it come to this?

The president's palms trembled with the force of his grasp as he leant down into the grips of his mahogany desk. He peered out through the glass, down towards the streets below.

His life's work, his father's, all of it, mankind's very future, the Order's own existence – they had never before been under such cataclysmic threat. And it had come under his watch. He pictured his father's disappointed expression with a grimace.

Sunlight had long faded, its beautiful orange glow against the spire of St Martin's Cathedral replaced by darkening grey clouds, interrupted only by the searchlight above, useless in its attempt to disperse the marching crowd.

Beautiful, yet dangerous. The only religion is science, he thought. No God could control the development of this species, only science. No God, short of those questionable fairytales, had saved humanity from disease and suffering, only science. It was imperative, whatever happened this evening, that the Order survived. Imperative, not just for him – he did not matter now – but for the survival of humankind.

He withdrew his gaze from the cathedral spire, and looked down at them, the thousands of degenerates and sympathisers slowly marching towards them to reclaim some fallacy of freedom.

Could they not understand what the Order was, what they were trying to do? Were their minds so utterly warped by their infantile perception of social morality that they could not understand that the human race was far more important than any one of them? The Order, Progeny, would help rid the world of needless disease, improve strength and intelligence - the essential next step to prevent human devolution.

Secrecy had been essential; he knew that now. Though it had not been part of the plan, their gamble had failed. To have allowed themselves to be discovered, to be exposed, had been a mistake. They had grown too big. They had underestimated their opponents, underestimated the Brocklands. How could he have been so foolish, so reckless?

"President, Sir..."

A timid voice crackled through his desk intercom, breathing heavily. "President, Sir..."

"Yes?" he responded, unsurprised to hear the weariness in his voice.

"Sir, the incompatibles. They've stopped marching."

The president turned back from his desk and looked out again towards the horde below. They had indeed stopped, a few hundred metres from where the Order forces were stationed, completely still but for the rippling of their banners in the evening breeze.

It had started to rain. With the slow flickering of the streetlights, the crowd looked impressive, even he had to admit, with their stolen weapons and those menacing masks.

"Yes," the president replied calmly. "I can see."

He released the intercom button with a sigh and turned to a cupboard nearby. He walked towards it slowly, and with a gentle press of his hand, the door hissed open to reveal his pristine white protective suit. He ran his fingers across the material he had helped to design for the first time in what must have been years. How had he allowed this to happen? He sighed and turned back to the intercom.

"Initiate protocol ADRB2."

"Sir?" came the voice, weaker still at the request.

"ADRB2 agent. Initiate immediately. Take the latest batch."

"But Sir, I want to…"

"Agent," the president repeated sternly. "ADRB2, that is a direct order. I will not ask you again."

He paused a second, turning back to look outside. "Too much is at stake. The Order must survive."

"Yes, Sir," came the voice again before cutting out.

The president recognised the reluctance in the young man's voice. He wanted to defend their mighty cause; of course he did. He almost felt guilty preventing the agent from having his chance to do so, but they needed to be prepared for whatever outcome.

"President, Sir…"

G had entered the room, flanked by two agents. He turned to look at her, resting his hands again against the sleek mahogany. He said nothing, offering only an inquisitive stare. Her face was flustered, bruised, and she was not wearing her suit.

"What's happened?" he asked. "Why aren't you wearing your suit?"

It had been G that had convinced him to embark on this foolish escapade. It was she who had convinced him that the ageing Simon Brockland would no longer be a credible threat, she who had convinced him to put the very survival of their organisation at risk.

"Sir," she said sheepishly. "Peter Brockland has escaped, aided by one of the Resistance and the defector, R24. They took my suit."

Her face was bleeding below the left eye; he must have goaded her into entering the cell, the fool. Even now, she stood tall, remarkably sure of herself in light of this failure. But then, he had trained her. She was a product of his teachings, his responsibility. He stared at her intently.

"It was only a matter of time," he muttered, more to himself than anyone else. He turned again towards the scene outside, his arms crossed. The agents remained still, awaiting orders. The sky had grown darker still, the steadily heavier rain the only disturbance to the city lights illuminating the battlefield below.

"Georgina," he said calmly, addressing her by name. "I have initiated protocol ADRB2."

Georgina's demeanour fell, not only at the news but at the use of her name; he was disappointed.

"But Sir," she pleaded, risking a move towards him. "We have them outnumbered, outgunned. We can't possibly be defeated."

"Don't be so naive," he snapped back, his gaze still fixed on the scene below. He knew responsibility for the day's events ultimately lay with him but he could not dissolve his anger - that she had been able to convince a foolish old man to change tact.

"Those people out there are organised, fighting for what they believe is a higher cause than our own. They fight to whatever end for their very survival, their parents' survival, their children's survival. Humanity has not evolved to extend that level of determination to protect the species; that's where we step in. We protect humankind from the dangers of degeneration. We cannot take any more risks."

He sighed again.

"Secrecy was our shield, it was our protection, their protection. I can see now that it was critical to our success. The people out there... just don't understand. They can't understand."

There was silence for a minute until...

"I'm sorry, Sir."

The president turned from the glass. Georgina stared down at the floor with that face he had known for so long might be his downfall, that face he still could not distinguish from the young girl whose parents had to die. He pictured the young recruit who had accepted, without argument, that her chance at a family was forfeit, that ambitious recruit so desperate to prove herself worthy enough to step into Simon Brockland's shadow, the terrified young girl he had protected from her failures for so long.

His desperate efforts to replace his former protégée had moulded her into what she was now: reckless and cruel.

"Georgina," he said calmly. "ADRB2, can you handle it? In the event of my death, do you have what it takes to initiate the protocol?"

She lifted her face and stared up at the president - the foolish old man whose dogmatic dedication to secrecy had for so long held back their true potential. She manipulated her face into a look of shame.

"Secrecy," he continued, placing two guns in his suit holster. "Secrecy, whatever you may think, is imperative."

"Yes, Sir," she said with a quick nod.

"Ok," the president sighed, looking intently at her. "I suspect Peter Brockland will be going for the mainframe, and with R24, his route will be a great deal easier. Kit up. He must not succeed. We must not lose those algorithms."

Georgina nodded again and turned out of the room, beckoning towards the other agents.

They turned to follow, but one held back, awaiting one final order. The president looked intently towards the agent, his face betraying a hint of pain. He nodded.

The agent nodded back obediently and followed the others out of the room.

The president turned back to the scene below and up towards the helicopter overhead, still urging the crowd to disperse, knowing full well they would not. They had come too far to turn back now. It was death for them either way.

He thought of Georgina and sighed. Whosever responsibility it may have been, she had become too reckless; she was too dangerous to them now. He knew she was no longer pure in their doctrine; she had twisted their beliefs to suit her own vision. She would not keep to ADRB2, he had known that before he had even asked. She had erred too far from the course now. It had to be done.

40

"Peter!"

Dux grabbed Peter's shoulder and pulled him back into a small alcove. They stood still, breathing heavily, concealed in a shadowed gap between two department stores.

They had managed to escape the labyrinthine passageways without further obstacles and, through a final concealed door, had exited directly into the second level of the Bullring shopping centre.

Gasping for air, they settled a moment. Peter rested heavily against the wall growing increasingly aware of the energy draining from him. He felt Rachael's concerned eyes upon him and an overwhelming desire to conceal his vulnerability. As Peter's quest for oxygen grew louder and sharper, Dux turned towards them. He motioned for silence before pointing towards the levels below.

Peter obeyed, his chest burning at the effort to calm his breathing and quickly understood Dux's urgency. From the ground floor below came the rhythmic march of Order reinforcements in perfect unison - the final wave of soldiers making their way to the battle outside.

Dux gave them both a telling look, instructing them to remain hidden, before he edged out slowly, his rifle poised. Peter watched, still trying to shake off the stars circling his head, as Dux scanned the immediate vicinity before moving closer towards the central viewing platform.

Peter had been to the Bullring once before whilst writing for the Chronicle but had only experienced within the stressful cauldron of impatient shoppers and goggling tourists. In the oddly serene darkness of the empty evening shop floor, he felt his inner artist purr.

The inside of the Bullring was remarkably large, separated over three floors by winding escalators, usually peppered by shopping bag-wielding enthusiasts. Its spectacular size was matched, perhaps even dwarfed, by the thick glass ceiling above, speckled by the showering of rain outside. As he stared up, a rain cloud shifted, releasing a glow of moonlight. It travelled at speed through the glass and directly down upon the ceramic flooring below, offering the only source of light against the darkness of the shop floor.

Peter saw another blinding glow from overhead and watched the raindrops dancing against the glass as the Order's helicopter passed overhead, its searchlight poised.

Dux turned back and motioned for them both to follow, startling Peter from his dazed appreciation of the setting.

"Come on," Rachael whispered, nudging him. Peter nodded and moved out from the alcove, only then realising that he had been clutching Rachael's hand.

They moved at pace, crouched low and pressed against the display windows of the surrounding stores, keen to avoid any unwelcome attention from below.

"Where are we going?" Peter whispered, gasping at the effort. "They said the mainframe was in the lower levels."

Dux did not answer, instead continuing his advance, clutching his rifle at shoulder level with Rachael closely behind him.

Peter slowed to a halt, and with an added appreciation for the glass support, felt himself fall into it. His breathing became more laboured as his body finally began to fail him. The adrenaline that had fuelled him since escaping his cell had subsided.

Peter's body felt heavy all of a sudden. His legs shook almost uncontrollably, and he began to slide down the glass.

Dux and Rachael continued, unaware of his discomfort, evidently having overestimated his physical competence after two months of near starvation. He tried to call out, but only a light wheeze escaped his lungs. With a clunk, he fell to the floor. Rachael glanced backwards and, noticing Peter struggling, prodded Dux.

Dux stopped and turned back. He nodded at Rachael, pulled something from his back pocket and handed it to her.

"I'm sorry," Peter gasped as Rachael jogged back towards him. "I've got nothing left, I can't move."

"Don't worry about that," she said, smiling as she reached for the object Dux had given her. "This will get you back up and running."

"What –" Peter gasped. But before he could finish, Rachael had crouched down and stabbed Peter in the neck, injecting him with a small volume of clear liquid.

Peter yelped, caressing his neck as Rachael pulled out the small syringe. "What the - "

His sentence was cut short by a sudden rush of energy. Peter felt his mind clear, felt the strength rushing back into his limbs. He was more alert than he had ever felt before; he could sense everything happening around him - every footstep of the marching agents below, every raindrop colliding against the glass ceiling above.

"Better?" Rachael asked, helping him to his feet with a smile as she put the empty syringe back into one of her holster pockets.

"Yeah," said Peter, with a relieved laugh. "What did you give me?"

"Come on," said Dux in a loud whisper a few metres away from them, and he waved at them both to hurry. Rachael winked playfully before turning to follow Dux.

With his burst of energy still flowing through him, Peter moved at a surprising pace. He followed Dux and Rachael towards a small side passage between two competing coffee shops and down towards a small door, labelled 'Security'.

Dux checked behind them for any sign of movement before he rapped on the door in what must have been a pre-rehearsed series of knocks. Peter heard a rustling from inside, and, within moments, it had opened.

"First thing's first," said Rachael, whispering towards Peter as she followed Dux into the small side room. Peter turned to scan the shop floor behind them too, before following her inside.

In his state of hypersensitivity, Peter was immediately blinded by the glare of six CCTV monitors. His vision swayed as he saw them stacked at a desk on one side of the dimly lit room, each displaying live footage of different sections of the Bullring. He blinked profusely, wiping tears from his eyes, and looked down to see a young man sitting in the chair.

"George?"

George Younger sat in the small desk chair, dressed in a borrowed security uniform, clicking and typing away in front of the CCTV monitors. Peter's eyes flickered quickly aside, and he noticed two security guards slumped unconscious, one undressed, tied up in the corner of the room.

"I don't think much of that beard," said George, smiling as he turned slowly in the desk chair. They looked at each other for a moment, beaming before George jumped up to pull Peter into a one-armed hug.

"George… the perilous time restraints," said Dux from the door as he continued to monitor the situation outside.

"Right," said George, laughing awkwardly.

George released Peter and sat back in the chair. He turned towards a small laptop linked to the central system and continued to work on whatever it was he was doing.

"What are we doing here?" Peter asked anxiously as George refocused his efforts back on the CCTV monitors, tapping away frantically. "We need to get to the mainframe!"

"Soon," said Rachael, looking towards the monitors.

All of them were focused on the escalating scenes outside. Peter saw them all, through the various angles, all the Resistance supporters who had braved the battle, thousands of them lined up in the distance, prepared to fight.

"George, is it ready?"

George nodded and continued to type lines of code into the laptop. "The camera will be live in sixty seconds."

"Camera?" said Peter, turning to look around the room again.

"Great," said Rachael, ignoring him. "Ok, now Peter…"

Peter turned from the monitors to look back at Rachael, utterly perplexed, only to look past her and see exactly what George had meant. Ominously waiting beside the door sat a video camera, perfectly positioned upon its tripod to record someone approximately his size.

"Probably a tad late for a shave," said Rachael, ruffling Peter's hair. "But there are people outside waiting for orders."

"What?" Peter spluttered. "Wait, now come on, what are we doing? We are supposed to be destroying the mainframe. We seem a little side-tracked here."

"Peter, those people out there are marching into a battle that most will never come back from," said Rachael sternly.

"Thank you for the reminder," Peter interjected with a frown.

"And," Rachael continued impatiently. "They are waiting for your signal. They need some inspiration from the man who started it all, the man they are still unsure is alive. They need this Peter. They need to know we have beaten them, at least this once."

Peter looked back directly into that fiery emerald glare, ruing the ease with which, in the short time he had known her, her passion seemed able to convince him of anything.

"But," Peter stuttered. "What do I say?"

"Thirty seconds guys," George interrupted, turning towards them. Peter looked back at him with an expression of sarcastic gratitude.

"Sorry…" George muttered, turning back to the laptop.

Rachael moved closer to Peter. She placed her hand gently on his chest and stared into his eyes with that same impassioned sparkle.

"Tell them what they are fighting for. Tell them that it will all be worth it. Tell them that there is hope."

"Twenty…"

Peter's eyes boggled. He had given speeches to small rooms of Resistance supporters plenty of times, most of them filmed, but never on such a scale or of such importance as this. None had been unprepared; none off the back of weeks of starvation. His mind, usually blessed with a journalistic spark of creativity, was blank.

Rachael pushed him in front of the video camera. "Your face will show up as a sort of projection on the outside of the Bullring."

"It is going to be epic," said George, continuing to monitor the laptop.

"Deep breath…" said Rachael, offering a comforting smile.

"Ten…"

"Peter," said Rachael, forcing him from his nervous daze.

Peter turned towards her, his face pale, his mind still maddeningly devoid of inspiration. She moved towards him and clutched the neckline of his suit, pulling him in.

For a moment, he felt complete shock and then... a blissful nothingness. The coming battle, his father's death, the Order - it had all been a dream; a mad, mad dream.

Rachael pulled away, taking his brief dose of euphoria with her, and pushed him back in front of the camera. Peter stared back, stunned, abashed, but emboldened.

"Don't screw it up," she said, smiling.

"Three..."

Peter gulped and desperately searched the recesses of his mind for inspirational battle speeches he had seen. Now was his moment. Though he despised that it was him and his stand against the Order that had inspired those outside to march towards their potential deaths, he knew, or at least hoped, that he could offer one final tincture of strength - one final push.

"Two..."

The reverberations from the lower floor had ceased. They must all have been outside now, lining up against the oncoming Resistance, in a passionate defence of the regime they placed so much faith in – their quest to save humanity from the perils of degeneration, at whatever cost.

"One..."

A red light began to blink in the corner of the video camera. Peter forced his face into a serious, and what he hoped would be encouraging expression, but his eyes flickered again towards Rachael, unable to forget the kiss.

Peter gave her one last embarrassed smile and looked back into the lens. He was ready.

*****

The atmosphere remained tense. The air was thick with anticipation, intensified by the bodies of the Resistance forces standing behind her. It was silent but for the rain falling against the ground beneath them, and the rippling of their banners in the breeze.

Claire Phelan's watch beeped – 20:00.

Almost instantly, reds, blues and greens erupted into the night sky above them. The outer surface of the Bullring had come to life, its colours jumping out from the aluminium discs to dance across the scene outside.

The lights strobed violently in every direction, and Claire was more than pleasantly surprised to find that their sudden appearance seemed to unnerve many in the Order ranks.

They turned, almost all of them, to look up towards the commotion, only to find that the light show was quickly followed by a deafening bassline. Music began to play out through what must have been huge speakers, reverberating off the brickwork of the buildings nearby.

"What is this?" Claire called out to one of the women standing beside her, as the low bassline turned to a succession of drums.

"I think it's Black Skinhead," she replied, turning her head only slightly.

Claire turned to look at her.

"Vintage Kanye..." the young woman finished with a shrug.

Claire shook her head with a wry smile and turned back. "Right."

Distraction and confusion.

The ground beneath them growled as the amplified bass continued to burst out from the Bullring. Claire turned back towards the Resistance behind her, noticing grave expressions, determined glares, and even a few nervous smiles. They were ready.

Suddenly, the music quietened. Claire turned back towards the Bullring to see that the lighting display had ceased. It had been replaced by a huge digital projection of a slightly dishevelled face across the outer walls. She dropped her gun to her side. It was gaunt-looking and sporting an unflattering stubble, but it was him; it was really him.

"I speak now to the Resistance," came the amplified voice of Peter Brockland. "All of you standing side by side here and across the country, standing up against the Order."

The atmosphere intensified. She felt the gasps of excitement chittering through the crowds; she shared it.

"I am alive," he continued.

The Order forces seemed openly restless now. Their commanding officers, standing to the side of the frontline, motioned to the agents to settle down, though it seemed even they were unable to resist nervous glances up at the two-hundred-foot digital projection of their number one enemy.

Claire noticed too that agents had been ushered back into the Bullring, she supposed to apprehend Peter and the others and cut the broadcast. They needed to move soon.

"You all know why you are here," Peter continued, his face etched with concern.

"If it were up to me, none of you would be risking your lives tonight. All of you would be with family and friends, secure in the knowledge that nothing and nobody was going to take that away from you. But life has not been so kind; this regime has not been so kind. If we are to regain the lives we have lost, the lives we have all, through false promise and fear, allowed to be taken from us, we can no longer allow it; we must fight back."

The crowd listened intently, nodding to his words, clutching their weapons ever more tightly.

"Whatever they have told you, I am one of you. I have always been one of you - no better, no worse, no more important and no more special. I stand with you now as you have stood with me, to destroy the foundations of what this regime represents, to reclaim the power to decide our own fates, our children's fates.

Look left and right, and you will see people who have shared your pain. You will see people who believe, as you do, that no one owns our freedom but ourselves. Nobody gets to decide who we love, or who is worthy of life in this world.

Those who stand opposite you believe they fight for a worthy cause, but to them, I say this. In the years to come, when they speak of what happened here tonight, what will you tell your children, your grandchildren? Will you tell them you fought for tyranny or will you tell them you fought for freedom, for the rights of those who cannot fight, for those who need us most?

To the Resistance… each of us might expect to fight one great battle in our lifetime. Find strength tonight that you do so beside others who share your same battle. We live and die together tonight fighting for what we believe in. Fight for your friends; fight for your family; fight for those you have lost; fight for those who, without you, may be lost in times to come!"

Claire felt the intensity of the atmosphere reaching its crescendo. Rachael had been right; they had needed this, a last push of inspiration to season them with the courage they needed to do what they knew they must. Every single person behind her now was ready to fight, whatever the outcome, for their freedoms.

The projection suddenly switched from Peter's face to the faces of others, many others, emerging and fading away. She recognised a number of them, faces of some of the victims whose lives had been cut short by the Order.

Claire heard an anguished cry from the crowd behind her as a young child appeared with a toothy grin that had long since passed. She turned to see the boy's mother consumed by her anguish, her face etched with a primal pain.

The boy's face faded away to be replaced by the now-iconic symbol of the Resistance movement – the shield entwined by a double helix. Claire slowly lifted her fist into the air one last time.

A rippling seemed to wind through the air around her as she heard the united movement behind her, all reaching for their weapons, lifting their own fists too. Claire's spine tingled; one last show of solidarity, one final stand, to the death if required.

A low, rushing came from above. They were coming - it was time.

Claire took a step forward, with another look down towards the photograph of her and her husband, beaming together as they clutched the sonogram of the child that had been stolen from her.

"Resistance…" she shouted. She turned to look at the crowd behind her, every face etched with passion. "We fight for our futures!"

The crowd behind her roared, stomping their feet against the ground and throwing their weapons above them.

"To those officers and soldiers defending the Order, believing it is your duty to do so…" came Peter's booming voice again. "It is not. Defending the innocent is your duty. Make sure that you are on the right side of history. Resistance…"

Silence fell upon the hyped-up crowd as his voice paused. "Give them hell."

On cue, two commandeered fighter jets emerged from the clouds above them. With ruthless efficiency, both pilots fired at the Order's front line and the guarding helicopter above.

The helicopter veered away in a harried retreat, but unsuccessfully; the bullets clanged against its metal shell, smashing through the glass windows. It spiralled as the pilots lost control and fell, as though in slow motion towards the forces below. As though in slow motion, it crashed only metres ahead of the Order's front line, skidding out harmlessly towards the Resistance forces, erupting into flames.

With one last message of defiance, the jets released two missiles towards the tanks that had turned to face them before pulling up in retreat. They heard the missiles whistle through the air before they collided with one of the Order tanks.

The air was suddenly rife with smoke, heat, light and panic.

Claire took one final glance down towards the photograph, lit by the glowing embers of the carnage ahead of them. She lifted it slowly to her lips and gave them both one final kiss before placing it carefully back into her chest pocket.

With one final roar, she, and the Resistance, charged.

41

"Where did that come from?" said Rachael, unable to hide a wide-eyed look of stunned admiration.

"We need to go," Dux interrupted from beside the open door. He peered out nervously towards the ground floor, where agents had begun to pile back inside.

"I guess I got a bit carried away," said Peter, abashed. "I may have borrowed some of it."

"Well, it clearly worked," said George, his glance fixed upon the monitors. They all turned to watch as Resistance fighters sprinted towards the Bullring, seemingly without fear for the tanks and awaiting troops just metres ahead of them.

The ground beneath them shook, and Peter felt the building reverberate again as the low whoosh of the returning fighter jets came from overhead, quickly followed by two further explosions.

"You didn't think we would come without a few tricks up our sleeve, did you?" said Rachael, smiling playfully in response to Peter's shocked glance.

"No," he muttered to himself. "I suppose not."

George closed the laptop, forced it into his backpack and ran towards Dux.

"Elevator," he said forcefully, pointing towards it.

More explosions came from outside, and Peter heard the shattering of glass.

"Mainframe now?" he shouted, trying to compete with the noise.

Rachael smiled and grabbed his forearm.

"Hang on," said Peter, turning back towards the two security guards.

He saw a pair of scissors lying on the desk and grabbed them. He crouched in front of the two guards and cut at their restraints. They stirred, gently nudged back into consciousness by the commotion outside.

"Should at least give them a fighting chance!" Peter shouted as he jogged back to Rachael, ignoring her look of scepticism.

"Elevator, now!" Dux shouted. He stepped back from firing shots down towards the agents amassing beneath them. Peter heard the clicks that indicated he had run out of ammunition and watched as Dux tossed the gun down towards them. Ducking a shot from below, he ran back towards them.

Peter ran from the security office, his arms flailing above his head in a vague effort to protect himself from incoming bullets. Rachael ran towards Dux and offered her own warning shots towards the agents below.

Dux pushed her back as she too narrowly avoided a stray defensive shot and jabbed his finger towards the elevator.

"In! Now!" he shouted. Rachael stumbled back towards Peter and George, as Dux pulled a pistol from his back pocket and fired one final rally towards the agents approaching from the top of the escalator.

Dux jumped inside the elevator, and George pressed frantically at the 'Door Close' button. The doors slid shut at the opportune moment, just as Peter glimpsed the rage-fuelled face of G emerge from below, flanked by other agents, all pointing and shouting towards them.

"Rachael..." said Dux, looking towards her anxiously. "Over to you."

Gunshots clanged against the elevator doors as Rachael calmly pressed a series of buttons in what appeared to be a code: 1-2-2-1-3-G. She completed the routine with the emergency bell icon, and the elevator gave an unnatural shudder. The lights inside darkened, and they began to move, not down but backwards, further into the interior of the building.

Peter stumbled backwards and clutched at the railing as they picked up speed. He turned and noticed that the back of the elevator had changed. Where it appeared to have been a mirror before, the glass had become transparent, displaying the hidden inner structure of the Bullring as they hurtled through the darkness.

Peter tried to shout out to the others, but the force of their movement had stolen the air from his lungs. Instead, he screwed up his face and stared towards a similarly anxious-looking George.

A minute's hurtling backwards had passed before the elevator slowed to a steady pace. Turning back to look through the glass again, he gasped. An eerie purple light illuminated the inside of the elevator, revealing the scenes below.

They continued to advance slowly into the centre of a vast circular structure. Peter looked out to see three levels, all protected by thick glass. They seemed to be deserted, all with walls of pristine white, lined by similar white, small-windowed doors, none offering any hint as to what lay behind them.

Peter looked down to see a separated fourth level hundreds of metres beneath them, the darkness interrupted only by hints of flickering purple light, outlining a large dome in its centre. Though Peter was unable to see the exact goings-on, even at that height, the opaque glass could not hide flickers of light betraying the activity within.

"That's it," said Rachael, standing beside him and peering down. "The mainframe."

Peter continued to look down towards the tiny flickering lights. Whatever was happening inside had been the cause of it all. Years of discrete sterilisations and murder, years of corruption, his father's disappearance, his father's death, the deaths of countless Resistance forces, all instigated by whatever lay inside that dome.

The elevator halted as they neared the centre of the structure, and it was only then that Peter noticed a clearer, almost invisible, glass pod feeding directly into the dome below and up out towards the top of the structure.

"Escape pod," said Rachael, taking her position as tour guide as she followed his gaze. "In case the worst happens, the protocol is to take the core algorithms and what data they can and escape. We need to stop them before they can."

Peter nodded weakly, still - he could find no other way to explain it - in complete awe. How had they kept this hidden for all these years?

Lights flickered ahead of him, and Peter noticed for the first time a huge digital screen, which seemed to react to their approach. The screen fed down from the top level right down to the foot of the third and seemed to be separated into three sections, each, he supposed, tailored to the activities of each floor.

"It's separated to give relevant information to each level," said Rachael, following his gaze and confirming his suspicions. "Level One is for the field agents: general briefings, a few training facilities. Level Two is for the lab techs: living quarters and lab facilities, and Level Three, well…"

Rachael looked awkward, as though admission of the horrors that lay in Level Three might unnecessarily incriminate her.

"What's in Level Three?" said George weakly from behind them as the elevator shuddered into its steady descent.

"Genetics," said Rachael ominously. "Engineering and testing."

"What do they do?" Dux asked, but Rachael did not immediately answer. Her glance was instead planted upon Peter, who looked down towards the third level with revulsion.

"Some of the incompatibles aren't so lucky," she said weakly, forcing her glance from Peter to look back at Dux and George. "Some are brought to Level Three to see if they can be 'cured' so to speak. They are trying to develop ways of genetically mutating, or replacing, human DNA to 'cure' their perceived abnormality, but, well, most don't survive the process."

She stared back at the three of them, all fixed with looks of horror.

"I suppose they think they are trying to find a way to help people," she said, in a tone that almost sounded as though she were defending herself, and it. "But-"

"It's barbaric," Peter interjected, still looking towards the level, darker than the two above. How many poor souls had been taken down to that level and painfully mutated, murdered even?

"Well… yeah," said Rachael before falling silent.

The four of them remained silent as the elevator approached the first level. So uneasy was it that Peter felt for the first time a longing for classic elevator music. As they stood awkwardly, he could not help but think it would have gone some way in easing the tension.

Even after everything she had done to help them, he struggled to accept her role in the Order. Every time his mixed feelings towards her reared up, it reminded him of his father and his unresolved guilt at having been unable to forgive him. Rachael, too, had turned her back on the Order, but how much of this had she been involved in? How much had she known?

How much had she believed in? Was it really so easy to shake off those beliefs?

Peter felt Rachael's gaze but fixed his glance ahead as the elevator bumped to a halt. Rachael moved towards the elevator doors and turned towards Dux.

"Your helmet," she said. "You'll need to look directly into this scanner. I can't use mine."

Peter looked at her again. Rachael had turned her back on everything to protect her daughter. She had risked everything to turn traitor, to help Peter and the Resistance. So why did Peter still feel that dull pang in his stomach whenever he looked at her? Why could he not shake his imagination of the cruelty that she might once have contributed to?

Rachael pointed towards a small sensor directly above the numbered buttons, and Dux crouched down. A thin green line appeared and scanned Dux's helmet before disappearing.

A few nervous seconds passed before…

"Welcome Agent K53," came a tinny female voice.

"Ok," said Rachael with a sigh. She cocked her rifle as the elevator doors opened slowly. "Welcome to PHROX HQ."

42

Ex-Chief Superintendent Justine Smith wiped away a trickle of blood from her mouth and slowly dragged herself to her feet. With a look of disgust at her opponent, she kicked the SCF agent's knife away, which lay harmlessly now beneath their lifeless body. With a throb of pain, she growled, as her skin tore painfully beneath her cargo trousers.

That had been close.

Emerging from her combative hyperfocus, she felt normality return with considerable discomfort.

Thirty minutes, perhaps more, had passed since they had begun their slow march up along The Victoria Embankment and towards Westminster, in homage to those murdered in the protests just a few weeks before. In that short period, bedlam had ensued.

The streets of London were rife with the sounds of civil disobedience as Londoners left the confines of their homes, offices and pubs to join the rebellious rabble outside. Whether they had emerged from their relative safety to join the cause, having watched the carnage unfold on social media, or to take advantage of the distracted constabulary, she was not sure. But the still-increasing sounds of violence surrounding her gave her comfort enough to believe that many had indeed come out to fight for the Resistance cause.

Screams of anguish; roars of passion; frantic cries for help – all combined with gunshots, smashes and explosions to add to the concoction of audible chaos.

Justine stumbled, battling an onset of weakness and disorientation. She grabbed for the riverside wall instinctively, desperate to regain her composure. She was far too old to be involved in this.

She clutched the side of her leg, chastising herself for being so slow to react, and felt the blood oozing through the fabric of her trousers. Had she been just milliseconds slower… she stumbled down the pavement and crouched behind a nearby statue, breathing heavily. She quickly regretted the short moments of mercy she had gifted herself as she looked up and, still gasping, out towards the desperate scene unfolding in the river.

She remembered a time when moonlight as bright as this would have glistened down upon a calm end-of-Spring Thames, meandering along amidst a backdrop of a vibrant, laughing Southbank crowd. Midweek punters would be revelling in the crisp evening air, and her gravest concern might have been those who were, perhaps, enjoying it a little too much. Now though, that same beautiful moonlight glow illuminated something altogether different.

Smoke and flame swirled upwards from all directions, and crowds battled beside the London Eye, fighting over the bodies of the dead, desperate in their attempts to reach the bridge and earn their chance to overthrow the Order's seat of political power.

Men and women, young and old, clambered for safety from the gunfight, throwing themselves into the river. Many struggled for air as they battled against the ferocious current and the lifeless bodies bobbing motionless in their path.

It was as though the scene was unfolding in the slowest of slow motions; her brain sought desperately to comprehend the horrors, to make sense of what had happened, what was happening. It was nothing short of hell.

SCF agents and police officers, soldiers and members of the public were tearing each other apart. She felt a particular pang of anguish at the sight of police officers fighting each other, killing each other, each side fighting for what they believed to be right. London, once the pinnacle of vibrancy and beauty, had become a bloodstained battlefield, tainted by the tragic stench of death.

A high-pitched scream sparked her back into life, speeding up the scene in an instant. Justine turned quickly and found its owner - a young woman struggling to stay above water as she fought against a lifeless body in her path.

The water surrounding the woman was growing increasingly scarlet as blood oozed from the body she clutched with apparent revulsion, desperate in her attempts to stay above water.

"Hey!" Justine shouted, finding her voice. She waved frantically at the woman, suddenly oblivious to the dangers surrounding her. "Hey!"

Spotting a lifebuoy nearby, she sprinted towards it and pulled at the restraints. Still screaming, the woman followed her sprint, her eyes widening at the last glimmer of hope.

Justine tugged at the lifebuoy again. After several moments of wrestling, it loosened from its restraints, and she turned back to face the woman. Staring back at her, the woman looked close to tears with relief. She pushed aside the safety of her chosen corpse, and swam towards her, as Justine tossed the lifebuoy into the river.

With a nod, Justine turned away, feeling her strength return, when she heard a gunshot, oddly separate from the others plaguing the scene. Her stomach sank. She knew what had happened before she had even turned back to confirm it.

Others in the water had already begun to swim towards the now vacant lifebuoy. The young woman had disappeared.

Justine looked away and saw an Order agent drop their aim. Noticing her defeated gaze, the agent quickly turned to point their rifle at her. Acting on instincts younger than her years, Justine threw herself behind the closest tree, only just large enough to protect her frame. She heard the gunshot shave the bark as it flew past her.

She felt her thigh vibrate, and after an initial panic at the prospect of a fresh wound, realised that it was her phone. She chanced a look around the tree and quickly moved back again as she noticed the barrel of the agent's rifle. Another gunshot collided with the tree bark.

She clambered at her trouser pocket and pulled out the mobile phone. She squinted at the screen – it was Claire.

"Claire?" she shouted, flinching at the sound of another explosion nearby – the Resistance had somehow managed to destroy one of the commandeered military trucks. "Claire, are you ok?"

"They're everywhere…" came a weak voice. Justine could hear in the background a scene perhaps even more violent than her own, but it was Claire's voice that troubled her most; she sounded defeated.

"Claire," she began, chancing another look from behind the tree and avoiding yet another gunshot. "Claire, you need to stay focused. How are you getting on?"

"Dux and Rachael are in there with him," her voice came again, still weak. She heard a rustling too, as though she was clambering to hide behind something. "There's too many of them, so many dead, we don't have a chance."

Justine could sense the resignation in Claire's voice and knew it was only a matter of time before it got her killed. They had to distract the Order long enough for the plan to succeed; Claire had to remain strong.

Justine turned from the tree again to look towards the Houses of Parliament. Within the windows of the upper floors, flickering lights of orange and yellow danced, but she had lingered too long. An intense heat spread through the side of her neck, and she pulled back behind the tree again, gasping.

Blood drained from her, spilling down her top to the ground beneath her. She dropped her gun and slid to the floor, clutching her wound to stem the flow, but she knew it was too late. Her reactions had been too slow; she had perhaps just minutes left.

"Justine?" came Claire's voice, more animated at the sound of the gunshot.

"We've breached Westminster," Justine croaked, and she coughed a spurt of blood. Holding back tears, she used every ounce of strength she possessed to maintain calm. "We're going to do it, Claire, you need to be strong now. Go."

She cut the call and tossed the phone away, feeling the strength desert her. She turned weakly to reach for her gun, preparing for one final stand but saw a thick white boot standing on top of it. She noticed too, only a metre or so away, the bloodstained knife that she had kicked away, agonisingly too late.

Justine pulled herself into a more comfortable position against the tree, still clutching her neck, and looked up towards the agent. It was only now that it struck her that this had been the tree she would always lean against as a rookie to catch her breath after a lunchtime run. She chuckled weakly at the memory, coughing up more blood.

The agent stared down at her. Justine was draining of life, and through her increasingly hazed vision, she could only see the agent's mouth beneath their visor. She chuckled painfully again as she saw it turn from a hint of confusion to a twisted, wry smile.

"Go on then," she spluttered, blood running more freely now. At least it would be quick.

A shot fired from elsewhere, connecting with the agent's visor. The bullet had rebounded harmlessly towards the river but had distracted the agent enough for Justine to take her opportunity. One final strike.

She released her grasp on the wound and threw herself towards the knife. Feeling it in her grasp, she turned back and thrust it with all her strength into the agent's boot. She felt the tip of the blade hit the concrete, and she was unsure if it was her blood or the agent's that stained the floor around them. As the agent winced, falling to their knees, Justine ripped the knife from the boot and thrust it upwards beneath the agent's visor.

The effort had been too much for her. She slumped back into the tree, hardly noticing the agent drop beside her, futilely clutching their own throat in a grasp at survival.

Justine's lips felt dry, her body cold. In her final moments, she felt a sudden appreciation of her senses, even amidst the battle still raging around her. Never again would she see the beauty of the moonlight shining down from above; never again would she feel the cool breeze against her face. But it had been worth it, she thought, with a weak smile. Her conscience was once again clear.

She saw a young red-haired girl running towards her, and smiled, picturing that same girl who always ran excitedly towards her from the bottom of the garden when she visited. That same young girl that, whatever difficulties she had faced that day, had always helped her feel better.

Could it really be her here now, in her final moments, helping her to feel better again?

She did not seem to feel the pain anymore; she did not seem to feel anything. Not the warmth of the blood flowing against her increasingly cold skin or the dazzle of the explosions and gunfire still lighting the night sky.

She felt, as though in a dream, someone clutch her hand and press down on the wound.

"Jenny," she muttered, her eyelids drooping.

She pictured her sister-in-law's garden, and there, amongst his prized bright blue cornflowers, was Frederick, tall and strikingly handsome. He beamed at her, his arms open, as Jenny led her by her hand towards him. Justine felt a single tear flow down her cheek as she approached him again, felt every enjoyment of her final breath, and smiled one last time.

43

"We'll need to be careful," Rachael murmured, edging out cautiously from the elevator. "They're bound to initiate ADRB2 soon; I'm surprised they haven't already."

Dux followed and scanned the floor outside with his rifle before pulling his visor down to analyse the route ahead.

Peter stared at George, who looked back at him nervously before they too edged out of the elevator shaft. Peter pulled down his visor, quickly readjusting to his digital view, clutched his rifle and followed.

A thick white wall blocked their route left, immediately forcing them to turn right and progress down the steadily declining circular path towards a second elevator opposite.

"What's ADRB2?" Peter whispered, catching up as they moved through the deserted pathway. They passed several white doors, whose windows revealed rooms with tables and chairs, television monitors and stray laptops. They even passed a small gym and gun range.

"It's sort of the final escape plan," she whispered back. "Take what data they can and prepare to start again. They'll destroy the facility, the mainframe, any Progeny tech that they can't take with them, and anyone unfortunate enough to still be in here," said Rachael with a grave expression. "The mainframe, even Progeny, can all be rebuilt, but the underlying data, the designs, the algorithms – that's hundreds of years worth of research, guidance and code. The algorithm is what drives them

– no prejudice, just science guiding their mission to save humankind. We have to get there first; we have to destroy the data."

Rachael continued forward, but Peter slowed to a halt. His visor had indicated a 'life form' behind one of the locked white doors.

"And they won't be far behind," said Dux, pointing up towards the elevator.

Peter followed his gaze. He was right; it had slowly made its way back towards the Bullring, where G and the other agents waited anxiously.

Peter ignored their haste and turned to investigate the life form identified in the room closest to him. He edged towards the room slowly. Through the small glass window of a white padded room, Peter saw a young girl, no older than 15 years old. She lay shaking, her knees tucked into her chest, dressed in a stained white gown.

"Hello?" Peter shouted, knocking on the door and peering through the glass.

The girl stirred at his voice, turning slowly. She offered only a fleeting, frightened look towards the cell door. The girl had dark blonde hair and bright blue eyes, with the same clear signs of malnourishment and neglect that Peter had come to know so well, in a cell strikingly similar to this one.

"Peter, what are you doing?" Rachael hissed, jogging back towards him.

She pulled at his arm impatiently, but he pulled it back. He lifted his visor and turned back to look into the padded room. The girl looked more intently at them now, confused. Peter desperately pulled at the door in his attempts to prise it open. "We aren't leaving innocent people in here Rachael."

He looked through the glass again and saw that the girl had got to her feet. Understanding, silent tears of relief crawled down her face. She smiled up at a face she had clearly now recognised. Peter smiled back, still pulling at the door uselessly, before turning to glare at Rachael.

"Oh, move over then," Rachael sighed. She pulled up her rifle and aimed it directly at a digital lock beside the door.

"What-" Peter started, but Rachael ignored him. He jumped backwards as Rachael fired three times at the device. The screen shattered, and stray electrical currents fizzed before the door clicked ajar.

"Little trick I learned," Rachael muttered, looking pleased with herself.

Before Peter had a chance to pull the door open, the young girl had flown out and, with a bout of strength that Peter had not expected, thrown herself at him. She clutched his waist tightly in a shaky embrace and sobbed silently.

Heavily winded, Peter held her for a second, staring awkwardly towards Rachael, before pushing her away.

"My name's Peter," he said, smiling gently, though he could see from her expression that his introduction had been unnecessary. "We're here to get you out, but you're going to have to be brave and help us, ok?"

The girl looked up at him and dabbed her eyes with the sleeves of her gown. She forced her face into a distinct look of determination and nodded.

"Ok," said Peter softly.

They could not allow her to go back up to the shop floor by herself; it would be a marvel if the pursuing Order agents did not just shoot her dead without hesitation. But they could not escort her back either; they had no time, and their task was too important. Peter reached for a gun in the back of his utility belt.

"Peter, come on," Dux murmured impatiently, staring up nervously towards the elevator shaft above them.

"Aim, and shoot," said Peter, handing her the gun and offering the most inadequate of demonstrations.

"Ok," said the girl, taking the gun from him and nodding back.

Peter smiled and pushed the girl gently towards the others when the lights began to flicker. Peter stared around them, growing increasingly anxious by the look on Rachael's face. The lights flickered again before extinguishing completely, leaving only the purple lights swimming from the central screen for company.

"They've initiated," said Rachael darkly, and even in the limited light, Peter could see her face etched with dread.

Seconds later, red filled their level, flicking on and off just as it had done in Peter's cell. Alarms blared, so loud that they all instinctively grabbed for their ears. Peter looked out towards the central screen again, his face straining against the volume of the alarms. The standard purple and black graphics had been replaced by an 80-foot projection of the president's face.

"Protocol ADRB2 has been initiated," came his amplified voice. "Protocol ADRB2 has been initiated. All remaining staff are to evacuate immediately, following protocol."

"Oh fuck," said Dux from behind him.

"Run!" Rachael shouted, pointing towards the next elevator.

They obeyed at once, staring down as they ran, as red lights switched on and off in the levels below. Peter had presumed they were deserted, but what agents had remained began to stir from their labs, grabbing what apparatus they could before escaping towards the elevator shaft.

"Quick," said Dux, holding the doors open as they reached the second elevator.

The four of them herded inside, breathing heavily from the sprint, before Dux followed, crouching down towards the elevator's digital sensor. The familiar green lines reappeared, scanning his visor vertically and horizontally before releasing a loud beep. The doors slid shut, leaving them in complete silence, but for the sounds of their laboured breathing.

Peter turned to look through the glass back wall, and down towards the scurrying lab agents. He did not need his visor's assistance to recognise the look of terror on many of their faces. Some looked up towards them and, without the protection of his visor, had clearly recognised the man approaching.

"Prepare yourself," said Rachael, cocking her rifle. "Some of them really don't like you."

"Fantastic," said Peter sarcastically. He pulled his visor back down as they slowed to a halt.

"Ready?" Dux asked, staring ahead.

"Ready," they mumbled back in unison.

Peter turned to look at George and the young girl, intent on offering some final inspiring look. George returned a look of readiness, but even behind his glasses, was unable to hide his own terror. The girl, though... looked almost as ready to go as Rachael did.

Peter gave her a consoling wink and turned back towards the elevator doors. The elevator shunted to a halt.

"Here we go."

After a brief moment, the doors slid open to reveal pandemonium.

Lab agents sprinted towards them, bumping off each other as they went, some clutching papers, some laptops, some carrying what must have been advanced genetic machinery. All though juddered to a halt as the elevator doors slid open to reveal Peter Brockland flanked by his Resistance forces.

The five of them had their weapons poised and, but for the young girl, their visors down as they edged out slowly. They moved towards the lab agents, who edged silently backwards. For a moment, both sides stood motionless, assessing the situation.

Peter concentrated on his visor as it analysed them, and heard his father's voice echoing through his mind. Some chose to be there, but some had no choice. Some had been forced into their situation just as much as Peter had been. His finger trembled nervously over the trigger.

After a minute's standoff, the lab agents appeared to accept their situation. Those nearest them subsided towards the walls on either side, quickly followed by the others, to leave a narrow route through them towards the remainder of the second level.

"Keep an eye out," Dux whispered through gritted teeth. They began to advance slowly and silently, the tension almost tangible.

The lab agents offered looks of fear, curiosity and disgust, helpfully narrated by his visor, but they soon passed the bulk of them. As soon as they felt safe enough to do so, the lab agents rushed into the elevator, desperate in their attempts to escape.

"Don't you dare!" Rachael shouted, breaking the silence. She jabbed her rifle in the direction of one lab agent, whose arm immediately stopped its slow advance towards the inside of his lab coat.

The agent stared back at Rachael intensely, and she jabbed the rifle more forcefully in his direction. With pursed lips and beady, panic-stricken eyes, the agent slowly lifted his hands above him, and Peter's visor highlighted the Beretta concealed beneath the man's lab coat.

Rachael rushed forwards and patted him down. She pulled the gun from his inside pocket, giving him a distinct look of dislike, before passing the gun to the young girl. Shoulder to shoulder, the two girls rejoined the tail of their advancing party, weapons raised, facing the agents passing by.

The lab agents continued to scarcen, and the advancing group quickened their pace to a light jog, nervously spinning back to check for any last-ditch attempts at heroism.

"Fuck," said Dux again, crouching down to the next elevator sensor between anxious glances to the level above.

Peter followed Dux's glance and saw what had drawn the curse. G, flanked by eight heavily armed Order agents, had stepped out of the elevator and into the first level. Peter caught G's eye through his visor as she stared down and pointed animatedly down towards them. Even in her green, digital outline, she looked angrier than Peter had ever seen her.

"Weapons," said Dux, distracting him as the elevator advanced slowly from the level below.

They stood a few metres back, their guns ready as the elevator approached, all prepared to deal with any straggling lab, or other, agents. Knowing what Rachael had told them about the inhabitants of the third level, Peter was almost certain that whoever came out of this elevator would not be as placid as those they had already passed.

He was wrong. The doors slid open slowly to reveal a middle-aged woman and a sickly-looking man. Both wore white gowns, similar to the one the young girl they had saved wore. The woman looked visibly strained as she tried to hold up the man, leaning on her shoulder, his mouth wide.

"Don't shoot!" she shouted, her eyes widening at the sight of the guns. She struggled to lift her remaining hand above her head. "Please, don't shoot!"

"Marcy?" said Rachael weakly.

Peter turned towards Rachael and saw that her face was overcome with shock. She instantly dropped her rifle to her side.

"Rachael?" the woman replied, staring up at her with equal disbelief. "But they said you'd been killed!"

Rachael rushed forward and grabbed the man's other arm, helping to support them both as they came out to the second level floor.

"Marcy, they're coming," said Rachael, straining at the effort. "They won't let you take him."

"What's happened to him?" George asked, staring at the man.

Peter looked too at the deathly-looking face, almost paper-white, his skin beginning to sag. The man's eyes remained tightly shut, and his mouth agape. Peter could only imagine what horrors he had been subjected to on the level below.

Marcy ignored George and instead looked imploringly towards Rachael, her eyes glistening. "I don't know what to do, I have to save him. Can you help us?"

Rachael smiled and, without answering, pulled them both towards the wall opposite. She pulled the man's arm from Marcy and laid him down into a seated position.

Dux looked at them, his expression stamped with impatience before he glanced up again towards the level above them.

"Rachael," he began softly, only for Rachael to wave his concerns away. Instead, she pulled Marcy into a tight embrace.

"Marcy, they're coming for us," she said as they hugged. "They'll kill you if they catch you trying to escape with him."

Marcy pulled away and looked at Rachael, her face overcome with exhaustion. She nodded reluctantly.

"You found him then?" she said, glancing up towards Peter. Rachael turned to follow her gaze and smiled.

"We're here to destroy it," she said slowly, turning back to face Marcy. "All of it."

Marcy looked stunned, but before she could open any further lines of enquiry, both had been interrupted by Dux's now angry bustles. "Guys, now!"

Peter glanced down at the man, who had begun to stir. His veins throbbed violently every few seconds, bulging not blue but lurid green. His eyes opened weakly for a moment as though it had taken all his strength to do so, to reveal two completely different, unnatural-looking, eyes. As the man tried to reach for Marcy's hand, all of them were distracted by the brilliant yellow and orange irises.

"Here," said Rachael, grabbing for a spare pistol.

She handed it to Marcy as the others made their way back into the elevator and helped pull the man to his feet. She steered them both towards the nearest room, where papers had been scattered across the floor and countless genetic testing machines, lab coats and laptops left behind.

"Hide in here until they've gone past. Take the lab coats and try to blend in with the others on your way out. There's fighting outside, so use that-" she pointed towards the gun. "Sparingly."

"Thank you," Marcy muttered as she helped Rachael to settle the man in the nearest chair.

They turned to look at each other again before falling into another tight embrace. Rachael clutched her for just a moment before pulling away. With a final smile, she rushed back towards the others impatiently waiting in the elevator.

"Good luck!" Marcy shouted as the elevator doors slid shut.

Dux stood back up from the sensor as it beeped its approval. The elevator closed its doors before lurching backwards and down towards the third level.

"She helped me with my daughter," said Rachael, breaking the silence with what she had correctly interpreted as a desire for an explanation. "She was part of a group of us who had wanted to turn on the Order and escape. She would have done too if she hadn't needed their help."

"Their help?" Peter asked.

"That was her husband," she continued. "Bowel cancer; terminal. The Order offered her their labs for experimental treatment. They were trying to cure him."

The elevator stuttered to a halt and the doors slid slowly open. Their weapons poised again and their visors securely in place, they crept out towards a deserted third level. Most of the doors leading along their path had been left ajar, and instruments were scattered across the floor. The geneticists had clearly been haphazard in their desperate attempts to evacuate.

"Cure?" Peter whispered, quickening to stand behind Rachael as they advanced.

"Yeah," she whispered back, her glance still fixed intently on their route ahead. "Some people come here by choice, one final hope."

She stopped at one of the doors which, like the others, had been left ajar and pulled it open. She proceeded to scan the room inside for a moment and, besides the scurries and screeches of a selection of haggard-looking caged rats, found nothing troublesome inside.

"I told you," she continued, advancing again. "This floor is for genetic engineering and other scientific experiments. CRISPR I think they call it, things like that. They aren't here to murder people, they're looking for cures, ways to improve strength or intelligence. The problem is that they just don't care how they do it, what laws they are breaking, or if people actually survive the process."

Peter stared at the back of Rachael's head.

For the first time since his absurd journey with the Order began, Peter felt his first inkling of doubt. Rachael's throwaway explanation, though he was sure not meant as a defence of the practices, seemed to resonate with him.

Peter cringed at his moment of weakness. Even so, this did explain at least in part the traction the Order had gained. Until the true brutality of their regime had been revealed by the Resistance, the promise of new cures to previously incurable diseases seemed, of course, on the face of it, an attractive prospect.

Within the levels of this complex, except for what materials the dispersing lab agents had taken with them, the five of them were about to destroy decades of research. But in the ashes of their victory, what might they destroy?

Had the Order developed the building blocks of a cancer cure? Amidst the barbarity, had their research discovered a method for the return of sight for the blind? Had they discovered fuel to reverse a degenerating mind, or treatments to eradicate the risk of hereditary disease? Was their fight to regain the fundamental human freedoms of choice flippantly condemning lives to come? Lives now?

"Peter!"

The young girl had screamed out, waking him from his confusion. But as he looked up at the growing green outline of a lab agent running out from a side room, their face determined, their gun pointed directly towards him, Peter knew it was too late.

He watched as a tiny glint of green sped towards him, felt his head forced backwards, heard a crack, a loud gunshot, a squeal of pain, and then nothing.

The bullet had rebounded painlessly off his visor, and he had recovered just in time to see the digital outline of the shooter slump to the ground as Dux approached. The digital confirmation of his being 'DECEASED' soon formed above his body.

Peter pulled up his visor, marvelling at his escape from death, and turned to identify the source of the squeal. With a look of horror, he saw the young girl leaning against the glass.

"I'm fine," she said, wincing as she clutched a slowly spreading scarlet at the top of her left leg. She tried to put weight on it and stumbled.

Dux ran towards her, catching her just in time.

"Steady now," he said, offering her a consoling smile. "I'm going to check the wound – just keep breathing, ok?"

The girl nodded, and Peter watched anxiously as Dux lifted the side of the girl's gown to reveal a wound in her left thigh. Rather than look discomforted, the girl looked disappointed, as though she had damaged their mission.

"Clean through," said Dux, ripping a line of fabric from his shirt. He wrapped it tightly around her leg and lowered her gown with a smile. "But you won't be running anywhere."

"What do we do?" Peter asked, staring back nervously towards the elevator above. Thankfully, it remained still.

"You three go," said Dux, with a determined look towards the girl. "We'll hold them off, huh?"

The girl nodded back, restraining any exhibition of pain, with that same look of determination.

"I'll stay too," said George, moving swiftly towards them both.

Peter looked down towards them, then back at Rachael. He could not see any other option. He nodded.

"Ok," said Rachael, with a reluctant nod. "Good luck."

"Good luck," they responded, in unison.

Rachael nudged Peter forwards and moved back towards the remainder of the third level. Peter nodded towards the three of them with a weak smile and gave the young girl a consoling wink. He turned back to follow Rachael, ominously aware as he did so that he may well have just seen the three of them alive for the last time.

Peter and Rachael wasted little time, as they continued through the dimly lit remainder of the third level, eager to avoid the distraction of any further horrors that lay within the rooms they passed until they finally reached the closing bend.

"Stop," Rachael hissed urgently, holding out an arm to stop Peter just in time.

Peter stopped immediately, groaning at the force of her outstretched arm, and they both moved backwards quietly.

"What?" he hissed back, rubbing his chest as they settled behind one of the open doors nearby.

"Look," she whispered again, nodding through the glass. Peter peered out.

"Fuck."

Two Order agents had remained behind, standing guard ahead of a clear glass chamber protecting the final elevator.

"Fuck," said Peter, again. "What do we do? Why aren't they with the others?"

"They're programmed to stay behind," said Rachael offhandedly, with another nervous glance out towards them. "To protect the mainframe, at all costs."

"Programmed?" Peter asked, staring at her.

"They aren't human," she said, still peering outside. "They're machines, robots if you want; I didn't believe they actually had them."

Peter continued to stare at her, dumbfounded. "Robots? Are you kidding?"

Rachael smiled at him playfully.

"I'm going to have to draw them away," she said, with a sigh. "You'll need to be quick before they notice."

"What do you mean?"

"I think it's the only way to get you past them," she snapped, preempting his disagreement. "I'll draw them away and try to help the others. Here…"

Rachael handed Peter a small black device the size of a fist, with a circular plastic cog encircling a small digital screen – it was a bomb.

"Set the timer by twisting this counter-clockwise," she said, miming the twisting motion. "Upload the virus then set this. Then find the escape hatch and get the hell out of there before it blows."

She pointed towards his pocket, and he pulled out his father's USB flash drive.

"Presumably George told you what you'll need to do."

Peter nodded, and his mind wandered back to George's passionate explanation. He smiled and gripped the flash drive tightly.

"There's another sensor on the right side of those glass doors, and another by the elevator. G's helmet should give you the priority access you'll need."

"Should?!" Peter exclaimed, forcing his squeak into a whisper. Rachael smiled again.

"Well if it doesn't work, you won't have too long to worry about it," she said, clutching her gun and dropping her visor. "Ok, Peter…"

She turned to face him. Peter looked up from the bomb in his hand towards her, his face fraught. "Don't die will you?"

And with that, she left the room.

"Hey!" she shouted, turning towards the robots, waving her rifle. Peter threw himself against the wall as she fired three shots.

Peter did not dare to look as he heard the bullets clang against the agent's, or robot's, armour. He heard a low mechanic whir and pictured the two Terminator-like figures turning their evil glares towards Rachael. Gunshots fired out almost instantly, this time from their direction.

Peter caught a glimpse of Rachael's boot disappearing behind a bend in the glass and was horrified by the rigidly efficient pursuit of the two mechanised agents, quickly gaining ground.

He suddenly felt an insane urge to shoot towards them, to save her, but Rachael had been clear – he did not have long.

Peter emerged from the room and moved swiftly towards the glass chamber. A sensor blinked in recognition of the incomer, and Peter noticed Rachael emerge from the bend opposite in the corner of his eye. He noticed, too, that the third-level elevator had reached its destination. G, flanked by her entourage, had made their swift exit out towards Dux, George and the young girl, hidden behind one of the open doors.

More ominous still, the sensor's recognition of him appeared to have signalled something to the mechanical guards. They seemed to slow their pursuit of Rachael. It was now or never.

Panicking, Peter crouched down to the sensor, pulled down his visor and faced the scanning green lights, desperately trying to calm his breathing. His imagination threatened to spiral as he considered what kind of biomechanical trigger the Order might have installed to identify signs of an anxious intruder. Thankfully, he had been paranoid.

"Agent G1, authority level platinum. Access granted," came a slow, banal voice from the sensor, and the doors slid open. Peter stepped forward, and the doors hissed closed behind him.

He noticed movement ahead of him again and looked up to see the agents shooting at the others. As much as he wanted to, as difficult as it was to restrain himself, there was nothing he could do for them now – he had his own job to do.

Peter crouched down to face the second sensor.

"Agent G1, authority level platinum," the voice repeated, but this time it faltered. "What is your purpose?"

What is my purpose? Peter repeated the question to himself in silent panic. What am I supposed to say now?

He noticed his heart rate increasing and desperately tried to calm his breathing. What was it that she had called it? ADB... ARD...

"Agent G1," the voice repeated in the same monotonous tone. "What is your purpose?"

Peter looked up, still panicked. The young girl lay motionless behind the door opposite – was she dead? Peter had not even asked her name in the chaos. Dux and George had retreated towards her. George dragged her back towards another room as Dux and Rachael, who had reached them now, offered cover fire.

What was that protocol called? AD… ADR…

Rachael turned towards him and caught his eye. She pointed frantically in the direction she had come from, towards the robotic guards he knew must be hastily making their way back to apprehend the intruder. He saw G staring towards him too, smirking at his apparent distress.

"Agent G1, what is your-"

"ADRB2!" Peter shouted back, laughing in relief. "Protocol ADRB2! I'm here to protect the mainframe. I'm here to secure the future of PHROX."

He breathed heavily, tentatively waiting for a response. He turned as something flickered in the corner of his eye. The robotic guards had reached him but had slowed to a halt. He had done it; he was in.

"Access granted," came the voice again, and the sensor glowed a shade of blue he would never forget. "Good luck Agent G1."

The elevator doors slid open. With one final look out towards the others, still cowering from the gunfire, one final look towards the now overtly animated G barking orders at her agents, Peter stepped inside.

44

Peter resisted his desperate urge to look back towards the fighting; had he done so, his resolve for the task ahead might well have disintegrated. There was no going back now; there was nothing he could do to help them.

Instead, he stared through the glass and down towards the chasm below. Peter took a few steadying breaths as the elevator juddered into action and lowered his visor, eager for the distraction of the technology.

This is it, he kept thinking to himself, gripping his rifle tightly. Everything that had happened, everything that they had built towards, it all came down to this.

The elevator continued its journey, faster and deeper beneath the Bullring - thirty feet, fifty feet, seventy feet. The digital statistics grew brighter against the darkness, indicating a descent deeper than he could have imagined. Ninety feet, one hundred feet. How had they built such a vast structure, beneath one of the busiest buildings in the UK, and gone undetected for so long?

He did not dare retrieve it this close to the end but Peter pictured the small, seemingly harmless object sitting patiently in his side holster and grew suddenly aware of his being in a tightly enclosed space.

Peter pictured his mission clearly to deter the growing threat of anxiety. He was so close now to avenging his father's death, to completing this surreal saga in his life. Perhaps if he was lucky, it might signal his return to some degree of normality, if that was even possible now, after everything that had happened. The idea that he could stroll back into the Chronicle building, settle into his desk and write about city-centre art exhibitions now, after everything, was absurd. Yet, he could not deny the warmth that the picture gave him.

120 feet, 140 feet, 160 feet.

Peter shook himself. He could not afford to think about his future now; he could not afford any distractions. The entire Resistance movement depended on him - the arts writer turned revolutionary. His focus had to remain on the task ahead.

The elevator descended further still, and Peter saw the budding outline of the dome approach, saw the sparks of activity as lights flickered across the outside of the structure.

Peter restrained the urge to lift his visor, unsure whether anyone might recognise who it was approaching. He pictured a large plasma ball, like the ones he had seen as a child at the science museum with his mother. It had been one of those rare days that she had not dropped her facade of happiness – one seemingly perfect day.

As the dome grew closer, the elevator shuddered and began to slow. "Approaching Level Four."

Peter gripped his rifle ahead of him as it juddered again to a halt. The tinny voice rang out again. "Level Four."

Peter stood still, staring out towards the outline of the dome as the glass door slid open ahead of him. Every move he made now had to give the impression that he belonged. Without hesitation, he stepped out.

Peter looked down at his feet and noticed a sparkling light below. Ahead of him lay a curving pathway, lit on either side by small, glowing lights, guiding him towards the entrance to the dome.

Peter advanced purposefully, clutching his rifle rather more tightly than was necessary as he disregarded perilous digital warnings of what would face him, should he stray from the path.

Peter soon noticed outlines moving frantically from inside the dome, carrying objects and papers, actuating their escape and the Order's future survival. As he neared, the figures slowed their movements. All activity ceased, and all those inside stopped and turned to investigate the agent approaching from outside.

Peter gulped, hoping that there had been nothing about his approach that gave him away. He walked directly towards what appeared to be another of the scanners upon a small knee-high post, ten metres or so from the dome entrance.

Peter leant down, his heart thumping in his chest. The familiar green lights scanned his visor horizontally and vertically before emitting its accepting beep. Sighing, he straightened up to look back towards the dome. It was all he could do not to gasp or fire his weapon.

Five metres from the dome entrance stood G, or so he thought. He resisted the urge to grab his gun, fraught, he supposed, by his desire not to incriminate himself, but it had been a close call.

Peter looked more closely at the translucent figure… translucent. It was not G at all, but an incredibly lifelike hologram. It appeared almost instantly upon the beep and rotated slowly to face the small entrance panel to the dome.

The frosted glass switched suddenly clear. Peter saw the digital outline of a lab agent inside, staring out wide-eyed and 'CONFUSED' at what must have been a recently-introduced security protocol. Indici had never mentioned this.

Peter walked towards the entrance with the authority he would expect G to have possessed. He could not allow any moment's reprieve for the lab agent to second-guess why G was here and not in the battle that raged above.

As Peter neared, he noticed with horror that one of the other lab agents had rushed towards the escape shaft inside, her hands full of documents. Peter had to stop her; he could not let them leave with anything.

He urged the door to open, desperate not to reveal himself too early with gunshots, but thankfully, his emboldened approach appeared to have had the desired effect. The lab agent rushed forward as 'G' approached and placed his hand on an area a few steps away from the entrance.

"Agent G," the man said as the door hissed open, with a squeak and a half-bow that indicated his evident fear of her. "Why have you -"

Peter ignored him. He pushed the man roughly aside and, without hesitation, fired a shot towards the agent at the escape shaft.

With a high-pitched scream, she dropped to the floor, spilling the documents everywhere as she clutched her calf.

"What the f -" came another voice, and Peter had only a few seconds to react before a vast outline rushed towards him.

Peter ducked instinctively, just in time, as the woman swung a keyboard towards where his head had just been. The effort of her intended blow propelled her past him, and Peter capitalised, planting a well-placed kick into the sizeable derrière.

The woman fell forward and collided hard with the edge of a nearby workstation before falling to the ground, unconscious.

Peter looked back towards the escape shaft. The lab agent, unsteady on her wounded leg, had reached for a gun. He reacted in an instant, before even his visor had warned him of the danger. He lifted his rifle again and fired a shot towards her.

The bullet hit the woman's neck, and she dropped her gun to the floor. She clutched desperately at the wound as blood spilt down her front. Without her arms to support her against the glass, her leg crumpled beneath her.

Peter spared no time for guilt and continued his search around the room for others. He turned to his right and saw a smaller lab agent holding a gun, his grip shaking, aimed directly towards him.

They both paused for a second, staring at each other. Neither moved as they assessed the other's intent. Peter wondered if the agent - twenty-six years old, five-feet-seven - was considering the reprimand awaiting him should he shoot a high-profile Order agent, but he quickly made his decision.

A flashing red 'EVADE' message popped up on his visor screen, and Peter threw himself sideways. He rolled behind a nearby workstation just in time as the lab agent nervously fired in his direction.

The bullets fired in succession, colliding with a tinny echo against the dome's interior, bouncing harmlessly off in various directions. Peter heard the gun click as the man's cartridge ran out, and he took his chance. He threw himself out from behind the desk, his helmet sliding off and rolling away, and fired towards the man.

Peter pulled himself up into a crouched position, his gun still aimed, and watched as a look of bewilderment spread across the man's face.

His momentary shock at seeing Peter Brockland emerge from beneath Agent G's helmet was short-lived. He glanced down at his chest to see the slow spread of scarlet.

Peter watched as the man offered a weak gurgle before he coughed up two spurts of blood and fell to the ground.

"No!"

An anguished scream burst out from behind a nearby workstation, and before Peter had been offered a chance to react, a woman had thrown herself at him. Though only slight in frame, she forced him to the ground, and his rifle slid away.

The woman fell on top of him, straddling his stomach, and Peter stared helplessly up at a face consumed by grief-stricken rage. She let out a deep, primal howl and threw punch after punch down at him as Peter held his arms up defensively.

I don't have time for this, Peter thought angrily, as the punches collided painlessly against his heavily padded armour.

"Enough!" Peter roared, and with a muster of strength, he forced the woman backwards.

She skidded towards the lifeless body of her colleague. Peter saw her turn to look at him through anguished eyes; perhaps they had been more than colleagues. His brief pang of guilt quickly evaporated when he saw the woman's eyes rest upon the dead man's gun. She grabbed for it, but Peter had been faster.

"Do not lift that gun, or I will shoot you!"

Peter stood opposite, his heart thumping again, his pistol raised. She turned slowly towards him, shaking. She had not yet lifted the gun; it remained gripped in her right hand, limply by her side.

"You?" she muttered, comprehending for the first time the man she had been tussling with. Peter could see her pallid grief replaced by a wave of growing anger. Her hand began to shake. "You killed him."

"Please," said Peter, pleading with the young woman. "I don't want to shoot you."

Peter stared at her imploringly, alert for any hint of movement. He held his gun tightly in both hands, his finger tensed upon the trigger. She turned back to look at the man on the floor, his face now devoid of colour and still fixed with a look of almost amused shock.

The blood surrounding him had begun to meander towards the woman's shoes, and Peter could see furious tears flowing down her cheek. He did not need the predictive support of his visor lying a few metres away to know what was about to happen.

Please don't, he pleaded silently. Please don't.

The woman trembled for a second before releasing an intense roar. She turned back towards Peter and raised the gun, but he had been ready. He fired one clean shot into the woman's forehead.

"Fuck," Peter uttered as she fell back on the other agent. "Fuck."

Assuaging a tingling of guilt, he looked around again for any more signs of movement. It was still, quiet. Satisfied that there was no further danger, he lowered his pistol and looked more closely at his surroundings.

The inside of the dome seemed like something he might expect to have seen in some futuristic film set. Without the imminent threat of gunshots, Peter could finally embrace the sensory overload as flurries of purple light shot across the inside surface of the dome in all directions.

Small workstations filled the room, each littered with what documents remained and kitted with various pieces of lab equipment. Peter walked around them and saw a selection of printouts of faces, missions, or genetic assessments. Many of the workstations had a series of test tubes too, containing the various genetic samples of the Order's victims.

Peter flinched suddenly at movement from above, but as he pointed his gun towards the roof above, he saw faces and numbers displayed on the glass panels. They all linked with the emittances of data, which he realised the pulses of purple light must have been, all feeding to, or from, the central mainframe.

Peter shook his head to deter his light-headedness. The interdimensional setting seemed to regurgitate feelings he had not experienced since his blurred nights of recreational adventure at university.

Peter moved slowly towards the central mainframe. It scaled up towards the top of the dome above, connecting everything inside. He circled it slowly, taking in the Order's prize asset. The mainframe was split into four sections, each side of the square pyramid structure. Each section had its own in-built screen, various buttons, and another small scanner.

Peter paused at one of the stations and stared. Various names appeared and disappeared on the monitor, presumably in the process of being analysed for their genetic compatibility. After a few names came and went, another appeared on screen and remained there a moment longer than the others had done. Peter leant in as a young boy's face appeared on screen, linking out from the name 'Ezekial Smith'.

More pop-ups appeared – numbers calculating, images of what must have been samples of the boy's DNA swirling before a further message appeared. 'ALERT… INCOMPATIBLE'.

A small red light flashed above the screen, and the inside of the dome switched from its calm royal purple shade to three pulses of violent red. The dome returned to its standard purple, but the screen remained the same, still flashing the 'ALERT… INCOMPATIBLE' message, as though waiting for further instruction from its user.

This was it? This was what it came down to? What had Peter expected, some strange chamber possessing secrets of an extra-terrestrial nature? Though the room certainly had its own futuristic feel, it seemed so simple - a collection of desks and workstations surrounding a, albeit unique, but harmless-looking computer. A few seconds' calculations on screen, and that was all it seemed to take for this young boy to be condemned to imprisonment, sterilisation, perhaps death.

The screen flashed again, 'Automatic processing in 60 seconds'.

Peter turned, panicked, and searched for the lab agent who had permitted him entry, desperate to stop the young boy's name from leaving the dome. He saw the man, conscious now, taking advantage of Peter's distraction to drag himself groggily towards the exit, his leg flailing behind him. Peter supposed he must have injured it from the force of his entry.

"Hey!" Peter shouted, running towards him. "No, you don't."

Peter grabbed the man by his injured leg and pulled him back towards the mainframe, where the red light still flashed impatiently.

"You have to help me stop this," said Peter, struggling against the man's remaining functioning limbs as he flailed in his attempt to break away.

Peter knelt on the man's injured leg and heard a sickening crack as the leg broke beneath him. With a scream of pain, the man held up his arms in retreat.

"I can't," he groaned, panting. "I don't have the authorisation to halt an incompatible process!"

"You're lying," Peter growled impatiently, and he exerted more pressure upon the man's injured leg. "I know you can stop this, I know it's been done before!"

He thought back to Indici's account of the events that had led to his escape - how he had stopped Peter's name from advancing to the PHROX agents. He had instead passed what turned out to be Peter's forged result to his father, starting it all.

"I can't, I swear!" the man cried out again, his face clenched in agony. "It takes four of us to halt a name progressing."

Peter released some of the pressure on the man's leg, and he continued. "And you've killed three of them!"

Peter turned to look back towards the lifeless bodies of the two young lab agents, to the unconscious, larger agent, and back towards the escape shaft. The lab agent lay against the glass, her lab coat stained with blood, her face drained of colour and resigned to her fate; she had succumbed to the neck wound.

"Besides," the man continued, scrambling back from Peter's brief release. "I imagine most of our agents are preoccupied, dealing with your lot."

The man nodded to a point behind Peter. He turned to see one of the panels inside the dome displaying footage of the battle still raging outside.

Peter looked back at the mainframe. The red light had stopped flashing. The message on the screen had disappeared. A purple light shot up from the mainframe, up and out of the dome towards the levels above them.

Peter sighed and held his forehead - Ezekial Smith had to be the last one. The recoiling lab agent might have had a point. Perhaps the boy was indeed safe with the PHROX agents distracted outside, perhaps not, but Peter was not prepared to risk any more names coming out. It was time to destroy it for good.

Peter pulled the flash drive from his pocket and turned it over in his hand. He stared at it apprehensively and hoped that the launch of the virus was going to be as simple as George had suggested.

"What are you doing?" came the weakened voice of the lab agent as Peter circled the mainframe, searching for a free USB port. "What is that?"

"I'm ending it," said Peter, still circling, until he finally found a slot beneath one of the mainframe stations. He held the flash drive and stared at it again before crouching down.

"Ending all of it," he continued, and he inserted the flash drive into the open port.

Nothing happened. Peter stood up and stared at the screen, pleading with it, anxiously waiting for something to appear, anything.

The lab agent behind him let out a cruel chuckle, but before Peter could retaliate, the screens finally flickered. The AutoRun function had begun.

A smaller pop-up message appeared – 'Would you like to open…' – and Peter pressed at the screen impatiently. Another message appeared, far more daunting – 'Authority required...'

A light flickered into life, and Peter noticed the outline of a hand appear on the scanner. Would G's authority be enough? He looked into the white, padded glove he had stolen from G, and stared at it. Would it even work? He breathed in heavily and placed his hand on the scanner.

The scanner analysed Peter's gloved hand two times, three times, four times. Peter held his breath. Nothing seemed to be happening. He looked around frantically for the lab agent's support.

The mainframe had been attempting a second scan at the station beside him. He turned back to his monitor, and his face drained of colour; a smaller screen above the central monitor had begun a facial recognition scan.

Peter ducked, certain that had it scanned him, the system would have shut down immediately.

"Throw me that helmet," said Peter, thinking fast, and with his free hand, he directed his gun towards the lab agent cowering a few metres away. "Now."

Reluctantly, the lab agent turned to his side and reached for G's helmet. He turned back with a growl of pain and slid it back along the floor towards Peter.

Peter picked it up, still ducked away from the prying eye of the mainframe facial scan, and hastily placed it back over his head. He pulled down the visor and stood up to face the scanner, urging it to work.

The mainframe scanned him inquisitively. After a few nervous seconds, the glove and visor appeared to have done their jobs. A visual of G's hand and face appeared on the screen, shortly followed by the indication of her platinum authority level.

'Thank you Agent G1', came another message on the screen, until - 'Additional authority required'.

"Fuck!" Peter shouted, panicking again. He turned aimlessly to scan the room for inspiration.

He had not been prepared for this level of resistance; why was it so difficult? Peter had been told, and without question had accepted, that the virus upload would be automatic – just plug it in and let it do its work. Had George intended, or perhaps hoped, that someone would be with him in the end?

His eyes rested back upon the lab agent who, in Peter's distraction, had again managed to edge slowly back towards the exit. Peter pulled his hand from the scanner and ran towards him.

"How do I get in?" Peter shouted, crouching down and shaking the man frantically.

He stared back at Peter with a smug smile, still panting from the pain in his leg, and refused to answer.

"How do I get in?" Peter shouted again, with increasing urgency. With a growl of impatience, he gripped the man's leg. The agent writhed around the floor in agony but still refused to answer.

Before any further physical persuasion was required, he noticed a lanyard emerge from the man's lab coat. As the agent continued to flail his arms to fight Peter off, the lanyard spilt, revealing the man's ID – Brian Sekandi, Authority Level Gold.

Peter stood up and pointed his gun at the man's head again. Would gold be enough? Had he got this far only to be thwarted by his haste to shoot the other agents? Did he really need the four of them?

"Is gold authority enough?" Peter shouted as the man scrambled away again. The agent looked nervously back at him, recognising his slip-up, and hastily thrust the ID card back into the depths of his lab coat.

"I'm not going to help you," he muttered, sweating profusely. "And you might as well put that gun down; you aren't going to shoot me. You need me alive. The scanner would know I'm dead."

Peter spun around and looked for something that might help him. His eyes rested upon a heavy-looking microscope and a small, but sharp-looking knife lying on one of the nearby workstations.

"Alive, maybe," he mumbled, and he walked towards the desk.

He had seen it many times before in sci-fi movies, the detached hand of a devious foe granting access to a secret lair, but did he have the stomach for it? He was not sure it would even work, but could he scare him enough into helping him?

"But perhaps not attached..."

He walked back towards the agent, who stared up at him, still breathing heavily. A dawning comprehension came over him as he quickly understood what Peter had meant, and he scrambled backwards.

"No," he stuttered, his eyes wide. "It wouldn't work, you're crazy!"

The agent recoiled as Peter approached. Peter hoped, desperately, that his act of derangement would force the man to change his mind before it had to happen. He could not have much longer down here alone before the others caught up with him.

Fixing a look of maddened determination, Peter lifted the microscope above his head and stood above the agent.

"No!" the agent screamed, and as Peter thrust the microscope downwards, he shouted. "Ok, I'll do it!"

With an exerting blow, Peter slammed the microscope down only a few inches from the man's outstretched hand and dragged him to his feet. He threw the man's arm over his shoulder, and the two of them stumbled back towards the mainframe.

Peter threw the agent into one of the chairs, and they both looked at the screen. It still displayed the same blinking message – 'Additional authority required'.

"Now," Peter growled, and he pressed his gun into the man's temple.

The agent let out a conceding sigh and placed his right hand on the scanner. After a few seconds, it released the familiar accepting beep, and the agent leant forward for the facial scan.

'Brian Sekandi', came the new message. 'Authority Level Gold… Dual Authority Level Granted'.

Peter pushed the man backwards, and the chair rolled away. He had lied, two was enough. Peter turned back to the screen, possessed by a newfound excitement, and saw a new message – 'Run programme?'

Peter pressed the 'Yes' option and stood back. The screens flickered again. Had it worked?

"You'll never get out of here alive," the agent sneered, suggesting the programme had indeed begun to work.

Peter turned back to offer his retort but grew distracted by the sight through the dome's frosted glass; the elevator outside was returning. G and the other agents must have overcome Rachael and the others.

With a pang of grief for what he presumed must have been their deaths, Peter turned back to the mainframe. The virus upload had indeed started – estimated completion time, ten minutes.

"My survival hasn't been a priority for quite some time, Brian," said Peter as Stage 1 quickly reached completion.

Peter walked towards the mainframe and carefully extracted the small black cube from his holster. Smiling nervously, he twisted the outside as Rachael had instructed, and set the timer for eleven minutes before placing it gently upon the mainframe station.

"But I suppose yours should be," Peter continued, stepping away with a sigh of relief that he had not exploded the room prematurely. He turned back to look at the agent, who stared back blankly. "Do you think you can manage with her?"

The agent looked past Peter with terror as he saw the timer counting down. He followed Peter's nod towards the larger lab agent, who still lay unconscious.

"Manage?" he asked weakly, but Peter had already rushed towards her. He knelt down, and with an intense effort, lifted her over his shoulder.

"Yep," said Peter through gritted teeth. "You've got less than eleven minutes to get the both of you out."

Peter moved gingerly towards the escape shaft and, less carefully than he had intended, lay the unconscious agent down on the small platform inside.

"Out?" said the agent, blankly, and Peter turned back towards him. "You mean, you're letting me, us, go?"

"I don't see much of a case for killing you," said Peter as he walked back and lifted the agent from the chair.

"Besides," Peter continued, with a gasp of effort as they moved towards the escape shaft. "If my final minutes are going to be spent down here, I'd rather they weren't shared with you. I can't say that I've enjoyed your company very much, Brian."

Peter said it so light-heartedly that he had surprised even himself at how casually he had seemed to accept his imminent death. He pulled Brian gently into the inside of the escape shaft and stepped back outside.

With one final pang of guilt, he pulled the dead agent resting up against the glass away, removing her lifeless arm from the opening. He rested her gently on the floor a few metres away. He turned back to see that the other woman had begun to stir, but Brian had not moved; he continued to stare back at him.

"Less than nine minutes Brian," said Peter, with an urging glance towards the touch screen controls inside.

The agent seemed lost for words. He nodded back weakly.

"Oh, and Brian," said Peter, and the man turned back from the controls to look at him, still wide-eyed. "If you do get out of this alive, do something better with your skills won't you?"

Peter forced a weak smile, hiding his disdain for the man, who nodded back, still unable to speak. The agent pressed the touch screen inside the glass shaft, and the door slid closed.

"I suppose a thank you was too much to ask," Peter muttered to himself as the platform began its steady ascent out of the dome above.

Peter turned back to look at the mainframe and watched as the upload continued. Stage 2 had completed, and with it, the lights shooting towards, and from, the mainframe had ceased. The virus had halted the progress of the mainframe data feeding up to the levels above. Some success, at last.

Peter stood for a moment, allowing himself some recovery time, and looked at how long he had left.

Six minutes until the virus upload was complete. He looked towards the bomb timer, still ominously counting down. Seven minutes to detonation.

Seven minutes then to hold off the Order agents, who now made their way towards the dome, guided by the purple pathway lights. Seven minutes to hold off G, who stood ahead of the others, her face livid, shouting orders towards her agents as she stared at Peter's outline through the entrance to the dome. Seven minutes to end it all.

45

Peter stood motionless, his arms held tightly behind his back. He watched on calmly as the agents fired their weapons hopelessly against the frosted glass exterior of the dome, desperate in their attempts to foil his plan.

G stood still, facing him, unperturbed by the bullets rebounding from the glass ahead of her. The glass between them was clear, and Peter could see her face clearly, taut with ferocious rage, staring directly at him.

After a few moments, she lifted her hand slowly and motioned for her agents to cease their gunfire. Their attempts to bypass the scanner had failed without an agent inside to permit them entry. Their force attempts had failed too; they were out of options. The dome's defences had held.

"I suppose you think you've won," G spat, her voice amplified by the dome's intercom system.

Peter turned away from her to look back at the mainframe. The virus continued its steady upload. He looked back at G with a wry smile. "Still a few minutes left before that."

She scowled and looked past Peter towards the mainframe screens. Through the, now clear, glass, she could see the notification - Stage 3 of the virus upload had been completed. All calculating functions ceased and, with it, the activity within the inside panels of the dome above emptied. The faces of the damned had disappeared.

"Don't you realise what you are about to do?" she growled, her voice tinged for the first time by genuine concern. "Don't you understand the damage you and your stupid revolution are going to do, to all of us?"

"I know exactly what I'm doing," Peter returned with steel. "I'm destroying it all."

Peter noticed the agents behind her glance up; without the images filling the panels above him, he could see that the vast digital screen above had begun to falter. The president's face had disappeared.

"All the algorithms, all the names," he continued, looking back at G. "Everything."

G stared back at him before flickering her gaze above his right shoulder. "Not everything, it would seem."

Peter followed her glance and saw that the escape shaft had emerged from the top of the dome, a bundle of lab coats the only thing visible now.

"By letting our people go, you are making the mistake that dooms you to failure," G sneered, her face easing. "You can delete everything we have here, but with our people, our ideas live on; our duty to protect humanity from itself will live on. Have you not yet understood our reach? We have people everywhere, sympathisers everywhere, history everywhere."

Peter stared back at her as her eyes bulged. He did not have long; he only needed to stall them for a few more minutes.

"Your actions here," she continued in a manic flurry of words. "Your Resistance's actions up there…" She nodded upwards. "Even if by some miracle you win this battle, you must know that we will not disappear. You must know that we will return."

She paused, as though waiting for Peter to respond and scanned his expression for signs her words had cut through. When Peter remained still, she smiled.

"I have fought for years to pull this organisation out from the shadows," she continued, her voice drenched with passion. "But we can return; we can build again in the darkness, build on the world's fears and selfish desires for survival, for order. You underestimate our dedication… my dedication."

She looked down for a split second, and her hand edged subconsciously towards her stomach. Peter remembered that she had done this before whilst interrogating him in his cell. With a cringe of revulsion, he finally understood.

She looked back up again and noticed that Peter had spotted her moment of weakness. She was not abashed at his discovery but instead smiled. She released the clips on her borrowed body armour and lifted the hem of her t-shirt to reveal a small scar beneath her navel.

"My test came early," she said lightly, stroking the scar with her fingers. "I was young, pregnant and frightened. I tried to hide it from the beginning, tried to pretend it wasn't happening, but there was only so long I could wait before they found out."

Peter was taken aback by the distinct change in her tone; she had softened dramatically. Her eyes appeared not to be concentrating on him anymore, but rather in a sort of daze.

"She was 30 weeks when they had her tested," she continued as Peter stared back. "And when she came back as incompatible, my whole life had collapsed. How could I, with everything I stood for, with everything I had done for the Order, have an incompatible child?"

She trailed off a moment as though the memory, or at least her speaking it out loud, caused her considerable pain. Peter wondered if it had been the first time she had spoken about the experience in years, perhaps ever.

"They forced me to terminate it, of course," she said, and with that, her release of what was evidently a deeply-guarded human side reverted back.

"And they were right. My dedication to the Order was tested, my duty to protect the future of humankind. I passed. The foetus was disposed of, and I had myself sterilised to avoid such a foolish episode from happening again."

The foetus was disposed of... Peter repeated her words in his mind. He struggled to comprehend the callousness with which she had recalled the termination of her only daughter, in what had clearly been a traumatic experience in her past, but it explained everything.

It explained her cavalier attitude towards murdering Raj's young daughter. It explained her dogged dedication to the regime. It explained her anger towards his father having, and hiding, a child, explained why she had become so obsessed with ensuring his father faced that same test, felt that same pain. For her, the Order had to be right, or else she had permitted the murder of her unborn child, for nothing.

Peter felt sick at the thought a mother could have the capacity for such cruelty, particularly when compared to the lengths his mother had gone to, to protect him. But had Agent G actually been given a chance? He knew her to be cruel, brutal, but had she been given the help that his father had done, had she been offered that same route out, might she have turned out differently?

Was this Peter's desperation again to find the good in anyone, or did she represent what his father might have become had he not been given his opportunity to save his son? Was this the future that awaited mothers and fathers everywhere should he, should the Resistance, fail?

"That's why I need to destroy the idea of you," said Peter, restraining his disgust. Whatever sympathy he might have had for the young mother forced to give up her unborn daughter was gone. She was not here now; he had seen first-hand what that woman had become.

Peter motioned towards the small black cube, still counting down upon the closest mainframe station. G's eyes darted towards it, and she noticed with horror the timer break the two-minute mark.

"Taking down this entire facility will show the people out there that you can be destroyed, that they need never fear your dominance again."

G's lips pursed, and her face drained of colour. She stepped back a few paces and grabbed her pistol before firing round after round towards the dome entrance, to no avail. Behind her, Peter noticed one of the agents stare at Peter's hand, still pointing towards the bomb, and saw them loosen their grip on their rifle.

G threw her pistol aside, having run out of ammunition, and pulled out another. As she did so, the agent behind her dropped their rifle. They turned, slowly, and ran back towards the elevator.

G, still shooting at the dome entrance, had not noticed their retreat, but the other agents seemed to be reconsidering their positions too. They turned to look at each other before edging away.

With a low whine and a flicker, the lights guiding the pathway back towards the elevator began to falter as the virus spread its destruction throughout the lower level. It seemed to be all the impetus they had needed.

Taking advantage of their commander's distraction, they turned away. Using the torches mounted on their rifles, they navigated their sprints along the pathway and back towards their escape.

G turned back at the sound of their clambering footsteps. "Where are you going?!" she screamed, her voice breaking with a newfound mania. "Get back here now!"

She turned from the dome, abandoning her attempts to break through the impenetrable glass, and fired towards the deserting agents, whose figures emerged and faded away in the darkness with the phasing on and off of the malfunctioning lights.

Peter saw two of them stumble as the bullets hit them, and, with a slight pang, heard their screams fade into nothingness with the lights of their rifles, as they fell into the depths of the chasm below.

With a final outburst of rage, G's gun clicked empty again. She turned back to look at Peter, her hair frenzied, her face drenched in an enraged sweat.

"You're prepared to die for this then, are you?" she yelled, tossing the gun aside.

"I have been for a long time," Peter replied calmly, and with a final glance towards the mainframe, he saw that the virus had completed its upload.

All light inside the dome died for a moment, plunging them into complete darkness before the mainframe screens flickered back into life. The only light inside the dome now came from the screens; all had been replaced by a white background, with a small shield entwined by a double helix in the centre. He had done it. He had actually done it; the mainframe had been destroyed.

Peter smiled weakly and looked down towards the bomb timer. It had entered its final minute.

"You don't have much longer left to get out," said Peter quietly. He turned back towards G, whose face seemed void of life. Her expression bore a strange blend of confusion, fear, rage and regret, and her eyes widened with a sudden and utter shock. It was as though she were seeing Peter clearly for the first time.

With one final look at him, his outline glowing spookily ahead of the white screens behind, the man who had just destroyed everything, the man who had rendered her ultimate sacrifice worthless, she stepped backwards and was lost to the darkness.

Peter felt no pity for her; a perfect serenity had washed over him as he turned back to look at the mainframe. Thirty seconds left.

Peter pictured the people fighting for their lives above him and wondered, hoped even, that the same image of the Resistance shield had appeared on the outer walls of the Bullring. He hoped it would give them the euphoric knowledge that it was over, that the mainframe had been destroyed. He hoped it would give them the faith they needed to keep fighting, to be rid of PHROX for good.

Twenty seconds left.

He thought back to his mother and the sacrifices she had made to keep him safe, to protect him, despite her grief and fear, from the truth. He thought of his father too and pictured his weak smile disappearing behind the sliding wall as he sacrificed himself to allow his son's escape. He felt a hot rush of sadness as the wave of their loss fell over him; he hoped they would be proud of him now.

Ten seconds left.

Peter thought of Rachael, of Dux and George, of Indici, of all of the Resistance survivors he had known who had sacrificed their lives to ensure that he and the Resistance would succeed.

Five seconds left.

He felt his body tingling; he had done it, really done it. Against incalculable odds, the mediocre arts journalist had overcome one of the most sinister organisations in history.

Three seconds left.

He felt his body weaken, preparing him for the end. With one final breath, he closed his eyes.

46

Rachael stumbled down the final few steps, and with a grunt that echoed back up the stairway, kicked through the fire exit door leading out to the underground car park. George groaned with pain.

"Come on," Rachael growled, lifting George from her shoulder. "Not far now."

Rachael dragged George through the doorway and rested him against a nearby wall, before turning back to the others. Dux was only metres behind, struggling through the small gap with the young girl hauled up in his arms. Rachael glanced around, struggling to capture her breath, and her eyes widened.

Bodies lay everywhere, Resistance and Order forces, sprawled against deserted cars or across the concrete floor. The battle outside had filtered into the car park, with the frightened and the wounded having sought solace in what they must have hoped would be relative protection. Instead, they had only found their end.

Rachael could hear the roars, bangs and screams tearing through the smoke-ridden air from the battle still raging outside and felt an intense, impatient desperation to sprint outside, to fight amongst them.

"Can you walk?" Rachael asked roughly, grabbing George's shoulders and pulling him up to face her.

"I think so," George groaned with a grimace. His leg was wounded, but not so badly as to put him in immediate danger - not compared with what waited for them outside, anyway.

"Can you fight?" she asked, unable to hide her hopeful tone.

Rachael did not wait for his answer but instead thrust a pistol into his hand; no, at this point, was not an option. George looked down at the gun. With a determined look, he looked back up at her and nodded.

"Fuck."

Dux released a low gasp from behind her, but as Rachael turned quickly towards him, expecting an attack, she could see that it was only then that Dux had taken the opportunity to assess the scene - to comprehend the bodies, dead or dying, strewn across the car park.

"We need to get out there," said Rachael, smiling weakly at George before turning to Dux. Her face had been abducted by an emblazoned passion that she knew Dux would understand.

Dux looked towards the ramp leading out through the smoke towards the battle outside. He nodded, with a twitch in his face that might almost have been verging on an excited smile. He motioned towards the young girl still nestled in his arms, who had only just begun to stir back into consciousness.

"Ok." Rachael stared around hopelessly, almost selfishly, searching for somewhere they might be able to leave her in some relative degree of safety. But nowhere was safe now.

Footsteps came from behind them, and Rachael turned to see two Order agents move out from behind a car nearby. Neither wore their customary helmets and as they emerged shakily their eyes locked with hers. Seeing their faces outside the veil of their visors seemed almost enough to humanise them.

"Dux…" she murmured, maintaining her stare.

The agents smiled as they noticed them all standing there, with a level of menace that quickly removed any threat of a human connection. They approached slowly, and Rachael heard the anticipatory pops against the hubbub outside as they cracked their necks and stretched out their arms. With some relief, Rachael noticed that neither of them had their guns.

"Get her out of here," she heard Dux mutter from behind her, and after a few scuffled movements, she felt Dux's presence beside her.

The agents began to speed up, raising their fists into a fighting position. Even disguised in their white armour, it was clear that Dux and Rachael were their enemies. Perhaps they knew her, perhaps they all knew who she was now, the agent who had betrayed them all.

"Ready?" Dux asked quietly as they too began to walk forward. Rachael offered a quick, confident nod before they ran.

Dux was faster. He ducked the opening swings of both agents and, using the full force of his body, threw himself into them.

They fell back, slamming into the concrete ground. Rachael did not wait for her follow-up and threw herself into an acrobatic cartwheel in an attempt to drive her knee into the face of one of the winded agents.

The agent reacted quickly, rolling aside. Rather than colliding with the agent's nose beneath her, she was instead forced to experience the painful crunch of her knee driving into the concrete.

Rachael heard the agent laugh between gasps for breath, and she made a concerted effort to hide her pain. She stood back up, ignoring the trembling in her kneecap, and turned angrily to face them, noticing just in time a white fist flying towards her.

Instinctively, Rachael threw her arm up in defence, and the agent's fist collided painfully with her forearm. She growled and stepped back, preparing her physical retort, when she noticed a huge frame approaching beside her. She jumped backwards just as Dux lunged between them, clutching his opponent by the waist.

With a sickening crack, he had driven the agent forward with immense power into a wall nearby. The agent fell to the ground, motionless, in the most unnatural of angles.

Rachael looked back towards her opponent, who, in her distraction, had thrown another fist towards her, this time successfully. The force of the punch knocked her backwards, and it was only instinct that allowed her to ignore the ringing in her ears and duck the follow-up blow.

Using the agent's lurch against them, she turned quickly and drove her boot into the agent's left knee. She heard another sickening crack, and with a howl of pain, the agent dropped to the floor.

As the agent sought to desperately scramble away, Rachael followed up with a twisting kick into the side of the agent's head. The agent's face vacated consciousness instantly. They rolled forward, motionless, on top of the other nearby.

Breathing heavily, her hands rested upon her knees, Rachael turned to stare at Dux with a weak smile, wiping away a small trickle of blood from the corner of her mouth.

Dux smiled back, his eyes blazing, but he was unable to hide his exhaustion. Rachael opened her mouth to utter a jovial dig at his flailing fitness levels but quickly stopped; Dux's face had tightened, his eyes alert.

"Move!" he cried. Rachael watched in horror as he lurched towards her, but he was too far away.

A gunshot fired out. Rachael felt a blazing heat graze past her ear as a bullet flew mercifully past her. Everything seemed to be happening at quarter speed. She watched as Dux continued towards her before she turned back to see another agent staring up towards her from beside a mound of bodies nearby.

Rachael had no time to react. Coughing up what seemed to be a final spurt of blood, the agent managed a final, cruel smile and pointed their gun for the second attempt.

Another gunshot fired out. This time though, Rachael felt no blazing heat; instead, she continued to stare down at the dying agent as a bullet passed her and collided with their face. Rachael watched the graphic structural collapse of the agent's nose, saw the eruption of blood; the agent's head fell back lifeless.

"I want to fight," came a young, determined voice from behind her. Rachael turned, wide-eyed, to see the young girl, no longer unconscious but pointing a gun directly towards the dead agent. "Not hide."

Rachael stared at her for a moment, then at George, who stood equally resolute. Rachael offered a look of astonishment towards Dux, who returned it. Rachael turned to the girl and nodded with a beaming smile.

"Grab weapons," said Dux, addressing them all as he knelt beside the agent's lifeless body.

They obeyed, and all moved quickly to grab guns, knives and anything else they could find that might kill an agent from the bodies around them. They stopped suddenly at the sound of a low, rumbling roar from outside.

It sounded as though the Resistance had somehow arranged for another fighter jet to fly over them, but as they listened more intently they could hear that the noise was… cheering.

All four of them looked at each other, united in their assorted looks of confusion and excitement. They smiled, nodded, and turned together to run towards the fight outside.

It felt as though life had again switched to slow motion as they sprinted through the exit and into chaos. Dux and the others continued to charge in different directions, roaring and wielding their weapons, but Rachael stuttered to a halt.

Thick smoke filled the air, swirling up and around the scattered array of smashed cars, aflame and smouldering, stacked up as a blockade in the road. The bodies of more agents and Resistance fighters bedecked the roads outside, their blood draining away as the rain fell.

Rachael swiped her arm to thrust aside a thick gust of smoke, and, through the momentary gap, noticed a glimmer of white.

Instinctively, she ducked to avoid the padded arm of another agent swinging at her. Still experiencing the scene in slow-motion, Rachael effortlessly overcame the attacker, avoiding the second fist with ease before thrusting a kick into the agent's stomach. The agent crouched, winded, and Rachael pushed the agent back towards two eager Resistance fighters nearby.

Rachael saw, in a flurry of madness, the outlines of people scuffling around her, their shadowed figures lit up in the smoke by the orange embers of petrol bombs nearby. Past the scuffles and through the briefly subsiding smoke, Rachael noticed some of the Resistance crowd stood still.

She moved towards them, preparing to urge them onwards, but they had not stalled in fright; they stared up towards the Bullring with their arms lifted, cheering. The atmosphere spreading amongst them seemed not to be despair or anguish, even amongst such death and destruction, but elation.

All of them stood with their weapons raised, screaming in feral excitement towards the Bullring. Rachael saw too that police officers and soldiers – more than had done at the start - stood alongside the Resistance, joining in the apparent celebration. They had unified, almost all of them, finally, in their allegiance to the people.

The sea of white Rachael had seen through the corridors of the Bullring seemed to be ebbing away too. Those that did not decorate the streets as lifeless sculptures seemed to cower at whatever unexpected event had caused such renewed vigour amongst the incompatible mob.

Rachael turned from the crowds to look up at what had caused such a reaction and gasped. Rising high above them, illuminated in the darkness of the grizzling evening sky, was a huge shield entwined by a double helix, projecting out from the bubble-like exterior of the Bullring.

Their plan had worked. The virus had been uploaded. They had destroyed it; they had done it. Peter… Peter had done it.

A brief moment's euphoria almost threatened to erupt from her, and the urge to join the others in their battle cry was close to overwhelming. But as the glimmer of the Resistance icon reflected in her eyes, she knew what its appearance meant, knew what was going to happen next.

Time quickly returned to normal speed as adrenaline began to pump through Rachael's body, and, fuelled by the sudden burst of energy, she saw another agent sprinting towards her. Rachael poised herself for the fight, her heart thumping madly, but the agent ignored her completely. Moving in a frenzy, they tossed their weapon aside and sprinted straight past her.

Confused, Rachael stared back towards the Resistance crowds. They still cheered as though they had already won, oblivious to what was about to happen. Rachael had to get away from the Bullring; she had to get them all away.

Frantically, Rachael ran towards what fighting she could see through the haze, ducking various blows swiped towards her, and saw Dux engaged in a ferocious struggle with two agents.

Rachael threw herself forwards and tackled one of them to the ground. She fell on top of the agent hard, elbowing their helmet and pushing their visor up slightly to reveal a strong, stubbled jaw. Straddling the agent's chest, Rachael noticed the agent move towards a hilt of a knife protruding from their boot. Without hesitation, she grabbed for it first. With one swift movement, Rachael turned and thrust the knife into the agent's jaw.

"We need to get them away from the building!" Rachael shouted, her voice fighting against the screams, bangs, and cheers as a rush of blood spilt over her.

Dux threw a punch at his opponent with such force that their visor cracked open. Swiftly taking advantage of the agent's stumble, Dux pulled out his gun and fired one shot into the gap his punch had left behind.

He turned towards Rachael as the agent fell, and looked back up towards the Bullring, quickly understanding.

"Ok," he shouted back, the shield still reflected in his eyes. "Let's go!"

"We need to move!" he shouted towards the crowds nearby, who turned to look at him, confused.

Dux jogged towards Rachael and pulled her back to her feet. As they turned back towards the crowd to intensify their efforts to hustle them away, an ominous murmur came from the ground beneath them.

They turned to look at each other, and Rachael saw her apprehension mirrored in Dux's eyes.

"Run!" he shouted frantically.

Rachael chanced a quick look towards the Bullring and noticed a small group of white collected together. She saw the president stare down at the ground beneath them before he too motioned towards the large group of the remaining agents nearby, ordering their retreat.

An immediate urge to run after him, to apprehend him, to ensure that it was finished for good almost took control of her. She was thwarted only by the rough thrust of Dux's arms as he pushed her away. "No! Come on!"

The ground rumbled again, this time with greater intensity; Rachael knew they had only moments. The two of them sprinted away, shouting at the other Resistance fighters to follow. Their cheers turned to confusion, then concern, as they recognised the danger, as Dux and Rachael pushed citizens and agents alike away from the Bullring, screaming out at the oncoming explosion.

The ground continued to rumble so intensely now that it took considerable poise for them both to remain on their feet, as others stumbled and dropped to the floor nearby.

And then, finally, it happened. BOOM.

A powerful surge of air flew through them. Rachael saw the crowds around her thrown from their feet. Rachael slammed painfully against the side of a nearby car as another surge of air, rubble, and dust tore through the streets. She slid to the ground painfully, to face the Bullring, or what was left of it.

She had not needed her hearing, stolen by the blast-induced tinnitus, to recognise the destruction. The glistening digital image of the Resistance shield had disappeared as the Bullring fell in upon itself. A mountain of flame and smoke erupted from the centre, lighting up the scene around them as the explosion enacted its disintegration of PHROX headquarters.

A stunned silence fell upon the crowds as the initial blast wave subsided. Everybody stared up in unison as the Bullring disintegrated into the ground beneath it.

The immediate barrage of smoke soon began to fade away, and they all continued to watch what little remained of the Bullring shopping centre, the facade that had covered up PHROX's operation; now reduced to rubble and flames.

Rachael's hearing began to return, and the silence was replaced by scuffles of movement around her. She stared up, still dazed from the force of the explosion. The remaining Order agents had begun to scurry away, retreating in all directions into the smoke, abandoning their fight.

The crowds began to stir again, noticing their retreat, and the shock of the explosion began to dwindle. The rain continued to fall, less heavily now, as dawning comprehension spread contagiously through the Resistance fighters; they had done it, they had won.

Rachael struggled to her feet and stared around, absorbing the sounds of the ecstatic cheers and anxious calls to loved ones. She watched as survivors hugged and grieved together, united in their understanding that they had been victorious against incalculable odds.

Rachael lay back against the car, exhausted. She stared at the wreckage of the Bullring. It felt strange to be surrounded by such displays of euphoria when her heart had sunk; she knew what its destruction meant. Peter Brockland, the amateur arts journalist who had risen against all logical reason to become the figurehead uniting the Resistance movement against the Order, was gone.

Rachael forced a weak smile towards a group of young fighters as they waved and cheered together, documenting the experience on their mobile phones.

She was not sure why, but Rachael felt a crushing sadness that she had not expected. Perhaps it was the oblivious elation spreading amongst her fellow fighters or her incomprehensible admiration of Peter's heroic sacrifice. Or perhaps it was just the plummeting loss of someone who had grown to be fundamental to their success, to her.

Her melancholy was soon interrupted by a loud chopping sound above. Pushing through the billowing smoke, a huge helicopter was escaping the scene.

Rachael straightened angrily as she recognised the president. He had removed his helmet and stared down through the helicopter opening at the scene below, his face overcome by their defeat.

He turned to look at Rachael and pulled back inside, noticing her gun. He wrenched the helicopter door closed as Rachael fired a succession of gunshots up towards them, but each bullet collided hopelessly against the armoured exterior. She had been too late. She had failed in the end; the president had escaped.

Rachael continued to fire senselessly as the helicopter passed over St Martin's Cathedral and into the distance. Her gun clicked uselessly as her cartridge emptied, and she only stopped when she felt a hand rest gently upon her arm. She felt the force of it guide her arm downwards, and she turned to see Dux staring back at her.

Amidst the still jubilated crowds, still yelling out, still relaying news of the Order's downfall elsewhere, still hugging each other beneath the downpour, she had found someone who, too, understood the sacrifice involved; he too understood the immensity of what they had both, what they had all, lost.

Dux smiled weakly and pulled Rachael into a comforting one-armed hug. They did not say a word to each other; there was no need. Both of them stared silently at the smouldering remains of the Bullring, offering their final respects to Peter Brockland.

47

"Best behaviour Rosy, ok?"

Rachael offered her daughter a playfully stern look before leaning in to wipe a smudge of leftover breakfast from her cheek.

Rosy nodded back with a smile, and Rachael winked. She pocketed the wipe and turned back into the leather upholstery of the back seat of the cab.

The moment she had been dreading for weeks had finally arrived.

It had been some six months since she had last walked down these roads towards what used to be the Bullring shopping centre. Six months since she had witnessed the devastating scenes of battle that had brought everything to a close; so much had changed.

Rachael had made a conscious decision not to revisit the scene to help with the immediate aftermath or to attend the impromptu 'one-month anniversary' held by key Resistance figures. She had not taken the decision lightly. But for the months following that now-infamous battle, not a night had passed where she had not woken in a terrified sweat, as the blackened eyes and charred remains of those who had perished swam through her nightmares.

Worst of all was his scarred face, staring down from the helicopter above as the president escaped without punishment.

As though she had sensed her mother's anxiety, Rosy leant over and rested her head upon Rachael's arm. With a grateful smile, Rachael reached her arm around to pull her closer. Her daughter always did seem to have a knack for making her feel better about anything.

Rachael took a deep breath as the cab turned off the A45 and out towards that ominously long stretch of road. She pictured the bodies that had laid there, their lifeless eyes, their blood washing away into the drains by the thundering rain. She squeezed Rosy a little tighter.

"Good lord," the cab driver exclaimed, slowing to a near halt. "Ark at that!"

The soft Brummy accent had intensified, and Rachael opened her eyes to stare at what had caused the driver's exclamation.

She gasped. The route leading to where the Bullring shopping centre had once stood was packed with people, all blocking the road leading towards St Martin's Cathedral.

This time though, they were not marching towards a violent, uncertain conclusion. This time they marched in cheerful solidarity, hugging and chanting together as they remembered, and honoured, those who had fought and died to defeat the PHROX regime.

"I think I'm going to have to drop you here, love," said the cab driver, with an exasperated look out of his window towards the marching crowds.

"That's fine," Rachael gasped, still breathless from the shock of the scene. "Come on."

She reached for her purse and handed the driver a twenty-pound note before releasing Rosy's seatbelt. "Remember what Mummy said?"

She gave Rosy another playful glare, and with her arms outstretched, Rosy nodded back. "Good girl."

She pulled Rosy into her arms and stepped out of the cab, closing the door behind her.

Clutching Rosy tightly, Rachael began to weave in and out of the slowly-moving people traffic. She marvelled at the sheer number of people who had made the journey, absorbing the unexpectedly electric atmosphere.

Rachael was not quite sure what she had expected to see when she turned up, in truth, but she had been almost certain of a setting at least a tad more morose than the carnival-type scenes that proceeded ahead of her.

The crowds were laughing and singing as they walked down the same road that only months ago, many of them had been walking down silently, their weapons poised. Camera crews watched from the sidelines as journalists interviewed passers-by as though they were reporting on a fun marathon, accompanied by drumming, trumpet playing, and wildly colourful placard displays.

The two of them continued to follow the crowd, weaving through musicians and dancers, Rachael pointing out the various unexpected attractions to the delight of her daughter. Rachael noticed several people handing out small green badges, which, when she looked around again, everybody there seemed to be wearing.

"Hey, can I get one of those?"

Rachael pulled Rosy up and edged towards a young woman clutching the box of badges. She beamed back at her, extending the box.

Rachael grabbed two badges, and, after fixing one to Rosy's t-shirt, looked at hers in greater detail. It was bright green, with a symbol Rachael had not seen for quite some time – the white shield, entwined by a double helix; the Resistance were on the march once more.

They continued to meander through the crowd, and it was not long before Rachael found a familiar face.

Fighting through the now almost stationary crowds, she made the final turn towards the cathedral and saw the towering frame of Dux, leaning against the door of one of the roadside stores. She waved up towards him as he stared down into the pages of that morning's newspaper.

He looked up and beamed back at her. He waved aside the nearby crowds, and with a growl of welcome, pulled them both towards the relative comfort of the small shop alcove.

"How are you guys?" he asked gleefully, making straight for Rosy. He pulled her towards him and lifted her above his head with a playful roar.

Rosy giggled, and Dux's newspaper fell to the ground. Rachael leant down to pick it up and stared at the front-page headline.

'New dawn for civilisation!' it read in bold print. As Dux pointed out a troupe of jugglers nearby to a thoroughly entertained Rosy, Rachael read on with interest.

'"January 1st welcomes a new dawn for civilisation,"' claimed Amelia Jackson last night, as, for the first time since the tumultuous downfall of the Progression Party, the UK welcomed a new government, following months of political turmoil.

"We must all come together now to rebuild society, one where each of us, and our children after us, are allowed to live the lives we want to."

Ms Jackson's speech last night comes just one week after the closely fought election victory for her new Prospect Party. The victory follows months of political instability, with a combination of Resistance leaders, ex-politicians and military leaders having taken temporary charge of the country following President Fairbarn's disappearance at the so-called 'Battle of Birmingham'.

"I hope the celebrations tomorrow remind us all what our family and friends died for last year, and of the freedoms we must all protect in the future."

Eric Haynes, 42, leader of the Resistance movement following the disappearance, and presumed death, of the key figurehead of the downfall of the Progression Party regime, Peter Brockland, declined to comment on Ms Jackon's victory, amidst reports of a rift between the two…'

Rachael looked up from the article and saw Dux staring back at her. "Still seems weird to read my real name," he said, handing Rosy back to her before taking the newspaper.

"So," he said in a whisper. "How is he doing?"

"Fine," Rachael replied briskly, staring around. "Come on, we'll be late."

Dux waved towards a few nearby ex-Resistance fighters, and they all trundled back through the crowds towards the cathedral, only recently restored from the damage imposed by that final melee.

Rachael stared at the construction site where the Bullring had once been; all that pain, all those plans, all that suffering that occurred was gone, soon to be replaced by some new Birmingham City Council project.

A small staging area had been laid out in front of the cathedral entrance, and, standing patiently with a large pair of token scissors, stood the newly-elected Amelia Jackson. She stood proudly against the backdrop of a large digital screen, projecting her smiles to the eagerly waiting crowds.

"We know we're back to normal when a politician is smiling, ready to take advantage of a good crisis," Dux whispered, as they nestled into a standing spot just a few rows from the front.

Rachael smiled back at him weakly and stared up as Amelia Jackson cut the small red ribbon to signal the reopening of the new society she had promised.

Rachael watched the growing passion spread across her face as she opened her speech, lamenting those who had died and celebrating their courageous victory before once again reiterating her dedication to build a better world for everybody.

Dux had clearly not bought into Ms Jackson, for whatever reason – he had never said - but as Rachael stared up at the fire blazing in the woman's eyes, she could not help but trust her. Perhaps the alternative, after all that they had gone through, however naïve she may be, was too much to bear, but Rachael could not help but take a distinct sense of hope from her performance.

The service continued as survivor after survivor was welcomed up to the stage, all given the platform to express gratitude to those they had lost, each more moving than the last.

Of greatest interest for Rachael were those that stood to pay their tributes to Peter Brockland. Almost all paid their respects to him, from those who had known him before it all to those who fought with him against the Order. The portly Editor of the freshly-independent Chronicle and ex-school colleagues all spoke of their admiration for what Peter had become, and how they would never have expected him to grow to be the dominant figurehead of the rebellion.

The standout eulogy came from a charming retired curator, who beamed with pride as he stepped up from his wheelchair to talk of the man he had come to think of as a son. Through sniffles of raw grief, he spoke of how he had always known Peter to have the strength of character to become the man he did.

The ceremony closed with an emphatic cheer and a few minutes of applause from the crowd before a presenter stepped on stage to introduce the first of the after-party music acts.

"Not staying?" Dux shouted as a loud guitar solo played out to an increasingly excitable crowd.

"No," said Rachael quickly. She was not quite sure what she made of the decision to throw a party to remember those who had died to preserve the freedoms of humanity. She stared down at Rosy, whose eyelids had begun to droop. "Bedtime!"

Dux nodded with a smile, and Rachael bade her farewells to him and her other Resistance comrades.

Rachael continued watching the celebrations unfold on her phone as they trundled along in their small train carriage. She clutched Rosy tightly towards her as she slept against the darkening skies outside.

She had been so close to losing her. If it had not been for him, perhaps she would have done. She watched with a smile as the crowds danced around a ten-foot makeshift effigy of Peter, merry now with alcohol-induced jubilation. She laughed, picturing Peter's embarrassed, bordering repulsed expression had he seen such a spectacle erected in his honour.

Rachael continued to listen to reports of the nationwide celebrations going into the night on the radio, as they drove back further into the suburban countryside, over a small field towards a remote, warmly lit cabin, beautifully poised in the moonlight against the glistening ripples of the river.

They slowed to a halt, and the sounds of the rocks crunched beneath the tyres. Rosy began to stir from the backseat, excited to have returned home. Rachael parked the car and pulled Rosy into her arms again.

Rosy wiggled out of her grip as she opened the front door and sprang towards a shadowed figure at the back door, lit against the moonlight, leaning against the small wooden fence outside.

The figure turned as the young girl bounded towards the back door, and Rachael beamed as Rosy was lifted into the air, laughing gleefully. Rachael leant against the wooden frame of the front doorway and just stared at them - her saviours, her future.

So much had been fought for; so much had been lost. Here though, in the warmth of the secluded cabin, as they both smiled back at her, she knew that it had all been worth it. She knew that the future for her and her new family was going to be nothing short of perfect.

THE END

Printed in Great Britain
by Amazon

47286051R00219